NEW YORK TIMES BESTSELLING AUTHOR

JESSICA PARK

Cover Designer: Damonza.com

Editor and Interior Designer: Jovana Shirley, Unforeseen Editing, www.unforeseenediting.com

Visit my website at jessicapark.me

ISBN-13: 9781508453420

ISBN-10: 150845342X

For Tracy Hutchinson, who proved to be strong, brave, loving, beautiful, and damn invincible despite the world screaming at her not to.
Sometimes, power surfaces after the intolerable trips us up.

CONTENTS

ONE
waiting for the blood to dry

I DON'T HAVE ON A COAT as my mother flies out of the house. I'm not convinced that she told me to get in the car or that she even remembers I am here. I just chase after her and manage to jump into the backseat before she races out of the driveway.

As we near the hospital, she throws her purse into my lap and demands that I locate her lipstick, so at some point, she has presumably decided that I exist enough to dig through her makeup bag.

"It's important to look your best, no matter what the occasion," she practically shrieks. "What? No, not that one! No one wears bright pink to a hospital. Good Lord, Stella. Find me something more neutral. The brown. And put some on yourself. But don't use mine. You look as white as a sheet. Did you bring blush? You didn't? What on earth is wrong with you? Pinch your cheeks at least."

I shift my focus from worry about my father and sister and the car accident they were in and lift my fingers to my face. My cheeks soon burn with pain, but I'm reassured that I am, in fact, still here.

The car peels out during a turn, and my head cracks against the window. It feels good, and I wish my mother would take all turns with as much vigor. But given my mother's inattention to the road, I'm still a bit surprised that my body is not in bits all over the asphalt between home and the hospital.

So, happy birthday to me.

I am alive.

My mother abandons me as soon as we enter the emergency room, and I overhear enough to know that my eighteen-year-old sister, Amy, is being examined and that my father is with her.

On my sixteenth birthday, I sit alone in the waiting area of the hospital.

I smell antiseptic cleaners and burned coffee. I smell chaos and misery. The truth is that I could very well be experiencing some similar crap even if there wasn't a car accident because that is about how life in my house goes. But I'd rather be at home where at least there is familiarity. I'm uncomfortable in new situations.

A few hours later, a nurse finds me. My father and sister are fine. The accident could have been much worse. Black ice totaled my father's Lexus, but he and Amy walked away from the accident.

The orange fabric on the chair that I am now sitting on is making me feel ill. It's hideous. The lighting in this claustrophobic room is hideous. The pile of wrinkled magazines with their airbrushed movie stars and neon lettering and overabundance of exclamation points is hideous. I want to put them all through a shredder and toss celebrity confetti. I would dance and spin under a cascade of shiny paper and forget where I am.

It's dark outside at only four thirty, but the streetlights shine enough that I can see that snow continues to fall. Chicago winters are not exactly peaceful, but I might prefer to be out in the cold rather than in here.

It is hours later when my mother saunters into the room, moving past me without stopping, and assesses the coffee situation. She frowns at various single-serve flavors, eventually settling on one that passes inspection.

As the coffee maker revs to life and begins brewing her cup, she turns and leans against the counter. She looks startled. "Oh, I didn't see you there."

One would never guess that my mother, Lucinda Ford, was in grave concern for her husband and daughter. There is not a wrinkle in her pantsuit, nor a hair not perfectly styled. She wears a matching jewelry set, and I glare at the green stones hanging from her earrings. I immensely dislike them, but my mother infuriatingly makes them look glamorous. Then, I notice her lipstick.

"You're wearing pink lipstick," I say. "You said not to wear pink. You put on the brown lip gloss that I gave you."

She sighs with exaggerated exasperation. "I did no such thing. And *why* you are concerned with my lipstick at this moment is beyond me. It's your fault that we're here in the first place." She whips around and simultaneously tears open three sugar packets before shaking them into the paper cup. With her back to me, she takes a wooden stick from a container and begins stirring her coffee. She stirs and stirs and stirs.

I drop my head and look at my feet. My boots are too small. They barely fit when I got them two years ago, and this year, I have squished toes and blisters.

"You do know that, don't you?" Lucinda asks. She is calm, eerily calm, and matter-of-fact in her speech. "That this accident is your fault?"

I can't begin to know how to respond.

My mother continues, "They were on their way to buy you a birthday present. *My* husband and *my* daughter. Do you get that? And they could have been killed while trying to get you"—she waves a hand in the air—"some sort of trinket to commemorate your birth." Suddenly, she begins to cry, and she clutches her hands to her chest. "Oh, if anything had happened to them, I don't know what I would have done. They are everything. You understand? They are my world. My *family* is my world. Stella, come here."

She opens her arms to me, and I quickly cross the floor and let her wrap my body against hers. Tentatively, I hug her back.

She is right about the lipstick. She must have asked for pink. She's always right.

"I'm so sorry about today. I don't need anything for my birthday. They shouldn't have gone out in this weather." Now, I shut my eyes and hold on to her more tightly. I want her to stroke my hair, to tell me everything will be all right.

She quickly pats my back. "This could have been much worse." Then, my mother pushes me from her hold, and her tone grows harsh. "Stop being so clingy. I need to get back to Amy. They're discharging your father but keeping Amy overnight just as a precaution. She's a bit batty and combative right now, but it's probably a concussion of sorts, nothing permanent. Considering what the car looks like, everyone is surprised that she's as perfect as she is. You're lucky they are both unharmed, don't you agree?" She smiles as she turns to pick up her coffee.

I drop back into the orange chair as she walks out the door. I sit, unmoving, for three hours. Maybe I fall asleep. I'm not sure. But I don't budge.

When enough time has passed, I leave the room and wander the hospital until I find a restroom. It smells worse in here than the rest of the place. My reflection in the mirror is alarming. I gather that I have been crying because my eyes are puffy and red. Or perhaps it's because I've just woken up—that is, if I did indeed fall asleep. The porcelain sink is cold against my hands as I grip it and stare at myself. My heavily streaked hair has lost its bounce from my early-morning round with the curling iron, and the blonde highlights have a green tint in this light. Sixteen is not looking very attractive.

I don't have my purse with me, so I can't touch up my smeared mascara or tear-streaked complexion. I just hope that my mother doesn't see me like this. It would only embarrass her. Running wet fingers under my eyes and over my cheeks helps a bit, so I rally as I take a deep breath and force a perfect smile.

There. Everything is fine.

But I lean forward and rest my head against the mirror as I think about my sister, Amy, and my father. What if I'd lost them? What if I were left alone with my mother? I squeeze my eyes tight and shake the thoughts. What horrible, selfish, ungrateful things to think.

It's not her fault that I am inadequate on every level. If I only listened to her and followed her lead with more skill, then perhaps I wouldn't be such a nightmare. Sure, she has her quirks, but Amy has her affection just fine, so I am clearly doing something wrong.

It's true that Amy is certainly worthy of adoration though. I cannot imagine having a better sister. She's an honors student, the vice president of her senior class, and a star lacrosse player. She dates any boy she wants, spends weekends with her girlfriends, and still makes time for me, the younger sister with little to offer.

I smile, for real this time, as I remember how she used to sneak into my bedroom when I was little. When the lights were out and I was supposed to be sleeping, Amy would silently open the door and glide noiselessly across the floor and into my bed. There, she would tent up the covers, turn on a flashlight, and read me books until I fell asleep. After three or four stories, when my eyes would finally get heavy, she would tell me good night.

And I always said, "I love you so *mush*."

And she always giggled and said, "*Much*, silly. *Much*. But I love you so *mush*, too."

Then, she would be gone, and I would sleep peacefully.

I bump my head against the mirror and stand back up to look at myself. "I do not love *me* so *mush*," I say out loud.

The hospital hallways are a confusing maze, and I can't find my way back to the waiting room, so I just keep going. I ride the elevator up a few floors and then more. Then, I take the stairs and walk a flight, counting the steps that take me higher. I walk another flight and then another. I continue until I reach the highest floor that I'm allowed on.

My feet throb, and I'm winded, so I plop down on the top step to catch my breath and remove my boots. I'm bleeding through my socks. It's disgusting. The idea of putting my boots back on is inconceivable right now, but I don't know what to do. I am, of course, in a hospital where I'm pretty sure there might be a bandage or two to help me out, but I'm too humiliated to go marching through the hospital, leaving bloody footprints behind me. There would be no good way to explain why my winter boots were too small for me, not to mention why I was compulsively running up flights of stairs. It would not reflect well on my mother, and no one would understand that she paid for these expensive boots, and that should be enough. It was my fault for not choosing a size that would last me until my feet stopped growing.

I will just sit here and wait for the blood to dry.

I want to find my sister *and* my father, but that would mean finding my mother, and I seem to be of little comfort to her today. What upsets me more though is that my father has not sought me out today. I know he was not hurt in the accident, and I know that he's probably been hovering over Amy…but I'm here, too.

I look at the blood congealing on my ankles. *See? I really am here. There's proof.*

Dad is loving and funny. It's easy with him, and he doesn't seem to feel that I'm any sort of monumental disappointment. Or if he does, he hides it better.

I wrap my hand around my left wrist and feel the imprint of the word engraved on my bracelet.

My father bought this for me last year when we were at a state fair. It was the sort of thing that my mother would never attend as she deemed it *low class and tacky*, but Dad had taken me.

I know that she loathes the wide leather cuff and the engraved metal plate on the bracelet that I have on at all times, and more than once, I've caught her wrinkling her nose at the sight of it. How the white of the leather stays white is unexplainable, but it never gets dirty. It says *Adored* in beautiful lettering. This bracelet is the one defiance that I allow myself, and I do not take this off because of her. I've developed a habit of tracing across the letters with my fingers in a near compulsiveness that I find comforting.

A clomping sound echoes throughout the stairwell as someone walks through the lower levels. I wait for the sounds of a door opening and closing, but instead, the clomping just grows louder. I scoot over on my stair perch and lean against the wall, letting my hair fall over my eyes, while I wait for the person to pass by me. I'm good at being invisible.

Instead, the loud footsteps stop abruptly, and I can tell the person has come to rest on the landing just below me. Perhaps I'm about to be murdered. My bloody feet will likely cause confusion during the investigation into my demise. It will appear that my ankles were savagely attacked prior to my being beaten to death in an unattractive hospital stairwell, and investigators will launch a manhunt for the ankle fetishist.

When I lift my head to meet my fate, I see a boy about my age, or maybe he's a bit older. I'm not good at guessing ages. His hands are tucked into the front pockets of his jeans, the hem of his white T-shirt bunching up near his wrists. A thin gold chain peeks out from under the collar, and I lift my eyes a bit more. The boy has twinkling eyes filled with mischief and happiness.

"Hi," he says with a smile. "Whatcha doing?"

"Just…sitting here," I answer dumbly.

He takes a small hop and lands with both feet on the first step. "Know what I'm doing?"

I shake my head.

His head falls to the side, and he lifts up and down on his toes. "I'm counting steps. Each flight has—"

"Eight steps," I finish for him. "I counted, too."

He hops to the next step. "Aha! But did you know that the two flights between the third and fourth level only—"

"Have seven."

The boy grins and hops again. He is getting closer to me. "Exactly! What does that mean? The third floor is one step shorter than all the other floors?"

I stare at him for a moment. "Or those steps are each a bit higher, adding up to the same height as the other flights."

He narrows his eyes and leans forward. "Very clever. You could be right. But then, why? Was there a secret purpose? Or was it a construction error and some step builder fouled things up? Other things might be fouled up in this godforsaken building, and we might be at risk. I mean, there could be a huge structural problem with this hospital."

"You seem rather paranoid," I mutter.

"Perhaps. Perhaps it's realistic." He jumps the rest of the steps until his feet are near mine. Then, he pivots and drops down, so he is sitting next to me. "Hi," he says again.

"Hi."

"I'm Sam. Sam Bishop."

"I'm Stella Ford."

"What brings you to the hospital today?"

I push my hair back. "My father and sister were in a car accident."

"Shit. Are they okay?"

"Yeah, I think so, but I guess it was close. Black ice and stuff. I haven't seen them, but my mother says they weren't hurt. Airbags and stuff."

"I'm glad."

We sit silently for a minute, and I'm growing more and more uncomfortable with every second. My experience with boys is pretty limited, and the fact that he is undeniably cute is not making me confident. He should probably go away and leave me alone, but it would be impolite not to ask him why he's here today, so I do.

"Oh God, it's ridiculous. I'm with a friend of mine. We're in Chicago for a class trip, and he snuck off to see a girl that he'd met. Ran into some kind of trouble and got himself banged up a bit. I can't see anything wrong with him, except that he's being loud and annoying."

His smile is endearing and mesmerizing, and I have to do what I can to avoid staring for too long.

"That's nice of you to stay with him. Are his parents here?" I ask.

"Nah. We're from Maine, so they're far away, not that they'd bother coming anyway. Not really those kind of parents, if you know what I mean."

I nod. "I do." Sam doesn't say anything else, so I add, "I've never been to Maine."

"Really? It's awesome. My parents run a big inn, The Coastal. It's right on the ocean in Watermark. It's a small town that's dead in the winter and packed in the summer."

"Lobsters," is all I say, and inside, I cringe. If I could disappear right now, I would.

"What?" For some reason, he just looks curious, not judgmental over my complete lack of social skills.

"Sorry. It's just, when you said you were from Maine, I immediately thought of lobsters. I've never had lobster, and I wouldn't even know how to begin with the shell and stuff."

"So, when you come to Maine, I will show you how to tackle lobsters, okay?" His arm brushes against my pants as he peers down and points to my feet. "Yeesh. What happened?"

Quickly, I try to tuck my feet into the corner of the step and yank up my socks. I wince audibly. "Nothing." I reach for the railing to stand. "I should go."

"How about I walk you downstairs, and we get someone to patch you up?"

"That's okay." I fiddle with my revolting socks. "I'm really okay."

Sam sets a hand on my shoulder and sits me back down. "Don't move. I'll be right back."

I watch with curiosity as he two-foot hops down to the landing. His hair is cut short, but it still bounces with each jump. The subtle auburn highlights are showing, even in this dark stairwell.

Sam stops and looks at me. "I'll be right back. I promise. You'll stay here?"

The way he smiles softly at me compels me to nod and to smile back only because it's impossible not to.

I listen to the sound of his ridiculous hops and then hear him open the door on a landing a few floors below us. I notice the quiet that surrounds me now that he is gone. As I fiddle with the bracelet on my left hand, I notice that my hands are smeared with blood. Perfect. How incredibly appealing.

I grab my boots and start walking down the stairs. I'm halfway down the second landing when Sam rounds the corner.

"Well, that's not staying." He looks disappointed.

"Sorry. I just…I didn't want you to…" I stammer. Finally, I hold up my free hand. "I'm kind of bloody. It's really gross."

"It's just blood." He pauses. "It's nothing to be scared of." Sam lifts up two paper bags. "I got you covered."

He gestures for me to sit, so I do. He kneels in front of me, and ever so slowly, he takes my right foot and then gently peels down the sock. The bag reveals alcohol wipes, gauze pads, antibiotic cream, and first-aid tape. For the next few minutes, I stare in a near trance as this boy, whom I do not know, cleans up my blood and puts me back together. Soon, I have clean white bandages covering my wounds.

"There. That's much better, huh?" He admires his handiwork and lifts his chin to me. "Hey? Did I hurt you? Why are you crying?"

"I'm not crying," I whisper.

The back of his hand grazes my face, and I feel dampness on my skin. I cannot move. Sam turns his palm to my cheek, and I instinctively lean against it, closing my eyes. He waits until an eternity passes, and I open them again. His hand moves to mine, and he begins wiping the blood smears until all traces are gone.

"Better?"

I nod. "Better," I manage.

He rolls up my socks and stuffs them into one of the bags. From the other, he pulls out a new pair of socks, and with the utmost care, he rolls them over my feet. There's no reason that I can't put them on myself, but I'm too busy looking at the shape of his lips. They are so smooth and full.

"I should go," I blurt out. "To find my family."

"Oh." He adjusts my sock one more time. "Sure. Sorry about the socks. It's what the gift shop had."

For the first time, I notice that Sam has dressed me in Wonder Woman socks, complete with stars and capes hanging from the top hem.

"I know. You probably hate them. It was these or frogs. Or fuzzy purple ones, but they looked a bit eggplantish. Okay, fine, there might have been a white pair, but—"

"I love them." I look up at him again. "I love Wonder Woman. And now…I…I have to go." I press my feet into my boots and move past him to the landing before I turn back. "Thank you, Sam Bishop."

He smiles. "Thank *you*, Stella Ford."

I exit the stairwell from the level below and then take the elevator back down to the floor I originated from. I locate a nurse who tells me where my sister's room is. Perhaps it's the Wonder Woman socks, but I am feeling better and desperately want to see my father and sister. No more of this waiting-around nonsense.

Amy's room is easy to find, but as I'm about to step in, my plans to run over and hug her and Dad are halted.

Amy is standing by the window, looking outside at the snowstorm that is now in full force. Her blonde curls tumble over her shoulders and down her back in a wild mess. Her face is extraordinarily pale, but what I notice more is her expression of fear.

My father, normally so happy and easygoing, is pacing the room. I don't like seeing him this strung out because he's the sane parent in the family and the one who balances out my mother.

"I'm so sorry, Amy. I'm so, so sorry. I didn't know what to do."

He steps into her to embrace her, and I am shocked to see her shove him away.

Dad freezes and then drops his head. "I would undo this if I could. Don't you know that? But what was the alternative? To let you go?"

Amy turns to him, her eyes flashing anger—or panic maybe. "What have you done? God, what have you done? How could you?" she screams. "I am seventeen years old, and my life is over!"

Dad walks slowly to the edge of the bed and sinks down. Very softly, he says, "Except that it can't be."

She explodes. "And what about that other kid? I saw it." She begins to sob and covers her face with her hands. "That poor kid. I wish we were all dead! What is this?"

"Amy, shh!" Dad pleads. "Stop. I didn't mean for any of this to happen. Believe that."

I have stopped breathing. Nothing they are saying makes any sense. Silently, I back away from the door and edge down the hall to the elevator. I cannot think and cannot feel anything right now. All I can do is make my way back toward the waiting room.

As I near the entryway, my mother walks past me, brusquely bumping into my shoulder, as she moves down the hall.

"Mom?" I call.

But she continues without stopping or acknowledging me, and she makes her way into the front lobby and out the door, car keys jangling in her hand.

I have been forgotten. Again.

When I catch up to her outside, she simply says, "You look bizarre. Wait over there for me," and she points to the far end of the parking lot. "I need to get some of Amy's things for her because the doctor has insisted that she stay overnight."

I have little reaction to what she just said, and I watch her march away through the downfall of wet snow. The snow, however real to anybody else, is basically nonexistent to me. The bitter cold should cause me to shiver, but I can't get myself to even bother with tucking my hands into my pockets as I head in the direction of my assigned pickup spot. The roaring wind bellows my name, and it's not until I'm halfway down the sidewalk when I realize it's not the wind but an actual person calling me.

I turn and see Sam.

Lights from the emergency room entrance highlight one side of his tall, lean body. His already damp hair, the shape of his silhouette, the way his posture delivers an air of such confidence and competence—more than all that, I see familiarity and safety.

Everything about him beckons me.

Without thinking, I run to him. I don't feel my throbbing feet anymore or the miserable Chicago winter or the way my heart is so full of pain tonight. All I feel is the desire to close the distance between us. Icy pellets hit my face and blind my vision, but I don't care. As I run to him, Sam

Bishop steps forward, hesitantly at first, but then he walks quickly and lets me crash with full force into his hold.

I wrap my arms around his chest and dig my fingers into his back. The warmth of his body passes to mine as he holds me, perhaps clinging to me as tightly as I cling to him. His arms are over my shoulders, crossing behind my neck, sheltering me from everything. If it were possible to stay in the dark and in the safety of his protection forever, I would.

I let every precious second here draw out. I drown in it, savor it, and commit it to memory.

The sound of a car horn makes me want to retch. I have to go. Reluctantly, I drop my hands and try to step away from him, but Sam only gives me a few inches.

With his arms still encircling my neck, he dips his head down, so we are nose-to-nose. "Everything will be okay. Good things last, and the bad things will fade away. So, go find your good." His lips touch mine, barely brushing against me, before he presses his mouth harder and kisses me.

Only seconds probably pass, but they are seconds that will stay with me over the upcoming years when there is no Sam Bishop.

"Go find your good," he says again.

But I can't. I'm not strong enough.

TWO
haze

IT IS FIVE YEARS LATER, and I have not found my good. Sam Bishop was wrong. The bad is what endures, what increases.

My father vanished a week after the car accident, and my mother has spent every day since pretending that he never existed. We are not allowed to mention him, to ask about him, to think about him, to miss him. As per her declaration, he was simply never here. My mother has the ability to erase whomever she wants, and it's by the skin of my teeth that she allows me any sort of place in her world. In her eyes, Amy has always been the good daughter, and in the years after the accident, that opinion inexplicably grew when Amy became insufferable and learned to loathe me.

I check my reflection in the mirror one more time. As of a few hours ago, my hair is now my mother's exact shade of rich deep red and styled in sculpted, tiered waves. For once, I am confident that my appearance will get her seal of approval. My lips are stained in dark mauve, and my eye makeup is immaculate. I flash my practiced smile and pose, readying myself to show off for her.

The pale-green top I'm wearing is something that she would have selected for herself from one of the many high-end stores she frequents, and my tan shorts and heels show off my legs. I turn to the side a bit. My shirt shows enough cleavage but not too much. I check my jewelry—small gold hoops in my ears and a matching bracelet. It's classy. Classy and seductive, the way she is.

While I'm in college, my mother has let me stay in the guesthouse above the garage on her property. I know she doesn't really want me here because she's hoping that my sister will move back home, but I doubt that will happen.

Amy likes her privacy—a lot. That's understandable, given her massive coke and prescription pill addictions. No one actually acknowledges that she has a problem—particularly our mother—but it's idiotically obvious. It doesn't take a genius to recognize that Amy's mental and physical states are the result of more than recreational partying.

I scan my room, memorizing the precise placement of the furniture. Then, I rescan and take mental pictures of the desk light, the alarm clock, the shelf of books, and the framed pictures. The floral wallpaper and Ralph Lauren patterned bedspread make me dizzy, and I touch the vanity behind me to steady myself. It takes a minute, but I refocus and slowly look from item to item. It's four o'clock on the dot, and I make sure to spend exactly six minutes reviewing every item in my bedroom.

Every time I leave the room, I have to go through this ritual. On more than one occasion, I have returned to my room, convinced that something is off in here. My perceptions are often muddied, so I work hard to pay attention to specifics.

I stare at my desk—penholder, laptop, magazine, scented candle, scissors, calendar on the wall behind it.

I go over this ten times until I'm sure.

I hear a car door slam, and I try not to rush as I grab my clutch purse and lock the guesthouse.

In the driveway, my mother takes shopping bags from the trunk of her ostentatious Mercedes while my sister sits in the passenger seat. The door is open, and her legs hang out. Amy stops examining her chewed fingernails long enough to catch my eye. She looks worse than usual. She might have on sunglasses, but I know that the bags under her eyes are particularly dark today. Her skin is pale, her badly bleached hair is stringy, and she is way too thin. The designer T-shirt hangs in a way that I can see her shoulder bones through the fabric.

I don't feel sorry for her though. I hate my sister. Not only has she routinely sabotaged the relationship between my mother and me over the years, but there is also nothing left of the childhood love we had for each other.

"Well, good Lord. Who the fuck are you supposed to be?" Amy talks loudly and snidely. "Oh, Lucinda!"

I have no idea why she insists on calling our mother by her first name, but she has for years.

"Lucinda, look what the hell the cat dragged in."

My mother shuts the trunk and looks my way. I can see her sigh as she struts toward me, bags bouncing against her legs.

I smile and touch my hand to my hair. "See? I got it done like yours."

My mother stops in front of me and runs her look over my hair and green shirt, managing not to meet my eyes. "Stella," she simply states. "Oh, dear. You just can't get it right, can you?" She makes no secret of rolling her eyes. "Amy, darling, tell your sister that her purple shirt is a joke."

Amy hops out of the car and stands in front of me. She smiles. "Stella, your mother says you're hideous."

I listen to the click-clack of Lucinda's heels as she heads into the main house. I don't say anything.

"Nobody likes you," Amy matter-of-factly tells me. "I just thought you should know that."

I'm disgusted with my sister. "Leave me alone," I whisper.

"Gladly."

My junkie sibling leaves me in the driveway.

I am not going to cry over this. I will not be some poor little rich girl standing in front of a mansion and manicured gardens, crying because life isn't perfect. How fucking cliché. Although, technically, while my mother might be rich—thanks to my father's money and her trust fund—I am not, so really, the cliché isn't even applicable. Nonetheless, I'm not going to let my sister get to me.

I inhale and exhale. I make myself smile and walk down the long driveway to my old two-door silver Civic that I always park on the street. My mother is understandably embarrassed by having this car on her property.

I sit behind the wheel for a while. A long while. Or at least I think it's a long while. I look at the clock. It's almost six. I don't know if I stood in front of the house for ages or if I've been in the car this whole time.

I watch the digital numbers change over and over. Finally, I drive.

I try to clear my head and attend to what I know is true. This is not easy for me, but I do this because I don't want to get lost again.

My name is Stella.

I am twenty-one years old.

It is a Tuesday evening in April.

I'm a junior at a small community college in Chicago.

That's...that's all I can come up with. Paying attention to facts is not easy when I'm in this state.

I drive for a while. Later, I park the car and go inside my boyfriend's third-floor apartment near campus.

You aren't anything to me. Don't you understand that? In my head, I hear the words that have been said to me so many times. *You are forgettable.*

Jay lets me into his place. After thirty seconds of small talk, we're in his bedroom. He's big on having sex as much as possible, and I'm big on forgetting it as much as possible. But I'm on my back in no time, and I let him go ahead and do what he wants.

I turn my head to the side. Today, I don't have the will not to fade off. It gives me pleasure to escape for a bit. The shades are open, and flashes of sunlight pierce through my closed eyelids, furthering my distance from reality. I let the rhythmic motion of him on top of me drag me into oblivion. If I'm lucky, I'll just disappear. If I'm really lucky, maybe I'll disappear far enough that I'll find myself in a world where I am happy, where my father did not take off in the middle of the fucking night and leave me with a screwed-up mother and a sister who went from angel to demon. Luck, however, does not seem to be my friend.

My thoughts shut down, and a fuzzy haze takes over. I like this space because time does not exist. My body does not exist. Most importantly, I do not exist. Nothingness is my salvation. Maybe I'm going crazy, but I don't care much right now because this is at least a degree of peace.

Then, I hear a noise, and I am ripped away from my alternate world.

A male voice. Oh, it's a groan.

My hands touch down beside me and run over cool fabric. Sheets. I am in a bed, on my back. My shirt is unbuttoned all the way, my bra still on. A breeze rushes in and crosses over my bare stomach. I reach out until my hand hits skin.

That's right. I'm having sex with Jay. Great.

I open my eyes. Jay is too busy fucking me to notice my spaced-out state. He's an asshole like that. But I want to be the kind of girlfriend who gets her guy off—one who is perfect in bed and out—so I need to do something other than lie on my back and battle the crazy swirling in my head.

Generally, I'm very good at hiding the fact that something is wrong with me, but I have lapses, like right now. So, I lift my hips and make appropriate noises of ecstasy, as though I am so totally caught up in the throes of sexual fulfillment that I can barely contain myself.

"That's fucking good, huh?" he mutters.

I nod and fake a smile.

I close my eyes again and let him crush his body into mine over and over.

When he's done, I grab my purse and escape to the bathroom.

My reflection in the mirror upsets me. Eyeliner is smudged, and my hair is a disaster. The linen shirt I have on is now wrinkled. I squint. I think it's pale green, but I could be wrong. My mother said it was purple. However, perhaps I misheard her. I look down and realize that I have no idea what color it is. For five minutes, I examine the fabric, looking for clues that will help me answer this. It's green, I confirm.

The color is green. That is a fact, I think.

But I don't know for sure. It's really just a guess.

I pull a small bag from my purse and begin the process of redoing my hair and makeup. While my curling iron heats up, I wipe away eyeliner that has traveled across my cheeks. I pause. It looks like I've been crying, but I don't remember doing that. I don't know if I hate Jay or myself more right now.

It takes a thorough primping process for me to make myself presentable until I can leave the bathroom.

I kiss Jay good-bye with a hundred times more sexual energy than I actually feel, and he slaps my ass as I get back into my car. The engine rolls over a few times before it catches and finally starts.

It's not particularly cold out, but I am shaking, so I crank up the heat. *What the hell is wrong with me?* My hand trembles while I touch up my lipstick in the rearview mirror.

Back home, I make it to my room in the guesthouse, undetected. I am exhausted. Every day is an exercise in faking happiness and sociability and enthusiasm for life, none of which I actually have.

I toss my keys on the nightstand and assess the glowing small lamp. It is supposed to be precisely in the middle, but for some reason, I cannot get it to stay there. It is clearly a few inches to the left of the center. I move it back to its spot. A routine check of my desk gives me pause. Something is wrong, but I can't tell what. The clock tells me it is past midnight. I didn't know that I'd been gone for so long.

Showering right now is a necessity because I must steam off the aftermath of Jay. The old tub doesn't drain well, but I don't mind because I find it comforting to stand in water while the scalding shower pours over me. It's like I'm a child again, playing in puddles with my sister.

I take the shampoo bottle from the ledge and immediately notice how light it is. It's empty, and I could have sworn that I just bought this a few days ago. Or maybe last week? It might have been longer. A month? The panic in my chest weighs heavily. I'm losing time, not properly tracking things—even the simple things, like shampoo. It's concerning.

Tonight, I will work on polishing a final paper. It doesn't matter that I've already gone over it a hundred times because I want to earn another A grade. I applied to other colleges and got into Wesleyan and Pomona, but my mother, of course, wouldn't pay my tuition. I didn't receive enough scholarship money to attend either, so I'm stuck at this local community college. Lucinda is only letting me live in the guesthouse because the money I did get won't cover housing. She tells everyone that she, a single woman, is more than happy to support her daughter's education, and, oh, what a blessing it is to have her girl still at home.

I pay rent with the money I make doing graphic design work. There is something satisfying in manipulating images. Clients keep finding me online—requesting graphics for websites, book covers, shirts, whatever—and I get to bury myself in design work and collect money. I like the anonymity. I also like that I'm very good at what I do.

Not to mention, I have been squirreling away money for the past three years.

The food I keep in the small fridge in my room doesn't cost much. I can barely stand to eat most of the time anyway. I don't have a stove here, and because the kitchen in the main house is off-limits to me, I have become an expert sandwich maker. After my father left, all food in *her* fridge, beyond the very basics, was labeled with her and Amy's names to be sure I would not touch anything that was not mine.

Another thing I can't get myself to touch is a large bank account, one my father left for me. I'm not taking anything from the man who pretended to be my hero and turned out to be my enemy. He broke my heart, and I will never forgive him for leaving.

I touch my bracelet—*Adored.* It's such complete bullshit. He doesn't adore me because he wouldn't have left if he had. Adoration means that you stay, no matter what. So, I don't adore him, and I don't adore my mother or sister, but I stay. Someone has to get my mother to pay her bills. Someone has to do the grocery shopping for her. Someone has to make sure that she can unleash her behavioral eccentricities in the privacy of her house, so the rest of the world does not see them.

So, the bank account remains as full as it was on the day my father left us forever.

I don't know what I'll do with my money.

Maybe I'll burn it.

Maybe I'll donate it.

Maybe I'll spend it.

Maybe I'll buy a gun.

THREE champions

"AREN'T YOU GLAMOROUS? And I'm delighted that you brought Stella with you today!" A woman wearing a shriekingly loud red dress air-kisses my mother while a crowd of gowned women swirl around us.

It's hard to pay attention to keeping a smile on my face and maintaining perfect posture when the smell of the buffet wafts my way. I am starving. The sweet scent of mimosas is unmistakable, and I inhale with the hope that I might get a secondhand buzz.

Surviving another insufferable charity gathering during which my mother will be honored for her dedication to various sorts of downtrodden is not how I'd choose to spend my Saturday morning. The bright blue dress that she had someone make for me itches like all hell, and I suspect that my body is rejecting the high-quality fabric. I coyly scratch my hip and wonder whether I love or hate my mother for buying me this dress. It might be both.

The red-dress lady leaves us, and my mother entwines her arm with mine as we make our way to our table at the front of the room. My mother's hair is pinned up in intricate curls, showing off her ageless face. She might be BOTOXed within an inch of her life, but in the expert hands of her dermatologist, her face looks surprisingly natural. Obviously, she tells everyone that she has been decidedly blessed with such incredible genes. She also lies about her age, but that's to be expected. Everyone at this event shaves off eight or ten years.

My ankle twists under me as I stumble in my heels, and my mother grabs on to me before I totally wipe out.

"Goodness! Are you all right, sweetheart?" She proceeds to make a spectacle of caring for me and helps me to my chair.

Our table is already full with other guests, so her fussing over me is not surprising.

"I'm so sorry. I'm not sure what happened," I apologize.

My mother laughs. "It happens to all of us."

The other women at the table engage us in enough small talk to make my ears bleed, but I manage to answer questions about my schoolwork while my mother chimes in with effusively supportive comments about how hard I study and what perfect grades I have.

She smiles at me with admiration. "Did you know that Stella was accepted at Pomona but wanted to stay near her family? It's such a testament to how close we are! I'm very fortunate to have *two* successful daughters."

Yes, I think, *one is a drug addict and the other spends half her time in a dissociative state. We are fucking role models.*

"Where is Amy today?" The woman who is running the event sits on my mother's other side. "I haven't seen her in ages."

My mother waves a hand. "She is rather late, isn't she? But I do believe that she was stopping by the children's center, where she volunteers, before coming here."

My stomach growls, and I excuse myself to load up at the buffet. My diet of homemade sandwiches has not been cutting it. I return to my seat with a plateful of cheese frittata, fruit, smoked breakfast sausage, and three éclairs. I'm going to make this meal count. Most of the time when I'm at these kinds of events, I don't get a chance to eat, or Lucinda nearly snarls if I eye lobster or another upscale dish.

I've barely made my way through a few bites before my mother whispers to me, "Go call your sister, and find out where the hell she is. She is supposed to introduce me when the ceremony begins in less than an hour. I bet you told her the wrong time. You always get things mixed up. Now, go! And when will you stop wearing that ridiculous bracelet? You look like a lesbian."

I tug down the sleeve of my dress to hide the bracelet that my father gave me. Calling people *lesbians* is one of her high insults. As far as I know, she's never been attacked by a mob of violent lesbians. In fact, I don't think she even knows any lesbians. It briefly occurs to me that I would delight in becoming a lesbian just to irritate her, but so far, I haven't found myself attracted to other women. One can hold out hope though.

In the privacy of the ladies' room, I try Amy's cell phone four times, and then I text her. There is no response, but she doesn't often reply when I try to contact her.

"Bitch," I mutter to myself.

Given the way our mother practically salivates over her—not to mention how she covers up Amy's narcotics habit to save face—my sister could at least pull her shit together long enough to be here today.

When I get back to the table, I can see how hard it is for my mother not to appear rattled.

She finishes her mimosa. "Drive to Amy's condo, and get her. Immediately." Her voice is quiet but unmistakably filled with venom. "And you've got chocolate all over your mouth. Clean up, for Christ's sake."

It must be frosting from the éclairs. I grab my napkin and blot my mouth. No chocolate appears on the fabric, so I dab again. Still nothing. Wait, I didn't eat yet, did I? But I look at my plate, and the éclairs are gone, so I must have eaten them before I called Amy. I'm still starving, but I can tell that my mother will lose her mind if I don't drag Amy back here in the next twenty minutes.

It's a quick drive to her place, and I leave the car out front, explaining to the doorman that I'm just running in to pick up my sister. He holds open the heavy brass door leading into the marble lobby. The elevator buttons glow as I ride up to the tenth floor, and I pray that I will get stuck in this metal box and be stranded here for hours, for days, for eternity.

Anytime that I have to go to Amy's condo, I find myself full of resentment and jealousy. My sister has had everything handed to her and lives in a pricey two-bedroom on Lake Shore Drive. She contributes nothing to this world, except for fueling the economy by spending our mother's money. I'm sure she drained the account my father left her years ago.

After I've pounded on Amy's door for longer than a reasonable amount of time, I locate the key buried in my wallet. She gave it to me before heading out on a five-day ski trip in Aspen last year, so I could let in the interior decorator. I unlock the door and immediately cringe at the smell. Her place is in its usual state of filth. Only, this time, it's worse.

"Amy?"

No answer. The kitchen is covered in empty liquor bottles, and I count thirteen discarded pizza boxes. *The diet of champions.*

"Amy?" I call again.

I walk through the living room, noticing that the couch cushions and throw pillows are all messed up. The giant oil painting above the armchair is crooked, and the wood floors look as though they haven't been cleaned in months. Apparently, Amy is not taking advantage of the housecleaning service her building offers.

I sidestep a plastic cup that was filled with God-knows-what and then go check her bedroom. Based on what I've seen, she's probably still asleep. I pop inside, but she's not in bed. Her comforter is scrunched up, and it's possible that she's lying beneath it, inebriated, but I just can't tell, so I double-check. A bottle of watermelon-flavored water and an empty zip baggie are on the bed.

"Amy, damn it! Where are you?" I say out loud to the empty room.

I'm beyond irritated when I don't find her in either the bathroom or the guest room. Out of desperation, I check the closets. Perhaps Amy went totally bananas and hid in one of them. I don't know. I'm anxious because my mother is going to flip if I return without the prodigal daughter.

While my sister is not buried among a pile of coats, the full-length mirror on the guest room door does reflect something that catches my eye. An empty prescription bottle is visible just under the bed. As I retrieve it, I notice another bottle in an open duffel bag, so I slide that out from where my sister has it stashed to see what her prescription drug of choice is these days. The label is unreadable, but it doesn't matter because what else I find in the bag takes precedence—razor blades, bags of unmarked pills in plastic bags, and what I can only identify as some sort of hunting knife.

Then, my breathing gets ragged.

There is a handgun—with boxes of ammo.

This leaves only two possibilities. It's either a suicide bag, or she's going to kill someone.

And I cannot find my sister—the person who used to be my world, who was vivacious and funny and loved me so hard that she sometimes suffocated me. It was eons ago, but it used to be the truth.

I repeatedly call out my sister's name as tears blind me. The feel of this gun in my hand is grotesque, yet I cannot stop looking at it, even as it shakes in my grip. I've never seen a gun in real life, much less touched one.

It screams violence, death, and tragedy.

If I'm honest, it also screams out the possibility of relief. I consider that for a moment. I could put an end to my life right now. It could be fast and painless.

Then, I hear a noise, like something is breaking. I shove the gun into the bag and push it back under the guest room bed. I have to catch my breath and reframe my thinking for just a second, but then I rally.

The distinct sound of my sister's laughter rings throughout the house, but nothing is funny about it. Her giddy cackle is clearly coming from her room. I crawl halfway across the floor before I get myself to her. Amy is in her bed, flat on her back, wild-eyed, and emitting moans and noises I've never heard. When I reach her, she is a mess of knotted, stringy over-bleached hair, and her skin is nearly gray. Her arms flail, pushing me away, as I try to calm her down.

"Amy, please. It's going to be okay. Please, please…" I beg. "Shh…let me help you."

"I saw him!" She slaps me across the face. "He's perfect!"

Great. She probably thinks she's seen God. Or Elvis.

While she is as skin and bones as ever, she is also surprisingly strong, and she shoves me aside, hard, as she rolls to hang her head off the bed while she vomits over and over and coughs with a hack that pains me.

In the midst of my tears, I call 911 and report my sister's overdose. On what, I don't know. A number of times, Amy tries to bat the phone from my hand, but she's still vomiting. And laughing.

"Don't call…" she sputters. "I gotta get back. Get away from me."

She hits me again, and I careen into the wall.

I slump against her dresser and watch what's left of my sister. She is in ruins, and I have no idea how to help her.

Soon, the sound of sirens rings outside the building.

My head falls into my hands. While something is atrociously wrong with Amy, something is equally alarming about me. I looked in this room earlier, at this exact bed she's in now, and I did not see Amy.

I am slowly losing my fucking mind.

FOUR
second time around

THE LAST TIME THAT I WAS IN A HOSPITAL, I had Sam Bishop to get me through a horrible day.

Today, I have no one.

If I had friends or a boyfriend beyond the superficial, then maybe I would feel less alone. As it is, I am left to manage my mother and sister by myself. Again, I curse my father for running off without a word—well, *maybe* without a word. A memory plagues me, but because I can't trust myself, I don't know if it's real or not.

Perhaps my father came to my room the night before he left and woke me with tears and regret.

Perhaps he kissed me and hugged me good-bye.

Perhaps he apologized for not being stronger, unable to live with what he'd done.

But I don't know. None of it means anything to me.

What does mean something is that he left, and there is no excuse reasonable enough for that. Parents don't abandon their children.

Today, Amy has been sedated. I look at her in the bed, and she appears pathetically childlike in the patterned blue hospital gown. Her color is better than it was, probably due to the fluids being pumped into her. Inexplicably, no drugs were found in her system, so she's probably going to be moved to the psych unit later today.

No drugs in her system. None. I don't get it. That's impossible.

Amy might be a bitch and a drug user, but she doesn't belong up in psych. I'm positive that when I first checked, she wasn't in her bedroom at the condo. I *know* that. I am sane enough to recognize when something doesn't make any sense.

Or so I thought.

Oh God, I don't understand what's happening—to her or to me.

Hours later, my mother flies into Amy's room. Immediately, she shoots me a venomous look and angrily hurls her purse at me. The zipper catches my cheek, and I wince.

"What did you do?" she asks with indisputable accusation. "What the hell happened?"

"I just found her."

"Shut up," she spits. "What did you do to her?"

"I didn't *do* anything. She was at the condo, acting all crazy."

"How could she do this to me? And today of all days?" My mother takes Amy's state personally.

"She didn't do anything to *you*, Mom. She tried to kill herself. She's suicidal."

My mother whips around and glares at me, utter confusion on her face. "Suicidal? Why would *Amy* kill herself? What a stupid thing to think. If anyone should be suicidal, it would be you."

Before I can react, she starts compulsively smoothing the sheets and adjusting Amy's hospital gown. "I had quite the juggling act to do at the luncheon. Imagine trying to explain your disappearance, Stella."

She delivers soothing words—lies really—to Amy. "You poor thing. You're probably dehydrated and worn-out. Look at you! Hospitalized for exhaustion, just like all those celebrities!"

I can't be around her right now, not when she's like this, so I set her purse down on the floor, next to my chair. It falls open, and the smell of sugar wafts out. For a moment, I just stare into her purse. Then, I push aside the tufts of paper napkin and see three éclairs unceremoniously stuffed into the main pocket.

My éclairs.

My head fills with fog, and I leave the room. Minutes or hours go by in the waiting area while I obsess about the éclairs. Sitting in the same waiting room I was in after the car accident is doing nothing to clear my thinking. The chairs are no longer orange, and now, a children's play area is set up in one corner, but it's the same damn room.

My chest is tight. I can barely breathe. Before I lose air entirely, I run from the room and instinctively find my way to the stairwell. Each flight sets me a bit freer, and by the time I reach the top, I am gasping, but at least my lungs are working again. And my shoes fit this time, so that's an improvement from five years ago.

I'm dizzy, so I hold on to the handrail and shut my eyes as I concentrate on breathing and grounding myself. This is not easy, considering that my blood sugar is probably low because I haven't eaten today.

Because my pathological mother stole my éclairs and told me that I ate them.

And I believed her.

As I extrapolate from there, images flash through my head—my empty shampoo, the shirt she told me was purple but was really green, objects in my room that moved around ever so slightly.

I open my eyes, and for a second, I see blood pouring from my ankles, so I blink until the vision that belongs to the last time I was in this stairwell disappears. Now, I'm just looking at my feet in heels.

My mother has so thoroughly warped my sense of reality—retelling facts and stories, insisting on my stupidity and forgetfulness—that I have now become someone who is trapped, dysfunctionally dependent on a shell of a family. I cannot continue like this, or I'm going to finally break until what's left of my psyche shatters into smithereens. I don't want that to happen. I want to thrive.

I walk slowly down the stairs and back to Amy's room. I peek inside to make sure that our mother is not there before going to my sister. Her fragility frightens me to the core. I don't stop myself from crawling into the bed and lying down with my body against hers and my head on her shoulder. I tug at her arm and pull it around me, so she's holding me like we did when we were little.

"I love you so *mush*," I say. "I love you so *mush*."

The room is quiet, dark, except for the lights from the surrounding monitors. I squeeze my sister.

A few minutes later, Amy squeezes back.

"I love you so *mush*, too." Her voice is tiny and hoarse.

I lift up to look at her through the murky darkness, and I can make out her eyes opening slowly.

"Where's our mother?"

"I don't know. I can go find her if you want."

"No, no." She holds on to me more tightly. "God, no." She takes a deep breath and coughs.

"Are you okay? Do you want some water?" I whisper.

She shakes her head. "Stella, listen to me." She's breathing harder now. "You have to get out of here, okay?"

I wipe my cheek. "What?"

"Out of Chicago. Leave, and don't come back. Mom and I…" Her chest rises and falls quickly. "*We're fucking toxic.* You have to get away from us."

"No," I immediately say. "I'm not leaving you with her."

She laughs. It takes forever for her to get out the words, "I'm too far gone. I can't leave. I have to stay. He needs me. So, you do me a favor, and you run for the both of us."

"Who needs you?"

"Doesn't matter. Just go."

I bury my head into her. "Let's go together."

"I want you to get the hell out of here."

"No," I protest. "No, I'm not doing anything—"

Suddenly, her strength is back, and she lifts my torso with her hands. Her voice is loud now, forceful and angry, as she says, "Oh my God, Stella! Get the fuck away from me. Do you understand? You get away. *You* get away—"

"She'll find me."

"No," Amy says decisively. "She won't look."

She's right, I realize. My mother wouldn't look for me.

Amy locks her stare on me. "I'll make sure."

For the first time in five years, my sister is showing me that she loves me.

"Go find your good, Stella."

I freeze and look into her eyes, now glowing in the moonlight streaming in through the window. Her words are Sam Bishop's words, and I can hardly breathe.

"What did you say?"

She abruptly turns from me and throws her arm over her face. "You and I are done. Break free from us. This family is cursed." In a minute, the sound of her sleep fills the room.

I back away from the bed and tiptoe toward the door, just an inch at a time at first. Then, the thought that my mother might show up throws me into action. I don't want to see her ever again.

I turn, and I run.

I am going to save myself.

FIVE
music and daydreams

EVEN THOUGH THE RECEPTION IN MY ANCIENT CAR is not very good, I crank up the fuzzy station and increase my speed. I can't remember the last time when I listened to music, and I've spent the past eight hours exploring everything from country to Motown to classic rock and newer pop. It turns out that I don't care much for jazz or classical. But the fun thing is that I get to choose what I listen to. That understanding is so stupidly simple yet so complex.

The roads are empty, the rest stops are quiet, and the highways belong to truckers and me. I like it.

The three caffeine-laden sodas that I've had are wearing off, and I'm exhausted. I tap my hands on the steering wheel and belt out a song that I've heard about seventy times since I threw some shit into my car and drove out of Chicago. My voice is hoarse and horrendously off-key, but I don't care because I am happy. I'm terrified and sick to my stomach but happy, and that's what's important. Also important is locating a place to sleep because I am wiped out.

Somewhere outside of Buffalo, New York, I pull into a cheap motel. The room smells like moldy cheese and body odor, but that doesn't matter. I lock the door and immediately take a step onto the bed where I jump up and down until I am giggling uncontrollably. I jump so hard that I actually crack my head on the popcorn ceiling and cause it to snow plaster all over the worn paisley quilt. When I drop down onto the mattress, I am out of breath but so full of exuberance that I manically roll back and forth on the now-plastered cover before grabbing fistfuls of blanket and wrapping myself up into a cocoon. In the darkness, I wait for my breathing to settle, for my heart to stop pounding.

"I ran away from home!" I scream into the blanket. "I ran away from home!"

This is, of course, a rather idiotic thing to say. I'm twenty-one years old, not twelve. I haven't done anything illegal or really all that interesting. One really can't *run away* at my age. It's pretty normal to move out of your parents' house, so this is not a monumental feat.

Yet it is.

When I left the hospital, I went home, raided the bathroom for my cosmetics and such, and tossed piles of clothes into two large duffel bags. My laptop and a few other items fit into a tote. I was almost out the door when it occurred to me that I might not want to take on a long drive in my ridiculous dress and heels. That piece-of-shit dress deserved to be burned, but instead, I wasted twenty minutes of good driving time to cut it into shreds and sprinkle those shreds all over my mother's room. I also stuck the godforsaken heels in the fridge, next to a glass jar of caviar labeled *Lucinda's*.

That was how I said good-bye. It seemed fitting.

I'm unclear whether it's the motel blankets or me that stink, but a shower is in order, so I steam myself and use the no-name shampoo and soap provided for me. My mother would be appalled with the lack of a high-end brand, so I wash my hair with the crummy shampoo a total of four times. I consider it a rather thrilling act of retaliation.

At six thirty in the morning, I finally fall asleep.

Although I wake up a few times, it is not until four the next morning when I start to fully come back to life. *Well, shit.* That was pushing twenty-four hours of sleep. I guess I was tired. For a moment, I wonder if I was actually asleep or if I blacked out.

After another shower, I unload my makeup and hairstyling items onto the counter and begin the process of putting myself together. I've had the same routine for years now, and I've never enjoyed spending time drying my hair in big rollers, applying makeup, and worrying about the position of each fucking eyelash. But I go through the motions because this is what I have always done. After I put on the cuff bracelet from my father and a selection of other jewelry, I dress in a navy silk button-down and tan dress pants, and I opt for slip-on shoes for driving.

I have at least ten hours of highway to cover today and no one to share stretches with, but that's okay. I can go this alone. While I drive, I'll make some calls and withdraw from school. I also need to change my cell number. I have a ton of missed calls. I haven't bothered to listen to the messages, so my voice mail is clogged.

I'll do whatever I have to do in order to disappear and start over.

I'm going to find Sam Bishop.

His parents' inn, The Coastal, is located in Watermark, Maine, and according to the Internet, they still own it, so that's a good place to start. For all I know, Sam is away at college in some other faraway state. However, I've never seen the ocean, so I might as well head to The Coastal Inn. Maybe that's not a reason to drive so crazily far, but I want to. For the first time, I'm going after what I want.

And what I want is Sam.

That one day I had with him was…well, I don't know what it was precisely. I just know that it was the last time I felt close to anyone.

It's almost as though I have no choice in the matter. Driving to Maine is a compulsion that I cannot ignore.

Music and daydreams propel me toward my future, whatever that might be.

One thing is for sure. I will eat a lobster.

peace

THE MAINE COASTLINE is dauntingly beautiful with rocky shores, jagged cliffs, seaweed-covered sand, and a deep navy ocean. The water is so dark, and white foam collects in spots as waves form and crash. From my seat on the restaurant deck at The Coastal Inn, I am essentially hanging over the water, and I cannot get enough of the cove.

It's chillier than I would have thought for the last week in April, but I should have known there'd be a cold ocean breeze. I pull my cardigan around me and cross my arms. No one else is on the deck with me, and I'm sure the server thought I was insane for wanting to sit out here, but I couldn't resist watching the sunset.

"It's a beautiful night, isn't it?"

I look to my left and smile at the woman standing next to me. "It's remarkable." It might be the two glasses of wine that I've had, but I am nearly delirious with joy right now. I'm a million miles from Chicago, but I've never felt more at home, at peace. I finish off my glass.

Her spiral curls bounce as she turns to take in the view herself. "It never gets old, even after all this time." She sighs with contentment and unties the apron from around her waist. "How was your food?"

"Perfect. I've never had clam chowder before, and I could have eaten another five bowls." This is true. It tasted like heaven.

"Really? You haven't? Well, come back anytime. We'll make more. Can I get you another glass of wine?"

"Yes," I say with a nod. "Another glass would be great." I see no reason not to get shit-faced. "You've worked here for a while?"

"Not only do I work here, but I actually own The Coastal. My husband, Micah, and I have for years. We live here in the building, too." She puts out a hand. "I'm Felicia."

My heart stops. This is Sam's mother. "It's a pleasure to meet you," I say, trying to sound normal and not all weird and shaky. "I'm Stella Ford."

"Lovely to meet you, too. Let me get you that glass of wine." She stops at the French doors to the main dining room. "I might grab a glass for myself, if you don't mind some company? Dinner service is about wrapped up, and the staff has everything under control. I'm calling it quits for the night."

"I'd love some company."

She returns with wine for the two of us and seats herself at the table, scooting back the chair and resting her feet on the railing. "So, what brings you to Watermark this time of year? A vacation or just passing through?"

I'm not exactly sure how to answer this. I take a big sip and set my glass back down on the table. The sound of the waves is soothing, and the salt air is fresh and smells of life. "I…well…apparently, I dropped out of college and drove across the country. Rather spontaneously."

"Aha." Felicia brushes what looks like flour off her billowy top and smiles. Crow's feet show as her eyes twinkle. "You're on some kind of adventure."

"I don't know."

"Are you running *from* something or *toward* something?"

Another big sip. "I don't know that either. Both maybe."

"Fair enough. That's an exciting place to be."

"It is exciting, isn't it?" I smile.

Felicia has the sort of relaxed, eco-friendly look that my mother would despise. I like this woman more and more every second.

"You've owned the inn for a long time?"

I sink into my chair and listen while she tells me how she and her husband gave up on a chaotic life in New York City years before and moved here.

"One Sunday morning, we read a piece in the paper about the owners were selling this place. It was falling apart really, but it'd become a landmark of sorts despite the conditions. We just…well, we'd both had it with city life, so we cashed out and threw everything we had into this place. I have no idea how we survived, but we built a family and a life here. Even bought a vacation house north of Watermark. So, maybe I understand what you're doing a bit."

The wine is making me tired, and I let the sound of her voice lull me into further relaxation. We talk for the next hour, and I enjoy hearing about all the work that went into renovating the huge old inn, including how they decorated each room individually. They built up the restaurant's menu, and eventually, they created a solid reputation.

"Our son works for us, too. He's basically the building manager."

I'm decidedly drunk right now, and I cannot lie to her. "Sam, right?" I say with a slur. "I know your son."

Her surprise is obvious. "You do?"

"I mean, sort of." I can't help from laughing. This is incredibly stupid and strange to be sitting here, talking to Sam Bishop's mother. "I don't really *know him*, know him. I met him once in Chicago, years ago. He was there for a class trip of some kind."

She lights up, presumably relieved that I'm not a full-blown stalker. "Yes, that's right. He was."

"Sam…helped me on a very bad day. I've always remembered how nice he was. So, Maine seemed like a destination." I rest my head on the back of the chair and look up at the dark sky. "Not that many people are nice, you know? I just kind of hate people a lot of the time, which sucks. I don't want to be like that anymore. All miserable and crazy and…and…hating myself. Sam," I say pointedly, "is a good, good person. You must be a happy mother. Proud."

She studies me with curiosity, but it's not in a bad way. "Did you come here, looking for Sam?"

"Shh." I hold a finger to my lips and suppress a giggle. "Don't say that. It makes me sound creepy."

Felicia laughs. "I won't say anything."

"I don't know what the hell I'm doing. I'm just trying to save myself."

She gives me a thoughtful look. "This is a good place to do that. You're going to stay in town for a while?"

"My plans didn't really include a lot of actual planning. I just…got in my car, and here I am." I look at her now. "I'm so sorry, but I think I'm a little drunk, and I think I should go to bed somewhere." Then, for some reason, in a horrible British accent, I ask too loudly, "Have you got room at the inn?"

Felicia laughs again. "For you? Absolutely."

She pulls me to a stand, and the world spins.

"I have a lovely room upstairs with a king-sized bed, a rose-colored comforter, and more pillows than you'll know what to do with. There's a beautiful view off the balcony. You won't want to leave."

"I already don't."

I scuffle next to her, and her arm slips around my waist to steady me.

"You're a much better mother than mine is. *Was*. Whatever."

Felicia makes me give her my car keys, and she asks someone at the front desk to retrieve my bags from the car. She helps me up a winding broad staircase that leads to the second floor and into the most beautiful cozy room. She pulls a bottle of water from a mini fridge and directs me to drink up. While she goes downstairs to help the person with my bags, I go to the bathroom and drunkenly decide that this is an opportune moment to check my voice mail messages. I hold the phone in the crook of my neck while I fumble for the guest-provided toothbrush and turn on the water.

"Stella! Where are you? How can you disappear on me now of all times?" My mother's voice bellows through the phone, and I roll my eyes. "I'm starving, so I need you to get me dinner."

Next message. "What the hell have you done? How could you do this to me? They're keeping Amy in the *psych unit* and putting her on suicide watch because you fabricated some story about pills and guns. Damn you, Stella. I will never forgive you."

Then, "Oh, sweetheart! I need you!" Lucinda is sobbing. "I am all alone, and I cannot get through this without you. What am I going to tell everyone? How humiliating."

I spit into the sink and keep listening.

"How dare you." Her voice is full of rage and disgust. "After everything I've done for you. And you *leave* me? Amy told me you're gone. You're just like your father—a coward, a child. A *bitch*. Well, you know what? Fine. That's just fine. Don't ever ask me for anything else. You're dead to me."

After this last message and after spending an evening talking to Felicia, I see so clearly that my relationship with my mother is not normal, not close to healthy. Lucinda has been emotionally abusing me for years. I suppose I've allowed it. Maybe I should have been stronger and seen that years ago. I could have fought for myself, escaped earlier, but she'd broken me too much. I hate her for that, for everything.

There are more messages, but I delete them, except for the one from Amy.

"You did it. Good. I won't call you again, and don't call me. I'm going to be fine. I'm not going to die or hurt anyone. I promise. Don't look back. Don't ever look back on us."

That's all she says. The sisterly warmth I got from her at the hospital is gone. She sounds logical and cold in this message.

So, there. It's done. I am effectively alone in the world.

I set down the phone on the marble vanity and gag a few times over the drain before I finish getting ready for bed.

When I stumble out of the bathroom, Felicia is pulling back the puffy duvet for me with a genuinely warm smile. "Hop in, kiddo."

She tucks me in. I am moved beyond words, but I say nothing and crawl into bed, fully dressed. Keeping my eyes open for even one more second is impossible, and I'm too tired to even thank her. But as I drift off, I feel her hand stroke my back and then tuck my hair behind an ear.

SEVEN
stay or go

THE NEXT MORNING, my headache is less excruciating than I expected. My embarrassment, however, is pretty significant.

I turn over, open my eyes, and pull the phone out from under my shoulder where I slept on it all night. The clock next to the bed tells me that it's only a little after seven. The light coming through the curtains is beautiful, and I roll off the bed to pull them open fully.

Jesus, I am still wearing dress pants and my silk top. I look like some business lady who got drunk at an office party and passed out under a desk or something. Fabulous.

I open the sliding door to the small veranda and am hit with a blast of cold air. The view, as promised, really is stunning. I understand how Felicia would never tire of this.

It's a beautiful place to start a new life.

Impulsively, I take the phone, still in my hand, and hurl it off the balcony toward the water below. I shut the door and then head for the shower.

An hour and a half later, after slugging through my usual routine, I am dressed and made up. I look terrible though. My eyeliner is all wrong, my long hair is frizzing in this salt air, and there's a run in my knee-highs. A knock on the door is the only thing that distracts me from my faulty appearance.

Felicia has delivered breakfast, which seems excessively kind, given my weird behavior last night. "Good, you're awake! And dressed…to run a staff meeting?" She winks and then walks past me before setting a tray on the dresser. "House omelet with local goat cheese, fresh spinach, and tomatoes. Bread from The Finicky Turtle, which is an amazing bakery right down the street. I know. The name is bizarre, but don't let that stop you. And a pot of coffee. I figured you might need it."

I hardly know what to say. Maybe I should confess my act of littering, flinging my cell phone into the Maine ocean. Maybe I should say that I'm a moron, and I'm driving back to Chicago right after I inhale this breakfast. Maybe I should throw myself into her arms and sob. Instead, I say, "Thank you." It's inadequate, but it's all I can come up with.

"I have to get back to the kitchen." Felicia places a hand on each hip, and her head tips to one side.

I can't read her expression, but it can't be a good one.

I look down. "I'm sorry about last night. I'm going to take off. You've been really—"

"Here." She cuts me off and steps closer. Grabbing my hand, she pushes a key into my palm. "You need a place to stay for more than a few nights. We have a house not far from here at the end of the road. The place needs some work, but it's quiet, high on a cliff, and surrounded by trees. I think you'll like it. The second floor is available to rent, so I'm giving you this key. Pay when you can. I left directions under your plate."

"Wait, what?" I protest. "I don't even know if I should stay." I still can't look at her. "What I said about Sam last night…driving here was insane. *I'm* insane."

"Check it out. If you like it, stay. If you decide to go, that's fine, too. Spend a few more nights in this room, if you like. Sounds as though you don't really have anywhere else to be, right? You might as well settle in someplace safe." Felicia walks to the door and pauses. Then, very softly and gently, she says, "Sam could use a friend. I think that friend might be you."

I notice that the crinkles around her eyes are not just from smiling, and her rough skin isn't just from the frigid Maine winds or too much sun. Felicia's face is washed with pain.

"Okay," I say. "Okay. Thank you. Thank you so much."

The door shuts behind her, and I realize that I didn't ask who lives on the first floor of the house to which she gave me the key. Maybe I already know.

I retrieve the breakfast she brought me and devour it while sitting on the bed. Felicia is right. I have nowhere else to be. I'm on the verge of something resembling happiness, and I've gotten myself this far, so I might as well keep going. In fact, now that I've ditched my phone, I'm feeling pretty damn good. Not to mention, this omelet is ridiculously delicious, and the bread is like nothing I've ever had. I resolve to check out the small town of Watermark and to make a point to stop into The Finicky Turtle bakery.

I decide to see my new apartment before buying groceries and other supplies. This is my first place on my own, away from my mother. As that understanding begins to take over my entire soul, I cannot wait to get there. I set the breakfast tray outside the door and toss a few belongings into my bag. When I check out at the front desk, I learn that my stay was on the house, and I'm again overwhelmed by the generosity and care Felicia has shown me.

It is indeed a short drive. I weave my car down the winding road running from the inn through the center of town. I know from the map I studied yesterday that Watermark is one of a group of towns that make up the Britannia Bay area. Ellsworth is about an hour away, and if I really decide to stay here, I might have to venture up to that larger town to find a big supermarket or chain store.

In the light of day, I am even more charmed by this waterside town, and I nearly miss my turn up the steep hill. Gravel and sand bounce under my tires, and a few low hanging branches brush my windshield. This is obviously a converted single-family house, and the structure has certainly seen better days—white paint is chipping off every surface, and there are a few missing shutters—but it's still beyond beautiful.

I park in the shady drive, and then as instructed per Felicia's note, I walk up the rickety stairs on the side porch leading to the upstairs unit. There are bay views—postcard views really—from here and the back of the house.

It takes a minute of fiddling with the key before I walk in. A small kitchen with an island opens into the living room. I check the ancient gas stove, and after a bit of clicking, it actually lights. Then, I open the cabinets and drawers. They're empty, so I will have to get dishes and whatnot immediately and definitely also some cleaning supplies. To say the place needs a thorough scouring is an understatement. Dust coats every surface, but at least the living room has a stone coffee table and an armchair. With some hard labor, the wood floor planks might be gorgeous. A cobbled fireplace takes up a corner of the room, the rocky frame climbing all the way to the ceiling. I have no idea how to start a fire, but I resolve to learn.

I wander around a corner toward the bedroom, which is surprisingly large, and I'm relieved to find a bed and dresser. Despite the dust, both are in good shape, and they are probably antiques. What I love most about this room though is that the doors open to a wraparound porch overlooking the water. I clap my hands and do a little jump. *Who has a view like this?* My smile refuses to be controlled right now, so I let my heart soar. The first attempt to fling open the doors in a celebratory move is less dramatic than I hoped because the hinges are nearly rusted shut, so it is only after much tugging and jiggling that I get them open. I step out and take a deep breath. It was worth the struggle.

The sound of a car pulling up to the house is the only thing that takes me out of my ocean daydreams.

He's here. I'm surprisingly calm, and I continue looking out over the seascape.

The clop of heavy shoes slowly moves closer as he walks up the steps to reach this side of the house, and soon, I can feel him standing at the top of the stairs. I'm terrified to turn and see him.

"I heard someone rented the apartment." His voice is deep and level, unexpressive. "I live on the first floor. Let me know if you need anything." He pauses. "I'm Sam Bishop."

"I know." Finally, I get myself to pull from the view and face him.

He looks almost nothing like the boy I met years before. While his body has filled out, chest and arms pulling tightly on the fabric of his shirt, his face is ashen, and his demeanor is anything but warm. Light-brown hair falls around his face, resting on broad shoulders. His eyes are dull, missing the life and exuberance I remember so well. I notice his work boots, dirty jeans, and flannel shirt tied at the waist. But he's still Sam, and he is still the reason I'm here.

"You probably don't remember me," I start to say, leaning back against the wooden rail. "We met a long time ago in Chicago."

Sam's brown eyes narrow, and he takes a quick stride toward me. "I wouldn't lean on that—"

Just as the wood behind me gives out, he slings a strong arm around my waist and pulls me in hard, throwing us both away from the edge.

I can barely catch my breath. "Holy shit."

"I guess my mother didn't warn you about this."

He is more muscular than I was prepared for, and I am struck by how enveloped I am in his frame. The last time I was this close to a male was when I was with Jay. The memory of him blazes through my mind, and I can't help but flinch.

"You okay?" Sam flashes concern for a moment.

I make myself relax. Sam is not Jay, and he's not hurting me.

"Yes. Thank you."

"My truck is full of lumber to repair the whole deck."

"Okay. I'm fine. You're fine," I say dumbly.

The truth is that Sam actually stinks to high heaven, and he's dirty and sweaty and frankly pretty gross right now, but I cannot stop looking into his eyes.

"You smell like fish," I say without thinking.

"Been up since before dawn on a boat. Extra money." His arm is still holding me against him, and he's matching my intent gaze, but he feels cold, closed off. "Technically, this house is mine, so it wasn't really my mother's right to rent out the top unit," he says, not concealing his irritation.

"I'm sorry. I didn't know."

"It needs a lot of work, and I haven't gotten to it yet." Then, for a moment, a spark of recognition appears in his deep brown eyes. "Stella?" His hand falls from my back. "Stella Ford."

I nod hesitantly. "Yes."

"What in the fuck are you doing here?"

It's perhaps not quite the reunion I was hoping for, and now, I don't know what to say.

"I just...needed someplace to go," I answer meekly. Then, because he doesn't say anything, I add, "I've never had lobster. You said it was good."

He doesn't seem much for conversation, but he's still studying me.

"I can go. I can find somewhere else if you want. I just..."

Sam moves away, and I watch his solid swagger take him across the porch as he calls back to me, "Stay, go. I don't really care. But I have to get to work. It's going to be noisy. Keep the windows and doors shut, so the apartment doesn't fill with sawdust."

Well, so much for the happy, caretaking solid guy of years ago. I've just had a rude awakening in the form of Sam Bishop.

I guess I'll have to figure out how to crack and eat a lobster on my own.

EIGHT
the perfect fit

AS I WANDER AROUND PICTURESQUE WATERMARK the next morning, I realize how utterly ridiculous I look in my full hair and makeup, not to mention my completely impractical shoes and fussy outfit. While I might have been here for less than twenty-four hours, the realization that I am coming off like some wealthy tourist bothers me. Somehow, it feels disrespectful to this beautiful town.

The couple at The Finicky Turtle bakery is covered in flour, wearing T-shirts, and they smile when they hand me the bag with bread and croissants. An older man at the small hardware and home goods store helps me find some household basics to get me through the next few days. He doesn't seem the least self-conscious about the tufts of hair sticking out from his ears or the limp that makes him teeter from side to side as he walks. I admire that about him, how he's so relaxed in what could be considered imperfections.

After I load some bags into my car, I hit the supermarket. It's actually less of a true supermarket and more of a very upscale gourmet-food shop with amazingly overpriced sauces, but I amass a collection of bottles and jars to put into my pantry. I have no idea what I'll do with them since I can't really cook. The butcher wraps up steak and shrimp in plastic and brown paper, ties it with string, and then kindly repeats cooking instructions, trying to reassure me that I can make dinner without any disasters. I buy two bottles of wine, a red and a white, in case I need to console myself. I don't really drink beer, but I also grab a six-pack of a Maine brew, supporting local businesses and all.

By the time I get back to my new home, I am exhausted and defeated. Part of me is wholly overjoyed at my freedom, bursting with a nearly manic sense of release that I do not have constraints and criticism and pathology bearing down on me at every turn. But right now, I am also completely lost and daunted at what I've done. Abandoning one's life without a coherent, logical plan does not exactly breed security, especially for someone like me who has barely detectable confidence.

After I load groceries into the fridge, I literally roll up my sleeves and put on yellow gloves, and then I begin the long process of disinfecting this place. It doesn't appear that anyone has rented the unit in ages, and there is not one inch that doesn't need cleaning. I start with the kitchen.

A few hours later, when I've decontaminated as best as I can, I hear Sam beginning work on the deck and on the railing that nearly killed me. I don't know whether to avoid going to my bedroom because he's right outside those doors. He hasn't been what one might call welcoming. Not that I blame him.

I barely have anything to unpack, but I put away the few things that I do have. I have a framed picture of me with my father and Amy that was taken only a few weeks before the car accident. I'll never understand what happened that day, including the bits of conversation that I overheard between him and Amy or the way he made such a conscious decision to disappear from our lives. Amy and I never spoke of the accident or our father abandoning us, and I'm sure we never will. Our mother taught us how to expertly block out the past, and I'm trying hard to do that.

I set the photo on the mantel because I can't help but feel a little comforted by the familiarity of two people who used to negate my mother's atrocities. My father had the kindest eyes, a thought which now seems unbelievably ironic. Kind people don't ditch their children. I move the frame facedown. I don't have the heart to trash the photo, but I can't look at what I've lost either. This is a nutty compromise, but it can stay on the mantel as long as I don't have to look at it.

I mop and polish, and then I decide to be brave. Maybe it's the fumes from the cleaning products that are making me aggressive, but I'm bothered that Sam was such a complete prick yesterday. Now that I've got gleaming wood and shiny appliances, I'm in a better mood.

It's well past lunchtime, but I make a roast beef sandwich loaded with vegetables and a pretentious flavored mayonnaise that I bought this morning. I grab the six-pack of beer and balance the plate when I crack open the bedroom door.

Sam has removed the entire railing and is wearing a mask while he uses an electric sander at the far end of the deck. I try shouting his name a few times, but I can see that he's wearing earbuds, and the sander is making too much noise. I stand awkwardly out of the sawdust blast and wait for him to notice me.

Eventually, he squats back on his knees and blows out air to clear his eyes, the dust around him settling slowly. At the sight of him, I immediately relax. I don't care about yesterday or that he's got the same cold look in his eyes now. Being in his presence is grounding, stabilizing, so I smile as I lift the plate and beer, questioning if he's interested. With the back of his hand, Sam wipes sweat from his forehead, takes out his earbuds, and nods.

I step over a power cord and hand him the plate. "Thought you might be hungry and thirsty."

"Thanks." He scoots to the edge of the deck and hangs his legs off the side.

I take a breath and brazenly sit next to him. Sam shoots me a slightly irritated look, but I cast my gaze out at the water and ignore it. He says nothing as he takes a napkin from me, and we sit silently while he eats.

When he's finished half of the sandwich, I take a bottle from the six-pack and twist off the top. I pass it to him but don't let go when he puts his hand on it.

Finally, his eyes are forced to meet mine. "Why are you smiling?" he asks.

I shrug. "I think I might be happy. Hard to know, considering how foreign that is to me, but I might be."

He tugs on the beer, and I let go. His long hair falls back as he takes an extended swig, and I admire his solid jawline, the ruddiness in his cheeks from hours of work, and the fullness of his lips as he drinks. Sam's wearing a worn sleeveless red shirt that's drenched in sweat, and it's impossible not to notice the definition in his arms. He is still the boy I knew from that one day, but he's also now a man, one who I don't know at all. I study him as he nearly inhales the beer. What's clear is that something has happened to Sam Bishop because a hardness and bitterness about him is evident in everything he does. He reeks of pain and darkness.

I have my own pain to heal, but Sam's is perhaps more jarring to me. Having seen the before and now seeing the after is difficult. He has hurt that is significant.

I open another beer for him and one for myself, and we sit without speaking for another fifteen minutes, dangling our legs off the side of the unfinished deck, while staring out across the ocean.

At one point, Sam slightly lifts his chin and points with the bottle. "Porpoise."

I squint toward where he's gesturing and see the figure bounding in the waves. I would never have been able to pick out the animal if he hadn't shown me. My smile might be permanent. The porpoise travels out of sight, and I shift my eyes to the ground below.

At this time of year, the yard is just coming back to life. It's not a huge garden under my feet, but what's there is rather unusual. I can see five distinct dirt circles carved into the grass, each probably three feet in diameter. Something about Sam's funny landscaping is quite charming, but I don't ask him what he plans on growing there. I want to be surprised. A set of tiered flat stones creates a small path to a long dock that leads out over boulders and into the water, and I make a note to take a walk down there soon.

The silence between us might be uncomfortable for him—I don't know—but it's not for me. On this scraped-up deck with the water view and the evergreen frame, I am filled with peace. While Sam isn't overwhelming me with conversation and enthusiasm, he hasn't pushed me off the deck. So, there's that, and I'll take it.

"I gotta get back to work." He returns the empty bottle to the cardboard box and wipes his hands on his jeans as he stands. "It shouldn't take more than a couple of days to finish up."

"I'm sure it's going to look great." A breeze blows, and I raise a hand to my eyes. For a second, I think I see movement in the foliage near the dock, but then it's gone. Clearly, my perceptions are still wonky, and I silently curse my mother for how I see or *mis*-see everything. "Is there a Laundromat here? I don't have that much with me, so I'll need to wash clothes soon."

He checks my outfit, covered in dirt and cleaning products. "There's a washer and dryer in the basement. The door is on the side of the house." Sam replaces his earbuds and mask and reaches for the sander. He starts it up as I walk past, but then he turns it off. After a few moments, with his head still down, he says, "Thanks for lunch."

"You brought me Wonder Woman socks, Bishop. It was the least I could do."

Even though he refuses to look at me and even from behind the shield of his hair, I can see him smile.

It's a start. And I wonder if he remembers more details of that day and if he remembers the way he took care of me and how I ran into his arms and how our teenage kiss was more than just that.

For the rest of the afternoon and into the early evening, I tackle the bedroom. While I do leave the French doors shut to keep out the noise and debris from Sam's work, I take down the formerly white curtains that are now covered in cobwebs.

I catch Sam's eye a few times as he walks past, but I try very hard not to stare.

The sheets and comforter that I pulled from the closet are worn and have a few holes, but they're soft and cozy. They're also rather musty, as I discovered when sleeping on them last night, but a good wash will fix those and the curtains.

Sam is now at the front section of the deck when I head out with an armful of bedding.

On my way back up from starting a wash, he calls down to me, "You should wear better shoes around here."

I have on ankle boots with two-inch heels. It is a little odd to be doing hard cleaning in these shoes, not to mention in the linen pants and patterned blouse right out of the dry-cleaning bag. Both of which will probably end up in the trash after today.

"I told you. I don't have much here."

"Oh. Right." Sam lifts a large bucket and relocates it to another spot. "The deck is going to be wet with stain for a while, so stay off of it."

I nod and go back upstairs.

After a thorough shower and an hour of primping, I decide to continue with my bravery and attempt to cook the steak and shrimp I bought this morning. Because my culinary skills have been limited to microwave meals, I'm thinking that I should have bought a cookbook, too, but this can't be that difficult.

Except it is because I burn the steak, filling the entire room with smoke, yet I've managed to leave the inside undercooked. And I stupidly forgot to remove the shrimp shells, which I didn't notice until I had a mouthful of them. I dump my inedible food into the trash.

Wine and bread, I decide, are a suitable dinner, so I open the windows to air out the place and curl up on the sofa with a glass of red wine. It's cold tonight, but I have to get rid of this smell, and I have no idea how to start a fire in the fireplace. I tear off a piece of sourdough, drink wine, snuggle under a blanket, and stare at the fireplace screen. I'm still crazy enough that I can picture flames. It's a fun side benefit of my mental issues.

Midway through my second glass, there's a knock at my front door. Immediately, my stomach drops, and the glass in my hand begins to tremble. I see the imaginary flames in the fireplace double in size and burst toward me. It's her. She said I was dead to her, but my mother has come after me. I shake my head and clear my thoughts. It cannot be her, and I will not live in a state of constant paranoia.

Sam is at the door with a stack of laundry in his hands. "Are you trying to burn the place down?"

"It's out. It's out. I promise." I look back at the fireplace. *Shit. Was that real? No. There are no flames. But maybe there were?* My voice is shaky. "I'm sorry."

"What were you trying to cook?"

"Oh." He means my burned dinner. My heart rate starts returning to normal. "Steak and shrimp."

"I can smell it downstairs." His breath is loaded with alcohol.

"It didn't go well." I shuffle my feet. "Did you know that shrimp have shells? They're clear. It's kind of deceptive, if you ask me."

"I did actually. You know"—Sam waves a hand around behind him—"Maine and all." He doesn't full on sway, but he's not acting as though he's on solid ground either.

"I know. Trust me. I'm embarrassed."

He holds out his laundry to me. "Here."

I blink at him. "You…want me to do your laundry?"

"Really?" He rolls his eyes. "They're for you. Some T-shirts and sweats and jeans. They'll be too big for you, but you said you don't have much, so…you might need something to sleep in or whatever. And you can't go around scrubbing floors in dresses and stuff."

My face heats up as he gestures to the long dress I have on. I take the stack of clothes from him. "Thank you. This is very sweet." I fidget with the tag on one of the shirts. "I'm going to order some clothes online tomorrow."

Sam nods and starts to leave, but then he looks back. "You doin' okay?"

I nod back. "Yeah, I'm doing okay."

That night, I sleep in a Red Sox shirt that is three sizes too big, yet it fits perfectly.

NINE
lobsters and breathing

IT'S NOT AS THOUGH THE HEAVENS HAVE OPENED UP and doused me in utter ecstasy, but my first two weeks in Maine have given me hope that I can save myself. No one is telling me what to do or how I'm doing it wrong or that I'm hideous and useless and pathetic. No one is clinging to me out of narcissistic need. I'm trying to shake off years of damage, much of it from my family, but I also fault myself for not being stronger. Jay, for instance, and what I allowed him to do to me was sick.

I'm trying to build a new life for myself, one that I choose and I direct, but I'm so paralyzed that I hardly leave the house, except to restock food. I'm a little tired of sandwiches, but I'll live. My apartment is still almost empty because I haven't the slightest idea how to decorate it. I don't know what I like, but I do know that I can't stand the sight of anything that looks like something my mother might choose.

Every day, I sit in the rather barren living room with my laptop and work on my designs, occasionally hopping on store websites to browse clothes. I've nearly bought about a million items before deleting shopping carts. It's just another example of how I haven't the slightest clue of who I am outside of the push-and-pull relationship with my mother. And that makes me want to vomit. Designing for clients who hire me to create graphics, book covers, banners, and all that—that's easy. I can do for others. When it comes to figuring out myself, I'm still rather lost.

I take a break to grab some coffee. I don't care that it's already seven. I don't sleep well anyway. Caffeine is the least of my worries.

As I walk to the kitchen, I catch sight of myself in the old mirror hanging by a scraggly piece of twine. Something about my reflection is vile, but I can't decide what. My hair and makeup are as they always are, and my navy dress and nylons are clean and orderly. Suddenly, I realize how fucking asinine it is that I am still dressing in these preposterous clothes that my mother expected and that I'm spending eons every morning on some stupid beauty routine that only makes me feel worse about myself. I can't stand to look at myself any longer.

As I stir sugar into my coffee, I become more and more agitated. While still in the kitchen, I pull the dress over my head and yank down my nylons. I stuff them in the trash can, and then I grab scissors from a drawer and head for the bathroom.

The water pressure from the sink is not great, so it takes a while, but I soap up my face and scrub until I can barely breathe under all the water that I'm splashing over my skin. I go through a few cotton balls of makeup remover to get the last of the eyeliner and mascara off, and then I really examine myself as I am—without gobs of shit all over my face. Right now, a stranger is looking back at me, one I'm going to have to get to know. My fingers run over my lips, my eyes, my forehead as I trace my features and feel what it is to be me.

Section by section, I hold handfuls of hair out, and the scissors chop through them. All I care about is getting rid of the weight that has been dragging me down. Dyed auburn locks fall over the sink and the floor, and I don't stop cutting until my hair is well above my chin. I run wet fingers through it and push it off my face. I start laughing with relief and exhilaration. This is better. My natural dark brown shows through at the roots, and I'm happy.

I dump my makeup bag into the waste bin, but then I think better of losing it all. I refuse to ever again be a slave to those products, but even I can't argue with putting on a little something now and then. Only if I want, only if it's fun for me.

After loading a trash bag with all my old clothes, I throw on one of Sam's sleeveless T-shirts and a pair of his jeans. I have to roll the legs and the waist, so I can walk without tripping, and my bra is totally showing on the sides, but I am so beyond comfortable that I don't mind how kooky I might look. It's now become imperative that I buy some clothes that fit me, so I'm going to have to go shopping tomorrow. With glee, I decide I want ninety pairs of jeans. I don't think I've worn jeans since I was a kid, and I plan to make up for that.

It's after eight when I hear Sam's truck rumble up to the house. I've barely seen him, but the sound stops me in my tracks every time he comes home. I've resisted my constant urge to race out of the house to catch sight of him. It's not as though he's given me the slightest indication that he wants any sort of friendship. Sometimes, I hear his music playing downstairs, and I'll lie on the floor and press my ear to the wood, trying to hear what he listens to. Maybe then I can find out who he is, why he's so angry.

I miss him, which is crazy and not based on reason, but I do.

The sound of his footsteps coming up the stairs is reassuring, and I wait to hear his front door slam. Instead, the footsteps continue, and then he knocks on my door. The second that I open it, he walks in with two large paper bags in his arms, and he goes right to the kitchen. I stand, dumbfounded, while he begins unpacking the contents onto my counter, and then he adds water to a large pot that he brought.

When I get to the kitchen, he's got a burner going, and he is chopping an onion.

"Hi," I say.

"Hi." Sam keeps chopping. "Do you want to open that wine for me?" His elbow juts out to a bottle by the stove.

The corkscrew shakes in my hand a bit, but I manage to get the cork out. I set down the bottle and stare at him until he looks at me.

"What?" he asks all innocently.

I keep staring.

"I'm cooking you things with shells. Steamed clams and mussels in a tomato-wine broth and then two lobsters."

I bite my lip and try not to smile. Sam, however, gives in and shows me the first smile I've seen on him. It looks good.

I cross my arms. "What if I've already eaten dinner?"

"Have you?"

"Well, no," I admit.

"Because you were too busy cutting your hair?"

Shit. Shit! I forgot. He probably thinks I look atrocious. "Are you making fun of me?"

He shakes his head. "Not at all. Short hair suits you. And…" His eyes travel over my face. "I like the new look. You don't need all that makeup."

"It wasn't really me anyway."

He smashes garlic with the side of the knife and then locates another good-sized pot under the counter. After a few minutes, he asks, "So, what *is* you?"

It's a simple question really and one I should be able to answer without my head swirling as I struggle to find a response. The room grows fuzzy in front of me, and I feel my anxiety level climb. "I don't know. I have no idea. I threw out all my clothes and don't know what to buy. I can't decorate the apartment because I don't know what I like." I can hear my voice rising along with my panicked diatribe. "I don't even know if I'll like what you're cooking because I've only had stuffed clams once at some stupid goddamn social affair that my fucking insane mother made me go to, and I couldn't even taste anything I was eating. I never taste anything. When I was out with my mother, she'd watch everything I ate. She often told me what I could and couldn't eat, what I liked and what I didn't. It was that way with everything—*everything*—until it got to where I truly had no idea what I liked and didn't. What I felt. What I saw. Who I was. Then, the other night, when I had clam chowder for the first time at your parents' inn, I actually got to really taste something and like it, all on my own. It sounds ridiculous, I know, but that was the first time I remember enjoying food, and it was probably a fluke. Something is wrong with me if I don't know what I like, and what if you make this and—"

"Breathe," he says calmly as he adds oil and the chopped garlic to the small pot.

"And why are you cooking dinner like that's a normal thing to do? You just march in here after barely speaking to me and act all blasé and cool? You don't even really remember much about when we met, do you? That day? It was a big day for me, and it was probably nothing to you, which I get. Why would it be?"

"You didn't breathe." He catches a tomato that almost rolled off the counter and then expertly begins dicing it.

I inhale and exhale dramatically. "Happy?"

Sam adds the tomato, sending a burst of steam into the air, and the smell immediately fills the room. For a few minutes, he just cooks as though I'm not there, as though I have not just blurted out monstrously huge and weird shit. But I can see that he is thinking. Then, he puts down the knife and faces me while I swim in confusion across from him.

He runs his hands through his hair a few times. "I've been an asshole. I'm sorry." Now, he's the one who takes a big breath, but he maintains eye contact while he blows me away with his words. "You up and ditched an entire life in Chicago, which is a big goddamn deal. I don't know what you left behind, but it was some pile of shit, I'm guessing." He looks away and busies himself with rummaging through a drawer.

I watch him take mussels and clams from a netted bag, and he washes them under the tap.

"I'm glad you're doing something for yourself. Healing." He pauses. "We should all be as smart as you are. As strong. You're pretty tough, you know that?"

In the few moments it takes Sam to say these words, he undoes so many knots of unhappiness that have been twisting inside me for years.

I also realize that this is a boy who knows deep pain.

We stand side by side in the kitchen for the next half an hour, our arms occasionally brushing while we cook, with no further discussion. Sam teaches me that mussels and clams are done when their shells are fully open, and we throw out a few that stay closed. I laugh when he takes the live lobsters out of a bag and strokes one with a finger, causing it to go limp.

"See? You can put them to sleep. You know, before you really put them to sleep." He winks and drops one into the pot that has a few inches of boiling water. "You do the next one," he insists.

I scream and whine as I hold the lobster as far away from my body as possible. Then, with half-shut eyes, I fling it into the pot. Sam claps the lid down.

Since I don't have a proper dining room table—or maybe as an excuse to stay close to him in the cramped kitchen—I suggest we just eat in here. I hop onto the counter while Sam pours the clams and mussels from the steaming pot into a large bowl. He rips off a piece of bread and dunks it into the aromatic broth. Then, he cups his hand under the dripping bread as he lifts it to my mouth.

"Good, right? This isn't that farm-raised shit. This is the real thing, straight from the ocean."

I groan and nod. I get that same salty depth that I got from the clam chowder I had at the inn. That reminds me that I've been avoiding stopping in to see Sam's mom, Felicia. I didn't know how to explain that Sam had not been particularly friendly. Well, until now.

"Is it really good, or are you just saying that?" he asks.

"It's delicious. For real." It is. I can taste and smell as I never have. It's as though my body is coming alive in all new ways.

"Intense, huh? Now, try this." He scrapes a clam loose and hands me the shell. "It's okay if you don't like it. Some people are weirded out by the texture."

I shake my head as I swallow. "No, it's so good."

Next, I greedily devour three more clams as if I haven't eaten in years. I can't get enough of the briny taste. The mussels are just as good—a smokier taste but wonderful. We pull out the meat and toss our empty shells across the room, making baskets into the trash bin.

"You'll be into oysters on the half shell soon enough, I bet," he says happily.

While we eat, I ask Sam about working at his parents' inn, and he tells me he loves when he gets to demolish a bathroom and redo it and when he replaced the roof last fall.

"Nothing better than walking on top of a three-story building."

"Yeah, if you have a death wish."

He holds back a smile, which I find confusing. "I don't have a death wish. Trust me."

"Okay." I study him for a moment. "You didn't go to college then?"

He makes a clamshell arc perfectly, and it lands in the center of the trash. "I did. I was at Colby for a few years."

"You dropped out?"

"Yeah. What about you? Did you go to college?"

I nod. "I also dropped out. About a day before I showed up here. Why did you leave?"

He shrugs nonchalantly, and I can tell he's trying not to make a big deal out of it, but a cloud of darkness washes over him. "I just...I don't know. I wasn't in a good place."

"Were you failing out or something?"

He laughs. "Actually, I was doing very well. There was...just...other stuff going on. Can we leave it at that?" The timer that he set on his phone goes off. "Lobsters are ready."

Sam walks me step-by-step through the process of cracking open lobster shells and pulling out the meat, leaning over the bowl to my left but staying close. The way he talks and moves is soothing, comforting. I notice how crystal clear everything is tonight—the colors, the sounds, the smells. There's sharpness to my world.

"Everyone is always crazy about the tail meat," he says, "but if you ask me, the best flavor is in these knuckles and the claws." He twists a red arm from the body and breaks it open. "Not only is the meat better, but there's all the liquid that you can't miss." Sam is inches from me when he brings a claw shell to my lips. "Drink."

I tip my head back a bit and let him pour hot liquid into my mouth. It's the richest, purest taste I've ever experienced. When he takes the shell away, I rub my lips together and smile. "More," I whisper.

So, he feeds me juice from the other claw. A rumble of thunder echoes just as I finish. I didn't even notice that a storm might be brewing, but I can feel the change in the air, the tingle on my skin. Sam's a bit distracting though. He steps in even closer, his waist moving between my legs. My eyes travel down the length of his muscular arm, to his hand that moves to rest on my thigh.

"More?" he asks softly.

"Yes," I breathe.

"You sure, *more*?" His voice is soft and teasing.

Now, I take in his broad shoulders, the way his shirt fits snugly and shows the shape of his chest, and mostly, the way our closeness, our sudden intimacy, radiates around us. Our draw to each other is palpable, yet this is much more than just sexual. I'm momentarily shaken by the inexplicable perfection of us being together. We hardly know each other, so my certainty about this should feel off. But it doesn't.

His hand gently cups my waist, and he moves his head in a bit. It only takes lifting my mouth a few inches before his lips come to mine. There is no hesitation and no tentative light kiss to feel our way around. Immediately, we have rhythm and instinct as though we've done this forever. He moves his mouth and tongue with an exquisite balance of confidence and tenderness, and I respond easily and naturally.

I touch my hands to his chest and admire his strength and solidity. His arm wraps behind me and pulls me in, so I slip my hands up to the back of his neck and let him bring us closer together. Each time his tongue slides against mine, a rush of adrenaline courses through me. I realize that I have been waiting for this since the exact minute when our last kiss ended all those years ago.

Right now, while burning heat and a certain level of aggressiveness come from both of us, it is also clear to me that this is not the precursor to sex. He's not going to clear off the counter and fuck me without care as if I mean nothing. And there is safety and security in his reserve. This is a kiss with meaning and feeling and not just an obligatory step before getting laid.

I know what that feels like, and this isn't it.

Even with my eyes closed, I sense the burst of lightning that flashes just before the thunder hits again.

Sam slows our kiss until his lips are barely brushing against me. "Food's getting cold."

He rubs his nose against mine, and I feel him smile.

"Okay."

"We can't let your first real lobster dinner go to waste."

"No," I agree.

But this is already the best meal I've ever had.

We get through the rest of dinner without me cramming my tongue down his throat, but it does take effort. I want to maintain the innocence in this night even though I know that it would be so easy for both of us to let it go further. I actually crack and shell the second lobster all on my own, and I feel a rather inflated sense of accomplishment that I *know* is inflated but that I nonetheless allow. We taste-test, dipping the meat in melted butter. He feeds me a chunk seasoned with a squeeze of lemon, and when he coats a piece in hot sauce, it sends me grabbing for bread.

I am drunk on flavor and drunk on Sam.

When we're done, he refuses to let me help clean and insists that I sit exactly where I am on the counter. "You just stay there and drink wine and look all kinds of cute in my clothes."

In between swipes at the counter with a dish towel, he leans in and gives me quick kisses, and it's all I can do not to wrap my legs around him and lock him against me. This all feels right—inexplicably, indescribably right—and he looks as giddy as I feel.

The wall that was between us has collapsed.

After everything is put away, my heart sinks when he helps me down onto the floor.

"I have to go. Early morning at the inn."

"Yeah. Of course."

"Stop by if you want. I'm going to be painting one of the guest rooms. My parents have a ton of furniture and stuff stored there, all different kinds of styles. Come pick out whatever you like, and I'll bring everything home in my truck."

"Really? That would be great. Thank you." I shiver as he strokes a hand up and down my arm. "And, uh...do you know where I can get my hair...fixed?"

"It doesn't need fixing. But my sister, Kelly, has a little salon in town on East Street. Tell her I sent you." When we're at my front door, he stops after he opens it. "Stella? I'm sorry things were so bad that you had to leave home. You've been through a lot."

I don't tell him that my mother's voice haunts me at every turn or that Amy's frightening drug-induced laughter keeps me awake at night or that my father's absence still hurts as much today as it did when he first left. Instead, I lift up on my toes and kiss him, very slowly, until I run out of breath, and my heels drop back to the floor.

"Wait here for a minute?" From the bag of clothing that I've discarded, I retrieve a shirt and bring it out to him. "Don't laugh, but I need you to tell me something." The fabric twists in my hands while I work up the stupid amount of courage it takes to ask him this. "What color is this? I need you to tell me. I need to hear it from you."

He doesn't laugh or act as though I'm completely crazy. Sam can tell that I'm not joking. "It's green, Stella."

I want to weep. I was right. It *is* green. "My mother insisted this shirt is purple. She spent her entire life trying to trick me and make me doubt myself so that I couldn't trust anything. Most of all, myself. This shirt thing was minor really. But who does that, right? She wasn't being funny or playing around. My mother…" I take a big breath. "My mother stripped me of being anything but a pawn in her game. But this shirt is green. And I am going to find myself."

"Stella…oh God."

Sam puts a hand on my face, and I lean into his palm just as I did in the hospital stairwell. Again, I am comforted and grounded.

He kisses my forehead. "I'm so sorry. I get why you left. You are very brave, and you deserve to find yourself."

"You deserve that, too, Sam. I don't know why, but you're so sad, aren't you?"

"Sometimes." The little smile he gives me breaks my heart. "But not today." He turns to leave and then stops and faces me again. "Oh, and Stella…I do remember that day at the hospital with you. Of course I do. And I remember the kiss. It was windy and freezing out. The lights barely cut through the snow, but I could still see you. I think I would have seen you anywhere. You ran to me, *right* into my arms, as if you'd done it a thousand times. I hadn't kissed a lot of girls, and I didn't really know what I was doing, but you made it easy. It felt crazy and unexplainable and perfect. Even though I was only sixteen, I knew enough to understand that it was one of the most important and most powerful moments I would ever have."

He pauses for a moment, and I can barely breathe.

"You were not just some unhappy beautiful girl in a stairwell. You were more. You *are* more."

Thunder roars, and lightning cracks sharply. Sam disappears into the dark, but what he's given me tonight stays firmly in my soul.

I hear him do his two-foot hop down each step.

He's right. Today is definitely not a day to be sad.

TEN
sun showers

NOW THAT SAM AND I ARE SPEAKING—well, and kissing and being all heated or whatever—I feel like an asshole while walking around town in his clothes. But the fabric of his old T-shirt is soft and worn, and it's shaped to fit him, so I like the way it feels on me. But after I stop in to see him, I'm going to make the rather long drive to a mall to buy myself more clothes. Girl clothes—not clothes borrowed from a smokin' hot neighbor boy who fed me seafood last night and then kissed me until I thought I might scream.

I'm energized and alert in an entirely new way today. My body is aware of every move I make, my skin reacting to air and touch with renewed sensitivity, and my mood is undeniably positive. Now, I just need to adjust my outward appearance to match.

The temperature is in the high sixties today, and the sky is a flawless blue. It's perfect weather for this seaside town. The traffic in Watermark is slowly picking up, exactly as Sam told me it would, as the town heads into true tourist season. It's strange to be back down at the inn again. The last time I was here was very different, but I'm no longer freaked out from having fled Chicago.

The Coastal Inn looks like the epitome of New England, and I take in the magnitude of the business Sam's parents must do. I don't know how many rooms it has, but it is quite the sizable building. Sam must stay busy. I'm not sure where to find him, so I start at the front desk. Felicia is just walking into the lobby when I get there, and she brightens so much at the sight of me that I relax any worries about my appearance.

"Stella!" Felicia has a clipboard in her hand, but she holds out her other arm and beckons me in. Her hug lingers for a second, and she quickly rubs my shoulder before pulling back to assess me. "It's so nice to see you. Things are settling in okay for you? You and Sam are…getting along?" She's clearly trying not to smile too broadly.

I'm standing in her son's clothing, so I can't really pretend otherwise. "Um…Sam just let me borrow some things." I clear my throat. "That's all."

"Mmhmm." She makes what I'm sure is an imaginary note on her paper. "Did you stop by to see him? He's working in room three twelve."

"I did come by to see Sam but also you." I feel shy now, unused to speaking to a maternal figure who hasn't so far shown herself to be mentally unstable. "That night I was here? You were very kind. I don't know how to thank you."

"You can thank me by being happy. That's all." Felicia pulls the glasses down from her head and checks me out again, wrinkling her nose at my hair. "And maybe by going to see my daughter."

"Kelly, right?" I laugh. "Sam told me. I'm on my way there this afternoon. Clothes shopping first."

"Enjoy your day, kiddo. I've got to get back to work, but you and Sam should come by for dinner on Monday night. It's usually quieter then, and we do a big family meal out on the deck. We'd love to have you."

"I'd really like that." I've never been invited on my own to a dinner party. "Thank you."

She directs me to find Sam, and my stomach is in knots while I make my way up the staircase to the second floor and then the third. What if last night was a fluke? What if Sam is a cold, angry silent boy again? What if he was just burning off steam with that kiss, with the way he let his hands hold my waist as his tongue and lips explored my taste and my feel and—

I'll just have to find out. A room down the long wooden hallway is open, and sunlight pours out. Before I am even through the threshold, Sam answers all of my unspoken questions. He drops the paintbrush onto a tray and is across the room in a flash, grabbing me by the hand and backing me up so that our bodies slam the door shut. I can't even get out a greeting because his lips are brushing over my neck. Hands entwine in mine, and he pulls them around his waist. Forming words is impossible because I am too engulfed in his touch to think clearly. His lips are so soft, and he trails them up higher until he kisses my cheek. He wraps his arms around me as he eases me in and hugs me, tightly squeezing me. I hug him back, struck by the security I feel. It's embarrassing how little experience I have with hugging, but he makes it easy.

After he finally relaxes his hold, Sam steps back, and I can see how bubbly he really is today.

"C'mon! Let's go down to the storeroom and see about hooking you up with some stuff for the apartment, okay? You're going to love it."

The storage area in the basement of the inn is massive, and it's also the area used for deliveries, as indicated by the large garage doors on tracks.

A man lifts a floor lamp from the back of a furniture pile and tries to make his way out.

"Dad! You're going to fall. Pass the lamp over." Sam frowns and shakes his head.

"I'm not going to fall. Stop acting like I'm three hundred years old." The man winks at me.

Of course this is Sam's father, I think.

His height and build, not to mention his sharp cheekbones, are the same. Gray colors his hairline, blending into the dark brown, and he moves with the same decisiveness as his son.

ELEVEN
the taste of love

MY TRIP TO THE MALL turns out to be less of a nightmare than I thought, and my car is filled with shopping bags. It's true that I had to keep veering away from the styles my mother would wear, but with a little determination, I am now the very happy owner of a decidedly comfortable collection of clothing.

If the salesperson at Banana Republic gets paid on commission, she was probably damn pleased with me. Soft cotton shirts, pullover hoodies, wrap sweaters, and flowy tanks and sundresses for the warm weather that's approaching. And jeans! I bought jeans at every store I went into. Jeans and I are going to have a full-on love affair. As much as I have a fondness for Sam's clothes, I feel good about the girl clothes that I wear out of the store. I also feel damn good about having a new phone with a new number that nobody knows.

Before my five o'clock hair appointment with Kelly that Sam made for me, I stop into Tail Spin, a small restaurant that reminds me of an Irish pub. I've never been inside any, but with all the wood booths and dark beer, it's what I imagine one might look like.

The owner, Pete, seems to take a liking to me and buys me a beer on the house. This is the first time that I've eaten today, and I inhale the fish and chips that come with malt vinegar and huge fries before getting a second beer, liquid courage for this hairy adventure I'm about to take. I let out an undeniably large belch and giggle. My mother would have a fit over my manners, but Pete gives me an air high five from behind the bar.

Just before I walk into Kelly's salon, Girl to Girl, I send Sam a text, so he has my new cell number. I sort of liked not having a phone, but it seems stupid not to. A new number, however, maintains my clean start. He texts back a picture of himself with white paint all over the front of his shirt with a message that assures me he will shower before dinner. I'm still smiling when I go through the front door. I mean, how can I not? The thought of Sam in a shower…all wet and soaped up…

Oh my God, I have to stop.

The salon is tiny, but it's got such personality with wild artwork hanging on every available inch of wall space. Each of the four client chairs is covered in black-and-hot pink leopard print, the front desk is littered with figurines and small toys, and various chimes and feathery things dangle from the ceiling. It's clutter at its best, and I have no doubt that Kelly is someone who knows herself well.

"Hi, I'm Stella. I have an appointment with Kelly," I say.

"Aha! The famous Stella. Come on over, and grab a seat. I'm Kelly."

Sam's sister is tall and striking. Thick jet-black curls frame her face and then fall wildly toward her waist. Not to mention, she has a body I'd kill for. If I could pull off wearing that outfit, I'd be thrilled. Her red leather pants and tight black tank top are practically glued to her body.

She stands behind me when I sit in the chair and rests her hands on my shoulders. "You're renting the apartment at Sam's place, huh?"

I love her husky voice. She's both assertive and warm, and I am immediately at ease.

"Yeah. I just sort of up and moved and landed here."

"Well, he seems pretty happy about it, so I'm happy about it." She runs her fingers through my hair. "What are we doing today? I gather you had a little fun with scissors."

I clear my throat. "I, perhaps, might have had a small fit and chopped off my hair, so I need to be rescued."

"Not rescued. Just shaped. And maybe we can get rid of the color on the ends. Just take you back to more of your natural root color? A dark brown with some lighter chestnut pieces? You've got nice curls for a shorter cut. Kind of a pinup-girl look but without being whorish."

The wide silver bracelets on each of her wrists make me think of Wonder Woman. I'm in good hands.

Two hours later, I stare at the mirror in disbelief at my transformation.

Kelly frowns and sets her hands on her hips. "Well, shit. You hate it. What's wrong?"

"Nothing. It's perfect." I'm too dumbfounded to say anything else. I feel like me, like how I'm supposed to look.

"Yay!" Her hands cheer in the air. "You look hot, not that you didn't look hot when you walked in here, mind you. But now, you look *really* hot. If Sam wasn't clearly obsessed with you and if I didn't already have a girlfriend, I just might hit on you. As it is, you're now relegated to hot-sister status."

I can't help from laughing, and I turn my head up to her and grin. "So, um…Sam is…obsessed with me?"

She shrugs. "My sullen, angry mopey brother is finally acting like a human being again. He won't admit that it's because of you, but I knew it had to be when he called and ordered me to take care of you. I couldn't get him off the phone. Even before that, over the last several days, he's been calling me and bringing me coffee and shit. I knew something was up."

Kelly looks at my reflection in the mirror, and I hold her eye contact.

"Your hair is on the house today. You gave me back my brother."

I try to figure out how I should respond, to ask how she lost him—or how he lost himself—when I am jolted by a terrifying crash, and the entire front window of the store virtually explodes in a firestorm of glass. Before I can react, Kelly grabs my shoulder and pulls me to the floor as crystal pellets fly across the room. Outside the salon, someone yells something that I can't understand, and the sound of a car peeling out echoes through the now eerily silent street.

"Goddamn it!" Kelly screams. Her fingers dig into me before she pushes herself to a stand. "You okay?" she asks.

My heart is pounding, but I look up at her and nod. I'm not hurt.

A slender young woman flies in from a back room. "Jesus Christ. Again?"

Kelly sighs angrily. "When is this shit going to end?"

"I don't know, babe."

Kelly reaches down, and I slap my hand into hers.

She pulls me to a stand and says, "Stella, this is my girlfriend. April, meet Stella."

April shakes her head, and neon-red hair falls across one eye. "Not how I wanted to meet Sam's chick, but hi. Are you okay?"

"Yes," I say, my voice shaky. "Just a little freaked out. Doesn't seem like the glass made it this far."

Kelly crunches over the wreckage in her black wedges and picks up a good-sized gray rock. "Fuckers. Last time, it was a brick. They could at least try for a bit of originality. You know, a big butternut squash or something."

"This has happened before?" I ask. "Do you want me to call the police?"

"No," Kelly and April answer back together. They look at each other with some kind of unspoken conversation.

April shakes her head. "It was a while ago, but Sam—"

"It won't do any good," Kelly cuts her off, shooting her a look. "Trust me. The cops can't fix any of this. I'll get Dylan down at the hardware store to help replace the window. It'll be okay."

"What…what's going on?" I move my gaze back and forth between them. "Are you guys all right?"

Neither says anything. Kelly is seething as she takes a broom and dustpan and then begins furiously sweeping glass.

April's face is now awash with sadness and concern. "Kelly, stop." But her girlfriend continues to maniacally push around chunks of glass, even as April softly touches her arm. "Sweets…stop."

"No! We have to clean it up. Now. I don't want him to see or hear about this."

"Look, I'll do it. I'll get it done fast. I'll call about replacing the glass, and we'll get it fixed tonight. Kelly, get out of here. You don't have to deal with this." She looks to me, her eyes begging for help. "Stella…can you…"

"I'll go with you, Kelly," I offer. I feel as though I'm suddenly caught up in something that is none of my business, but I do want to help if I can.

Kelly stands still in the pile of glass, her fingers white-knuckling the broom handle. "Okay."

Pete from the bar appears outside the storefront as we're leaving. "Aw, Kel. Damn it. I'm so sorry, my girl. Get out of here. Drinks are on me. I'll help April."

She nods as he pats her back.

Kelly storms a few doors down to the bar, and I have to scurry to keep up with her. It's hard to tell if she even wants me to stay with her, but now, I feel an obligation to watch over her, so I slip into the booth. She strums her nails on the table until two tequila shots arrive. I'm not particularly in the mood to drink any more, but I sling one back with her. She raises her hand for two more, and the bartender nods her way.

"Do you want to talk about what happened?" I ask softly. "Or not. That's okay, too."

Kelly can't seem to look me in the eyes. She's tapping the empty shot glass on the table and taking slow deep breaths to calm herself. After drinking her second shot and mine, which I passed to her, she lifts her head. Although I can see that she's fighting them, tears fill her eyes.

"The rock through the window? That wasn't because of me, and it wasn't because of April and me. In case you were wondering, this is a gay-friendly town, and no one gives us any crap. Half the tourists this summer will be gay. You'll see."

"You don't have to explain. I understand if—"

"You need to talk to Sam," she says firmly. "It's his story, not mine."

Another round of shots arrive, and again, I pass even though I could probably use it.

"He needs to talk. God, he needs to talk. He won't let me help him, but he might let you."

An hour and a half later, I pull up the driveway to the white house on the hill. I don't bother to unload my bags from the car because I just want to find Sam. He didn't answer my texts or calls, so I rap on his front door. I still haven't been inside his place, which suddenly feels extremely strange. I listen for sounds that he might be working outside, but it's eerily quiet this evening. Still, I sense that someone is watching me, yet I don't see Sam when I turn and scan the front area of the house.

I check the wraparound porch, and while he's not there, I do see his silhouette out on the dock. The sun is setting now, the light spectacularly beautiful, and the shape of his figure is so immediately relieving. Before reaching him, I can tell his mood has changed dramatically from what it was earlier today. A bleakness in his aura is palpable. He must have heard about the window, and I'm dreading this conversation. The incident in town has me nearly sick to my stomach.

Old dock boards creak beneath my shoes, but Sam doesn't turn back. He won't even look at me when I sit down next to him and hang my feet over the lapping water. He holds a half-empty bottle of whiskey in one hand. My worry only increases when I touch his arm, and he pulls away.

"Sam…" I start.

"You know, don't you?" he says flatly. "Kelly told you."

I shake my head. "I know something happened, something happened *to you*."

Sam takes a too-long drink and then corrects me, "I *made* something happen."

I touch his arm again, and this time, he lets me.

"I'm going to tell you because you'll find out anyway. That's inevitable even though I pretended it wasn't. Then, you're going to hate me, the way most people in this town do."

"Sam, I could never hate you."

"Yes, you will."

Now, he angles his face, and I can see how pained his expression is.

"For about ten minutes, I got to feel good again, good with you, and that's going to end. *Of course.* And I can't fucking stand that, Stella, because you are a relief in this fucking insane world. I felt it the second I saw you, and it scared the hell out of me. But it was there, as clear as day."

His eyes are red, and I'm not convinced it's from the booze.

"For reasons I can't begin to understand, I am whole again with you. After everything, I get to feel whole. And now, it's all going to blow up. Another bomb detonating in my life." He laughs, but it's filled with anguish. "My fucking life."

The slight slur in his words tells me that he's had more than enough to drink, so I take the bottle from his hand. Sam must know he's had enough, too, because he doesn't stop me.

But he does begin telling me his story, "I used to have a best friend, Costa. We grew up together, here in Watermark. We were practically brothers, especially because his parents were complete dirtbags. It was that classic shitty situation with abusive parents, neither of who gave a shit about him. My parents loved him though, and he slept over all the time and ate dinner at our house most nights. The whole nine yards. He was so awesome. Charismatic and funny and all"—Sam waves a hand around—"hero-like, you know? I looked up to him. Costa became sort of stupidly iconic in my head. I mean, his energy, his constant need to push limits, to be the life of the party…he always was, too. Everybody worshiped him, including me.

"When he was nineteen, and I was off in college, he was still living here and working on the lobster boats. He got his girlfriend, Britney, pregnant.

She took off after the baby was born, which was probably for the best." He leans in and whispers, the drunken edge evident, "I didn't like her much."

Sam lies back on the dock and squints into the glare of the setting sun. "He had a little boy, Toby. He was the cutest damn kid ever, and Costa was so crazy about him. Toby had Costa's eyes, the same deep, deep blue. Like little storms. Little storms of mischief.

"Costa had an apartment right near the inn, and my parents and Kelly helped him out a bunch. Costa took that kid everywhere he could. He even drove up to see me at school once. Who brings a baby to a college dorm, right? But Costa did.

"I loved Costa, and I loved Toby. When I was home from college on a short February break, I took them up to this cabin that my parents have a few hours from here, in Willow, just to get Costa out of town, take some time to be together with him and Toby. It was supposed to be a weekend that brought us back together. But there was an accident."

Sam throws an arm over his eyes, maybe because of the sun and maybe to protect himself from his words. "Toby was a little over a year old. Just a tiny guy. He used to run everywhere all the time. We were always chasing that kid around, and he never tired out. One morning, I was supposed to get up with Toby because Costa…because Costa wanted to do an early ski run. He woke me up before he left, but I passed out after that. I'd been up drinking hard the night before, and I just…I just crashed.

"Costa came back…and I can still hear him screaming. I can still hear him screaming because Toby was gone. I was supposed to be watching him, but instead, he got out of the house, probably looking for his dad. When Costa and I were running around outside, both of us frantic and calling Toby's name, we saw his little footprints in the snow, going down toward the lake. That kid could walk and climb over everything. He was so smart. The lake…it was iced over…or it looked iced over. At about ten yards out, there was…a hole in the ice. A little…kid-sized hole."

"Oh God, Sam."

"We broke through more ice, and we went into the water, trying to find him. We did everything. Stella, we did everything, and he was gone."

Sam rubs his arm over his eyes, and my heart breaks for him.

"It was a weak spot in the ice, but the rest was too thick, and they couldn't dredge the lake then. And in the spring…even then, they couldn't find his body. There could have been bears or…other animals. God, he was so little…" Sam's voice cracks and sounds increasingly ragged.

"Costa left Watermark soon after. I can't say that he hated me or that he didn't love me anymore even though he should have, but he certainly couldn't stand to look at me. I was his best friend and the person who should have been comforting him, but that was obviously impossible. I don't know. Maybe he did hate me. Maybe he just hated the world then.

"I stayed here because my family couldn't stand for me to leave when I was such a mess. So, I drank my way through it and slept with too many tourists who floated through town, which just kept making it worse. And that's it. I lost everything."

Without hesitation, I rest my head on his chest and hold him. There are no words to make his story any easier, so I say the only thing I can, "I told you I couldn't hate you."

It takes a moment, but then he says, "You must. Everyone else here does."

"The window at Kelly's? That can't be how everyone feels. Sam, you never wanted this to happen. It was a horrible accident."

"What I wanted to happen, who I loved, and what I tried to do? That doesn't matter. It only matters that my best friend's son is dead. And everyone knows it. I'm not allowed to be sad. I'm only allowed to be hated. But Costa will always have it worse. Always," Sam speaks so softly now that I can barely hear him. "It's wave after wave of pain. Just when I almost forget, for even a short time, I am hit in the face with what happened. I stay in town because my parents and Kelly want me to. They try to make me forget. When you came, you brought me to life. But you'll go away, too."

He sounds exhausted and drunk, and I can only imagine how miserable he is. This is not the kind of pain that anyone can get over. Maybe it can lessen some, but it can never disappear. His hurt and his self-loathing are brutal, and I would give anything to take those feelings away. I can't, I know that, but I'm aware of my need to show him that I'm not scared off, that I don't think of him differently. *How could I?* We all have something miserable in our pasts. I'm no different.

Sam has shown me raw pain, so I can show him mine.

I tell him my truths, letting them pour out of me in fragmented bits, "When you and I met? My entire world came undone that day at the hospital. My father had given me this bracelet." I put his hand on my wrist. "The bracelet is a lie because he vanished with no explanation a few days after the car accident he was in with my sister, Amy, and I was left with a mother who never should have been a mother.

"She grew to hate me—hate everything really—more than she already had, and she nearly destroyed me. Amy became a mess of a selfish, mean drug addict. She tried to kill herself. I mean, it was so bad that she wanted to die. Not just escape temporarily, but actually die. She was done. I don't believe it was an accidental overdose. I think Amy couldn't tolerate this world any longer. As difficult as she is and as hard as our relationship is, she is my sister, and I can't stand the thought of her dying."

I inhale and feel the shudder when I release it. "Then, she asked me to leave, so I did. I left Chicago to save myself from falling down a rabbit hole of crazy that I might never get out of…so I wouldn't try to kill myself, too, or slip into some kind of permanent delirium. To get away from the guy I was sleeping with, the one who made me shut down and disappear every time I let him fuck me. I let him…I let him use me and treat me terribly. It allowed me to escape the real world.

"I wanted to save myself when I left. The only thing I thought to do was to go to the one person I knew who I could intrinsically trust. You." I brush his hair back.

"We all have pain of some kind. You lost two people who meant the world to you. You went through hell, and you're still here. You get to hurt. But it *is* going to be okay." I lift up and ease my mouth over Sam's. "It's going to be okay because while you get to hurt, you also get to heal. And you get to be you again."

I kiss him with everything I have, drowning in some messed-up hope that I can ease his devastation. While he tastes overwhelmingly like whiskey, he tastes even more like love.

I pull back enough to whisper words into his mouth, "Let me be your good."

Sam's body tenses, and his heart pounds against me. "Can you let me be yours?"

I answer by continuing to kiss him, and he relaxes under me, letting my body sink into his.

TWELVE
safe

BY LATE JUNE, the Bishop family has had me to dinner four times. I've taken a liking to beach clambakes more than I would have imagined, and April and I have perfected making a fire pit out of hot rocks.

April is from Nebraska and only moved out here a few years ago, and Micah finds it very funny that the two girls with little oceanside experience dig a better clambake pit than his own kids. It's easy to see how someone could have the Bishops as a second family, the way that Sam's friend Costa did. They give generously and love unconditionally. For people like me, who are essentially alone, being taken in and embraced is so foreign and so needed.

Then, there is Sam himself. We can't seem to get enough of each other. Since that day on the dock, we've been inseparable. When boundaries fall and truths come out, it can bring a closeness that is unshakable. Despite our emotional intensity, we haven't slept together. In fact, we haven't done more than kiss. I think that it's because of how strongly we feel for each other—how quickly that connection hit us—that we've almost been scared to take our physical relationship further as though it would be too much. As extensive and heated as our kissing and groping has been, we've always let it wind down in a way that feels natural.

I don't know. Maybe we feel an obligation not to jump into bed after revealing so much to each other. Sam let me in on something very painful, and I think it's hard for him to trust that I still see him as *him*, not as a monster responsible for a child's death.

So, really, I guess that I'm not sure why we haven't slept together, but I'm over whatever has been holding us back.

Right now, Sam is in my kitchen, finally cooking that risotto dinner that got delayed. I'm in my bedroom, fussing over what to wear. More specifically, what I want him to rip off me because I cannot take this much longer. I go with a deep purple-and-black push-up bra and underwear set. There's a hint of lace—just enough to avoid being slutty, but enough that I'm going to get him to cave on this whole holding-out thing. That was fine and probably smart, but now, it's time. I pull on a loose top and straight-leg pants, both of which should take about three seconds to remove.

I step through the doors and outside to the deck to take in the view. I could never grow tired of overlooking the ocean.

Sam's garden of circle plots catches my eye, and I smile at the flowers that he's planted—dahlias and calla lilies, I think. The soil is dark, and I can tell he must have just watered them today. I squint. The grass around them though is nearly dead, which is quite odd.

The salty air gusts cause me to shiver, but for a few minutes more, I stay on the deck, searching the wooded area by the house, as I compulsively rub the bracelet that remains on my wrist. Again, I sense that I'm being watched. I think it's my phobia over my mother finding me. Not that she would ever do something as undignified as to hide out in shrubbery, but still, I'm allowed to be paranoid. An obsessive part of me needs to check and recheck the area outside the house until I'm sure she's not there.

I finally go back into my room, and I shut and bolt the doors. I back out of my bedroom, afraid to turn my eyes, and try to shake off the spooked feeling. When I get to the living room, I'm already feeling better. Each time I walk in here, I see the furniture that Sam brought up a few weeks back. He angled the giant chaise toward the fireplace, set the lamp that I love next to it, and placed a tall bookshelf just off the kitchen area. Every item in here feels like home.

I brush my fingers over the main wall and smile. Sam has insisted that I let him repaint the apartment, but I can't decide on a color, so every day, he slaps a splotch of a new paint shade for me to assess. There are fifteen up right now, and I still haven't decided. But he has the patience of a saint, and maybe I'm reticent to choose because I'm growing rather fond of the paint-sample routine. I stop though. Something new is on the wall that he must have done while I was getting ready. I run my fingers over the paint colors as I read what Sam has written under each sample.

THIS BLUE IS THE COLOR
OF THE SKY ON THE DAY
YOU CAME TO WATERMARK.

A SOFT WHITE
BECAUSE THE FIRST TIME
YOU WERE IN MY ARMS,
AFTER YOU ALMOST FELL
OFF THE DECK, YOU SMELLED
LIKE MAGNOLIA.

WHEN WE KISSED IN THAT
SUN SHOWER,
THE LIGHT CAST A FILTERED
PINK GLOW ON YOU.

THIS IS THAT EXACT SHADE.

A SILVER GRAY FOR THE METAL
ON THE BRACELET THAT
YOUR FATHER GAVE YOU AND
WHITE FOR THE LEATHER THAT
NEVER SEEMS TO DIRTY.
YOU HAD THAT BRACELET ON
WHEN I FIRST MET YOU,
AND YOU ARE VERY MUCH ADORED.

THE SAME GREEN AS YOUR SHIRT
BECAUSE YOU WERE RIGHT ALL ALONG.
THAT'S IMPORTANT.

Every single paint swatch is *for* me, *because* of me.

I catch myself resting a hand over my heart, and I practically roll my eyes at how much I'm swooning. I don't care though. I keep tracing his words with my fingers, stunned by what he's done. How deeply he knows me and cares for me is so evident on this wall. Not to mention, it's just freaking adorable.

My feelings for him border on overwhelming. He's the first person I've been involved with romantically who lifts me up instead of smashing me to the ground. Sam has a gentleness and loyalty about him that is irresistible, and I'm proud of myself for responding to such a healthy relationship. It means that *I'm* getting healthy. Maybe I'll never be able to explain what propelled me to Maine, and my impulsivity and urgent need to see him again defy explanation, but from the first moment when I saw Sam in that hospital stairwell, my draw to him was powerful and eternal and impossible to deny.

I glance to the open kitchen and take him in—his broad shoulders, the start of a summer tan on his forearms, his hair again falling into his face and hiding those gorgeous eyes. The way he concentrates on what he's doing, the way he can focus, arouses me.

Sam glances at me and quirks a smile.

After I've read and reread everything he's written five times, I drop my hand and go to him. I come up behind his tall frame, and my arms encircle his chest. "Bishop—" I start.

"I love when you call me that. You're the only person who does."

There's a shyness and sweetness in his voice that I adore.

I nuzzle my face against his back.

"Okay, so the basic risotto is done, and this is where we flavor it. We're doing lobster, caramelized onions, parmesan, fresh basil, and a hit of heavy cream."

"Bishop," I say again. This time, I press against him and ease my hands down to his stomach.

"Yes?" By the tone in his voice, I know he's smiling. He empties small bowls with ingredients and stirs the rice mixture.

I'm sure this dish he's slaved over will be really amazing. But lifting his shirt from under his belt is more enticing, so I do that. I also slip my fingers under the waistline of his jeans. And because I can't stand not to, I inch a hand lower. He's definitely hard.

Sam shuts off the stove and turns to me. "Stella."

"The wall..." The words to thank him escape me.

He steps in and twirls a finger through one of my curls. "You have trouble with colors. I was just helping."

He leans in and kisses me, and it only takes a second before we are both breathing hard. I can feel the shift in our passion tonight. The urgency is upped, the need for each other demanding and no longer able to be delayed.

As we fumble toward the bedroom, he walks behind me and keeps his hold on my waist. Once there, I lean back into Sam while his hands roam over the front of my shirt, and I catch my breath when he slowly travels his fingers over my breasts. His mouth is on my neck, his lips and tongue wetting my skin as his kisses grow more aggressive.

A wonderful shiver rips through me when his hands start to move under my shirt and over my stomach. There's no way that I'll be able to stand for very long, so I turn to face him and wrap my arms around his neck. When he grabs my ass and pulls me against him, I can't help but let out a sound. It's probably in the whimper category, but I don't care.

God, I want him so much.

I walk us backward and sink onto the bed, and he crawls over me, keeping his weight on his arms but settling his waist between my legs. I lift up into him, desperate to be closer.

But then, he freezes. "I don't think…Stella, we should probably wait."

His expression is so sweet, yet it shreds me.

"Wait? Wait for what, Sam?" I can't hide the confusion in my voice.

"It's just…" He softly kisses me, briefly, on the mouth.

"You don't want this?" Could I have fabricated what I thought was between us? I *am* still recovering from my past and prone not to understand things as they are, so maybe that's what I've done.

But I'm looking into his eyes, and I know—*I just know*—that I am right about us. We both feel this connection, this inexplicable bond. Now, only concern and warmth are on his face.

Sam tips his head and gives the hint of a smile. "I'm dying to be with you."

"So, what's the problem?" My legs wrap over his, and I pull him back onto me.

"What you said a few weeks ago. About the last guy you were with. About disappearing during sex. It kills me that it was like that for you because that means that whatever happened was all kinds of fucked-up wrong, Stella. It's not okay, and it's not how it should have been for you. I keep thinking about that, and it's really been bothering me, so I don't want to rush things." Sam pauses and drops his head onto my shoulder. "He hurt you, didn't he?"

This is an impossible question for me to answer. Physically, no. But Jay hurt me, I hurt me, my mother hurt me, my father, my sister…the list goes on and on. "I'm okay."

He hesitates and then says, "You flinch sometimes when I touch you. Just at first."

I didn't realize this. *Okay, fine*, I think. *Maybe* I've caught myself a few times, but I thought I hid it better.

I slip my hands up next to my head and work them under his palms. "That's not about you. It could never be. This is different. *We're* different."

"You don't have a good history, and I want to be careful with you."

I love that he says this and that he sees more about me than just what I've told him.

"You will be careful with me. I know that. You have a history, too. Everyone does. A slew of one-night stands with tourists probably isn't how it's supposed to be either. We both have damage, but I want us to be together so much. You have to believe that. Sam, it feels like we've been waiting *forever*, not just weeks."

"I don't want you going through the motions, sleeping with me, because you think you're supposed to or something. You can't...you can't ever feel like I'm using you. Or that...God, I don't want you to think I'm some asshole guy who just wants to get laid. If you want this and you're ready, then I am. Just promise, you won't disappear on me, that you'll stay present and...grounded."

"I won't disappear. You can give me something that I haven't had before."

Sam thinks for a minute. "You'll let me show you what it's supposed to be like when you care about someone?"

I'm glad that I left the light on in this room, so I can see how fucking gorgeous he looks when he says those words. "Yes."

He smiles back and grinds into me. He is definitely still hard. "When you really, really care about someone."

"Yes."

Sam kisses me, letting his lips barely touch mine, before he puts his mouth to my ear and whispers, "When you love someone."

Again, he's left me virtually speechless, but I whisper back, "Yes." Every part of me is electrified and totally aching for him, for his body, for his heat, for his entire being.

"And we can stop anytime you want. You just tell me."

"I won't want to stop," I breathe.

"You might change your mind. That's okay."

"Bishop, please fuck me."

He laughs softly. "I'm not gonna fuck you until you promise. It's important."

I push on his chest and make him look at me. "I promise. I promise you everything. I want you in a...in such a pure, clear way. For no substantiated reason, I drove halfway across the country to find you. I could have gone anywhere, but I drove to you. I want *you*, and I want *us*."

Now, I've left *him* speechless.

But only for a moment.

Sam sits up and lifts his shirt over his head.

Jesus, he is so beautiful.

"And to clarify," he says, "I'm not *fucking* you tonight. I'm *making love* to you."

He tosses his keys from his pocket and undoes his belt, and I nearly come apart.

Then, he gives me a mischievous smile and asks, "You ready? Because this will probably take a while."

Oh God, I am totally ready.

He eases off my shirt and ever so slowly slides my pants down. Then, he runs the outline of my bra with one finger. I put my hands on his arms while he takes his time kissing me and teasing my skin with his tongue. By the way he touches the fabric of what little I have on, Sam—I can tell—is a guy who appreciates lingerie.

After he's had his fill, he finally pulls down my straps and undoes the hook in the back, and I finish taking it off. His touch on my breasts is both gentle and confident, and I love watching him move over me. I also love how my body shivers when he takes my nipple between his fingers with just the right pressure, and then he grazes his mouth over it.

It's as if I've never had sex before, which certainly isn't true. But I've never had sex with Sam Bishop, and this is clearly an entirely new game.

He teases and delivers with every move, and it's fucking hot. I find that I'm almost intoxicated by how he touches me. His care is unparalleled. I put a hand over his, feeling each movement and pattern, trying to comprehend this mix of tenderness and raw sensuality.

A deep rumble of thunder rolls outside through the cove, and rain starts to patter against the deck. The last time we kissed when there was thunder, we stopped. This time, we won't.

Every move Sam makes is slow and deliberate, and I know it's going to be a while until he's inside me. But I can wait because the way he touches me is exquisite, and I could stay like this forever.

I close my eyes and feel his mouth continuing to explore, and he is thorough and perfect when kissing my neck, my shoulders, down my arms, over to my stomach. I curl my hips up, wanting more, wanting him to move his mouth lower. I crave what I've never had before, what Jay never did for me.

With Jay, sex was about control and power and getting what pleased *him.* He had no interest in my pleasure. It was why I tuned out and faded away when we were together. Or maybe I sought out someone like him to punish myself for all my inadequacies. But I should have been stronger. I should have stopped him and protected myself—as I should have done against my mother's words and actions.

You are useless.

Such an unpleasant person to be around.

The way you forget and mix things up? I don't know what in heaven's name is wrong with you. It's a good thing you have me.

"You still with me?" Sam asks.

I nod.

He is lying beside me, propped up on an arm, his free hand caressing my shape. "Open your eyes."

I do what he asks.

"Look at me," he says, placing a hand on my face and turning me to him. "You with me for real?"

I find deep familiarity and comfort when I meet his eyes. It's like coming home to a place I never knew I had. This is where I'm supposed to be—with him.

I smile now. "Yes. If I watch you, yes."

"Then, keep watching."

After his fingers have moved over my waist and legs, he runs the back of his hand between my thighs but only for a second, only enough to make me miss it terribly when he moves back to my breasts. I touch two fingers to my lips and then to his, passing him a kiss so that I don't have to take my eyes off him. Just as he kisses my fingers, his hand glides smoothly beneath my underwear. Now, he smiles when I gasp under his touch. He starts very slowly, moving lightly, taking his time with working up my arousal, until I am breathing hard and digging into his shoulders.

Sam pulls my underwear fully off and strokes my inner thigh. I'm so wet now that I think I might finally go legitimately crazy if he stops, but I can tell by the look in his eyes that he isn't going to stop.

"Stay with me," he purrs, easing two fingers inside me.

My back arches, and my vision gets blurry, but I stay with him. His pace as he begins to slide in and out is steady, letting me get used to the care in his touch. I reach up and rest my hand on his face, keeping my eyes locked on his. Even when he curls his fingers a bit and hits a spot that makes me nearly go blind and even when he starts to move a little faster, we maintain eye contact.

"You are so beautiful," he murmurs. "You are so beautiful, Stell." He tilts his head up. "Look in the mirror."

My head falls to the side, and our lovemaking reflects back from the old mirror that Sam polished and hung in my bedroom. I study myself, the way my body intuitively responds against his hand. I watch him move his arm under my neck as he cradles me and keeps moving his hand.

The storm is on us now, and lightning flashes into the room through the French doors. Thunder growls, and driving rain hits the window.

"Watch yourself come," he breathes into my ear. "Watch how gorgeous you are, how safe you are, how free you are."

And so, I do. Even when it gets nearly impossible to focus because my body tightens and shudders over and over, I watch myself. Then, I meet Sam's eyes in the mirror. It's so clear in his expression that he's giving me this to show how much he feels, not for any other reason. It's not because he wants something physical in return or because he's taking advantage of me. This is new, but after tonight, I couldn't ever accept less.

Eventually, my body begins to calm after the heightened waves of my orgasm. Now, I turn back into him, and he lowers his mouth to mine, kissing me deeply. I reach between us to finally unzip his jeans.

"We can still stop. You know that, right?"

"You're insane if you think I don't want you inside me."

I tug on his jeans and boxers, and he helps me get them off. With my hands on his sides, I pull him to roll on top of me.

"One sec. I have to do something first." Sam rubs his nose against mine, and his eyes sparkle.

So, it's only for a moment that his cock brushes between my legs before he is kissing his way down my body until his mouth is on me. Maybe Sam is trying to prove all the ways that he can make me come, but I'm not complaining because his mouth feels incredible. I'm fighting so hard for my sanity, and now, I'm on the brink of losing it again because his tongue is the most perfect thing in the world. It wouldn't be a bad way to go.

I am still breathing hard and shaking when he crawls back up. I wouldn't protest if he had a list of other things to do, but I'm really beyond ready for him now.

He laughs when I throw an arm off the bed to yank open the nightstand drawer, revealing three boxes of different condoms.

"Well, I see you're prepared."

"I was going with a build-it-and-they-will-come philosophy, and one of us already has. Twice."

"Very punny." He reaches for a box and shakes out condoms before tearing one off with a hand.

"Oh, one-handed, huh? Show-off," I tease.

His smile is ridiculously cute. "In case you haven't noticed, I'm quite good with one hand."

"Oh, I noticed," I assure him.

Together, we lift up until he is kneeling in front of me, and I'm sitting. I set one hand on his chest and touch my other to his cock, wrapping my hand around him. It's my impulse to lean in, but I don't. The truth of how much I hated it when Jay made me go down on him, how sick he and I both were, hits me. I'm not ready to do this even though I know how different tonight is with Sam, but he doesn't seem to mind. In fact, he doesn't seem to expect it.

I do, however, feel more than comfortable using my hands on him, learning how he feels. He doesn't press against me or push on the back of my head to try for more. He simply lets me touch him at my own pace, which seems to work given the sounds he is making.

When he starts to get a little breathless, he rips open the condom and puts it on. For a moment, I lean in and kiss his stomach and his defined abs as he rubs his hands over my shoulders and through my hair. I am so…joyful…for what we're about to do, for the closeness we're going to have. It's something I never imagined I could experience.

I look up to Sam as I lie back, and he lowers himself. He wraps our hands together and kisses me. Then, I feel just the tip of him against me as he lifts to look me in the eyes, and the head of his cock slides inside me. And he stays there, making sure I'm okay. Neither of us moves for a minute. Slowly, he slides in just a bit more and then pulls out. Then, in again, pushing deeper, and he stays there. He slips a hand under my lower back and keeps it against me, holding us still.

The rain is torrential now—the thunder and lightning and wind all loud, I'm sure—but the only thing that I hear clearly is Sam.

"Stay with me," he says, pushing fully inside me.

He couldn't lose me now if he tried.

THIRTEEN
did you miss me?

I HAVE NO IDEA what time we finally fell asleep last night. There was sex—outstanding, beautiful hot sex that I need much more of—and then there was heating up risotto on the stove and feeding each other and being schmaltzy and gooey and completely awesome. It was like we were in some hideous Nicholas Sparks movie. It was more than I could have dreamed of.

When the power went out, we moved to the living room and cuddled in front of the fireplace, watching flames dance into the early morning. I fell asleep easily, safely, without worry. God, to be able to drift into slumber without any weight breaking apart my night? It was the best feeling ever.

The storm hit the electrical lines among so many things that hit last night. Who needs electricity? I couldn't care less if it ever came back on.

And goddamn, if choosing that huge chaise wasn't the smartest thing I'd ever done. Right now, I am stretched out on it, next to Sam, our warmth defying the chill in the air. I've never thought of myself as sexy, but Sam makes it impossible to deny that I feel attractive and desirable. Even when we had a rather practical conversation about me being on the pill and both of us making sure we were clean and whatnot and deciding to ditch the condoms, he managed to remain adorable and keep me feeling hot and sensual.

He's got a gift, this boy—or more accurately, many gifts.

He has on only light sweatpants, and I'm in a silky tank top and underwear. I've found that while the days are warm here in Maine, the nights are still quite cold, but the heat from his chest flows into mine, and I snuggle more tightly into his hold.

While he sleeps, I study his face and the peace that radiates from his slumber. I suspect that while I slept, I looked as settled and fulfilled as he does now. I doubt that I've ever felt this way—perhaps as a child before chaos invaded my life and before I understood the destructive nature of a mentally ill parent.

One of the things that I find most comforting this morning is that while Sam provided a safe harbor, *I* am the one who has been making choices that are helping me find myself. I am healing because of me, and *that* is letting me trust and risk and love.

I am proud of myself. It's a beautiful feeling and one that I plan to hang on to.

Finding reality and clarity is no small feat when one has been subjected to emotional warfare for so many years. It's embarrassing, whether rightful or not, to have fallen prey to the cruelty of my family's disintegration. I probably idealized life before my father left, but it was certainly his departure and Amy's delving into narcotics after the car accident that together sparked my rapid descent into turmoil. My mother has always been nuts, always manipulated me, but without my father and sister to buffer her behavior, I was left defenseless. It's hard not to feel as though I should have done better, been stronger and smart enough to circumvent their dysfunction.

Now, however, I can reclaim myself.

Sam stirs a bit, and I roll in closer, breathing in his smell. His wide shoulders and muscular arms provide what feels like an unbreakable and protective armor from harm, and I press in a bit more to kiss his chest, reveling in this moment of freedom and levity. Lightly, he lets out a small murmur. When my hand runs over his bare skin, then travels to his waist, and then over the front of his sweatpants, that murmur grows a bit deeper.

"Good morning," I whisper.

Sam smiles and opens his eyes a hint. "I missed you while I was sleeping."

He grinds into me, and my every nerve ignites. The weight of his body moves over mine, and in a flash, I am on my back, laughing, with Sam above me, growling and making me giggle as he kisses my neck.

Mere seconds later, I raise my waist and run my hands through his hair, desperately intent on getting what I crave on such a basic level. Our mood becomes more serious, more real. While last night was incredibly gentle and romantic, it's clear that what we both want this morning is raw and intense. It's so easy to let myself move against him, to find a rhythm and flow between us. It's not awkward or uncomfortable at all. It's as though we were made for this, for each other.

The rain begins *again* just as we begin again.

As I start to push down his sweatpants, both of us stop short at the sound of another male's voice in the room.

"Did I come at a bad time?"

Sam pulls himself up from me. His entire body freezes, and I see terrible fear in his eyes when he looks into mine. He knows the voice. That's clear.

Slowly, he turns and moves to the end of the chaise, sitting as if to shield me. His voice trembles. "Costa."

Now, I am the one frozen with fear, but I don't fully understand why.

"It's been a long time," Costa says in a voice so kind that it unnerves me.

Costa's hair is black, neatly cut, and pushed off his face. He has penetrating navy eyes, framed by sharply arched eyebrows. Tall as Sam but thinner, he's clearly well built. Even under his black leather jacket, he looks to be solid and strong. Leaning against the kitchen counter, smirking and staring at Sam, he waves jovially, and under the circumstances, it strikes me hard as ludicrous.

"Why…why are you here?" Sam pushes into me even more.

I see his chest rise and fall quickly. I hear his breathing escalate. The heat he radiated before is gone, replaced now by a cold tremor.

Sam's voice is ice cold. "What do you want?"

Costa stops about ten feet from us and gives Sam half a smile. I study him, fascinated by the person before me. He's…cocky, flirtatious even, I think. When he finally tips his head in my direction, I am both chilled and entranced.

"You must be Stella," he says calmly. "It's so good to finally meet you."

Sam leaps off the chaise and positions himself to my left, directing Costa's attention his way. "How do you know her name?" His voice is stronger now.

Costa keeps smiling and moves a bit closer.

"*How do you know her name?*" Sam repeats. This time, it's a demand.

"She's really cute, Sammy. Nicely done." Costa blows me a kiss.

Before I can react, Sam barrels both hands into Costa's chest, throwing him backward and hard onto the floor.

"If you touch her, that's it." Sam stands over him now, enraged and ready to attack. "Is that crystal clear? She is off-fucking-limits with your game. I swear to God, I'll—"

Costa laughs. "You'll do what?" He slowly returns to his feet and then brushes his hands together. "What can you possibly do to me?"

Sam steps back, creating distance between them. "What the fuck do you want?"

"God, I've missed you, Sam, so much." Costa drops his head to one side and smiles.

He's so relaxed, so eerily at ease in this exchange, while Sam and I are anything but.

"Did you miss me?" Costa puts his hands in the back pockets of his jeans. "Sam, did you miss me?" he asks more insistently. "It's been forever since we've seen each other, hasn't it? I want us to hang out again, like we used to."

Sam's hands tremble as he defensively holds them up. Against what, I'm not sure, but my stomach drops because Sam sees something coming that I don't.

Sam shakes his head. "Costa, don't do this. Please."

"We had so much fun, Sammy. Remember when it was just us? Tell me that you missed me the way I missed you." His words and tone are harmless, but Costa is most definitely not. "Let's get back what we lost, shall we?"

That smile again, and this time, it sends ice through my veins. I scramble to the edge of the chaise, panicked now. "Sam…"

"Stella, don't! Stay there!"

Sam throws out a hand, and I do what he asks, holding still only because I'm afraid to make the situation worse if I jump between them.

With immeasurable steadiness now, Sam says, "Costa, please leave. I'm begging you. Don't you do this to me, not now."

I look back and forth between them, trying to decipher what they're talking about. Tension throttles the air, all of us on high alert.

Then, Costa slips a hand from his pocket and raises a gun to Sam.

I scream and lurch forward, but again, Sam yells for me to stay.

He stares at the gun and inhales loudly. "You don't want this, Costa. Please."

"Sam, we were so good together. So, so good. You remember, right?"

I don't know how to defuse this, and my heart is in my throat anyway. I cannot think or speak anymore. All I can do is see the gun and the inexplicably sultry, seductive expression on Costa's face along with the pleading look on Sam's.

Sam shakes his head, silently conveying so much to Costa.

But Costa simply stares directly at Sam and cocks the gun. "You owe me this. For fun."

In slow motion, I watch Costa pull the trigger, and my world explodes.

I think I'm screaming. Or maybe I'm trying to. I might be choking.

Through my tears, I see Sam's chest turn red.

Costa steps in a bit and fires off another round.

I find myself on the floor, crawling toward Sam through my hysteria. In a blur, I make out Costa's boots next to me, and I feel his hand on my back. He calmly says something that I can't understand before he walks away.

My hands reach for Sam's chest, and I clamp down, hard, soaking my skin with his blood. Everything is red. My hands are so wet that they slip, but I move them back to the source of the blood, and I resolve not to fail again. I'm aware that I cannot breathe normally. Vacuous white noise floods the room, and I can't see anything but death. Because God—*oh God*—Sam is bleeding out, right in front of me. So, there is only the static sound in my head, the internal chaos, and the splintering destruction of everything that makes sense.

This cannot be happening. There cannot be all this blood draining from the boy I love. I won't tolerate it.

"Stell…"

Sam's voice breaks me from the saturation of blood, and I look up. He's trying to smile, and that just drives this horror deeper.

"Stell, you give me such light. In a dark, dark world, you give me such light. Don't…cry…"

Thick crimson liquid trails from his mouth, so the attempt to console me rings as horribly impossible.

Even with the pressure I'm putting on his gunshot wounds, I can't begin to control the bleeding. "No, no, no," is all that I can say. There is no stopping the word. If I say it enough, this will end, so I'm relentless. "No!" I keep repeating, my voice broken and wrecked. My body won't let me stop.

"It doesn't hurt…really. I feel so good. It'll be fine," he manages to say. "I promise."

I can only respond with a sob.

Sam is going to die. I know that.

"Say you…trust…me." He coughs, and his eyes roll up. "Say…trust…"

I have never been so scared in my life. It's only because he's struggling so much—and he so clearly needs this from me—that I can give him this one last thing. "I trust you." My words are garbled, but still, I say them. "I trust you."

The uselessness of trying to dam the bleeding is undeniable now, and I move up and cling to him while I fall apart. It takes every ounce of strength I have, but I lift him so that I can wrap my arms around him and hold him fully. I won't let him leave this earth anywhere but in my embrace.

"I trust you. I love you. I trust you. I love you." This is the first time I've told him that I love him, and every word devastates me further. "Please, no, no, no! Sam, I love you."

For a split second, his hand is on my arm, and then it falls to the floor.

In my love, his breathing halts, and his body falls lifeless.

Repeatedly, I scream his name. I scream until my throat hurts, until I cannot produce any more sounds.

This death cannot happen. *It can't.*

Instinctively, I lay Sam's head back onto the floor, place my hand under his neck, and tip his head upward. With my mouth covering his, I pinch his nose and try to blow life into him. I try to breathe for Sam. I pump his chest, but more blood just seeps onto both of us. Then, my mouth is back on his, and having to exhale and fill his lungs might be the only reason that I can even breathe at all, yet I breathe for as long as I can stand to because it might be the only salvation.

Minutes go by, and all I can taste is death. I pull myself from Sam's body with the clear decision to get help. Staying here is giving up on him, and I can't do that. Some crazy part of me thinks that maybe—*just maybe*—I am wrong, that he can be saved. I refuse to have it be too late.

"I'll be back. I'll get help. Do you hear me? This will be fixed. I can fix this. I can fix *you*! I can!" I'm screaming to no one, but I scream anyway. "You taught me that I can do anything I fucking want. I'm going to prove you right. Watch, Sam. Watch me."

Panting, I rush to find my cell phone in the bedroom. After I stumble and catch myself, the comforter is soiled in blood, but I keep going and grab my phone from the dresser.

Micah and Felicia or Kelly and April—they'll help me. They'll know what to do. But I've got no fucking cell signal because the storm blew out service.

I'm barely dressed when I step out onto the deck off my room and hold up the phone. Still nothing.

Jesus. I suddenly realize how serious the storm was, the kind of trouble we're really in.

Trees are down everywhere, and a few trunks are torn up at the roots. From here, I can see how wild the ocean is. Waves rise higher, and with more density than usual, they crash into the cliffs with relentless force. The wind is still strong, the sky gray like steel and showing no breaks of light.

I try to protect my eyes with one arm as I make my way through the debris on the deck and race down the stairs. I can't find a signal, no matter what I do, so I have to get into town. Given the aftermath of the storm, my little piece-of-shit car will never make it, but I can run. Sharp pain sears through my foot, but I don't stop until I'm halfway down the driveway and faced with a nightmarish tangle of live electrical wires. I might be blind with panic, but I've got enough sense not to run through them.

Think, I beg of myself. *Think. Focus.*

Sam's truck.

Driving off-road will be rough, but it'll be a lot faster than trying to navigate on foot through the newly downed trees, dense foliage, and rocks. I can barely see through my tears, and I'm in the driver's seat before realizing that I need the keys. I shake out the visor—not there. I have to go back upstairs.

Every second counts right now, so I need to remember where they are. A picture flashes through my head—the floor of my bedroom, almost under the bed.

I will find the keys and get help. I will motherfucking undo what has been done, and Sam will not…Sam will not…

Sam will *not.* The end.

He just won't because I cannot handle even the thought, so I will fix him.

I'll drag Sam into the truck and crash through tree limbs, and I will…I will…I will fucking turn back time, so Sam and I are in each other's arms, and there are no guns and no Costa and…

Costa might still be around, but he didn't kill me earlier. He won't kill me now.

And if he does? If Sam is gone, then I don't care what happens to me.

I'm still getting us out of here.

Except…except I start to understand, there is no point. Nothing I do will change what has happened.

I cannot force life where there is none.

A wall of clarity slams into me, and it's a miracle that I do not collapse against the brutal force.

Sam is dead.

I felt it happen.

The only reason that I'm in this truck right now is because my demons resurfaced to confuse my reality, to let me deny the truth.

Sam is dead.

I walk back into my apartment. I want to lie on the floor next to him and hold him. It's the last time I'll ever do that. But I can't even look up as I enter the living room because I'll see Sam and the blood and the mayhem.

My face falls into my hands, and I let myself sob until I'm brave enough to look up and accept that Sam is dead. When I finally gather the strength, the floor of my apartment is empty.

There is no Sam.

There is not even a trace of blood.

I shut my eyes. I was wrong that I could see truth because I must finally be going solidly crazy. I'm having a coping reaction or…maybe I don't want to see what hurts too much. I don't know anymore.

I have a glimmer of hope. I've made mistakes before. I remember. I did *not* see Amy when she was clearly in bed on the day she attempted suicide. Sam could be here. It's a force of will, but when I look again, he is still gone.

No body, no blood.

Nothing.

What the fuck is happening to me?

I look at my hands. They're clean.

No, it's not possible.

I look down and see my shirt is also clean. Any trace of Sam and of violence and death is gone.

My knees give out, and I drop to the floor. I pound the old wood boards with my fists until my own blood colors my hands, and I feel something resembling human.

I stumble to the bathroom and intentionally avoid looking at the wall with Sam's words. I lean on the sink and stare into the mirror.

"You are crazy, Stella." Calm envelops me now because I understand the only truth there is. "You are totally fucking nuts, and you cannot save yourself, so go hide. You'll never make sense of the world because you are too broken and too far gone."

There is only one explanation for what I've seen. There is no Sam Bishop. I made him up.

I'd chased after some psychotic fabrication because I was so weak and pathetic that I needed to create someone to hold on to. But if I can stay crazy, then I can keep Sam alive because I just can't survive his death if he ever were real.

Except that he can't be real. If he were, his body could not have simply disappeared, blood and all. If someone inexplicably dragged his body out of the apartment, I would still have blood on my hands, and there is nothing.

To keep him, I need to disappear back into the dream world that I know how to create.

I back out of the bathroom and immediately crawl into bed where I can wrap myself in his smell, imagined or not. I won't look in the living room or the kitchen again. I won't go downstairs to see his apartment or his truck. I won't hang off the bed and reach for his keys that should be there from when he tossed them from his pocket. If anything about him is gone, then this reality that I've created won't hold up.

My brain went wonky enough that I killed him off in my daydream world. But I know about fucked-up realities more than most people, so I can get my Sam world back.

I can dissociate.

I can believe anything.

I can trust myself to fall down the rabbit hole again.

The covers go over my head, and my legs pull into my chest. I let myself disappear. There is no line between truth and fiction for me, and I'd rather be crazy and get to keep Sam than find sanity and lose him.

FOURTEEN
rock you like a hurricane

THE DAY PASSES WITH INCREASING QUIET. The winds peter out, the hard slap of waves against rocks slows, and my mind easily slips into nothingness. I might just stay in this bed forever. The only thing keeping me from totally vanishing is that my wrist is inexplicably burning under my bracelet, and it's as if the heat is trying to tell me that I'm alive and that I'm not allowed to disappear—or die. I won't kill myself. No matter how delusional and crazy and miserable I get, I won't. I twist it and scratch beneath the leather, irked by the feel, yet I won't take it off.

I will myself to ignore it and hide under the comforter, so I can black out the world. Sleep is impossible, but I can easily stay in this hypnotic zone.

I try to make Sam appear, to resurrect what my imagination created, but no matter how hard I try, he is frustratingly elusive. After hours of focusing on him, on working my mind to rebuild the one I love, I've got nothing to show for it.

Finally, when I've had enough, my anger and pain reach a limit that propels me out of bed. I grab fistfuls of sheets and tear them off, howling and crying in pain, and then I ball them into a messy pile. I shove the mattress half off the frame and throw pillows across the room.

Sunrise starts to show through the French doors, and I drastically resent the onset of light. Without thinking, I take a vase from the dresser and hurl it through the glass as though that could make the sun retreat. Fresh post-storm air fills the room, but I don't feel it on my skin.

I catch sight of myself in the dresser mirror, the one where I watched while the nonexistent Sam made love to me. My chest is heaving, my eyes are bloodshot, and my hair is plastered to my head with sweat. Just as I'm about to throw a heavy antique clock at my reflection, I hear a sound on the deck.

Or I think I do. Maybe I'm just making it up.

But the glass from the shattered door makes a distinctive noise under footsteps.

"Stella."

Blankly, I stare at the person in front of me. I should be elated, but I can't stop shaking my head. Sam is wearing the same sweatpants that he had on when he died. But there are no gunshot wounds, no blood, not even any scars. There's no indication that *anything* happened. He's whole. He's perfect. This vision cannot be trusted because I don't know if I can make it last.

I look at Sam and wait for him to disappear before my eyes.

Instead, he steps through the doorframe, sidestepping the jagged shards of glass clinging to the wood. "Stella," he says again.

Now, I turn to the mirror and send the clock in my hand smack into the image of my head. Fragments of me fall to the floor.

I look back at Sam. "You're not really here. I know that. But come in anyway."

"I am here. And I'm going to explain."

"It's okay," I say calmly. "Losing my mind means that I don't need things explained to me. I can just roll with it. As far as hallucinations go, you're a pretty good one. So, come on in, and let's see what my fucked-up head does with you next."

"You're not crazy, Stell. I really am alive."

"No, you're not. You never were." When I take a step, I feel something sharp. It takes a moment, but I look down as I lift my foot.

The keys to Sam's truck. They can't be real, and to prove it, I slam my foot down on them. But I cry out because the pain shooting through me certainly seems to be real enough.

Sam rushes forward and grabs my arm to prevent me from stomping my foot again. "Stop, stop."

I stare at the floor. My voice sounds far away as I talk, "If your keys are real, then you are real. But you also aren't. It seems that I've concocted keys, too. So interesting." I sigh. "I can't quite figure this all out."

"Oh God." His hands go to my wrists, and he lifts them to his face. "Stella, look at me, touch me. I am real. You didn't make anything up."

His voice is so kind, so sweet, but my mind must be doing that. He moves my hands over his face, down to his shoulders. I know every inch of his body, and feeling it again breaks my heart.

I flash to seeing him in the moonlight—shirtless, muscular, and perfect—as he showed me how to trust in him and in myself while he made love to me.

"I know this doesn't make sense to you right now, but I'm going to tell you everything. Please stay with me. Please don't disappear."

Suddenly, he takes me in his arms and tightly holds me. My arms stay at my sides, listlessness and exhaustion winning out over everything. I'm having a weird fantasy. Then, his arms squeeze me hard.

"You died in my arms," I murmur. "There was lots of blood, lots of screaming. Well, *I* was screaming. You were rather calm. And now, you're alive. So, no, none of that is real. It's very simple. But I can pretend."

Sam pulls back and takes my face in his hands. His eyes search mine, clearly trying to assess how far off the deep end I've jumped. I could save him the time and tell him that there's no hope for me, but it seems like a lot of effort.

"I did die," he says. "You're right. Costa shot me. Twice. And I told you to trust me, that it would be okay. Remember?"

I nod. "I remember that."

"And I came back to you, right? I'm here."

I laugh dryly. "Yes. That makes *complete* sense. You know, given my state of mind."

The anxiety and concern on his face is clear, and it starts to cut through my numbness. I feel badly that I'm disappointing my fantasy Sam. I should play along better.

"I came back to you," he says firmly, "and now, you're going to come back to me."

Sam swiftly leans in, and when his lips reach mine, it's as though I've been hit by lightning. And truth. The taste, the feel, the rush of him is full of clarity.

Sam is real. This kiss is real. I know that.

He was also dead. I know that, too.

My sobbing separates us, and I collapse against him, grabbing at the front of his shirt, as I bury my wet face in his chest. I'm nearly hyperventilating while I do what I can to trust him.

His hands rub my back, and he tries to soothe my emotions. "Breathe, baby, please. Just breathe."

He holds me and waits for my storm to calm. Sam has patience, and he doesn't falter in his hold or his words, talking to me, while some semblance of sanity reenters my mind.

He sits us down on the bed. "This is the bed we slept in two nights ago. On the sheets that you found in the closet when you moved in here. You didn't want new ones, you decided, because you liked how soft these were from age. It took three rounds through the washing machine to get out the musty smell. Remember?"

I nod again. "Yes. I used scented fabric softener that smelled like lavender."

"Right. And the keys you stepped on?"

"Those are for your truck? It's outside?"

"Yes. Do you want to see?"

"Yes."

Sam stands and lifts me, carrying me to the broken French doors and outside over glass. My arms are around his neck, my head resting against his shoulder. He takes us along the wraparound porch to the front of the house, and in the driveway, I see his truck. The driver's side visor is down from when I searched for the keys nearly twenty-four hours ago.

"I tried to get help," I say. "I think electrical wires were down on the road."

"There are. I saw them. I managed to get a signal and texted my family so that they know we're all right." He carries me back inside and sets me down on the bed again. "It's freezing. We need to get you dressed." He turns to retrieve clothes from my closet.

"Bishop, don't go, don't go…" I am panicked.

"I'm not leaving you, okay? I'm right here. Watch me. I know you're scared. I know. But I'm not leaving. I wouldn't lie to you. You know that, right?"

He does tell me the truth—always. I'm sure of that. It's one of the few things I believe.

My eyes stay glued to him when he pulls a shirt from a hanger and takes pants from the dresser.

"I'm sorry that I broke the mirror." It's a stupid thing to say, given the circumstances.

He smiles. "If you'd died in front of me, I'd have broken a mirror, too."

"There's also the glass from the door. I broke that, too."

"I'll fix it. It'll be like it never happened."

"Will it be like you never bled to death?" I start crying again. I can't help it.

Then, he is kneeling in front of me, holding my hands. "I'll fix that, too." He kisses each of my fingers and then wipes away my tears. "You must be cold."

A sweater slips over my head, and then I am stepping into soft pants.

When he stands, I quickly grab on to his hand. "Don't let go of me again."

"I won't." He scoops me up in his arms and takes me from the cold room, down the hall, and stops in the living room, next to the wall of paint colors.

"See these? I made these for you. They're real."

There are a few bumps in the paint, and I run my fingers over them as if I'm reading braille.

"Feel that?" he asks.

"I do." But I'm hesitant. I reread the lines he wrote for me, and it seems implausible that I would fabricate those.

With great care, he sets my feet on the floor and leads me to the kitchen. "Tell me what's in the fridge."

I'm not sure if this is a trick, and I'm scared to answer. I think for a moment. "That rice thing?"

He smiles and swings open the door with one hand while holding me steady with the other. "Risotto. Exactly. And you loved it."

Now, I smile just a bit. "We ate in front of the fireplace." I pause. "After…"

"Yes. After we made love. That was all very real. You couldn't make up something that fucking outstanding, right?"

Sam is trying to get me to laugh, but I'm not there yet. He does have a point though. Next, he takes me back to the living room, back to the chaise where this nightmare started, and I lie down on his chest.

"You didn't imagine anything," he continues. "Everything that you've seen and felt since you got to Watermark happened. I know it *seems* crazy, but *you're* not crazy."

I'm nearly paralyzed by confusion. I feel a powerful deep relief that I am in Sam's arms, but I am still desperately trying to clear the fog. I don't even know what to ask him. None of this makes any sense.

"I've never…this is hard to…" Sam fumbles to find words. "I've never had to explain this before, so just bear with me, and I'll start at the beginning." He pulls a blanket from the floor and covers us. "We call it death tripping. There's no language, no one to learn from, so we just call it death tripping."

FIFTEEN
not for the meek

SAM TAKES A DEEP BREATH and rubs his temple.

I can tell that what he's about to say will be difficult. I have no idea how to support him because I feel lost and traumatized, and I'm doing what I can to avoid disintegrating. I swear though that I will stay here and listen and not fall apart. I rub his hand with mine. It's not enough, but it's all I can manage in my shaky state.

"You know that Costa was my best friend for years, practically my brother." Sam falters and takes a moment before speaking again, "But by the time we graduated high school, we'd drifted apart a ton. He didn't come over often, if at all, and he was partying way too much. Or so I thought.

"I went off to college, and I suppose I'd mostly given up on him by then. As much as my family and I had tried to undo what his own family did, I figured that it hadn't been enough to change his life. I got caught up in school and friends, and I assumed he had whatever he had going on. It happens, right? People lose each other. So, I didn't see him when I was home on breaks or anything. I didn't even know where he'd gone.

"Then, one summer, right after college got out for the year, I was rock climbing, alone, on Mount James. It wasn't the smartest idea because it had rained. The rocks were slick, and the terrain was muddy. I thought I was kind of a badass, and it didn't really occur to me that I could get into trouble. I was doing a hard uphill climb when I slipped and fell way off route. I think I broke my ankle on the way down, but I managed to catch hold with both hands and stop myself from going into the ravine below.

"But I was hanging off the side of a cliff and in horrible pain. I…I've never been so scared in my life. I couldn't get a leg up over the edge, and I didn't have enough strength to pull myself to safety. All I could do was hang there with jagged rocks and…and certain death if I let go. It was my own damn fault, too. I'd been incredibly fucking stupid, and I deserved to die. I wasn't harnessed in, and I went out without a partner. There's no excuse. Anyway, I was panicking enough that I wouldn't have been able to hold on much longer."

I'm grateful that Sam pauses here for a bit because I already feel sick. There's no denying that this story is not going anywhere good, and the details will likely be excruciating.

He blows out a long breath. "That was when Costa showed up. Out of nowhere, it seemed. He's always been stronger than he looks, so when his hands clapped around my wrist, I knew he'd be able to pull me up. And he did. He hugged me. I hugged him. And it was as though we'd never fallen away from each other, as though we were still brothers, and he'd somehow magically known that I was in trouble. It felt so amazing for all of three minutes. While he was holding on to me, he asked if I trusted him. And of course I did." Sam slows his storytelling now, his voice getting quieter, his tone growing darker. "Then, he said, very clearly and calmly, 'It's a good day to die, my friend.' It was very Costa of him. Then, he threw us both over the edge and onto the rocks below.

"I remember falling, and I remember feeling terrified, but Costa didn't let go of me, even when we hit the rocks. That sound, the sound of bones breaking…yeah, that first time still echoes in my head. Sorry. You don't need to hear that…"

"It's okay," I say although my head is spinning and I feel sick to my stomach.

"It's not. None of it is okay." He tightens his arms around me. "The thing is, I wasn't in pain from the fall—at all. The opposite, in fact. It felt good. I realize how that sounds, but the process of dying was like a drug. It didn't take long, probably only a few minutes, but they were an indescribably awesome few minutes.

"First, I watched Costa. His face was a mess, blood and…but it wasn't frightening. I just closed my eyes and drowned in pleasure. It was like I was floating, flying, or…I don't know. You just want to be absorbed into that, if that makes any sense. Then, I died, and everything went dark and murky, like I was swimming through a dense gel of some sort. I couldn't see much. I don't know how long that part took.

"Understanding where I was, what happened, was impossible. I just sensed that I was dead, like dead for real but in some kind of in-between space. A fake death. Or on my way to heaven or hell, if I even believe in those. I don't know. There was an urge to escape, to *land* somewhere, but I couldn't get a handle on where to go or even how to move.

"Then, I saw Costa, and he wrapped an arm around me and pulled me up. Like surfacing from deep water into breathable air, it's lighter near the surface. I wouldn't have been able to get there without Costa. I can do it now on my own, but that first time, I never would have without him.

"When we surfaced, there was this rush, this relief, and this fucking euphoria that nothing could ever compete with. Ironically, it was like I was so full of life. We had no injuries, no scars. There was no blood. We were whole and perfect. Everything looked gorgeous and bright. I was full of energy…and aggression. And I was starving. I mean, crazy hungry. So, first, I beat the absolute shit out of Costa." Sam stops for a second and actually laughs.

"Then, I made him take me out for pizza. I ate two larges by myself while he iced his eye and plugged his bloody nose with tissues." He strokes my fingers with his. "Costa tripped me because he was so lonely. In it all by himself, I guess. I understand that, but…"

I sit up and face Sam now, crossing my legs over his. "But he did this to you."

"Yeah. He needed me. Desperately. Dying and surfacing…we've found out that they're so much better with someone. Being under is nothing too interesting really, but sometimes, the longer we stay under, the more intense the surfacing is. We call that a surge, the rush you get when you surface. You come back really wired, and you're totally id-driven. Freud would probably love the whole idea of death tripping because it's all about food, sex, and aggression when you trip hard. You're driven by primitive instincts."

"How is Costa a…*death tripper*? Was he…born this way? I mean, is it genetic at all?"

"The short answer is that someone tripped him. He found another death tripper, a stranger he caught in the act of tripping, and Costa somehow convinced this guy to trip him. Costa's never seen him since. The only information that my adrenaline-junkie friend walked away with is that we can trip anyone, turn anyone into a death tripper. Essentially though, we've had to learn everything on our own, and we still don't know much."

"What…what happened after…Costa *tripped* you?" This language of Sam's sounds crazy coming from me. "You must have hated him."

"You're right. I should have hated him. But I couldn't because death tripping felt so goddamn good. We loved it. It felt like he'd given me a gift, not a curse. He stayed in town, and we spent the summer death tripping. We started out just dabbling—you know, like recreational drug use. We fucked around with dying slowly, trying to stay under for as long as we could, trying to control where we surfaced.

"I showed up in an IHOP twenty miles from here once, seated with two parents and their three kids. It was…you know, rather embarrassing. Surfacing is a pretty loud, intrusive process. Floors smashing apart and reassembling themselves…it's nuts. The family was a little freaked, needless to say, so I paid for their breakfast and left."

I can't help but smile.

"It was the least I could do, right? It's hard to control where you surface sometimes although I can always find my way home. We got totally out of hand. It was disgusting and wrong—killing ourselves over and over. Guns, knives…Costa was big into knives…

"It's sick. I know." He looks away before continuing, "Death tripping is an addiction, just like any other. You can get run-down and you need more and it's never enough. Never. As suicidal as it sounds, it isn't really dying, and it isn't about trying to die. There's no death wish. Ironically, it's the opposite. We're after an enhanced sense of life. We trip over death, but don't take it. The process, the ritual of this, is all for the thrill and the power from the pleasure that seeps into every part of you during dying and surfacing. The intoxication is nearly impossible to fight."

Thank God my mind is so used to being fucked with. My ability to cope is the only thing keeping me from screaming that this is all impossible. "All of this…this is why you left college?"

Sam doesn't say anything.

"Because you were…*death-tripping*…so much?" I offer.

It takes a long time for him to answer. "I dropped out after Toby died. The summer before, Costa and I had both been out of control, tripping way too much, but I'd quit abruptly. I'd known it was a problem. My family had started to notice something was wrong. *I* had noticed something was wrong. I had to go back to school, and I couldn't be all tripped out, so I'd stopped. But Costa hadn't. Couldn't. He'd wanted to know everything about death tripping. He was addicted.

"When I had come home that winter, I had gone to the cabin with Costa and Toby. They were family, you know? I'd just wanted to help Costa, to be there and get him to slow down." Sam strokes my hair for a few minutes. "Of course, the opposite had happened, and being around Costa had reminded me of how good it was. I'd wanted the surge, that intensity.

"I was supposed to be watching Toby…the details don't matter. You know what happened. I'd fucked up. After Toby had gone through the ice, we'd tripped over and over, trying to find him, so we could, in turn, trip him, but the kid was gone. Stella, he was just gone. He wasn't anywhere under, and we'd looked. It was why we'd kept tripping and surfacing—thinking that if we died again, maybe we'd somehow enter into the right location and be able to get to him. Toby was nowhere. I swear to God, we had done everything we could." He sniffs and wipes his eyes.

"I don't think kids can be tripped. Toby is dead, truly dead. Costa was devastated. Obviously. Absolutely wrecked. But even then, even in his grief, he loved me. I don't know why, but after what happened, he didn't hate me. He could have."

"And you had to tell a story that the rest of the world would believe, one that could be real. So, you left out the death tripping."

"Yeah."

"I understand."

"You can't *possibly* understand. *I* don't understand. I've been in this long enough now that it should make more sense, but as I'm telling you this, I realize how insane it sounds."

"The addiction piece. My sister, Amy, has been hooked on…well, I don't know exactly what, but she's been using for ages. Coke, I'm sure. Pills. Definitely too much booze. I know what it can do and how it can control you."

"Toby died. Amy almost died. Death isn't a joke. But here, Costa and I were acting like death meant nothing. Because it didn't to us. Until it did."

"How were you supposed to know how to handle this? It was an impossible thing to deal with."

"Toby is dead. That's all that matters. Tragedy. That's the only outcome from death tripping, and it's why I haven't willingly tripped since. And I wasn't planning on doing it again. But then Costa showed up yesterday."

"Bishop, why is he back? Why did he do this to you? Why did he bring you back into this…this addiction? Especially after Toby…"

Sam rubs his eyes again. "I have no fucking idea. He must have been watching us though because he knew who you were."

The times when I felt as if someone was nearby but out of my eyesight—now, it makes sense. I push back Sam's hair to examine him. "You are really here. I believe that now." I kiss him, keeping my hands knotted in his hair and pulling him closer, until I am dizzy with his taste. "Why didn't you come back right away? When you surfaced?"

"God, I'm so sorry. I was under for a long time because I hadn't tripped in a while, and it got me pretty drugged. I wanted to surface back here, but it's just…I told you how I'm all kinds of id-driven when I surface? It's primal needs, urges." He looks intently at me. "I made myself surface eight or nine miles from here, so I could walk it off. There was no way that I could come back to you in the state I was in. I don't know what I would have been like with you, and letting you think I was dead for real was better than what I might have done."

I force a smile. "Eaten all the food in my apartment?"

He shakes his head.

I bite my lip. "I didn't think so. And I don't think you would have surfaced and wanted to fight me."

"Exactly. I would have been…" He clears his throat. "Very sexually aggressive. I wouldn't have hurt you, you know. Or…or God, I'd never force myself on you, even when I'm like that. But I wouldn't have been myself. With your history and with us just getting together and…Stella, I would never do that to you or ask you to give up part of yourself to be with me, to give me what I want just because I'm in a surge state. I wouldn't have been able to explain."

He probably did the right thing by waiting. If Sam had returned as anything but the calm, even person he's been today, he might not have been able to break through my own disorientated state.

But I ask, "Are you still in that place? With those…urges?"

"No. I'm okay now."

My hips slide, and I crawl up his chest until I am straddling him. Sam is the most gorgeous, desirable creature I could fathom. My connection to him is stronger than ever. Losing him and getting him back have solidified how much he means to me.

"Are you sure? No residual needs hanging around?"

Sam puts his hands on my waist. "I could get there. Easily."

"Good." I move against him. "Because you scared the absolute fucking hell out of me, Bishop. The only things I care about right now are that I am not delusional and that you are alive and here with me. That's enough for today." I can only process so much right now. The rest will have to wait.

"I'll get it if you want to run from me. This is messy and scary and massively dysfunctional. Anyone would want to escape the shit you just saw. You've gone through too much."

"Death tripping is not for the meek, is it?" I lean into his body to soak up his warmth and his heartbeat.

"No, it's not."

"I don't understand how you and Costa can hurt yourself like that."

"There is no hurt, no pain," he reminds me. "That's the nature of death tripping. Not until we can't fix the aftermath, then there is pain."

"I can be strong enough, Sam. I can do this with you. I can be here for you, and we'll figure out what Costa is doing."

"You're very strong, Stell, stronger than you know. But Costa's strong, too." He pushes gently against my shoulders so that I'm sitting up, looking into his eyes. "I made you doubt yourself and question the reality that you fought so hard for. That's unforgivable."

"You were protecting me. That's everything."

Sam slips his hands under the back of my shirt and presses his fingers into me—running them up and down my skin, undoing my bra—and then he moves his touch to the front. Through the thin fabric of my pants, I can feel that he wants me as much as I want him. He sits up, too, and embraces me.

"I missed you, Stella," he whispers, his breath and words dancing against my ear.

"And I missed you, Sam."

SIXTEEN
light in the dark

SAM DRAINED MY FRIDGE AND PANTRY OF FOOD, so we moved downstairs to his place. We haven't spoken much since he finished laying out his story. It's hard to know what to say.

Instead, we're eating pancakes.

He is frying up a batch with fresh blueberries, and I am sitting on the counter. This seems to be my spot whether we're at my place or his, and I like it because he often reaches out to brush my leg with his hand or sneak a kiss.

Sam flips a pancake over his head, and I catch it, tossing it between my hands until it cools some. It's strange, I think, that what has happened over the last twenty-four hours plus—all that I've seen and learned—has not broken me. I can make peace with this somehow.

I will.

It's beyond my imagination, beyond what should be reality, but I refuse to let it undo my sanity or destroy what I have with Sam. The simple truth is that because I've been living with such a mangled sense of reality for most of my life, I can probably integrate this more easily than I otherwise might.

My mother is a bigger bitch than this death-tripping thing, and I survived her.

Besides, now, he's hand-whipping heavy cream for the pancakes. Not everyone can do that, so that's reason enough to stay.

"You must be starving," he says. "I bet you haven't eaten since our risotto night, have you?"

I shrug. "I guess not."

"Whipped cream?" he asks.

"Sure." I crinkle my nose at him. "If you do anything weird with that whipped cream, I'll have to dump you."

"Hmm...like this?" Sam wipes a finger full across my lips and then licks it off.

I giggle. "See? That's precisely what I'm talking about. Whipped cream has gotten such a terrible name when it comes to romance, being all corny and whatnot. We need to class it up."

Sam lifts his eyebrows. "You mean, like, with jimmies or something?"

I laugh. "No! And they're called *sprinkles*!"

"Jimmies!"

Sam wipes more whipped cream across my lips and then sinks his tongue into my mouth until I've forgotten that I don't believe in mixing food and sex.

He eases back a bit, and I taste his words when his lips tickle mine as he says, "They're jimmies. Always."

"Fine. Jimmies. You win." I lean back on the counter, but I wrap my legs around his waist, holding him to me. "Do you always get your way?"

Sam looks serious now. "Nope. I don't."

"Shit, Bishop. I'm sorry. That was dumb."

"It wasn't dumb." He picks up a pancake and dunks it into the whipped cream.

"Can I ask you something?"

He squeezes my hand. "Of course. You probably want to ask me plenty."

He's right. I have a million questions swimming through my head, and it's hard to know where to start. But I do. "How do you feel about Costa now?"

"You think I should be afraid of him? Hate him?"

"Yeah. Maybe."

"I'm not afraid of him, and I don't hate him. I was afraid of how you would react if you found out about me, what I am. But…I love him, even now. I don't know if I can explain it in a way that would make sense, but he and I have a friendship that survives even death." He smiles a bit. "A lot of death. I don't always like Costa, but I'll always love him. He feels the same way about me. We're unbreakable."

Unbreakable. I understand it now, how powerful their friendship is. It might not be logical, but life isn't always logical.

"I hear you, Sam. He's a part of your life. He's a part of *you*."

"Yep. It's not always easy, as you might have noticed."

I laugh. "I did notice. Can I ask another question?"

"Anything."

"Death tripping has caused you a lot of problems even though some of it…has felt good."

He nods.

"Can you die? I mean, for real? Like, not in a death-tripping way?"

There's a long silence before he answers, "I don't know. I have no idea. It's a strange feeling, not understanding my own mortality. I'm aging though, so time goes on, but…I don't know, Stell."

I can tell this is a particularly uncomfortable topic for him, so I try to find something positive. "I know you say that it gives you a rush, but is there anything about it that's just…I don't know…fun?" I shrug. "Something harmless and not so violent?"

Sam quickly eats another pancake. He wasn't kidding about death tripping making him hungry. "It's kind of embarrassing."

"What is?"

He takes another pancake from the pile on the plate and crams it into his mouth. Then, he helps me down from the counter. I follow him out to the porch that overlooks the ocean.

Sam points down to his garden. “See that?”

“I think it’s sweet that you have a green thumb.”

“Don’t you think it’s odd that I made a series of the same-sized circular plots and that only the flowers are watered?”

“Actually, I did notice that.”

He rests his hands on the balcony and stares at the garden. “I can make it rain in circles.”

“Seriously?”

“Yep, a three-foot diameter. I actually measured. Every time I surface, I come back with a…power, an above-ground skill. Whatever. Each time I trip, I lose it and get a new one with each surface. The rain power was the last one that I surfaced with, and the only thing I could think to do with it was to water circular plots.” He looks at me and smirks. “I know. It’s not very alpha male of me.”

“I find it kind of hot. Artistic talent and such.” I actually make him blush slightly. “Wait. Does this mean that you have another power now?”

“Oh. I guess so.”

Sam starts down to the dock. It seems to be where he goes for comfort, peace. I follow and slip my hand into his as we step over downed branches.

“I’ve never found the powers to be very interesting. It’s always something pretty lame and useless. One time, I could move small objects a foot or so. Like I said, stupid stuff.”

“I don’t think it’s stupid. So, what can you do now? How do you figure it out?”

“Usually by accident. Or it sort of comes to me in passing.”

“I look forward to seeing what it is.” I nudge his side with my elbow. “Maybe you can water triangular gardens this time.”

“Very funny.”

We sit quietly on the end of the dock. I have a hundred questions that demand answers, but I also can’t bear to ask them right now. I instinctively want to withdraw, but I don’t.

The sound of the waves is hypnotic, and I am now overwhelmed with exhaustion, both emotional and physical. I fall against Sam, and together, we lie down, the worn wood beneath us somehow softer than it should feel. He entwines his body with mine, and we continue comforting and stabilizing each other.

Sam says sleepily, “I can’t stand burdening you with this, but it’s a relief that you know.”

“It’s not a burden. Knowing brings us closer.”

With that, I am able to drift asleep.

It must be hours later when I awake because it's nearly pitch-black out. And I am alone on the dock.

In an instant, I am shaky and sick. Sam's gone. My world is going to implode again. It's happening. I'm sure.

"Sam!" I stand and stumble on the knotty wood. "Sam!"

"Hey, hey. It's okay. I'm here." His voice immediately brings me down.

But I can't see him in the dark. My only vision comes from the moonlight reflecting in the lapping water.

"Where are you?"

"Here."

A luminous ball appears about ten feet from me. It's the size of a baseball, amber-colored and glowing. Sam's face comes into view behind it. There's enough light now that I can see his smile as he holds the swirling globe out in the palm of his hand.

Stunned, I take a few steps toward him. "You did that?"

"I guess so." He tosses it into the air and then catches it.

"Fire?" I ask.

"No. It's not hot."

Entranced, I move closer. "That's beautiful, Sam."

"It kind of is, huh?"

I squint as I examine the colors. I stand next to him and take his hand in mine. "I think you've come back with a very cool power this time."

"I don't know what to do with it really, but I guess it's sort of cool."

"Can I touch it?" I ask.

"I don't see why not."

Slowly, I inch my hand to the globe. The shape breaks apart a bit at my touch, and when I move gently through the colors, what looks like pops of electricity fly off, like one of those glowing static balls.

I smile with delight. "Did you see that? Like sparklers! Try it."

Sam takes a turn passing his fingers through, but he yanks me back hard when a strong burst of light erupts in his hand. "Shit. Are you okay?"

I laugh and lean back against him. "I'm fine. Just startled. You're right. It's not hot."

Sam nuzzles my neck and kisses my chilly skin. His tongue moves against me, and I close my eyes.

God, I have him back. "Don't die on me again, okay?"

"I don't plan on it." Suddenly, he lets out a noise and shakes his hand enough to send the glowing ball into the water. "Okay, maybe it can get a little fire-like after all. That burned pretty good."

"C'mere." I lie on my stomach at the end of the dock. "Give me your hand. We've got an entire cold ocean."

He lies down next to me, and I dunk his hand in the salt water. The orb drifts in front of us, and we both watch as the current slowly takes it farther into the cove.

"Well, I guess it floats," he says, still in disbelief about what he created.

I rest my head on his shoulder. "I'll miss that glow-ball thing."

His free hand goes out in front of him, and he holds it steady. "Pick a color," he says.

"What?"

"Pick a color. I want to try something."

I stare at his palm. "Um...blue?"

He's thinking, focusing. Within seconds, a blue orb materializes. This one has a much stronger light than the first one. He smiles.

"Red," I say softly.

Sam rubs his lips together, and I wait. The ball changes color, the blue fading and quickly seeping into deep red hues. I laugh as I clap my hands together, and I list more colors. The orb turns purple, then green, and then diamond white.

He takes his burned hand from the water and puts it next to his other. The weightless ball doubles in size, and I gasp. Sam bounces it in his hands and sits back on his knees. For a few minutes, he tosses the orb. Then, he holds it in both hands and shakes the ball hard, creating a glittery array of colors that spin and streak.

"Huh," he says to himself. Finally, he turns and winks at me. "Watch this."

With the ball in one hand, he extends his arm behind him and pitches the orb into the air. It disappears into the dark, and for a moment, I think it's gone, swallowed by the night.

But then, the sky ignites in flashes of color, like fireworks exploding above us and showering the sea with falling colors.

Under the illumination, we kiss and drown in our reunion, in relief at purging the truth, and in hope for the future.

SEVENTEEN
the cat came back

THERE'S SOMETHING TO BE SAID FOR ANONYMITY. Having no contact with family or other people from my past is incredibly freeing. It's remarkably easy to disappear. Hiding online is simple, and that safety is immeasurable.

It does occur to me that my mother and sister could find me if they wanted to, but I've heard no word from either of them. Part of me has been waiting for them to snap into shape, for the shock of my absence to have shaken them into mental health. It's unlikely. I know. However much I like the emotional and physical distance between us, I have thought about calling them. Guilt washes over me each time I consider it, but I suppose it's normal to wish I could have a relationship with my family. I've taken to doing online searches for my father, and I can't tell if I'm happy or tormented that I can't find one thing about him.

What helps counterbalance disappointment in my own family is the joy of having Sam as part of my new world.

Sam and I just had dinner in town with Kelly and April, both of whom I absolutely adore.

Now that we're into July, the streets have filled up with vacationing families, couples, hiking and boating enthusiasts, and weekenders looking to escape Boston or New York for a long weekend.

The inn has been packed, so Sam has had plenty of work to do. I go in and help out, too, a few days a week. It's an excuse to spend time with Felicia and Micah, whom I've grown very fond of, and I like working the dining room and readying guest rooms. Felicia scolds me because I won't take her money, but I haven't been able to get Sam to cash any of my rent checks, so fair is fair.

At his parents' insistence, Sam has the day off tomorrow, and because I just finished three graphic projects for clients, I'm giving myself a day, too. Sam raved so much about the work I'd completed until I was full-on blushing and actually feeling quite proud of myself. Sam is going to take me on a short hike to Seal Cove, and if we're lucky, we'll actually get to see seals sunning themselves on rocks, which I would absolutely love.

I'm watching Sam fold laundry now, noticing what neat piles he makes as he stacks shirts and pants on the couch in his living room. The dichotomy between the side of him that is so rough and rugged and dirty when he works on the house or helps on fishing boats with this softer, more domestic side intrigues me. It's the death tripper in him versus the sensitive, gentle human being.

I lean back into the armchair and look up at the ceiling. "Nice job with the lights, Bishop."

He smiles. "Glad you like them."

Hundreds of pale white and pink glowing balls hang in the air above us, spreading a soft hue over the room. Each is smaller than a golf ball, and they move a bit as though not entirely stable, but it gives them a look of life and personality. Over the past few weeks, Sam has been playing around with his new light power, and he's found that he has a lot more control than he has had in the past. I also enjoy pushing him to try new things, and I find what he can do utterly enchanting.

"Think you can light up the fireplace, too? It's cool again tonight."

"It is not that cold, silly. But whatever the lady wants…"

He focuses on the hearth, and I turn to watch. Eight deep purple and pale violet orbs appear and bounce in the fireplace. Sam sets down the sweater he's folding and goes to the lights. When he swipes a hand through them, they burst like bubbles and shift to look like flames. Immediately, I feel the heat radiate, and I move next to him by the fire and lie down on the rug. The colors are beyond beautiful, vibrant. It's unlike anything I've ever seen in the real world before.

It's taken work for me to process that death tripping is real, to reconcile that the world as I understood it actually includes something as unbelievable as what Sam and Costa can do. But my only choice is to accept it, which I can do because of how much Sam means to me and because he's made such an effort to ground me even in this whirlwind.

Sam lies down behind me and puts an arm over my waist. "Too hot?" he asks.

"Maybe a little."

An arctic blast shoots from the fireplace. "Sorry, sorry!" Sam puts out a hand, and the temperature levels to a comfortable warmth. "Got a little carried away there."

I roll onto my back and look up at Sam. "You're the best boyfriend ever."

"Because I make light?" The corners of his eyes crinkle adorably as he smiles and leans in to quickly kiss me.

"Because you make everything." I brush back his hair, now streaked with more blond and auburn because of his time in the sun, and I run the back of my hand over his tan face.

"Stella…" he starts. "I can't believe you're with me. After everything."

"You're with me, too. After all *my* everythings. I told you before that we both have a past."

"And one of us has a rather strange present."

"*We* are the present, and it's beautiful." I tug on his T-shirt and bring him close.

Every time we kiss, my whole being reacts so strongly, like it's the first time that we've done this. I can't get used to the strength of our attraction, but I don't mind. While there is familiarity and comfort in his kiss, it's also equally exciting and dizzying.

"I love you, Stella. With every part of me, I love you."

This is the first time he's said that. I said it when he was in my arms, bleeding and dying, but I haven't said it since. I didn't know if it was allowed, if I should dare say it outside of a crisis. But now, he's said it. He's made it real.

"And I love you, Sam. I am so clear when I'm with you."

"Even with the world I've shown you?"

"Yes, even with that."

"It's done, you know? You don't have to worry. I'm not going to trip again."

I nod. "Okay."

"I'm not, Stell. I don't want that. I don't need it."

"I know, Sam."

"I just need you." His hand moves to my leg, and he pushes my dress up. "And I can't tell you that enough. But maybe I can show you."

He leans over me and kisses his way up my thigh until I can feel his breath over my underwear. He slips it down and then with one touch of his tongue, he quickly sends me into sexual oblivion. Only Sam can get me this crazed so fast, and I let myself take in every sensation of his mouth. He pulls me against him, showing me how much he loves this. He is slow and methodical in what he does. First, his tongue barely moves over me, something he now knows gets me squirmy and breathless. Later, in the heat of it, Sam's hand and mouth work faster and harder until I can't control the way my thighs tremble, and he makes me come so hard that I'm nearly blinded by the force of it.

I'm still panting when he crawls up, but I grab him by his waistband and hold him against me while I catch my breath.

"You okay there, sport?" he asks, laughing lightly.

I nod. "Holy shit."

He lets me recover and kisses my neck and shoulders until I can breathe again.

"Sam?"

"Hmm?" His mouth is still exploring my skin.

"Sam? I need to tell you something. For real."

"Anything." He moves onto his side and props himself up on an elbow.

Now that he's waiting on me, I'm uncomfortable. But I need to say this. "What you just did for me? I…I haven't done for you yet."

"Stell—"

"No, it's true. You can't pretend it isn't. I feel like I spend half the time I'm awake with your mouth between my legs."

He smiles flirtatiously at me. "I like it down there."

"Well, I do, too. Trust me. But..." I hate what I'm about to say. "Before, when I was with Jay, he made it...awful. I know it wouldn't be like that with you, but I have this bad association."

"That's not how it's ever supposed to be. And I'd like to go a round or ten with that asshole for how he treated you." His expression softens and is so full of understanding. "You don't ever have to do anything that you're not comfortable with. You know that, right? I don't need you to go down on me in order for me to be crazy about you or to be crazy about how good it feels to be with you."

I roll my eyes. "You might be the best guy in the world, but you're still a guy. It's kind of normal to want a blow job now and then."

Sam is trying not to laugh, and he bites his lip. "Okay, sure. I can't say that I don't think about it ever. But who cares? It's just not that big of a deal to me. I want you to be happy and comfortable. And occasionally in ecstasy." He brushes his lips over mine. "And, Stella? You don't have to justify this to me. What you want or don't want is up to you."

I move a hand to the top of his pants and undo the button. Then, I ease down the zipper. "I'm telling you this *because* of how comfortable I am with you. You make everything safe. You make me want what I didn't know I could have." I press against his shoulder and move him onto his back. "I want this for me." His pants and boxers come off easily, and I move to hold myself above him.

When I run my tongue over his length, Sam groans and runs his hands through his hair. "Are you sure? It's okay if—"

I stop him by putting my mouth around his cock, and a rush of pleasure runs through me. He feels so good. I didn't want to do this until I was sure that it would feel right. The last thing I wanted was to get myself in a situation where I might feel negatively about doing anything with Sam. I am immensely grateful for his understanding, so I plan on showing him just how grateful.

There's not one part of me that is not fully absorbed with touching him, tasting him, and feeling how he grows harder in my mouth with each move I make. I wrap one hand around him and move along with my mouth. Sam finds my free hand, and his palm presses against mine. His fingers hold on, tightening, as I bring him closer. It's his way of telling me to stay present, that he's here with me, and it makes me want to prolong this as much as possible.

So, I slow down. I tease. I learn to enjoy what was once about being dominated, controlled, used, what used to make me choke and gag and hate myself. Sam's response to me—the subtle way he lifts his hips in rhythm to my mouth, the connection he solidifies by holding my hand, and the perfect sounds of sexual pleasure he lets out—undoes the damage from my past.

When I can't wait anymore, when my urge to hear him and feel him go over the edge are too much, I increase my pace.

Sam moans. "Stella…" He moves to push me away. "You need to stop, or I'm going to come."

I love that he's said this because it shows how cautious and watchful he is over me, but I keep going because this is exactly what I want. And when he does come, he is perfect in how he moves and sounds and tastes. I'm not sure which one of us is more fulfilled by what we've done together, but he reaches under my arm and pulls me to lay on his chest.

"I have to hold you."

His heartbeat pounds into me, and it's the best sound I could hear. It is life and love.

The door to his apartment bangs open. "Who wants tequila?"

Fuck.

Costa is back.

EIGHTEEN
tequila sunrise

SAM IS STILL SHIMMYING BACK INTO HIS PANTS as Costa slams a bottle onto the kitchen counter.

"Remember, we don't need to be scared of him," Sam reminds me. Then, he snaps at Costa, "There's such a thing as knocking, asshole."

"Jesus, you two are like rabbits, huh? Every time I come by, there's all kinds of sex going on."

Sam glares at him. "Then, stop coming by."

"Aw, don't be so salty, Sammy. Look!" Costa waves his hands around. "No gun this time!"

I scramble to make sure that my dress is pulled down all the way—and to control the fear that is taking over. I can't help it. Sam stands, and I put a hand on his leg. He looks down, and I see that his face is relaxed.

"It's okay. Don't worry." Sam strides from the living room, pulls a fist back, and slams it squarely into Costa's jaw.

Costa reels back and catches himself on the small dining room table. "Fuck, Sammy. That hurt."

"Probably not enough." Sam takes a second swing, hitting the exact same spot.

This time, Costa hits the floor. It takes him a minute to sit up, and he wipes his bloody mouth on the sleeve of his hoodie. "Glad I wore red."

Neither of them moves for a bit. Eventually, Costa looks up at Sam, and I see something in his eyes that makes me think he might be more than just a murderous prick. Apparently, Sam does, too, because he lets out a loud sigh and reaches a hand down to Costa. He hesitates but then claps his hand into Sam's. They stand face-to-face, and I'm afraid they're going to erupt into a full-out brawl.

Instead, they both start laughing and throw their arms around each other.

Sam messes up Costa's perfect black hair while holding him in a bear hug. "You haven't changed."

"Neither have you. But, dude, get a haircut."

"So that I can be all pretty boy like you? I don't think so."

They are both smiling—and not killing each other—so I stand up and wait awkwardly until they separate. Costa looks shyly my way. He covers his mouth and clears his throat. Then, he walks toward me. I instinctively take a step back when he's close, and he stops in his tracks.

"Sorry. Really. I didn't introduce myself properly last time. Costa Jorden." He drops down on one knee and extends a hand. "It's a pleasure to meet you, my lady."

His eyes are the darkest blue I've seen, and his skin is fair and smooth with barely a hint of stubble showing. I don't care how handsome or charming he is.

I'm still pissed, and it's all I can do not to snarl. "Your apology needs work."

He cracks a smile. "Agreed. Sorry I shot and killed your boyfriend with no warning. It was horribly rude."

I can't help but smile back. "Better. Pour me some of that tequila, and you might be halfway there."

Costa looks back to Sam. "I like her."

"Not sure she likes you yet."

He hops to a stand. "She will. Everybody does."

Sam pulls down shot glasses from an open shelf. "It's goddamn true." He sits down in a chair at the table. "Are you pouring or what?" Then, he nods at me, giving the signal that all is safe.

I slip past Costa and stand in the embrace of Sam's outstretched arm. "If that's cheap tequila, you're going back to the liquor store for something high-end."

"Oh, she is not going to be easy to win over, is she?" Costa flips a chair backward and straddles it.

I glare at him. "No, *she* is not. But if you brought limes, you'll help your cause," I say as I sit down in Sam's lap.

Costa taps the side of his head and raises his eyebrows. "I'm no dummy." Then, he pulls a lime from each pocket of his red hoodie and proudly holds them up.

Sam tosses him a pocketknife, and Costa catches it with one hand. He pours a shot and skims it across the table to me.

I shoot it straight with no salt or lime. I send it back to him, and with the knife, he stops it from flying off the table. I nod, and he pours another.

It's three shots in before I've gotten over wanting to strangle Costa myself, not that it would do any good. The whole death-tripping thing is rather problematic. Sam keeps rubbing my back, reminding me that he's here, that things are okay.

"So, man, what's up with the lights?" Costa jabs a finger at the living room ceiling. "Tell me that's not what you came back with."

"I was happy with the limited rain power, but…"

"Dude." Costa leans over the table and whispers, "It's kinda lame."

"Lame?" I throw a lime wedge at him. "Sam, show him."

"He'll still think it's lame."

I grab Sam's hand and hold it out. "Costa, pick a color."

He leans back and grins. "Tequila sunrise."

I squint at him. "Okay, smart-ass." I smack my hand back against Sam's chest. "Easy. Do your thing, Bishop."

Sam groans. "Okay, fine. Here." He shakes out his hand and then holds it steady.

The lights on the ceiling black out, and a small colored droplet begins to form in his hand, soon growing to be nearly a foot in diameter.

"You made a pretty ball." Costa claps slowly. "I worship you."

Sam stares at him with irritation and hurls the globe over Costa's head. Just before it lands, it explodes, and the entirety of Sam's apartment is coated in thick tiers of red, orange, and yellow.

"Holy fuck, Sam." Costa rises from his chair and grins. He spins on his heels, his dark eyes electric with fascination. "Okay, show-off, I'm definitely impressed. You've gotten stronger. You never could have done that before. Interesting."

"You asked for tequila sunrise. I gave you tequila sunrise." Sam hugs both arms around me.

Costa sets his hands on his hips, and his face softens as he studies Sam—and then, Sam and me. "I really, really missed you. I shouldn't have left."

I can feel Sam's anxiety. "You had to. I get it."

"I think it was a mistake. I just…" Costa takes a seat again, the orange light covering his skin and somehow making him more striking. "I couldn't look at you. It hurt too much."

I slide from Sam's lap and move back to my chair, but I take his hand in mine.

"I didn't want to look at me either."

Costa pours himself another shot and licks the side of his hand. "It wasn't your fault, Sam." Slowly, he sprinkles salt and pauses before he takes the salt and tequila. "We were both in a whole shitstorm, and it wasn't your fault. Everything was fucked up." He bites a lime wedge and winces. "You were my best friend, and nothing will ever change that."

"No," Sam says. "Losing Toby changed that."

At the sound of Toby's name, Costa visibly tenses. "No, he didn't. Even with everything that happened, I needed you. Leaving was a mistake, and I want to be back. I want *us* to be back."

"You're my brother, Costa. You can come home anytime you want."

Costa puts his hands behind his head. He flashes a cocky grin that I'm already familiar with. "I'm too fuckin' sexy to be your brother."

Sam laughs and shakes his head. "So, we're back to normal, I see."

"If normal is disco lights and overpriced tequila, then yes."

"These are not disco lights, moron. But since you asked…"

Sam claps his hands, and the room goes black. He grows six silver drops in his hand, and he tosses them to the ceiling. Within seconds, glittery balls spin overhead and send white light patterns across our faces.

"God, you're such a prick," Costa says, not able to hide the amused tone in his voice. "How do you put up with this guy, Stella?"

"Simple." Now, it's my turn to grab the bottle. "Best sex of my life."

Costa winks at me. "So far."

"Hey, hey, watch it there." Sam claps his hands on the table. "You and I just made up and all."

"I'm just kidding. Seriously, you two look very happy together. And, Stella, you're much better than those skanks he went after when he was surging."

I can't keep from laughing, but Sam groans.

"Costa! Seriously?"

"Kidding, kidding. You were an altar boy, no matter how great the surge." Costa looks at me and not so subtly shakes his head.

"Can we change the subject, please?" Sam begs.

"Fine. But, dear God, do you remember that horrid girl with the crow tattoo across her neck? Some tourist from Michigan. You're much hotter, Stella."

I try not to snort. "Thank you, Costa. I'm flattered."

"Let's toast to starting over." Costa pours three more shots, and we each take one. "To old friends and new. I think we're going to make a damn good trio."

Sam nods and raises his shot glass. "Here's to that."

While I'm sucking on a lime, Costa hops up and turns on Sam's stereo. "And since we have disco lights, I think we must dance, yes?"

He holds his hand out to me, and I'm drunk enough to agree. When "Stayin' Alive" starts playing, I crack up. Costa's charm really is hard to resist. I let him spin me around, and I giggle when he pulls out a few good moves from the '70s. I catch sight of Sam watching us dance, and he looks so happy. After what he went through with Costa—and with Toby—it's good to see these old friends finding peace with each other. We spend hours listening to music, thankfully ditching the disco hits early on, and talking.

By one in the morning, we're all impressively drunk and sprawled out in the living room. Sam made another light-orb fire in the fireplace, this one turquoise and gold. I stopped drinking a while ago, but tequila has a way of sticking around, keeping me warm and awake. The boys are reminiscing about death tripping, and it's a good thing I'm not sober, or the stories about the various ways they used to die might be too much. But maybe I've had enough time to incorporate Sam's reality into mine because I'm not entirely freaked anymore. Maybe I'm still a bit concerned but curious to know more.

I'm on the floor, and I lean back on my arms and look between Sam and Costa, now both on the couch. "So, you went skydiving and just didn't pull your chutes? Didn't you feel bad for that skydiving company? I mean, that poor instructor! And the pilot!"

They both start laughing, and Sam lightly smacks Costa's arm.

"That was totally your idea, and it was awesome." Sam apologetically looks at me. "I know, I know. It was wrong. But our packs and chutes disappeared with our bodies, so…it was like it never happened, right? Okay, fine. It was mean."

"But also awesome!" Costa screams. "Come on, Stella, say it was awesome."

"I'll admit…it might be just a teeny bit amusing. In a totally sick, awful way."

Costa hangs upside down off the couch. "You do have yourself a bit of a bad boy, Stella. Get used to it."

"Ah, my bad-boy days are over," Sam says. He gives Costa's feet a good hard push, sending him toppling to the floor.

"Sammy, for real? You're gonna…what?" He scrambles to a teetering stand by the fireplace and waves at the colored display Sam conjured up. "Make pretty lights forever?"

"Death tripping doesn't lead to anything we need, Costa. You know that." Sam gets up and stands near me.

My hand automatically lifts to stroke his leg. He wiggles his fingers at the lights, making them flare up and singe Costa's pants.

"Hey! Not funny!"

Sam shrugs. "A little bit."

"Ah, really? You could do with a much better power." Costa's tone moves from playful to more serious. "You deserve better than this. Don't you agree, Stella?"

"What do you mean?" I ask.

Costa shrugs. "You know, your boyfriend never would have been able to do something like this before. He's different now. What if he could fly?"

"Oh, shut up, Costa," Sam says. "That's ridiculous."

"We could make you some sort of cape or whatnot." Costa opens his arms and beckons to Sam. "Come here, my favorite superhero. Give me some love!"

Sam dramatically rolls his eyes, but he reluctantly steps into the hug and puts his arms around Costa's neck. "You're crazy."

"And you're strong." His arm moves a bit.

Then, I hear a sound that I can't place.

Costa's voice turns serious. "You can do anything, Sam."

"Goddamn it, Costa," Sam whispers, but I can hear the emotion. "Again?"

Costa moves his arm, and I see the pocketknife in his hand while it is now sticking into Sam's stomach.

"No, no, no..." I repeat softly, unable to move, aware that I can't stop this.

"You have to knock this shit off." Sam grabs on to Costa.

Costa lowers Sam to the floor and against the couch.

He looks at me over Costa's shoulder. "Stay with me, Stella. Remember, it's going to be fine."

Even though blood is once again pouring from the person I love, this time, I try my best not to panic, and I listen to his words.

Costa runs a hand through Sam's hair and then lifts his chin to look into his eyes. "And it feels good, Sam, doesn't it?"

Sam smiles at him, virtually drugged, clearly euphoric. "Yes."

"Tell her you'll be right back," Costa purrs.

Sam shifts his eyes to mine. "Listen to me. Listen, okay? I'll be right back. Don't worry." He's not lying to me. He wouldn't.

Costa kisses his forehead. "Good boy. Enjoy your trip." Then, he digs the knife in deeper and lifts it upward.

Sam lets out a groan that sounds all too much the way he did earlier while we were alone and half naked. And I can't stop staring at him. I hold his eye contact as he takes a few shallow breaths.

"Stella, tell him that you hear him," Costa says, "that you're all right. You'll give him a good surge if he knows you're not freaking out."

It takes everything I have to control my trembling when I go to him and take his hand. I even force a smile. "I hear you, Sam. I hear you. I'm all right."

Sam slightly nods.

And then, he dies.

Costa pulls the knife from Sam's gut and leans against the couch, leaving one arm draped over his friend's shoulder.

Now that I don't have to control myself, I straddle Sam's body in order to lunge at Costa and slap my hand across his face as hard as I can. "You're a fucking asshole! You're a fucking asshole!"

Costa grabs my arm with one hand as I remain kneeling over Sam, panting and shaking, while his blood colors my dress.

"Settle down," Costa says firmly. "He's fine."

"He didn't want to trip again, you fucker!"

"Yes, he did." Costa is inappropriately calm. He wipes Sam's blood off on his jeans as though it's nothing. "We always do."

I yank my hand away and slap him again. At least he winces, and I shake off the sting.

"That wasn't for you to decide. Just like turning him wasn't for you to decide. It was selfish!"

But what I hate most right now is that I think he might be right, that Sam did want to trip.

"Stella," Costa says evenly, "Sam is not in any trouble. He'll have a good trip, and he'll be back."

I try to control my breathing. Sam's body is still slumped against Costa, and I can hardly stand to look with all the life sucked out of him, but still, I curl up against him and take him in my arms.

"He'll be gone in a minute."

I cling to Sam. "How does it happen? That he…disappears?"

"Wait."

Knowing his death is temporary, that he will return to me, does little to lessen the searing pain caused by seeing him like this. I drop down and rest my weight on Sam's legs, hoping that maybe my heartache will ease once his body is gone.

"Nothing's happening."

"There. Look at his hands," Costa says gently.

The tips of Sam's fingers are becoming sheer, like a gel. There's light movement though, like water swirling in the current of a stream. It moves to his hands, up his arms, to his chest, and down his torso. I touch my fingertips to him. He's still solid, but the man beneath me quickly becomes a blur of deep colors. Then, like sand falling through a sieve, he disintegrates, and I drop fully to the floor.

"Oh God, you're not going to cry again, are you?" Costa is busy examining the knife.

I look down and see that my dress is clear of blood, and so are Costa's pants.

It's just like last time, I assure myself. *It all vanishes, and then he'll return.*

"Tell me again that Sam is coming back to me."

"He's coming back to *us*," Costa says. "Got that? I wouldn't do anything to hurt Sam. Come on, Stella. You have to know that, right?"

"I don't know anything," I spit out.

He puts down the knife and turns to me. "I was just fucking around. Really. Look, Sam's a death tripper. That's not changing, okay? It's not. This is who he is, and if you love him the way I think you do, then you're going to have to accept that. Death trippers, we want certain things. We need them the way you need food and water. We need to die. We need the rush of death and the rush of the surge."

"Sam went ages without tripping. He was fine."

Costa drapes his arms over his knees and rests his head down. I can't deny that there is genuine kindness beneath his obnoxious attitude.

"If either of you thought that hiatus from death tripping was going to last forever, then you were both fooling yourselves. I know how strong the pull is."

I don't know what to say to this.

"Stella, I'm not trying to scare you. I'm telling you so that you can fully understand who Sam is. He's going to need to trip now and then."

"He was tripping too much before." I pause. "Your son…"

Costa takes a long breath.

"I'm sorry," I say quickly. "That's none of my business."

"It *is* your business. You're with Sam, so it is." He runs a hand through his hair and stands up. "Come on. Sam's going to be hungry when he gets back. Let's see what we can rustle up for him."

I don't hesitate when he extends a hand and pulls me to my feet. It's odd that I'm relying on Costa to get me through this trip when he's the one who caused it. "How long will he be gone?"

"Dunno. Depends on where he surfaces. It can be a bitch sometimes because you can't always control where you come up. Sam's out of practice, but he should be okay. Generally, the more we trip, the faster we can come back. I don't think more than a few hours."

"Really?" I am hugely relieved. "I thought I was in for another long one, like last time." I follow him into the kitchen. "Fuck you for that, by the way."

"It was a bit dramatic, wasn't it? With the gun and all?" Costa smirks.

He turns and places his hands on my waist.

I let him set me onto my usual spot on the counter—but not without question. "Have you been watching us?"

He doesn't answer.

"Costa, have you been watching Sam and me? You know this is where I sit, don't you? With Sam. And you knew my name when you showed up at my place."

He fills his arms with food from a cabinet. "Maybe."

"Why?"

He sets a can of tomato sauce down. "I don't know. Look, I didn't know what I was walking back into with Sam. We didn't exactly part ways under the best of circumstances. I was wrecked. He was wrecked. So, I wanted to feel things out."

"And you decided that the best entrance was to shoot him in front of me?"

Costa shrugs.

"Look at me."

I wait until he stops fussing with a can opener. There is such sorrow in his face, and I'm now hyperaware that the last time he saw Sam—before he shot him in the living room—was right after his young son died.

"Were you…punishing Sam? For Toby?"

"No," he immediately says. "No. Besides Toby, Sam is the only person I've ever given a fuck about. And I hate that he has to live with how Toby died. It must be all sorts of hell. This is a small town, and people will always talk. I know how they've treated him. When I came back and I saw him with you…how happy he was, how *really* happy he was…"

"And you wanted to punish him."

He slams the can hard onto the counter, and red sauce flies everywhere, half of it landing on my dress. "Shit!" He wets a dish towel and starts wiping my arms.

I'm fascinated while he cleans off my hands and then rinses the cloth. I look down and see red liquid seeping through the fabric on my legs. I feel it on my skin. He stands in front of me again, and I am shaking and engulfed in nausea and fear.

"Costa…"

"Sorry," he says.

"Costa…Costa…"

He finally looks up at me. "Jesus, I'm sorry, Stella. It's not blood, okay? It's not blood."

"Get it off me. Get it off me…" Speaking feels nearly impossible. "Costa, please."

With one hand, he pulls me off the counter, and with the other, he lifts the dress over my head and then tosses it aside. "I'm sorry. I'm so sorry." He brushes the towel over my legs. "Don't look down. Just look at me, okay? Look at me."

So, I do.

He soaks the towel again and returns, setting one hand just under my chin so that I can't see the blood.

The sauce. The blood...

"You were right," he starts. "What you said earlier. I was probably punishing Sam. I guess I didn't think of it like that, but maybe I was." Costa moves the cloth over my thigh, but he's respectful, not roving once. "I've probably always been jealous of Sam. He's everything I'm not. He has everything I don't. And now, he even has you. It's stupidly easy to see that he is in love with you—all the way. I haven't had anything close to what you two have."

When he throws the towel into the sink, I start to ease out of my fog. It dawns on me that I'm nearly naked, but before I can say anything, Costa is unzipping his hoodie and slipping it over my shoulders. He tucks my arms into the sleeves and zips it. All the while, he does this without a lurid look, which I appreciate. He seems like someone who could be an asshole about this, but instead, he's very sweet.

"I know Sam loved Toby as much as I did, but this is an impossible situation. I can't forget what happened, but I can't hate him. Sam is the best thing to happen to me, next to my kid. But maybe I did need to lash out." He grins. "Passive-aggressive, I'll admit."

"You two boys always seem to be unraveling me with dramatic bloody displays and then dressing me," I mumble. "It's quite gallant. And sickening."

He smiles. "Sorry that the hoodie is red."

"Sorry everything looks like blood to me right now."

"You'll toughen up," he says.

"I hope so."

"You don't have a choice."

NINETEEN
the surge

AFTER I CHANGED INTO A CLEAN SKIRT AND T-SHIRT while Costa finished preparing a lasagna with both red and white sauces before setting it in the oven, I check the clock. Killing time has not been easy.

"It's been a while," I say.

"Distract yourself," Costa says. "Tell me something, anything."

"I just spent the past hour summarizing every season of *Sons of Anarchy*. It's not acceptable that you haven't seen that show, by the way, considering you have a fondness for murder."

"Maybe it's not acceptable that you *have* seen that show. Pick another topic."

"Okay, Costa Jorden," I say. "Do people call you CJ?"

He wrinkles his forehead. "Uh, no, they do not."

"Then, I will."

"No, you won't. What else?"

I pace the floor outside the open kitchen and blow a stray hair out of my face. I can't think of anything to discuss that will make me stop thinking about Sam. "I have a crazy mother," I spit out.

"So do I. Sucks, doesn't it?"

"And my father left us years ago. Although I'm not really sure, I think he kissed me good-bye in the middle of the night. I haven't seen him since. We weren't allowed to talk about him."

"You don't know where he is?"

"No. And I don't want to."

"I don't know where my parents are either. And I also don't want to." He fakes a smile. "Isn't it great how much we have in common? The start of a beautiful friendship."

"Yep. Lifelong friends, you and me."

"Next topic," he says. "I got an apartment in town, above the bakery. My place smells like snickerdoodles all the time."

"Lucky you."

"You should come over one day. Check it out. I'll shuck oysters for you."

I glare at him. "Nice try."

Costa takes the tequila bottle from the table and hands it to me. "Have a drink. You've sobered up way too much."

I slug down a shot. "Happy, CJ?"

"Your crazy mother. Is that why Sam was worried about you before he tripped? Why he told you to stay with him? What does that mean?"

His questions feel like a violation, and I don't want to explain too much. "I get…messy sometimes."

"Messy?"

"My mother did a number on me."

Costa takes the bottle and drinks. "Messy, like you can't see things clearly?"

I'm surprised by what he understands. "Yes, actually."

He walks the floor for a minute, seeming lost in thought, and then goes to the stereo. He scrolls through his phone until he finds music he wants, and then he takes another drink. "Dance with me."

"I already danced with you."

The music is slower this time.

"Dance with me again. It'll help pass the time."

"Fine." I step into him, somewhat reluctantly, but the truth is that I also welcome physical closeness and comfort because I'm beginning to falter in my faith that Sam will be okay. I put an arm over Costa's neck and a hand in his. "What are we listening to?"

"Matthew Mayfield. 'Heartbeat.'"

"Ironic."

Costa's hand moves to the small of my back, and he pulls me in hard, his waist pressing into mine. "Feel."

I push away. "Don't be a shit again."

"No, not *that.*" He repositions me against him. "Feel my heartbeat. I've died way more than Sam has. My heartbeat is still strong, so feel."

I lean the side of my head on his chest. Even with music filling the room, I can hear, and I feel a little better—only a little, but it helps. I let Costa rock us back and forth to the lyrics. "Who tripped you?" I asked.

"Some guy."

I step on his foot. "Say more."

He laughs. "About ten miles north of here, there's a place where people go cliff diving. It's illegal, but it's fun. I never jumped, but I used to go sit and watch from a distance. I caught him there, alone—*the death tripper.*"

Costa makes a dramatic ghost sound, and I smile.

"When he jumped and crashed, I saw him die. I saw him and the blood on slabs of rocks. Then, I watched his body disappear. I thought I'd made it up. I stayed there all day, trying to convince myself that I wasn't crazy."

His heartbeat continues to keep me calm.

"I understand that."

"He came back just before nightfall and did it again. He *tripped* over death. It was awesome. I don't know what he calls it, but Sam and I go with *death tripping.* Nice ring to it, huh? I watched him a few more times, and then I asked him if could make me what he was, if that were possible. He said he could do it to anyone. So, he did it to me. Made me a death tripper. End of story."

"Just like that? But why did you want to be tripped?" I ask with skepticism. "You went up to some stranger and—"

"End of story, okay? The point is, I got what I wanted, and I never saw him again."

"This doesn't make any sense." I step back just slightly and look up at the raven-haired boy who I know damn well is holding back the full truth. "You hardly knew anything about death tripping. You still don't. Why didn't you ask him about it? I mean…if there are rules or whatever? Will you and Sam ever die? Are there more death trippers? There have to be, right? Shit, Costa, why would you ever choose this?"

He stops dancing and holds me still. "You, more than anyone, should understand wanting a way out. That's what I got. I got my out. Death tripping gave me a life. Until it took my son's."

I don't know what to say to this, so I move into his body and make him keep dancing with me. Three more songs play before I speak again, "What the fuck is this song we're listening to?"

"Hey, be careful there. This is Bret Michaels. 'Every Rose Has Its Thorn.' Don't mess with Bret."

"Fine, fine. Sorry. I had no idea this was so important to you."

"Ballads from the eighties are very important to the world. And this is the updated country version. It's hot." He steps back and gets on one knee while he serenades me.

"You're so weird."

"And you love that about me."

"I *acknowledge* that about you."

"Same diff." He stands back up and continues our dance.

"What power do you have now?"

"I don't," he says simply.

"Only Sam has powers?"

"I used to have them. After I tripped Sam, they disappeared. Apparently, there's a trade-off."

"That's a big one."

"Maybe. Maybe not. Death tripping got to be lonely. I needed someone."

"So, you sucked your best friend into this nightmare?"

He slowly turns us. A haunting new song fills the silence. Finally, he says, "Yes. I did that."

I shut my eyes.

"I shouldn't have," he continues. "I know that. I was lonely. And I needed Sam with me. I'm not justifying it. I'm just telling you. I can't take it back, so the only thing to do is have fun with it."

I place my hands on his shoulders and push, creating a good distance between us. "Yeah, it's a fucking joyride. It's been over four hours now. Where is he? Where the fuck is Sam?"

"What? You're not having fun with me? Of course you are. Stop worrying."

"No. No, I'm not going to stop worrying. You don't know shit about this. Is there some…some book of rules I don't know about?"

"Well, no, but—"

"But nothing. Maybe there's a limit on how many times you can die. Maybe his limit is different than yours. Maybe he's dead for real this time." I am incredulous—and increasingly furious—that Costa chose death tripping without having any real grip on what it is.

"Stella, he's not—"

"You don't know that!" I'm full-on yelling at him now, but I can't stop. "My life was a complete fucking disaster until I came here and found Sam. I pulled my shit together, and for once, everything felt clear and normal. Then, you show up and blow it all to hell!"

"Stop, okay?" He looks broken, but that doesn't slow me down.

"He didn't need this. He wouldn't have chosen this. You're like me. Your life was a disaster, and you *needed* death tripping. People like you and me have to escape somehow, but Sam wasn't like that until you made him need this. You tripped Sam, and Toby died because of that, so losing your son is on *you*." Before the words are out of my mouth, I regret them—deeply.

Costa reaches for the bottle again and leans against the wall. He cracks his neck and then takes a long drink. He's stoic, but he can't hide the hurt. "Well, that was brutal. Do you feel better now?"

"No." I walk to him. "No. I'm sorry."

He takes another drink and wipes the back of a hand over his eyes.

"Really sorry. Costa, that was awful. *I'm* awful." I nod at the tequila.

He holds the bottle to my mouth, and I drink more than I should. But it's what I want—to feel numb. Then, I put my arms around his waist and hug him close, attempting to undo some of the damage that I've just inflicted. He doesn't move, but I don't let go.

"There's no blame in any of this. I'm sorry for what I said. And, God, I'm so sorry your son died. That's unbearable. It's the only thing that matters in all of this. Sam told me what a great father you were and how much you loved Toby."

Costa moves a hand to my back and drops his forehead onto my shoulder. "We couldn't trip him. We tried. He was nowhere."

"I know. Sam told me that you did everything you could. You both did."

Together, we stand like this for what feels like forever, yet it also feels like no time.

Later, he takes out his cell and shows me a picture of a toddler with hair as dark as his and eyes just as intriguing. The child is holding a raggedy stuffed lion over his head and smiling at the camera.

"I miss him every second of every hour." He tucks the picture away. Then, Costa says something that nearly breaks me, "I lost Toby. I can't lose Sam, too."

I grab fistfuls of his shirt in my hands. "Sam's been gone too long, hasn't he?" It hurts to even ask.

"Truth?" It takes him a minute to answer. "I thought he'd be back by now."

"Oh God, Costa." My voice breaks.

"I know. I love him, too." He rubs my back. "Look, you can't always control how long you're under or how long it takes you to pull it together when you surface. He's different now. He was off for a long time before I tripped him a few weeks ago. It's been a while, so he might still be getting back into the swing of things. And his powers seem different and stronger, so his trips might be different. Maybe he surfaced far away, but he'll call if that happens. We're just going to wait, and Sam will be back."

For another forty-five minutes, Costa holds me and tolerates my tears. I don't disappear into my alternate world, but I'm not entirely in this one either. Costa must know this experience because he doesn't force me to choose. The only thing he does do—just when my fear and anxiety have peaked—is turn me around in his arms and face me forward, so I can see Sam, who has just come through the door. The *real* Sam. He is whole and beautiful and alive.

I let out a choke of relief, and my legs begin to buckle. Costa catches my body and holds me up, and I fall against him. Sam strides to me, his expression intense, his eyes nearly on fire with lust. I'm not sure that he's even aware of Costa. Maybe he's not aware of anything or anyone but me, which I understand because the only awareness I have is my equally fervent and immediate desire for Sam—to be entwined, engulfed, and in love with the person I am so tied to.

It's only with Costa's support that I am still standing when Sam reaches me. His hands slam against the wall behind me as he presses his full body against mine and kisses me more powerfully than he ever has. He is soaking wet with ocean water, and while his body should be cold, it's anything but. I twist my fingers into his hair as I arch my back into him.

I'm vaguely aware that there are hands on my waist—not Sam's though.

Oh, I realize fuzzily, *it's Costa's*.

His touch is firm as he runs his hands up and down my sides. Sam's mouth is so tight over mine that I can barely breathe, yet I also can't get enough. He tastes like salt water and sex. Sam hits the wall hard with a fist and grinds into me. I have to pull my mouth from his to let out the gasp that's been building. He puts a hand to my throat and tips my head back so that I'm resting it on Costa's shoulder, and then he starts working his mouth and tongue over my neck.

"Do you feel his heat? His need?" Costa says, his mouth next to my ear. "He's so hard, isn't he? Sam wants you so much that it'd kill him if that were possible."

All I can do is whimper in response. I can't think. I can't stop this.

I don't *want* to stop this.

I pull the back of Sam's drenched shirt from his pants, slide my hands under the hem, and move with his hips. I want him closer. He's so close against me that I can't get my hands between us. I push against him, but he's too strong, and he stays bonded to my body. However, Costa gets Sam to pull back, and all I feel is gratitude when Costa moves his hands from my waist to Sam's, easing him away just enough that I can get my hands to Sam's front button and zipper. He practically growls as he pounds the wall again with his hand. I hear plaster crack.

"Easy, Sam," Costa says soothingly.

Sam takes his mouth from my skin and looks at me. He's so drugged on death tripping, even I can see that, and I want everything he's feeling right now. I want him to pass it to me. I lower his pants just enough and wrap my hand around his cock. Sam groans and braces his hands more firmly against the wall. I can tell that he can barely focus, and it just makes me need him more. The way he's so intent on being inside me, on his need for me…I keep moving my hand up and down over him until he's wet and harder than ever.

"Go on. Take what you want, Stella." Costa lifts my skirt on both sides and then firmly wraps one hand around my waist.

I press on Sam's shoulders and groan as he shoves down my underwear. They drop to the floor, and I spread my legs apart a bit. Costa puts a hand under my ass and raises me just enough. It's all I can do not to scream when Sam brushes the tip of his cock against me. When he pushes inside, the feeling is almost too much.

The arm Costa has over my waist moves up to rub over my ribs as it lifts me higher and then comes to a rest just beneath my breasts. "Breathe, Stella."

He's right. I need to breathe, so I make myself inhale and exhale.

Sam pulls out and then roughly slides back into me. I drop my head back onto Costa's shoulder and close my eyes while Sam holds still inside me. I'm drowning, but it's a different sensation than what I'm used to, and it's magnificent. I feel completely consumed by Sam. He pulls out and slams into me. It's aggressive—and he's strong—but it's not too much. It's just what I want. Then, he starts to settle on a hard rhythm, taking me to a place where I'm almost as high as he must be, totally lost in this heat and primal lust.

I hear Costa's voice again, and then I look in time to see him pushing Sam's hair away from his face. He lingers, tucking a lock behind an ear, before running a thumb over Sam's jawline.

"Sam's so fucking good, isn't he?" Costa's husky voice echoes through me.

"Yes," I manage. I turn so that my mouth is against Costa's neck.

"Watch Sam. You want to see him fucking you."

So, I do what Costa says. It's hard to focus through this haze, but I watch how Sam moves, how his arm and chest muscles are taut each time he enters me, how his intensity is unparalleled to how he's been with me before, how he drips ocean water on me every time he thrusts. He's always amazing—perfect really—but this could be addictive. Yet even this is not enough. I'm hungry to go further.

"You went way under this time, didn't you, Sam? I can see it," Costa says.

Sam says nothing and doesn't stop moving inside me.

"More," I murmur. "More, Sam."

"Sam can't hear you now. He's too driven, too consumed with you."

I feel Costa smile against my cheek.

"He's surging hard."

I squirm between them and push my hands into Sam's shoulder, wanting my hips higher so that Sam can go deeper. "More." I'm begging now.

"Sam…Sam, listen to her. She wants more." Costa's voice is deep, directing, and cuts through Sam's haze.

Sam puts both hands firmly under my ass and gets me higher so that he can go deeper. My back is flat against Costa's chest, but my ass is right over his pants, so I know how turned on he is, too. But I don't care. This is not about his pleasure. It's about Sam's and mine. When Sam is fully inside me, he slows his rhythm and kisses me again. This time, it's more controlled, more teasing—exactly how he's fucking me now.

"The surge is raw," Costa says smoothly into my ear. "It's basic instinct. It's overpowering. And it's how much he loves you."

Sam's tongue is hot against mine, and he tastes more like himself but more extraordinary than ever. I tighten my stomach and move against him, increasing the tension and my need. I'm starting to breathe too hard, and I have to take my mouth from his. I know that he wants to keep kissing me, but I'm too heated, and I need air.

But Costa doesn't. So, while I rest my head against him, Costa leans forward just a bit, just enough to direct Sam's attention to his mouth. I take a hand from Sam's shoulder and touch it to his face while I watch them. Costa is gentle in the way he kisses Sam, sensual and slow, giving him just enough to take the edge off. My fingers go to the kiss, and I ache to run my tongue over their lips. I want to feel them, taste their connection. I'm not threatened at all. It's just different than what Sam and I have. And it's wildly erotic.

I move Costa into Sam a bit more and catch my breath when I see him slip his tongue over Sam's lips. I'm starting to get lost in their kiss, but Sam moves away and looks at me. He half-smiles and thrusts into me, hard. Then, he kisses Costa again, harder this time—full tongue, no holding back.

I smile to myself. Sam's doing this for my benefit, and it's working.

I'm so close. I just need a little more. "Put your hand on me." It's so hard to talk.

And Sam's so lost in me again.

"Sam, please…"

From the corner of my vision, I see Costa end the kiss.

"The surge is still too high. I think he can only hear another death tripper." Then, Costa moves *his* fingers between my legs. He finds just the right spot and rubs against me.

It only takes moments until the build is inevitable, and I'm clenching my body as my arousal climbs. Sam watches, taking me in. His eyes are sharper, steadier. Costa takes his hand away now, and I think Sam is starting to see more clearly.

I know I'm right when he tells me, "I'm with you." Those words send me over the edge and into an orgasm that leaves me shaking, trembling, and dripping in sweat.

Sam smiles again. "Told you I'd come back to you."

"Now, come *for* me."

Sam moves with a smoothness and pace that rings less of pure lust and more of pure emotion. Even when he's on the brink, when his sounds tell me that he's seconds away from coming, the tenderness and care in his pacing overwhelm me. He softly kisses me and then holds his mouth just near mine when he needs to let out a groan. When he comes, he shudders, his release reverberating through me and into Costa.

Costa releases his grip on me. He kisses his fingers and touches them first to my lips and then to Sam's. "And that, my friends," Costa says with no hidden satisfaction, "is what we call the surge."

Sam laughs lightly, and he's still breathing hard when Costa slips out from behind me.

Costa walks backward and winks at me. "Welcome to death tripping."

The front door shuts, and I lean back against the wall to look at Sam. "A simple muffin basket wasn't going to do it, huh?"

"Go big, or go home, I guess." He strokes a finger over my shoulder and trails it down my chest. "You okay?"

I think for a minute and nod. "I don't like muffins anyway."

TWENTY
the power of three

WE DON'T TALK ABOUT THAT NIGHT, not until days later when we are on the beach in the late afternoon.

Sam's parents put together an early picnic dinner for all of us, and I'm absolutely stuffed after three lobster rolls. They have to get back to the inn for the dinner rush, but they've made sure that we'll all meet up once a week even during this busy season.

April is stretched out on a rock reef that juts into the ocean, watching the tide roll out, and Kelly and Costa are stomping through wet sand, looking for clams. I raise a hand to my eyes to block the sun and look out at the scene before me, complete with people who are in my life, whom I care about and who care about me. I'm so peaceful today, so entirely relaxed.

Sam sits, propped up against a boulder, and I lie on my side with my head in his lap, enjoying the feel of his fingers as they run through my hair. Whenever we're together, we are inevitably touching. It seems impossible for us to break our physical connection.

Even when he got sick the day after his surge, I sat on the floor of the bathroom, holding a wet washcloth on the back of his neck. Costa had been smart to make that lasagna. Sam ate half and then immediately puked it up, but he went right back and polished off the rest. Then, he slept for twelve hours.

Costa came back that afternoon. He explained that death tripping could give a bit of a hangover sometimes, so he stayed and watched over Sam while I did some online work. He said that Sam wasn't in bad shape, likely because it was only his second trip in a relatively short time. I could certainly vouch that Sam was perfectly fine when he woke up because we took a forty-five minute shower together, and I never got around to washing my hair.

"Stella, about that night," Sam starts.

I breathe in the salt air and roll onto my back so that I can look at him. I'm surprised he's bringing this up. "What about it?"

"Do you understand now why I had to stay away from you after that first trip during the storm?"

"I think so."

"I was damned if I came back too early and damned if I came back too late. But I had to protect you. You see how it can get to be a little…much?"

"You didn't hear me complain, did you?"

He smiles down at me. "No."

"Is it always like that?"

"The surge? No, not always. And that was the strongest I've had. The thing with all of this is that nothing is really consistent. I know that sounds crazy. But dying, going under, surfacing, surging…they're never the same. I think mood affects each stage—who I'm with or not with, how long it takes to die, how often I've been death-tripping." He shakes his head. "Not much is clear."

"That last surge was pretty clear." I run a hand over his tanned bare chest. As much as I love these family gatherings, I can't wait to get home. And all this talk of Sam's intensity isn't helping my patience.

Sam clears his throat. "That surge was pretty out of hand. Are you all right…with what happened?"

I sit up next to him and pull my legs in. Sam wraps an arm around me, and I softly kiss him.

"Yes. Are *you* all right with what happened?"

"Yes." He kisses me back. "Just so you know, that was the first time it was like that."

"You and Costa don't go around surging and seducing love-struck women on a regular basis?"

He laughs. "We do not."

Sam looks out at the water when Costa starts whooping and yelling. "Oh God, what is he doing?"

Costa is in the middle of a ridiculous dance that involves lots of knee lifts and finger-pointing toward the sand. Then, he jumps up and down several times. "Kelly! Hurry! Clam! Get it before it eats me!"

Kelly shakes her head, but I can see her amusement from here. She heads his way, carrying a long bar with a claw on the end that she's been using to dig in the sand, and Costa swings his bucket with exaggeration as though he's a little kid.

Sam touches his head to mine. "He looks so happy, doesn't he?"

"He really does."

"It's been a long time since I've seen him like this."

"You're glad Costa's back. I can tell."

"Yeah, I am."

"You two have been hanging out a lot this week. I think that's good—for both of you."

"It's good he's working at the inn. Everyone missed him. He and Kelly have always gotten along really well. And of course, my parents worship him. He's around family again."

"You know…Costa's crazy about you," I start.

Sam looks at me. "I know."

He also knows where I'm going with this, but it has to be asked.

"Is he in love with you?"

"Nah, not really." He looks back to the water. "Maybe. I don't know. We have a complicated history, an emotional one. Both of us have hero-worshiped the other at certain points. And both of us have despised the other, too. I think Costa's a little bit in love with the idea of you and me. He's got some sort of infatuation with us being together. Maybe it's what he wants for himself. And about that night?" He digs his feet into the hot sand until he hits cool mud. "Costa loves women, I know that, but his sexuality is probably a little more fluid than most. He'll go where there's fire. And do not underestimate the tequila factor. I saw how much you two went through while I was gone."

I rub my feet next to his. "Waiting for you might have required some liquid courage, yes."

"There's another piece you should know about. He told me that you know about him losing his powers after he tripped me?"

I nod.

"Well, because of that, he's become a bit of a thrill seeker. It's a way to compensate, I guess. He used to hit up a racetrack a few hours from here a lot. Fast cars, danger, speed. He loves it. He also likes more elaborate death stunts than I do. The more blood and gore, the better. Diving from buildings, crashing stolen cars. Knives and guns, as you know. Costa's done it all. The thrill seeking probably explains why he killed me in front of you—twice—and probably why he didn't leave the minute when I came back surging the way I did. He knew where that would lead. I'm id-driven when I'm surging. Costa's id-driven all the time." Sam is quiet for a minute. "Do you hate Costa for what he's done?"

"No," I say, "of course not. He's a little fucked up, but he's lost so much. I get it. I like a lot about him, and anyone who cares about you the way he does—with his sincerity and his loyalty—is worth way more than any wrongs he's done."

"Good. I don't want you to hate him, but I'd understand if you did."

"We make allowances for people who matter. But I don't understand *how* he can trip after Toby. He still loves it."

"I know that it doesn't seem to make sense, but it's wired into us. It's who we are and what our bodies ask for. We're drawn to tripping because of something that changed in us. It's like our body chemistry makes the need intrinsic." He pauses. "We can't really fight it."

"You did."

"And it probably made me worse off, but I'll always fight it."

We listen to the ocean and the sound of seagulls flying overhead.

"You good?" he asks.

"I'm good." I tousle his hair. "I *found* my good, remember?"

He puts both arms around me now and exhales with relief. "I've been so fucking terrified that I hurt you during that surge, that I scared you, or that I made you feel like I could have been that way with just anyone…or that you were at all uncomfortable with it."

"What? Sam, Jesus. Why didn't you say something to me earlier? I assumed we hadn't talked about this because it was awkward, not because either one of us was worried." I rise up on my knees, kneeling next to him, and put both hands on his chest. "I thought you knew that I was fine, that *we* were fine. We are amazing, you and me. Sam, look at me, and listen very closely. The truth is, I loved that night, and I loved how you felt. I loved everything that happened, *how* it happened. Sam Bishop," I say with my most flirtatious smile, "you rocked my motherfuckin' world. If that wasn't obvious, if you couldn't tell how much I wanted you…Sam, really. You know me better than anyone—in bed and out. You know I loved every second."

With uncharacteristic shyness, he asks, "Really? It wasn't too much?"

"Apparently, I'm as fucked up as you death trippers because I don't regret anything."

He's still not convinced. "Even that we weren't alone?"

"Even that. Maybe I'm supposed to be embarrassed, but it just happened the way it did. I wasn't freaked about it at the time, so I'm not going to be freaked about it now. The truth is that Costa…" I struggle to figure out how to say this. "He *translated* for us. He…facilitated it."

"Yes, he brought us closer," Sam says definitively. "I can't deny that." He smooths out the towel underneath us. "Costa likes you a lot, you know?"

I smile and raise an eyebrow.

He laughs. "No, not just because of that night. Despite what happened, he doesn't look at you as more than a friend. He'll always be edgy and nuts because he's Costa, but he likes you for *you.* Because of your strength, your compassion…because of how you love me."

"Did you two talk about what happened?"

"Nope," he says. "And we probably won't. He and I are totally fine. Just another weird thing that happened between us. Add it to the list." Sam wiggles his toes in the sand and squints into the sun. "Surges and drives. It's part of what makes up death tripping."

"You do, however, have some id drives, even when you're not surging." My hands follow the lines of his arm muscles and roam over his shoulders. All this talk about his sexual appetite is getting to me.

Sam bites his lip. "You know, we are in public. During daylight. And my family is just down the beach from us." He takes my wrist in his hand. "And I'm wearing swim trunks that are not going to hide anything."

"Sorry," I say with a laugh. "So, can you talk during a surge?"

"What do you mean?"

"You didn't say anything at first when you came back, surfaced. I was just wondering…"

"Talking isn't always the easiest thing when surging, but seeing you fed into my sex drive so much that I was pretty much in a zone. Speaking, hearing…well, they weren't really options." Sam smiles. "Normally, I have a bit of function, but seeing you got me a little crazy. And just so you're aware, you also have strong id drives of your own—for which I am immensely grateful." His eyes look down over the front of my bikini. "I plan to make use of them when we get home."

"I do indeed have a drive—for you and only you. I can't get enough. You changed everything for me, Sam. You made sex beautiful. You made it about love. You let me be able to feel it and enjoy it. I'm learning about myself because you've given me a place to do that."

There is so much care and truth in his face when he looks into my eyes. "My surge, the level I was at…it was about you. Costa was right that I needed to know you were okay before I died, and it made going under and surfacing smoother than ever. But I think that knowing I was coming back to you also influenced my surge in a way I haven't felt before. I don't know how else to explain it, but I believe the power was because of you. That surge had meaning." Sam pulls me so close that the rest of the world fades away for a minute. "You're doing something to me. I feel it all through my body. I love you, Stella, so much."

There are kisses that arouse, there are kisses that deliver love, and then there are kisses that transcend both of those things. That's how Sam kisses me—with his entire soul. He gives me all that he fights for and against, all that he fears, and all that he hopes. He kisses me with his past and his present and his future.

I am so in love with him.

"Hey! If you two do it on the beach, watch out for sand! Ew!"

Hollering from the water's edge makes us separate, and I can't help but giggle at Costa's shrill squeal.

"Fuck off!" Sam yells back. But he's got a smile plastered on his face.

Costa throws both hands on his hips and takes an outraged stance. "Language! Honestly, I'm appalled. There are families here!" He gestures around the cove that is empty, except for our crew. "As restitution, one of you needs to come clamming with me. Kelly ditched me."

Sam groans, but I stand up and stretch. "I'll go, or we'll never hear the end of it."

"Tell Costa he's a dick."

"Will do."

The truth is that I like clamming. Stepping on the wet sand, waiting for squirts of water that tell me a clam is somewhere under there—it's just so

Maine. I feel very comfortable that this is now my home. I give Sam a quick kiss and head for the shoreline, and Costa cheers when he sees me coming.

He's adorably free and unrestrained, but I'm struck with sadness.

God, he must have been a wonderful father.

I run faster to him. I reach out for the bucket. "Let's see what you've got."

Costa whips it behind his back. "Tell me what Sam's power is."

I laugh. "Nope."

Costa has been trying to get Sam to reveal his new power, but Sam is determined to torture Costa for as long as possible.

He narrows his eyes. "You're mean."

"Well, Sam says to tell you that you're a dick."

He wiggles a finger. "Ah, I think Sam meant to say that he *likes* my di—"

"No!" I laugh and scramble for the bucket, but he's too fast.

We stomp in the mud and clam until my toes are freezing. The Atlantic Ocean, even in July, is frigid, and I cannot believe there are brave people who actually swim in this.

"I'm getting cold."

"You only got three clams, you big wuss."

"CJ, I'm cold," I whine.

"Stop calling me CJ! Let's make a deal. If you get eight more, then it'll be enough for me to cook dinner for you two. Death trippers are good cooks because we eat like we just came back from the dead."

"Very funny. And it's tempting…"

"And if *I* get eight more, then you tell me what Sam's power is."

"I am not agreeing to that."

"How's this instead? You tell me what Sam's power is, or I'll dunk you in the water."

"I am also not agreeing to that."

"But I am."

He drops the bucket, and I immediately turn for dry land. Before I can take more than a few steps, Costa scoops me up and heads for the water.

I kick my legs, and I cannot stop laughing, but I seriously do not want to get dropped in this bitter ocean. "No, no, no! Please, Costa!"

Water is lapping at his knees when he stops. "So, you'll give it up?"

"I think I gave it up the other night."

"Ha! But that's not what I meant." He lightly tosses me in his arms, but he catches me just before I go in. "Tell, or you'll get dunked."

I give him a fake scowl. Then, I make a point of whispering, "Sam, forgive me, but I'm not going in this ocean. I love you, but I hate cold water more."

Sam yells from his spot on the sand. "Stell, don't you dare!"

"Sorry, too late," I say softly.

Costa looks at me with curiosity. "No way."

I continue whispering, "Besides, Costa would have found out somehow. He's a sneaky bastard."

Costa smiles. "Shut up. Hearing? He's got super hearing?" He lowers his voice so that it's barely audible. "Sammy? This can't possibly be true, or you'd hear that I've got my hand on the hook of Stella's bikini top, and it'll only take one flick of my finger to pop it open. Also, your sister's not really a lesbian. It's all a front to hide the devastatingly erotic and disturbing things she lets me do to her."

"You are so going to regret that!" Sam shouts, his voice echoing over us.

I giggle and cup my hand to Costa's ear. "Oh, and Sam? Costa has massive penis envy and told me that he's hugely jealous of how big your—"

Costa flings me into the waves, and I scream. The cold burns, but I'm still laughing when I surface. And I'm just in time to see Sam tackle Costa, sending the two of them careening into the water.

TWENTY-ONE
no limits

"THIS IS REALLY BECOMING A GODDAMN PROBLEM." Poised on the end of the deck, Sam hurls a rock into the water. He's not in a good mood. "Everything. I mean, I hear *everything*. It's just getting worse."

Costa reels in his fishing line and wiggles his feet as they hang over the edge of the dock. "Then, trip again. Simple. You'll come back with something cooler."

Sam spins around. "Really? That's your answer? Screw you. I'm not tripping again. And neither are you. It's too addictive, you know that."

"Then, live with it." Calmly, Costa casts another line. He's not going to catch anything from the dock at the house, but he seems to like fishing from here anyway.

I stretch out on my towel and pull my sunglasses down. "There must be some way to deal with this besides another suicide run."

"It's not *suicide*," Costa growls. "You of all people should have an appreciation for the beauty of death tripping, Surge Girl."

He does have a point. But Sam has progressively become more miserable. His hearing power seems to be increasing, and it's a special kind of torture at work. He's plagued by every conversation throughout the inn, which is beyond intrusive.

"I'm going to go crazy." Sam throws another rock. He likes being here on the dock because the water brings a degree of white noise that helps stifle other sounds.

"You're still only hearing people's voices though?" I ask. "No other sounds?"

"Thank God, no. If I had to tolerate every single sound within my earshot, then I'd certainly be flinging myself in front of the closest oncoming truck."

Costa sighs. "Man, that sounds fun."

Sam flings a small rock at Costa, and he winces.

"Well, that wasn't very kind."

"Neither was killing me."

"Okay, fine. I'll let you two in on a little secret, one that is right in front of you, but you're both too lovesick to see it." He sets down his fishing pole, takes off his T-shirt, and lies back to take in the sun.

Sam crosses his arms. "What? You have some brilliant fucking idea to make this shit stop?"

I hate seeing him like this—so angry and restless.

"I do actually." Costa lowers his sunglasses as though he's not being stupidly calm in the face of Sam's agitation. "Maybe I'll make you guess what it is."

Immediately, Sam moves to sit on Costa's chest and clamps his hands around Costa's throat so that he's all but cutting off air. "You're a fucking douche bag, you know that? Tell me."

"Sam, stop!" I scramble toward them.

No matter how hard I try, I can't pull Sam's hands away, and Costa is definitely having trouble breathing.

"Stop! You don't want to do this," I say.

Sam tightens his grip.

Even while losing air, Costa smiles. "Do it, Sam," he gets out. "Come on, kill me."

"You do not want to do this, Sam," I plead. "This is not who you are. Don't let him get to you. He's just screwing around."

"Kill me, baby," Costa begs. "Send me under…"

For a moment, I'm distracted. It's a draw to watch and to be in the presence of Costa's pleasure in his own pain. Or what maybe isn't pain. Maybe it's all pleasure. He turns his eyes to me, and all I see is the hypnotic look from his rush because he's dying. Right in front of me, he's dying.

"Sam!" I scream, shoving him hard. "Enough!"

Finally, he drops his hands and sits back on Costa's chest, keeping him pinned to the dock.

Still smiling, Costa coughs and gasps. "Damn it. So…close," he sputters. "Almost there."

Sam is panting, and he puts his arm over his face as he calms down. "Sorry. Sorry."

Gently, I guide him a few feet away from Costa, and we sit. "You okay?"

"Yeah. Really, I'm sorry. I'm being an asshole."

Costa rolls over onto his side. "He needs a fix. That's why he's doing this."

"Shut up, Costa. He's not tripping. This hearing thing is the problem," I spit out.

"Look at him, Stella. He got all fired up just from nearly killing me. You feel a little better now, Sammy?"

"Fuck off," Sam says coolly.

I can see though that Costa's right. Sam is already more peaceful than he's been in days.

"Okay, I'll tell you what I think." Costa props his head on his elbow. "Your powers and your surges now? Stronger than ever. That's because of Stella. She's making everything about tripping bigger and better."

"What do you mean?" I ask.

"You're Sam's…power augmenter," he says.

"What the fuck is a power augmenter?" I look to Sam.

He shrugs, but something seems to be dawning on him.

"I've been watching you. It's so easy to see." Costa's voice is seductive now, smooth and enticing. He really *does* enjoy watching us. "You two are magnets for each other. Anybody can see that. The power with the light, Sam? Did you ever try using that when Stella wasn't with you?"

Sam shakes his head.

"I saw you that night on the dock. What you did was amazing. And I don't think you could have done that without her. And this hearing thing? Stella, do you remember what you said before Sam went under?"

I freeze. "Oh my God…"

"That's right," Costa says. "You said, 'I hear you, Sam.'"

"No way." Sam appears to be in as much disbelief as I am.

Costa sits up and rubs his throat. "And now, you hear."

"The storm…" Sam starts. "It was a near hurricane."

"What?" I ask. "The night Costa first showed up?"

Sam says, "I could only make it rain in small patches before."

"No," I tell him. "There's no way. You didn't make that storm."

He turns to me, and it takes him a bit to respond. "*I* didn't make it. *We* made it."

I flash back to that night—to Sam and me in bed with the lightning, the thunder, the way the storm grew as our connection did the same. "And the sun shower. Outside the inn." I pointedly look at him. "Sam, the lights you could make. 'In a dark, dark world, you give me such light.'"

"See? You're his power augmenter." There's too much delight in Costa's words and not nearly enough intimidation over this realization. "I made up that term, by the way. *Power augmenter.* It has a certain ring to it, doesn't it?" He literally blows on his knuckles, and I want to scream at him for being so cavalier. "Your surge the other night? How you stayed under longer than you should have? That was Stella."

"I don't understand." I'm in shock. But what Costa's saying feels right. It makes sense in this nonsensical world. "How?"

Costa stands up, fully recovered—maybe even energized from his near-death choking. "The point is that Stella might be able to help you tone down the noise you're hearing. She can get you to focus it."

"I'm desperate," Sam says. "So, let's go with your theory. I don't like it one bit because I don't want her sucked more into our shit than she already is, but…this has to stop."

"If I can help somehow, then I want to," I say.

"Sam, you can only hear voices within a certain radius, right? That cliff up there. Out of range, right?" Costa asks as he hops into the rowboat tied to the dock. "I'm gonna row myself out there just like a distinguished sea captain. When I'm far enough that Stella can't hear me talking but you still can, you're going to try to block me out."

"What do you mean?" Sam asks.

"Cut me off. Stop my yammering. With Stella here, I'm betting she can help you focus your power, so you can be stronger and have more control over it." He throws on a life vest. "I know. A *life* vest. Ironic, huh?"

As he rows out over the small waves, I have to admit that it's not a bad idea. If I can somehow influence Sam's hearing ability and he can turn off the incessant noise of people's voices, it will be worth admitting again that Costa is right.

"This is crazy," Sam says.

"I know. But we both know he's right, don't we? There's something here, something between us, that connects with death tripping. Costa might be difficult and half insane some of the time, but he sees a strength between us that we haven't."

"Okay."

"You're shivering, Stella. It's eighty-five degrees out." He looks worried.

"I'm fine. Let's just do this." I don't tell him that I find Costa's power-augmenter idea daunting.

He knows anyway. "I'm so sorry about—"

"Stop. Don't apologize. We don't need to do that with each other. Death tripping is here to stay, so let's get a handle on it."

He nods and takes my hand.

It's a relief when Costa's screaming version of Poison's "Talk Dirty to Me" vanishes for me, but based on Sam's wincing, I can tell he still hears Costa. I wave a hand to signal that the boat is far enough out, and Costa stays where he is.

Sam frowns. "He's intentionally singing radically off tune. And…oh God, now, he's ad-libbing weirdly and stuff. We have to stop this."

"Good. You're motivated!" I squeeze his hand.

"Yep. He's moved on to 'Unskinny Bop.' Let's make this work."

"So, now…I don't know. There isn't exactly a rulebook here, but I'm going to focus on you, and you focus on blocking out Costa's wretched singing."

I close my eyes while the ocean air breezes over me, through me, and I concentrate on Sam and my love for him. I think about the first time I met Sam in the stairwell of the hospital—his touch on my skin, the sweetness he brought to such a horrible day, the impulsive way that I ran through the sleet to be in his arms.

I get dizzy and take a step back.

I see Sam angry on the deck the day I moved in, feel the strength of his arm when he caught me before I fell. Then, I remember the night he first cooked dinner for me, how he started to let me in. I feel the hard shift when every wall between us dissipated and how we fell in love with so much work and fear but also with such ease and trust. There are no conditions and no limits on my love for this boy who stands next to me.

His voice takes me from my thoughts. "It's so peaceful when he shuts the fuck up, isn't it?"

I smile. "You did it? You blocked him out?"

He nods. "I did. Shit, I really did it. You *are* making me stronger, Stella."

I throw my arms around him and tightly hug him. Everything about him impresses me—not just his powers and how he's gaining skill, but also how he handles so much in his life and the way he loves and lets me love him.

Besides all the syrupy feelings, I think definitively that I'm going to fuck his brains out tonight. Then, we're going to order pizza and eat in bed and get crumbs all over the place and have an awesome time.

Slowly, Sam turns to me, his face stunned. "Oh my God."

Confused, I ask, "What's wrong?"

He looks incredibly unhappy as he asks a very simple question, "So, what kind of pizza are we getting?"

I shake my head. "No. That's not possible."

"It seems that anything is possible."

"You heard me? I mean, you *heard* my thoughts?"

"Apparently, you power-augment hard. You amplified my hearing so much that I can hear you in every way." He pulls his hand from mine and turns away. "This is too much. It's too weird."

"Sam," I start. But I don't really know what to say. This is…incredible.

It's much more than what Costa suggested.

So, I just think, *We'll deal with this later, but let's look at this as a beautiful thing. We have to see it like that.*

"Stell, don't. Don't talk to me in your head. It's like I'm invading your privacy. This is awful."

"Sorry. I understand."

"I don't know what to do. And I don't want Costa to know."

"Why not?"

"I don't know. Just…not yet, okay?"

What this all feels like for Sam is a mystery to me, and I'm at a loss about what to do or how to make him feel better. I move into him, lean my head on his back, and wrap my arms around his waist. We're both staring into the sun that is just beginning to dip.

"I love these afternoons in Maine. The light is more beautiful, the air fresher than I've experienced before. I love everything about Watermark."

"Even now, with all that's going on?" Sam fiddles with my bracelet while he inhales the sea breeze and runs his fingers over the letters as though he's reading through touch.

"Even now. The air here? I can breathe again without feeling like I'm inhaling toxins. Before Maine, every move I made hurt. But now, I have a new life with this new air that smells like freedom and love. It makes me want to float into it."

Sam turns into me and brushes his lips over my shoulder. "I don't know how you're so positive. Most people would run screaming from this shit, not want to float in it."

"I'm not afraid of this. I just want you to have peace, Sam."

"I will have it. Because of you."

TWENTY-TWO
it won't hurt

THE ROWBOAT BUMPS THE DOCK, and I start to tie it off while Sam reaches to Costa and helps him out.

Costa immediately claps his hand repeatedly on Sam's back. "It worked? Dude, no way. You are completely awesome."

"I don't know that I can stop all the voices I hear when I'm at the inn or somewhere else though. One person is probably easier. And I can't exactly strap Stella to my back and cart her around with me all the time." Sam smiles, trying to hide his mood from Costa. "This power is going to take work to live with."

"Then, don't live with it." Costa backs up and reaches into the rowboat to pull out a small net. "Look! I caught two fish while you were busy being all death trippy and magical. Seems Stella is good luck for me, too."

We head back to the house, and I kick off my shoes on the deck while Sam goes inside to get us drinks.

"It's going to cool off soon," Costa says. "You need a sweatshirt?"

"Yeah, probably. I'll get one in a sec."

"I'll get it for you."

I smile at him. "Thanks, CJ. There's one on the couch in my living room."

"You got it. Then, maybe we can see what else Sam can do. This is cool shit." He trots down the stairs, yelling, "Fish for dinner! Fish for dinner!"

Alone, I lean over the railing and see that Sam's garden is suffering now that his watering power is gone. I find something terribly sad about the dry plots, and I resolve to bring them back to good health. There's enough death around us without losing the flowers.

Costa hangs my sweatshirt next to me.

I pat his arm. "Thanks."

Silently, Costa takes the knife from his pocket and squats on the deck. Water from the netted bag runs over the wood and drips off the side. I can't stop looking at it. The pattern it is making is thick and heavy and crawling toward me. Something doesn't feel right. I'm nervous and edgy all of a sudden.

"Hey, you okay?" I ask him.

"Fine," he says dryly. The net is tangled, and he rips the knife through it.

He's not fine. That's clear. He's anything but, and I know from the way my stomach knots that something is urgently wrong.

Sam, get out here. Now, I think.

I wince when Costa slices open one of the fish and starts gutting it. "Do you have to do that here?"

"Can't take a little blood, princess?" His hands are filthy, and he shoots me a cold expression. "I thought you'd like the head."

"Hey!" Sam is at the door, three open beer bottles in his hand. "Watch your mouth."

"Just a joke." But Costa's mood has changed. "Relax. This hearing thing is making you touchy. Maybe you're right. Maybe this power is a bad idea."

"I'll figure it out." His words are loaded with tension.

Costa takes the second fish and swipes the knife through its belly. "It's pretty fucking simple, Sam. If you hate this hearing power, then trip. Poof! You'll be all fixed."

"I'm not tripping again, understand?" When Costa doesn't say anything, Sam throws the bottles over the railing and takes a step closer. He's angry now, and the tension between them is high. "I asked if you understood me, Costa. Enough is enough. No one is tripping anymore."

"Christ, Sam! I heard you, okay?" Now, Costa stands up. He's not as big as Sam, but he can definitely be intimidating when he wants to be. "You don't want to trip. I get it. So, don't. I'll leave you alone. Everything's cool." He glances down to the yard. "Do you want to replace those perfectly good beers you trashed?"

"Sure." Slowly, Sam backs up, keeping his eyes on Costa, until he's inside.

"What's going on with you, Costa?" I ask.

"Nothing." He slices through the second fish head. "I just think Sam's being a little goddamn thoughtless."

"What do you mean?"

"Has it occurred to you that I don't get to have powers like Sam does?" He holds up the hand with the knife to stop me before I say anything. "I know, I know. My own fault because I tripped him. But it doesn't mean I don't want what he has." Costa's look is hungry and heartbroken and frightening.

I don't know which of the three is stronger.

"Sam is being stupid, Stella. He has a gift. And with you? I mean, we didn't know for sure until today that there were people who could power-augment, and you sure as hell do that for him. And he wants nothing to do with it? Or with death tripping even? We've started to figure out what else might be possible, and Sam's ready to just bag this all and pretend that we aren't who we are? That's bullshit." He points at me. "And you know it's bullshit, don't you?"

"I don't know what to say to that."

"Why not? You're in this now. You're part of us."

"I'm part of *Sam*," I correct him.

"Really? Then, prove it." Costa wipes his knife on his shorts and stands in front of me, much too close.

Inside my head, I scream for Sam.

Glass breaks inside, and he's on the deck. He's fast, but he's just not fast enough.

Costa has positioned himself behind me with an arm around my neck, his back to Sam, while he faces me toward the ocean.

Stay where you are, Sam, I plead. *Don't move.*

"Stella, it's going to be okay." Sam's voice shakes, and I can tell that he's trying desperately to sound calm. "What's going on, Costa?"

When Costa turns us around, it hurts me to see the fear overtaking Sam's face.

Sam puts his hands on his head, and his knees start to buckle. "Oh God, no, Costa. No, no, no. Don't."

The knife at my neck hasn't broken the skin yet, but it's pressed hard enough so that I know this is serious. "Sam…" I start.

Costa's hand is steady, his grip on me solid, but his entire body is relaxed. "Here's the thing, Sam. You and Stella—there's too much potential in death tripping for us to ignore this power-augmenter piece. We need her. *You* need her. I think we both know that this has to happen."

Sam keeps shaking his head. "Please don't. Anything else. I'll give you anything else that you want!"

When he takes a step toward us, Costa pushes the blade a bit more. Now, I feel blood.

"No!" Sam stops in his tracks.

Costa continues, "We have to see what Stella can do. That's the only option here. Both of you need to try to be happy about this. It'll make it all easier." He moves his lips to my ear. "It's not going to hurt. You think it will, but it won't, so don't be scared. Then, you'll come back and be just like us."

"Please don't do this to me." I can only whisper now, "We're friends, Costa. We are. You don't want to do this."

"Yes, I do. I have to."

Stop him. Don't let this happen. Oh God, Sam, I'm scared. You can stop him.

Sam lets out a sob. "Baby, I can't stop him. You know I would. He's too fast. I can't. Goddamn it, Costa!" He's helpless, and he's fully aware of that.

"Sam is correct. He can't stop this. So, you both need to accept what's going to happen."

I might die. Forever. I don't want to die. I don't want to disappear.

"You're not going to die, got it? I won't let that happen."

Sam is determined, but I don't know that he can guarantee anything.

Costa hugs me and puts the side of his face against my hair. "Sam and I have done this hundreds of times, and we're just fine. You will be, too."

Tell Costa that he'll lose you for good.

"You'll lose me, Costa. We'll never get past this. This is unforgivable."

"I'm not going to lose you, Sammy."

When Costa starts to move his hand with the knife, Sam collapses, falling to his knees. I know he sees my blood now.

"No! No! Stell, I will get you. I'll be right there. I swear to God, I will be right there. I'll make this okay. I'll get you. I'll get you…" Tears fall over his face. "Costa, you're a *fucking psycho*! Fuck you for making me trust you."

"That's not very nice, Sam," he responds evenly. "Sometimes, we have to do things that are hard. This is one of those times. You'll thank me later. Really."

"Never. I'll see you in hell," Sam spits out.

Costa laughs. "If we ever make it there."

"*You* will. I'll find a way." Sam's hatred is full-on.

My body is trying to cry, but any move I make brings the knife deeper. *Sam, save me.*

"Stella, listen to me." Sam's hands are tight in his hair, and I know that he's trying to make me less terrified, but his own fear is showing so profoundly. "It isn't going to hurt. Look at me. You'll be okay. I'll surface you, and we will end this. It'll be like it never happened."

I love you. You have to get me. Promise me. I love you.

I wrap my hands around Costa's arm, which is keeping me pinned close, and I cling to him. He's the only kind of physical comfort I have now. I thought we cared about each other. I wanted us to. Maybe I can remind him that I mean something to him. But maybe he's irrevocably broken, and now, I'm just a tool in his thrill seeking and his addiction, in his never-ending quest for fulfillment that he'll never find.

"I'll be there. I love you, Stella. I love you so much." Sam is falling apart. He's not getting closer to us because he's trying to prolong these last moments. "Don't be afraid. Just keep looking at me. Don't be afraid. I'll surface you, and we'll float in the Maine air that you love so much. Just like you wanted. I'm coming for you, but you have to go first. I'm so sorry. I'm so sorry. Keep looking at me."

It would be impossible for me to look anywhere but into his eyes. Right now, all my faith is in him and our love.

"Here we go," Costa says softly. "It'll be fast."

There's no time for me to cry. The blade is digging in deeply now. I'm surprised at how easily Costa glides it across my neck. I feel the pressure it takes him, the strength, but the act of slitting my throat is, for him, so simple and smooth. It's a strange sensation, and I can feel everything about the knife moving through me, but it doesn't hurt. I have awareness, and each nerve reacts—only not with pain. Instead, warmth and love run through me, starting at my neck and radiating to the rest of my body. And there's pleasure, electrifying intense pleasure.

Blood is seeping over my chest, and it's such a lovely sensation. The thick liquid massages my skin and coats me with joy. Dizziness overtakes me, and my vision becomes blurred, but I want this to last forever. Every part of me feels perfect and light and beautiful, whole and heavenly really. I have never been happier or filled with more love.

God, I adore Sam. I feel my love—my worship—for him so sharply.

"It feels so good to die, doesn't it?" Costa's words float in front of me, beautiful script letters that travel before my eyes. He lowers me to the ground and kisses my forehead.

Yes. Don't stop.

It's too short, Costa. I'm fading too fast. Keep it going. "More…"

"Next time, love," he says.

The last thing I hear is Sam screaming in agony, and the last thing I see is Sam hurling himself at Costa.

And I'm gone.

TWENTY-THREE
the first cut

IT'S DARK AND PROFOUNDLY LONELY. All the good feelings that I had…are gone. If I could scream, I would. But I can't speak or hear anything. While moving feels possible, it's difficult, and I can't get my feet on anything solid. I'm drowning, yet I can breathe.

Wait, I'm not breathing.

There's no need for me to inhale and exhale because I don't need air. All I can see is deep gray, like a dense fog but only thicker, that suspends me. It's like floating in blood maybe.

Blood. God, feeling my blood run down my skin was so good.

It shouldn't have been. It should have been terrifying and painful. It was the opposite.

Slowly, I'm able to get my hand to my neck to feel that there is no gaping wound. Part of me is waiting to die fully because none of this can be possible, and part of me is crumbling under the weight of waiting for Sam. Thinking comes with difficulty, and there's no way for me to tell how far I am from the surface or even which way is up or down.

But it's Costa who crashes through the viscous substance we are in, and his shoulder slams into mine. Before I can panic, I am blinded by brightness overtaking my vision, flashes of electric color dancing in front of me. Soon though, they settle, falling like diamond dust, and the darkness is back. I reach out, willing to grab on to even Costa. Cognitively, I know I have vile hatred for him, but I can't feel that now. I'll do anything to eradicate the nauseating loneliness threatening to sink me deeper into the fog. Finding him feels hopeless because I can't see or move, but nonetheless, I do what I can to feel around me.

Sam will never find me in this gel. How could he? But I remind myself that he's done this so much more. He's more skilled, and he has experience that I can't begin to imagine. I'm on trip one. He's on trip infinity.

I don't know if I'm moving a few inches or covering great distance, but I don't stop trying to kick and claw my way through this underworld.

My sense of time is violently fouled up. I might have been here for hours, days even.

Out of nowhere, my heart begins to ache for my mother, and I am tortured by wanting her to save me from this increasingly frightening experience. She's the last person in the world I should need. She would tell me that I'm weak and not worth surfacing, so I shake off my heartache.

And next, it's Amy who creeps into my being, and I can almost hear her voice. She's singing, and then she's laughing. It's her old laugh, the one that was musical and uplifting, not the devastating, piercing sound she made the last time I heard it. I don't understand why I'm hearing her.

Before I can question that further, my father's presence intrudes. My conflicted feelings for him trigger a searing blunt headache. The pain makes me cry out, but there's no sound. No one will hear me.

Except one person. Through my hurt and disorientation, I'm able to remember Sam.

Find me. I'm here. Please find me, and get me up. Sam, Sam…

My thoughts call his name over and over. Concentrating on him is the only thing that gives me some hope that this will end.

Costa floats near me, and I flail trying to grab his hand. His eyes are open, but he isn't moving or responding in any way. My fingertips brush his, and my body convulses among waves of light again. He spasms as much as I do, and then he's gone.

Hurry. Please hurry. I'm so alone.

Just as my desperation begins to be unbearable, I feel Sam's arm around my waist. Relief floods me, and I try to get my own arms around him, but it's an arduous process that takes every ounce of energy I have. His hold though is strong, and when he sharply turns me, I realize that I've been upside down. He evenly moves us through the density, swimming us toward what must be the surface.

Just when I begin to see lightness, when the murky gray becomes sheer and I can get a sense of distance, we pound into some kind of ceiling, and we hit this boundary hard. Or rather, *I* hit it. Sam's hand goes through it and disappears, and his face contorts as he fights to bring it back under. His shock and fear is too strong for him to hide, but he lowers us back and tries again and then again. It's no use. Each time, I'm stopped.

What's happening? God, why can't you surface me?

Finally, he looks at me, and his expression scares the shit out of me. He doesn't know. Sam takes his arm from around my body and holds up his hands, telling me to stay.

Don't leave me. Don't! Don't!

Sam takes my face in his hands and kisses me, but then he abruptly pulls away. He throws his hands over his ears and releases a silent scream. I'm too scared to touch him, and there's nothing I can do but wait until whatever is happening subsides. When he's recovered, he holds his hands up again. This time, I nod.

I'll stay. You're going to come back. Very soon.

Sam blows me a kiss and disappears into the dark.

Because I must survive this, I accept that time has no clarity. My inclination is to do what I normally do when my mind can't take what is happening. Slipping into my old state of near unconsciousness would let me avoid terror, but even now, I refuse to let that happen. I won't go back to that place—not unless I have to, not unless I am trapped here forever.

Later—maybe much later, maybe only a few seconds—Sam returns, and he's dragging Costa with an arm under his chin. When they're close, Sam starts to shake him, but Costa remains glassy-eyed and drugged. Sam grabs my arm and pulls me to them, setting my hand on Costa. We both have our touch on Costa, who slowly starts to rouse.

Maybe Sam thinks that it will take two death trippers to surface a power augmenter. I can only hope. It's with that thought that I feel a bit stronger, only I'm still barely able to move.

Then, Sam lightly rests his hand on me, and the substance I'm in becomes manageable. I can move a bit more now, so I grab on to Costa's shoulders and do what I can to make him alert. I lift both feet, kicking him in the chest, until he at last focuses on me. Sam slugs him across the jaw, and I know that's not just to ensure that Costa is conscious. It's obvious that Costa is confused, but when Sam points up and to me, Costa nods groggily. Reluctantly, Sam pushes me into Costa's arms, and the three of us head toward the ceiling. Just before we hit the light, Sam takes his touch from me, and my world goes dark again.

There is a noise that sounds like waves crashing against a rock wall, and with great speed, Costa and I push through the surface, to the real world. Wood floor erupts up in the few feet around us, snapping and flying across the room, and I gasp for real air. We fall over, hard, and I hear Costa's shoulder dislocate when I land on top of him.

I'm shaking and panting, but we are on the floor of Sam's apartment. Before I can even begin to grasp what has happened, the floor outside of Sam's kitchen breaks open, and I watch with disbelief as Sam's body shuttles through, and he stumbles to a stand. Then, with great noise, the floor underneath Costa and me and also under Sam rebuilds itself until there is no indication that anything was ever destroyed.

I reach for my throat again.

Sam staggers over and lifts me from Costa.

I still can't catch my breath, and I am roaring with a level of energy that I cannot contain. Sam's body is hot and sweaty, and it's calling to me. I have to have him—now. I run my hand over the front of his shorts and pull his mouth to mine. Sam lifts me and walks us to the kitchen counter. The only thing that stops us is Costa's voice. I forgot about him the moment that Sam appeared.

"So, we're doing this again, are we?" Costa says with a slur. "Let me just pop my shoulder back in."

Brusquely, I shove Sam away, my sights now on Costa. "Bastard!" I scream. In a flash, I've pulled a knife from the chopping block and circled out of the kitchen, heading straight for him.

"Don't, Stell…" Sam tries to say, but his voice is weak.

He's surging, and I suppose I must be, too.

But he can't stop me, and I barrel into Costa, who is now halfway to a stand. I run against him until I've pushed him into the wall.

"I fucking hate you." I don't even recognize my own voice.

He's smiling. "How's that surge going for you?"

"I'm going to kill you."

He trails a hand through my hair. "Bring it, darlin'."

The knife in my hand plunges into his gut, and Costa and I both groan.

He tightens his fingers in my hair. "I see you have a thing for knives, too."

"Fuck you." I grip the handle and shove it in more. "I want you gone."

"Now…" He has to pause for a few seconds. "Now, lift the knife just an inch but not too much."

I grunt and edge the knife higher. His sound is so markedly erotic, and I'm powerless to deprive Costa of pleasure. I can't stop.

"More." He starts to slide down against the wall.

I rip the knife up until Costa smiles again and looks into my eyes.

"You're so good."

His bare torso is leaking blood down his frame, and impulsively, I put my hand against him to feel. Slowly, I start rubbing blood across his skin and up his chest, admiring the brilliant color and the sheen.

Without warning, Sam shoves me aside, and I catch myself on the back of the sofa as Sam yanks out the knife from Costa's gut.

It takes no time before he's got it to Costa's neck. "You don't deserve to surge and die at the same time."

"Oh, Sam…twice in one day? All those times…I asked you to kill me…"

It's an effort for Sam to focus. Even in my state, I can see that. Costa's allure is strong right now for both of us, his dying undeniably feeding our surge.

While the surge is powerful, Sam's rage is stronger and allows him to slur out words, "Better me than Stella."

Through blurry vision, I see Sam slash Costa's throat, and Sam lets him fall unceremoniously to the floor. Sam's eyes are half open when he walks to me, knife still in hand, and I immediately lift my shirt over my head and meet him halfway. In a flash, he has my shorts undone, and I shake them down while he slides the knife under my bra and cuts it off with a swift movement. His hand covers one breast, and his mouth goes over my other until he's sucking hard on my nipple. I look down and barely register the blood coloring my chest.

After he moves up, when I start to kiss him, to devour him, I hear the knife fall.

Then, when he's on his knees in front of me, my peripheral vision catches sight of Costa's body sinking into the floor. I run my hands through Sam's hair and push my hips against his mouth.

Later, he's sitting on the sofa, and I'm on top, grinding on him, while his hands dig into my ass, moving me up and down on his cock. The primal part of me is in charge, and every physical sensation that I seek comes from an animalistic urge to take everything I can from Sam and to give him everything that I have.

I am insatiable.

Sam and I are my only concern.

So much so, that the couch floating four feet in the air is of none.

TWENTY-FOUR
after under

THE TABLE IS COVERED in nearly everything from Sam's fridge. I already ate half of a leftover roast chicken and two pita pockets stuffed with hummus, green peppers, and olives.

Now, I'm halfway through an apple pie from The Finicky Turtle. "Do you have any more milk?"

"You drank the two gallons I had." He opens the fridge and rummages around, emerging with a bottle of vitamin water. "This helps."

I wipe my mouth with the back of my hand. "Do you need it? Did you get enough to eat?"

He raises a beer. "I'm good. The pizza did it for me."

I forgot about that. Still straddling him, I'd located the phone in between the couch cushions and called in a delivery for three larges.

"Why aren't you and Costa morbidly obese?"

"Death tripping seems to burn a lot of calories."

I burp and wave my fork at him. "Plus, sometimes, lots of fucking happens after. Must help." I'm pretty sure I'm still slurring a bit.

He gives me a soft smile. "There is that. You might want to slow down. Nausea is a problem."

"Oh. Okay." I drop my fork. "I feel a little weird still."

"I know." He's not smiling anymore. "It's going to get worse before it gets better."

I set my elbows on the table and drop my head in my hands. "I tried to kill Costa."

"Yeah."

"Why did you stop me?"

"That wasn't really you. It was the surge. You're not meant to kill. I knew you'd feel bad about it after."

"No, I wouldn't have. You should have let me."

"Stella…"

"Fine. You're right." I rub my eyes with my palms. I can't bear to think about what I did with that knife, how easy it was and how good it felt. The connection I had with Costa in that moment…I wish I could erase the memory. "You never tripped him before today?"

Sam waits to answer me. "No."

"Why not? He's tripped you enough."

He starts clearing the table, and I sit up.

"It should be up to the person to trip themself. Among the many things that Costa likes, tripping me—and apparently, you—is one of them. But what he's wanted for ages is for me to kill him. As you probably noticed, there's a certain kind of pre-trip high that you get when someone else does it." Sam carries dishes into the kitchen and sets them on the counter before he vomits into the sink. He hears me move my chair back, but he waves me away. When he's emptied his stomach, he splashes water on his face. "Fuck."

"You all right?"

"No, no, I'm not all right. I'm prone to hangovers. Costa, of course, isn't. I can't believe I have to explain this shit to you. It never even occurred to me that Costa would trip you."

A loud crash from the living room makes me jump, and I'm frightened that Costa is surfacing. Instead, however, it's the coffee table that dropped from the ceiling.

"Should we try to deal with the rest of the floating stuff?" I ask.

Sam shrugs. He eyes the rest of his furniture that's still suspended around the apartment. The sofa is about five feet off the ground, but a number of other pieces are plastered to the ceiling. We got his small dining table down, but we accidentally shattered picture frames that landed too hard. The smaller items were harder for him to control, and both of us decided to try later when we weren't such a mess.

"I can make things float." Sam tosses up his hands. "What the hell am I going to do with that?"

For the first time since I was tripped, I smile because I understand something. "You'll help me float in the Maine air."

"That's right." Sam's face softens. "We made this power."

"I know. It's crazy." I rub my arms. I'm restless and edgy, and my body doesn't feel like my own. "Sam? When we died or whatever…where were we? What is that place?"

"I can't really answer that. We just call it *under*. We're dead enough to be out of the real world but not dead enough to go anywhere else—if heaven and hell even exist."

"I didn't like it there."

"I don't blame you. It can feel really awful. I know. Hey, are you crawling out of your skin?" Sam asks.

I nod and realize that I'm tapping my foot on the floor.

"Come on." He holds out a hand, and I go to him. "A shower helps for that."

In his bathroom, Sam helps me undress.

I feel tremendously weak and tired now, so I let him run the hot water and get me into the shower. "Don't leave me."

"I won't." He takes off his clothes and steps in. "Come here."

I fall into him, and I let him hold me while the water rushes over us. "This feels nice."

"Good. It's a tactile thing. Sensory stuff gets screwy after tripping. Sometimes, light touches feel good, and other times, you need deep pressure. It sounds weird, but I used to rake a comb over my skin to bring me down. Another time, I blew bubbles and let them fall over me. Oh, and once, I slept with bags of rice on my back. You learn to get creative. Showers usually work though, no matter what."

My emotions are mostly numb, but now that the surge has mostly passed, the reality of what happened sets in. "Sam…" My voice breaks.

"I know, I know." He keeps me against him and soaps my back using gentle rhythmic strokes. "This is too much."

"I can do this," I say softly. "I *am* doing this."

"You shouldn't have to. And you had a horrible first trip, which is patently unfair."

"I assumed mine was bad. Otherwise, you guys would have never gone under again."

"You were tripped under shitty circumstances, and that can strongly influence things. I tripped badly, too, but it's why I could get to you so fast. I was alert and not all drugged up. If it'd been good, I could have sunk a lot lower and been the way Costa was."

"I don't understand. Why was his trip so good?"

Sam glides his hands over my shoulders and down my arms, and his touch is soothing my nerves. "Costa probably had a highly intense trip because I killed him, and he'd wanted that for years. Then, *you* gutted him, and he'd just tripped you. The combination of the two of us…well, he'll be under for hours and hours. Death tripping is very often tied into emotion. No two trips are ever the same because no circumstances are ever the same."

"So, yours was bad because of how it happened also?"

He nods. "I ran my body into Costa's and threw us over the edge. He hit his head on a rock, but he didn't die right away, which he loved. I wasn't thinking clearly though. There was no reason for me to trip him, but watching what he had done to you…I broke my rule about not tripping others. I couldn't stop myself." Sam stops to kiss me.

His passion and love are the only things letting me keep it together at all.

"I can't think of a worse way to go into a trip. I understand how you felt, watching me die. I don't ever want to see that again. That's why I went crazy and launched myself at him. Unfortunately, I wasn't hurt enough, so I had to get back upstairs."

"How did you—"

"I really don't want to talk about it. I saw more blood today than I cared to."

"When you were under with me," I start, "something happened to you."

Sam turns me around again and takes his time lathering my hair with shampoo. "This feels okay?"

"Yes. The light touch is helping me. Thank you." He's being so sweet to me, but I need an answer. "Sam? Tell me what happened when you covered your ears during that trip."

He sighs. "I didn't know about this, but it seems that I can keep my powers when I go under. When you touched me, I was entirely focused on you and how much I wanted to make everything better for you, how much I love you. Then you…you power-augmented me when we were under. I could hear everything."

"Everything where? What's to hear when you're under?"

He hesitates. "Other people."

"Oh my God, Sam…other death trippers?"

"I don't know. The noise was excruciating. But I don't want to go back under. Neither of us is going back. This is over."

Sam tips my head under the spray, and I have to catch my balance when I shut my eyes.

"Easy there. Dizziness can be a problem, too."

I can tell that Sam doesn't want to talk about this anymore. He just wants to take care of me, and I'm too drained to let him do anything but.

"I'll be fine. Maybe I need to sleep for a bit."

"Okay." But he wraps me in his arms once again and tightly holds me. He shivers against me, and his voice trembles when he says, "I'm sorry I couldn't surface you, Stella. I'm so sorry. I've never had to surface anyone, and it didn't occur to me that it would be a problem."

"It's not your fault." I hug him with all the strength I have left. "I gather, it's a good thing you tripped Costa though."

"It scares the shit out of me to think what would've happened if I hadn't. The person who first trips you must be the person who surfaces you." He lets out a sigh of disbelief. "Costa was right when he said that we don't know nearly enough about this. But I don't want to know more. What if I hadn't gotten mad enough to attack him? I didn't even mean to kill him. I wasn't thinking. But what if he hadn't been there? What if I hadn't thought to have him try to surface you? What if—"

"But that didn't happen." I put my mouth to his. "That didn't happen, and I'm okay. I'm breathing, I'm in love, I'm back where I belong. Home."

While surge sex is pretty damn impressive, kissing after death tripping is equally remarkable. Everything about the beauty of tasting Sam is magnified, and this closeness, this total intimacy in the shower, clears my mind more than I could have thought a few hours ago.

Sam turns off the faucet and reaches for our towels. He wraps both of us up and brings me to his bed. I slip into one of his shirts and crawl under the covers. I very much needed to be in this familiar bed.

"Are you tired, too?" I ask him.

He gets in next to me. "I am. But I'm going to stay awake."

I don't have to ask why. Sam is watching for Costa. "You're going to have to sleep sometime."

"True. But it's not going to be tonight."

"You said he'd be under for a long time."

"I'm not taking any chances."

"He'll come back, won't he?"

"Yes." Sam cuddles me in close. "But he did what he wanted to today, and he'll need time to come down."

"So, sleep with me."

"Later. I'm okay."

Dawn is breaking, and in the light, I see how overwhelmed and spent Sam is. But there's more. "Something else is wrong," I say. "Tell me."

"You need to rest. And you're shivering now. The detoxing does that. You've been through a lot."

"Sam, what is it?"

He sighs. "I don't know. I just…I don't like that you were tripped at all, but I particularly don't like that it was Costa who did it, who turned you into a death tripper. There might be a…I don't know…a tie between you two now."

"There's nothing between me and Costa. Don't say that."

"Romantically, no," he says with a smile. "Sexually, yes. You've felt how strong death tripping is. It fucks with your emotions. It creates sexual tension, and don't protest because I know it was there. I don't blame you." He slides his hands up under my sleeves and warms my skin. "If I'm honest, I probably have some kind of tie myself with Costa because he tripped me. We were close before that, but it added an entirely new dimension. You might have that with him, too."

"I have a tie with *you*. End of story. And if it makes you feel any better, you can look at the fact that Costa tripped us both. That's another thing that ties you and me together."

He laughs lightly. "So, Costa's kind of our daddy?"

"If you'd like to think of yourself as my brother, then a number of things are going to have to change."

"Okay, scratch that," he says quickly.

"Good. Because I won't give you up. I can't. And I might not know much about this, but if I'm your power augmenter, that has to mean something much more significant than who tripped me." I nestle in more. "Maybe Costa is right about one thing."

"What's that?"

"That making me a death tripper needed to happen. It makes some kind of crazy sense, doesn't it?"

"Don't say that, Stell."

"You know it's true."

"I'll never be able to justify what he did. Nothing in the world is worth doing this to you. That trip you went on was a one-time deal." His body heat engulfs me, traveling easily from his core to mine. "At least your surge had some good moments. I mean, after the stabbing-Costa incident. Not sure it makes up for all the other downsides though."

"I don't know. That was some pretty good sex."

"Pretty good?" he says with mock irritation. "Seriously?"

"It was insanely, amazingly good."

"I know, right? Sex when both of us were surging? That idea never even occurred to me."

"So, *you* would have tripped me if it had?" I tease.

"Funny, funny. Besides, sober sex with you is more than I could ever ask for. The surge is great. It is. But—"

I finish his thought, "It's fueled by the wrong things."

"Yeah, it is. And it's addictive."

"I'm already addicted," I say, "to you, to making love with you, to being in love with you."

"Good. Because I am equally addicted to you."

"Even the new me?"

"Yes, Stella. Of course."

"Show me." I squirm against him. I have leftover surge powering me, but I don't care where it's coming from. I need release. "Let's just enjoy the surge. We know there's good underneath it."

"You're not too tired?" But he's already rolled me on to my back and positioned his body over mine.

"For you? Never."

TWENTY-FIVE
fight or flight

SAM TOLD HIS PARENTS THAT I HAD THE FLU, and he stayed with me for the few days following our trip. After that first fourteen-hour sleep, I was really fine, but I knew Sam was standing guard for Costa.

On the third morning, I set an alarm for Sam and shoved him out the door. I spent the day on my design work, completing three book cover jobs that were already late. I got back into my daily schedule, refusing to let what had happened interfere with a normalcy that I'd fought so hard to find. A publishing house even contacted me, wanting a thriller cover done for a book they were putting out next year. The good news? They wanted blood and gore on the cover.

I could do that.

It's been nearly two weeks since that night and since we've seen Costa. I know he'll be back though. Sam and I both do. The only solace I have is that Costa's already done the most damage he can. There's nothing else left. Although I hate what he did to me, I hate the way he destroyed his relationship with Sam even more, and that makes my hatred complicated. I don't understand why Costa tripped me, knowing that it would end his friendship with Sam—a friendship that I'm damn certain Costa values. Theirs was the only true deep relationship he had left in this world, and he blew it all to shit when he slit my throat.

And I cared about him, too—still care really. I can't say that I don't. I'm confused and hurt and furious, but Costa's past and his sadness prevent me from seeing him as entirely despicable. Sam, however, won't even talk about Costa anymore, choosing instead to latch on to his anger, not the sense of loss and betrayal that I know haunts him.

Maybe Costa is scared of the good, so he ruins it before he can lose it.

I don't have answers. I just have the aftermath to deal with. To add insult to injury, I don't seem to have any powers. If I could fling fireballs, I know who my target would be.

I'm walking into town this late-August evening to meet Kelly for dinner. Sam is still working at the inn, and he's going to meet up with us. Kelly and I have become regulars at a small bistro that opened this summer, and we've been getting together every week for lunch or dinner. We've worked our way through the menu, but the chef also runs daily specials that are delicious.

Kelly waves to me from an outside table, and I wave back. Her wild black curls are woven into two thick French braids, and I'm suddenly wishing that I hadn't hacked off my hair last spring. Dining out with Kelly is always fun, but she's so pretty that we're constantly interrupted by guys slipping her their phone numbers and sending over drinks.

Tonight, however, she has on a shirt that simply says, *Thanks, but I'm a lesbian. AND I have a hot girlfriend.*

I laugh when I hug her. "Nice shirt."

"Thanks. April made it for me. I think she's hoping Costa will see it. Where's he been anyway? Dad said he called in a few weeks ago and said he was traveling for a bit."

I take a seat and pick up the menu, eyeing the appetizers. "Did he say when he was coming back?"

"I assumed you and Sam would know."

"I'm not really sure where he went. I think to visit someone," I say vaguely.

"Visit who?"

"Just…I don't know."

Kelly pushes my menu down. "What's going on? Costa doesn't have any friends outside of Watermark."

"Oh, fine." Obviously, I have to lie to her, but I do tell her a partial truth, "He and Sam had a bit of a fight."

"Shit. Really?"

"Guy stuff, I guess. Costa isn't the easiest person to get along with."

"That's an understatement." She flags down the server. "I'd hate to see that friendship fall apart again."

To start with, we order crispy pork belly with peach chutney and also charred Brussels sprouts tossed with pancetta and balsamic. My mouth is already watering.

"What do you think about Costa?" I ask.

Kelly blows out a long breath. "Oh, Costa Jorden…he's self-centered and a shithead some of the time, I know, but I saw how he grew up. I saw what his parents did to him. I swear to God, I've never seen parents care less about their kid. It was like he didn't exist to them most of the time. When he was only eight or nine, they'd leave for days on end with no food in the house, no working phone, nothing. When my parents found out, they threatened to call child services, but his parents gave some bullshit sob story about how they found work out of town for a few days and had to go. Costa begged Mom and Dad not to make the call. Instead, they got his parents to agree that Costa would stay with us when they couldn't take care of him. He was with us more often than not."

I drink half of my grapefruit cosmo to try to ease the sick feeling in my stomach. "Jesus. I didn't realize it was so bad."

"I know. My parents would go over to his house to clean and leave some food. I went with them one time when Costa was eleven or so.

Liquor bottles were everywhere, and trash was piling up. Costa's room was no place for a kid—no sheets on his bed, almost no toys. It was disastrous.

"By high school though, Costa was basically living with us and barely had any contact with those people. He had clothes, a warm house, and a family. Finally. Holidays were at our house, and he got presents on Christmas. His parents were nuts. I know they were addicts. Mom told me it was why they never gave those people actual cash. They would have blown it on booze or drugs. Costa grew up in hell. I hate to think about what that kid's life was like before he had us."

Everyone's an addict, I think to myself. "Thank God for all of you."

Kelly seriously looks at me. "He and Sam can't fall apart. You do whatever you have to do and make sure that doesn't happen."

"Kelly, I don't know if I can—"

"Promise me," she says strongly. "Costa is family."

"I'll try," I say with more resolve than I expected.

She sits back in her chair and folds her hands together. "Whatever garbage is going on now, it's meaningless in the scheme of things. They got through losing Toby. This summer has been the best either of them has had in years. A lot of that is because of you, but it's also because they're back together. Costa has earned a lot of slack, so Sam needs to give it to him. And vice versa."

"Sam's done a lot for him," I point out.

"He has. But Sam has advantages that Costa doesn't. We all need to do what we can. I've tried calling him, and he won't pick up. Maybe he'll talk to you."

"I can't call him."

Kelly studies me. "Something happen with you two also?"

I don't say anything.

She reaches across the table and puts her hand in mine. "I don't care what it is. Fix it. You're the only person who can."

I squeeze her hand. "I'll do everything I can. I swear."

"Good. Now, let's order more food." She takes a sip of her beer. "And why are you smiling?"

"I was just thinking about how truly horrified my mother would be that I'm holding hands with a lesbian."

"Yeah? Well, we could take a selfie of me tongue-kissing you, if you'd like. Just don't tell April."

I laugh. "It's a good thought, but I don't talk to my mother."

"At all?"

"At all."

"Is that permanent?"

"Yes."

She studies me. "You get Costa, don't you?"

"Unfortunately, in many ways, I do. And I want the zucchini noodles with seared shrimp."

"I'm sorry about your mother. And I want the pork chop with the red-wine glaze and wilted spinach."

I smile at her. "I'm glad we got together tonight."

"Me, too. Now, let's dish before my brother gets here." She leans over the table. "Did I tell you what April and I did the other night?"

Her eyes gleam, and I can tell there's a good story here.

"You did *not*," I say, my interest piqued. "Shoot."

We talk and eat over dinner, and we trade stories that must be whispered. I wish I could tell Kelly about the death tripping because she's become such a good friend, but I obviously can't. It has to be contained.

The sun has set by the time Sam shows up to drive me home. "Aw, you got me dinner to go? You girls are the best." He gives Kelly a noisy, long sloppy kiss on the cheek until she screams and pushes him away.

"You're disgusting. *Boys* are disgusting. I don't know how Stella tolerates you."

Sam kisses her again anyway. "My penis and I are repugnant. I get it. But I love you anyway."

"I love you, too, you weirdo." Then, Kelly hugs me. "Good luck."

"Thanks. Talk to you soon?"

"Yep. And you need a dye job again. Come in next week."

Sam's truck is parked down by the waterfront, and we hold hands and pop into a few of the shops as we make our way down the tourist-filled busy street. I've relished the simple things like this ever since I got to Maine but now even more so. My appreciation for good food, amazing friends, the beauty and feel of a small town, a place to call home, a boyfriend to hold my hand and guide me through a crowd…I won't let anything undo that. *Anything.*

Maybe I should feel differently than I do. Something freakishly wild has happened to the very center of who I am. I don't even know if I'm still considered human. *Are death trippers human?* I have no clue. But I should feel wobbly and jarred. And while I do to some extent, there is a significant part of me that feels as though this was supposed to happen. I'm not a big believer in destiny, but it's hard to ignore the idea that it's coming into play here. There's also the undeniable feeling that, as a death tripper, I am closer to Sam.

Now that we are the same, yet another wall has come down between us.

Sam and I stand on the pier and watch the boats for a bit. Their lights remind me of the ones that Sam used to be able to make, and I'm surprisingly melancholy about him losing that power. There was something so incredibly sweet and pure about it. We haven't done much with his floating skill, except help him control it and stop our togetherness from sending things flying into the air. I follow the path of a small fishing boat decorated with twinkle lights, and my sadness swells again. The time of the lights seems so simple now.

"It's beautiful out tonight," I say. "I never imagined loving a place as much as this."

"Watermark is a pretty special town to live in, I agree. Come with me. I want to show you something." He leads me down a set of wooden stairs that takes us to a small beach area.

"Sam, it's kind of dark here. What are we doing?"

"You'll see." With a swift movement, he scoops me up into his arms and carries me a number of yards away until we are in the most remote area of the shore, none of the streetlights reaching us.

"Sam…"

"Shh…"

He kisses me, and my arms encircle him in response. It's one of those kisses that melts me, that's filled with adoration and devotion, and that pushes aside anything even mildly troubling.

Gently, he takes his lips from mine. "Look."

When I turn slightly from him, my eyes fill with joyful tears. We are hovering three or four feet over the water, fairly far from shore.

"You wanted to float in the Maine air," he says.

"So, you made it happen. Oh, Sam…" I take a deep breath and feel the air coursing into my lungs along with the salty wind dancing on my skin. I look down and see the ripples of small waves below us. It's just the two of us and the night right now, and I'd happily stay in his arms, sheltered from so much—forever. "You are amazing."

Even Sam, who is prone to brushing off the intriguing and fantastical nature of his powers, appears to be enjoying this. How could he not?

We jerk up a foot higher, and I squeal and clutch on to Sam. His mouth finds mine again, and my nerves settle as I relax into the feel of him. Kissing when floating, it turns out, is pretty remarkable.

Slowly, he takes his tongue from my mouth and whispers over my lips, "I'd better take us down. I don't think we're up for night swimming." He rubs his nose against mine, and he floats us over the water and back to the shore.

He sets me on my feet, and I playfully swat his arm. "We could have been seen."

"Whatever. It's Friday night. Everyone's drunk." He hops up and down. Then, he picks me up by the waist and spins me around in the dark. "You and I should go home and get drunk and have some more fun."

"I'm totally into that idea. Dirty martinis?"

"You got it. Extra olives."

"Deal."

"And extra mini swords?" I ask.

"I'll spear as many olives as you like."

"Maybe you can make them float from the jar into the glasses?" I suggest.

"For you, anything."

I keep my hand on his leg while he drives up the hill to our house on the cliff. The contentment that fills me each time we pull into the driveway will never get old.

We're strolling up the gravel path toward the steps when Sam sharply drags me back.

"What?" I look at Sam and find fury on his face. I turn to the house.

Costa is sitting on the porch under the spotlight, his back against Sam's door.

Sam's body lifts from the ground, and with surprising speed, he *flies* the twenty feet it takes to reach Costa. In an instant, he lifts Costa under the arms so that they are both off the porch. Sam floats them back a few feet and then rams Costa against the door. And then, he does it again.

"Sam, no!" I scream, running to them.

But Sam pounds Costa into the old door one more time. Under his strength, it splinters down the middle, and they fall through the threshold to the floor of Sam's apartment. When I reach them, Sam has his hands positioned to snap Costa's neck.

"Don't do this. There's no point." I'm trying to control my panic. I might be new to this, but what Sam is doing seems to fall outside the boundaries of death tripping. "There's no point!" I say again.

"He'll be gone for a while. That's a good point."

I look at Costa, who is barely resisting Sam's aggression. He is clearly exhausted and broken.

"Let him go. For me."

Costa speaks softly, "Please don't kill me. I've been sober from death tripping since that night. Please."

"Fuck you." Sam is seething.

Then, Costa says something that makes even Sam's violent impulse break apart, "We might be able to surface Toby."

TWENTY-SIX
dirty martini

SAM RIPS COSTA OFF THE FLOOR and charges him across the living room until his body is pinned up against a wall. "What the fuck are you talking about? Don't you dare use Toby to try to repair what you've done."

I quickly get to Sam, but I can't pull his hands from Costa. Appealing to his non-death-tripper side is the only hope I have that Sam won't kill him. "You are not a murderer. You're not. Please."

Sam pulls his hands back, and Costa catches his balance before he falls. Sam's face tells me that I'm right, that he was on the brink of going too far. He doesn't kill people when he's sober. I know him. It's a line that he cannot cross without hard repercussions, but this is now the second time that he's come close. The day on the dock when his hearing power was making him edgy, he nearly choked Costa, and I was barely able to stop him.

Costa's leather jacket is off one shoulder as he stands fully and runs a hand through his hair. There is a ragged and unfamiliar air about him, and he strains to sound casual. "So what? You can fly now? That's kinda badass."

Sam makes a slight move, and Costa holds up his hands to block him. "Okay, okay. Sorry."

I have to work to pull Sam back and move myself in front of him. I hate the mood between them, between all of us. "What are you really doing here?" I demand. I can hear Sam pacing behind me. So far, this is much less fun than martini night would have been. "You want something. So, what is it? What else are you trying to take from us now?"

Costa is noticeably thinner and paler than usual, and dark circles leave shadows under his eyes. "Can I sit down?"

I hardly recognize his voice. He's shaky and emotional and nothing like I've seen him before. He's even pathetic-looking. But I'm still suspicious of his motives. I wish to all hell that I could blindly trust him, but he's ruined that. I know broken and crazy well, and I'm willing to forgive. Only, Costa has been pushing it beyond reasonable limits.

"Please. I don't deserve for you to hear me out. I get it. You feel like I've wrecked everything we ever had. You're right, but I'm going to ask you to just listen to me anyway."

Sam can't even begin to form a response, so I figure that separating them for the time being can only help. "Sam, why don't you get him some water?"

Sam scoffs but goes to the kitchen.

There is too much tension for any of us to think reasonably. And Costa's mention of his son has made it impossible to throw anything solely hateful his way. Losing a child will always take precedence over any other pain there is to be felt.

Costa and I sit silently in the living room, and being alone in his presence, even for a few minutes, is unsettling and confusing. I am at a loss about what to believe or what to say. Sam returns with a plastic cup and keeps as much distance as possible while passing it over.

Costa chugs the water and then keeps his head down while he fiddles with the cup. "I'm so sorry. Really, I'm so sorry." He rubs his fingers over his eyes. "I need you both. You're the only chance I have."

"What are you talking about?" Sam throws himself into an armchair and glares at his friend. "Spit out whatever crap you're here to tell, and then you can get the hell out. I can't do this anymore with you. Every single time you show up, you rip out some piece of my heart. No more." Sam is now consumed with his emotion. "I can't stand it. It hurts too much. I am begging you, Costa. Please get out of my life. Stop shredding me. I have nothing left to give you."

Costa breaks down, hiding nothing from us. For once, I see honesty and not some kind of manipulative display. Costa is raw and unrestrained when he cries and lays out his pain, and it's excruciating to be present in his grief. "I don't know how to explain it all," he says rather helplessly.

As much as I want to destroy him for what he's done, I also want to heal someone who's been broken. I had to be healed, and I didn't do that alone, so I try to ease him into his story, whatever it might be. "Start with why you came back to town," I say.

He looks at me with gratitude. "Yeah. Okay. Last spring…I came to see you, Sam. I missed you, but I was scared to see you again, too. After the ice…the drowning…when I had been away and alone, I'd needed you so much, but I hated you at the same time. It was impossible. Losing Toby was my worst nightmare, but I couldn't do anything about it. My whole life had been eviscerated, and maybe I'd deserved it because I probably hadn't deserved that miraculous kid in the first place. But I'd had him and then lost him, and there's nothing like that. There's no way to explain exactly how my world fucking ended. But I did what I could. I just kept going because there was no other fucking option. I couldn't die, right?" He laughs, but his laugh just hurts all of us.

"Except, eventually, I got an idea. It was vague, nothing really thought out, but just an idea that maybe Toby could still be alive. Sure, at first, it was just wishful thinking. That's normal, I guess—the denial stage of grief. But there is truth in it. I mean, we never found his body, Sam. Nobody did."

I glance at Sam and see that a good portion of his fury has subsided. Now, he is trying to hold it together while Costa talks about his little boy.

"I came back home, back to my lifeline," Costa continues. "You, Sam. So, I watched you for a while, just to get used to the idea of seeing you again. It sounds weird, I know, but I did. I'd see you water the garden circles every day. I liked that." He gives a light smile.

"But you looked as fucked up as I felt—angry and miserable. Part of me thought you deserved to live in such agony, but most of me just hated it. I hated that you were suffering, that everyone around here saw you as some kind of monster that I knew you weren't.

"Then, Stella showed up, and I saw you two together. Right from the start, it was so obvious that there was something really strong between you two." He pauses and taps his fingers over his knees while he fumbles to stay with this narrative. "Then, holy shit, you two made that storm. I knew it because you were together that night. Your rain became the storm. I figured there was a power connection between you two."

"You watched us the night of the storm?" Sam's anger resurfaces.

"I know, I know. I'm sorry. I didn't hang around or anything. Really. Just listen, okay? Please. I knew immediately that Stella was influencing what you could do. So, I tripped you to test it out. Then, there were the fireworks and everything else from the glowing lights." Costa rubs his jeans. "That was because of you, Stella."

I nod. We know this to be true. There's no question. It makes me uncomfortable, but he's right.

"So, all of this drove me to the idea that if Sam were somehow…strong enough…that we could trip and find Toby. And I think I'm right. I know he's supposed to be dead, but I can't accept that—not just because I don't want to, but because I don't *feel* it, you know? I don't. Toby is still with me too much. I don't care how little he was. His body would have turned up sometime, especially after the thaw in the spring."

Sam shakes his head, but it's not entirely with disbelief. It's also with understanding—and maybe hope.

"But to do it," Costa continues, "we need Stella. She makes you stronger when you're not tripping, and if you had a…I don't know…" Now, he stands up and walks the room, agitated. "A vision power or something, then Stella could get you skilled enough that we could trip and find Toby. You know how hard it is to see when we're under, right, Sam? I can't do it alone. But you could take your power with you and maybe be able to see where I can't."

Sam is now slumped in his chair with his head in his hand. "Why didn't you just come to me and ask? I would've done anything for you."

"Shit, Sam. You haven't tripped since Toby! And I knew you wouldn't. No matter what I said, you wouldn't have believed me. I tripped you to get you going again, give you a taste of what you'd been missing, to prove how gifted you really are. You've never appreciated what we have."

Sam doesn't move. "And what else? Say it. Say what you mean."

Costa drops his hands to his sides and meets Sam's eyes. "And you let Toby drown in that frozen lake. You killed my son."

"And you had to retaliate."

"Yes."

"You saw me happy when you weren't."

"Yes."

Sam looks off to the side for a minute and sniffs. "Fair enough."

"What I did wasn't right. I know that."

"And why Stella? Why did you drag her into this shit?"

"I thought she could make you more powerful if she tripped with you. It was a stupid idea. I can see that now."

I look to Sam, and he nods. He knows that he has to tell Costa. "It's actually not a stupid idea."

I go to the kitchen and shake up three strong martinis while Sam explains how significantly his hearing power has increased since he tripped to get me.

"You had your hearing power when you were *under*? Wait, did you *hear* him? Did you hear Toby? You'd know his babbling as well as I would." Costa is at Sam's side when I return. "Anything?"

"No, no, Costa. It was just all noise, way too much to decipher. I could hardly take it. It was so loud. Nothing distinct. Just chaos."

He doesn't mention all the other voices, I notice. Sam gladly takes the martini from my hand.

I give one to Costa and sit back down. "There's no way to know if this would work."

"It could," Costa says. "If there's any chance—"

Sam finishes, "Then, we have to try."

"And we found out that you couldn't surface Stella," Costa says. "That has to be because I tripped her."

Sam shifts his eyes away. "So, I'd have to surface Toby."

Costa nods. "Sam, I'm sorry. I get it now. Finally, I get it. I was still mad and hurt…and…bitter when I got back to town. I did a lot of crap I shouldn't have. I've been sober for two weeks. I've been trying to calm down and get my head on straight about everything. Toby was not your fault—not really. Sometimes, I try to tell myself that you're solely to blame, but…we were *both* tripping hard and way too much, and we were *both* out of control with it. It was just an accident, a horrible accident. We didn't understand tripping then like we do now, and—"

"We don't understand shit now, Costa. Every move we make is a guessing game, so this very likely won't work, and you have to be prepared for that." Sam takes a drink and then another. "And if I'm supposed to have some kind of amped-up vision while we're under, this means that Stella would have to trip again, too."

Nervousness crawls through me. I dread the idea of tripping again.

But I also can't wait to.

Sam downs the rest of his drink and sits silent. Eventually, he looks at Costa. "If you're lying to us about any of this, I will dismantle what's left of your world."

"Hate me all you want. Just help me get my son back."

"I'll do anything you need," he says.

TWENTY-SEVEN
binge

FORGIVING COSTA IS WHAT WE DO. As we see it, it's our only option. His heartbreak is too much, and perhaps it grants him license to lash out in illogical ways. I can't begin to understand his loss.

Sam, however, does.

Sam's willingness to allow Costa back into his life and mine didn't come with total ease, but his devotion to his friend was, as he said, unbreakable, even under the worst of circumstances.

"I could have been Costa. I would have done everything that he's done if I'd lost my son."

Sam and I have to be all in or all out. There's no middle ground.

So, we're in.

And now, we work.

We all agreed that a vision power was the right choice. While Sam and Costa are experienced enough with death tripping to be able to move well and have a sense of orientation, neither of them can see very far. Sam has been tripping for two weeks now, and despite both of us focusing on the idea of vision before he dies, he hasn't been able to surface with the power.

He was a wind-maker for one day, which quite delighted me, and I even bought a kite at one of the souvenir shops in town. I wasn't sure that Sam was entirely amused by my flying it in the living room even though he kept it aloft and let me play for a few hours. He also accidentally blew off a section of roof tiles from our house, but he was utterly exhausted, so it was understandable that he got sloppy.

Costa is up on the roof right now, repairing the damage, and I do find it slightly funny that death tripping seems to come with a lot of home repairs—Sam's front door, a hole in the wall from that intense night with the three of us, the mirror and glass door that I broke.

Right now, I'm watching Sam pummel the shit out of the sandbag hanging from a sturdy tree limb. He surfaced a few hours ago, and he's still surging and trying to work it off.

He insisted that we come up with a plan to handle his surges because he was not going to let me offer myself up each time he came back. As much as I love Sam—and sex with Sam—I had to agree. Something felt very creepy about the idea of throwing myself in his path just so that he could discharge his trip energy. Because he made me promise, I try to make myself scarce for at least the first hour or so after he's back. So, we have the punching bag.

And both of our kitchens are positively stocked to the brim with food. Costa has two good black eyes, courtesy of Sam, from when he tried to help himself to some of the food I'd cooked for Sam. I'm not convinced Sam couldn't have stopped himself there, but he punched Costa a few times and then finished an entire chicken and serving bowl of mashed potatoes.

Sweat pours down Sam's back and chest as he continues fighting imaginary targets, repeatedly slamming his fists into the punching bag. Watching him is not easy for me. He's lost weight, and there are dark circles under his eyes. He's been going to work in the mornings, coming home in the afternoons, and then tripping. Keeping his trip time down to just a few hours or less has gotten easier, so he's been able to work off the surge and get to bed at a reasonable hour, but this amount of death tripping has taken a hard toll on him. I've cleaned up more vomit and washed more laundry than I care to admit. When the surge ends, there's also the shaking, the clammy sweat, and the near delirium—and the nightmares. I'm not sure how much longer he can do this, and I can't figure out why we can't get him the vision power. I've been trying to get him to slow down, to let his body recuperate, but he's refused.

"If we can get to Toby," he said earlier, "then this tripping binge is more than worth it."

Costa comes down from the roof and gives me a nod, so I head into my bedroom and watch through the French doors as Costa gently guides Sam away from the sandbag. Sam leans against him and lets Costa untie the boxing gloves. Costa wipes him down with a towel before they walk slowly inside his first-floor unit. He'll eat the four Italian subs I made, drink at least a gallon of milk, and probably polish off the rest of my chocolate chip cookies that he's become fond of post-trip.

I've forced myself to stay near him because that has seemed important for getting a certain power, but watching him die over and over feels like it's killing me, too. He was killing himself at first—with pills mostly—but he asked Costa to take over and do it. In his worn-out state, Sam said he just wants it to happen faster, and he doesn't have the energy to get creative or dramatic.

Among the many things that worry me is that I'm not sure Sam's explanation is true. I think he dies better and with more pleasure when Costa does it. The bond between them has intensified with each kill. I see the way they look at each other when Sam is losing blood. The truth, however, is that I don't hate that look. In fact, I enjoy their connection. But Sam compromising on his belief that a death tripper should trip himself tells me how worn-out he is.

Costa texts me when Sam has finished eating and has had a long shower. I wipe my eyes and take the wraparound porch to the stairs, using these few moments to brace myself before I get to Sam's bedroom. Costa is just pulling up the covers, and he looks almost as ashen as Sam does.

Sam groans and rolls on his side, reaching out to wrap his hand over Costa's arm. Costa leans in so that he can hear and then shakes his head. He has to peel Sam's grip from him, but at least I know that Sam still has some strength left.

"No, Sam. No! It's way too soon."

Sam groans again and turns onto his stomach, pulling his legs under him so that he is hunched in a ball. Costa winces in reaction.

I step fully into the room and sit on the edge of the bed. I'm not sure Sam even knows that I'm here. "Why don't you go get some vitamin water, CJ? I'll stay with him."

Begrudgingly, Costa rounds the bed toward the door but pauses by me. He starts to say something but stops.

"I know," I say. "We're trying. I swear. I don't know why we can't make this work."

Costa's eyes are the darkest I've seen them. "He has to stop. This is breaking him."

I'm reluctant to agree, but it's the truth. This is too much. Sam is too sick.

"Did he just ask you to kill him again?"

Costa nods. "I won't, not until he's better. He's too doped up now. And…" Costa hesitates. "He doesn't just want to trip. He needs it. His body is asking for it, and he can't tolerate not tripping."

Sam shudders, and I scoot over to his side to put a hand on him. He's burning up now.

"Sam is addicted again, isn't he?"

"We're always addicted. But now, he's using. It's my fault this time. Last time was his, but this time, it's on me."

"Sam chose to do this for you. He insisted."

"This trip was one way too many. He can't trip again until he's clean. That's at least a week. And he's going to be a real mess for a bit, so he can't go to work."

"I'll go talk to his mother and make up some excuse for why he won't be at the inn. It's mid-September, so the season is over really, right? They'll be okay without him."

"Thanks, Stella. I'm going to clean up the kitchen and the bathroom."

"Don't. I'll do it in a bit. You've done enough. Go rest. Get something to eat."

He tries to wave me away.

"Please. I can't have both of you down."

"Okay. Maybe you're right." He gives me a weak smile before he leaves. "You can try the ice, if you want. It might help this time."

I reach over Sam and grab two of the heavy ice packs. I set both on his bare back. He whimpers and scratches his nails into the sheets. The heat radiating off of him now is strong, and I can only imagine how high his temperature is. We've got another ten ice packs in the freezer, and I suspect we might need them.

I spend a while moving these two around, pressing them against his skin, and giving him some of the water that Costa brought in. Sam had made me promise not to give him any medication to help him sleep, but I'm tempted to ignore that promise right now. His fingers trickling over my skin had helped me, but me doing the same just agitates him, and he shakes me off.

When he's warmed the ice packs, I switch them out for new ones and turn him onto his back. He struggles against it, but I get three on his upper body and another on his forehead. For a while, the cold and the weight of the packs seem to help although he starts muttering in a half-sleep state. I can't make out any clear words, but he does cover his ears at some kind of invisible distress that's plaguing him. Putting pressure on his legs and his arms appears to help, so I lean my weight into him and work over his body.

Just when I think that maybe the worst has passed, Sam breaks into tears and puts his hands over his eyes. "Stella, please make it stop. Please."

"I'm trying, Sam. I'm trying." I have no clue how to console him.

"Everything hurts." He begins to choke and turns to hang his head off the bed. The ice packs fall to the floor, and he empties his stomach once again.

"Just get through this, and it'll be over. No more. You're done."

"No, no, no. Toby." He is pleading with me, but he can't possibly continue death tripping, especially given that we are no closer to getting a useful power to search for Toby.

Some power augmenter I am.

"I'll be fine," he says.

I wipe his face with a wet cloth. "No, you won't. This isn't working."

"Do me a favor?"

"Anything."

"Just trip me again, Stell. Just trip me. Please." His desperation is excruciating.

"No, Sam. I can't. It'll just be worse after."

"Then, I won't stop. I'll just keep tripping and tripping…" He laughs, but there is nothing the slightest bit funny about what he's saying. "I can't do it myself, so you have to help me. There are scissors in that bureau over there."

"You need to sleep. Please just sleep. There's not going to be any more dying."

He begins to sob. "Don't say that! That's not fair!" Sam, usually so strong and rational, is like a child now. "The screaming won't stop, and the headache won't stop. You just have to kill me. You have to kill me! I would do it for you!"

"I can't. I can't." This is a nightmare.

I use towels and the mop we have stashed in the room to clean up the floor for the umpteenth time.

He rubs his arms and then looks at me, his eyes red and weary. "I'm sorry. I'm so sorry."

"It's okay. This isn't you. It's not your fault."

"Can you…can you get me some more water?"

"Of course. I'll be right back."

As much as I don't want to be away from him when he needs me this much, I also can't deny that I could use these few seconds to take a breath.

Costa is at the kitchen table when I get there. "How is he?"

I try to smile. "Tough."

"Thank you, Stella, for everything that you're doing. I know I've been an asshole."

I nod. "You have. But it's part of your charm."

I wash my hands and face and then take a water bottle from the fridge. Just as I shut the door, a loud crash comes from the bedroom. Costa flies out of his chair and runs through the living room with me at his heels.

"Shit!" Costa yells, moving like lightning to Sam.

Sam is on the bedroom floor, surrounded by shards of broken mirror.

"Sam, no!" Then, Costa screams at me to get over there.

I finally make my feet move. He's sitting on Sam, pinning his arms to the floor, and Sam is kicking and trying hard to maneuver out from under Costa.

"Let it go, Sam!"

Sam is clutching a jagged shard in his blood-soaked hand. "Fuck off!" he spits out.

Costa releases one arm just enough to slam it back onto the floor. Sam swears but doesn't let go.

"Stella, get a pillowcase from that closet. Cut it into strips." Costa nods at the scissors on the floor, the pair Sam wanted earlier.

I do what he asks, noticing the blood on the scissors. The blades are dull though, and cutting up the pillowcase is slow-going.

"Now, wrap up each wrist. Make 'em tight."

It's only then when I notice the precise slices on Sam's wrists. The scissors must not have been sharp enough, so he broke the mirror. I guess we're even now because I destroyed a mirror myself not that long ago. Wounds that lead to a death trip are gone upon surfacing, like Sam's gunshot ones, but these on his wrist will take time because they have not caused his death. It'll be an unpleasant reminder of this week. I wrap up one wrist while Costa holds him down. I'm trying to block out the fact that Sam is furious with me.

"Why are you helping him? You should be helping me! I thought you loved me!" he keeps repeating.

"I do love you, Sam. I love you so much."

"Fuck you! You're such a bitch!" There is venom in his voice.

Costa is angry now. "Hey! You're the one being a little bitch. Keep your mouth shut, or you're gonna say something else you'll regret later."

I move around them to get to Sam's other wrist, and I slide the fabric under it. Before I tie it though, I'm compelled to stop and rub my thumb over his cuts. The blood doesn't scare me now. In fact, it calls to me.

How could I have ever been repulsed by something so perfect? I wonder. *It's beautiful.*

I start to get a little dizzy, a little high, as I smear the wetness onto my other fingers.

"Stella, snap out of it! Keep moving," Costa orders.

Slowly, I look at him. Costa is so handsome, I notice. And he's so in charge right now. When I look down again, I see my fingers on Costa's arm, painting him with blood. The contrast against his fair skin is stunning, so artistic. I wonder what my own blood would look like on him. Plenty of sharp objects are across the floor, and I begin letting my eyes drift over the many choices.

"Stella!" Costa jars me enough that I pull my hand away. "Listen to me. It's just the blood getting you crazy. And Sam reeks of death. It's making you trippy. Just shake it off, okay? Shake it off."

I nod.

"Bandage up his wrist," he says sternly. "Do it now."

So, I do. It seems to take eons, but I do it.

"Now, get out of the room. Go outside, and wait for me. You need fresh air."

Some piece of me knows he's right, so I get up and walk through my fog and out the door to the porch. The salt smell hits me hard, clearing my nose and throat, letting reality seep back in.

"Shut the door," Costa says. "And go wash your hands."

I feel better already—embarrassed but more myself.

Costa is still on top of Sam, and he's talking. I don't know what he's saying, but he looks calm and even. For twenty minutes, I watch through the door window as Costa talks, and finally, Sam's body relaxes until he's not struggling at all. I take a step back when Costa releases Sam's arms, but Sam just lifts his wrists and looks at them. He shakes his head and puts an arm over his face. Then, Sam holds out a hand, and Costa takes it in his. They stay silent and unmoving—just holding hands and breathing—and eventually, I walk away.

Later, when it's dark out, Costa calls to me.

"I'm up here," I answer.

"Where? Are you on the roof?"

"Yeah."

I hear Costa stepping up the ladder to reach me. "You're as crazy as we are, huh?"

"Good spot to stargaze," I say blandly.

He makes his way up the sharp angle of tiles on the roof to the small flat spot I'm sitting on and hands me a beer. "Good place to fall off and break your neck."

I don't acknowledge how appealing that sounds, but I gladly take the beer.

He studies me for a minute. "Oh. You've got it bad, don't you?"

"I'm fine."

"No, you're not. You need a fix."

"I don't want to talk about it. How's Sam?"

"Dead asleep." Bright moonlight shows me the smile that he flashes. "Pardon the overly appropriate clichéd phrase."

"You're a riot." The beer tastes beyond good right now. "Costa, what are we going to do?"

"I don't know." He hangs his hands over his bent knees and swings his beer. "I really don't know. He could be detoxing like this for days. I've never seen it this bad. He has to stop tripping, but he also *can't* stop tripping. Toby…I mean, it's for *Toby*, you know? How do I tell Sam that I'm giving up on my kid, so he should quit?"

"You can't," I agree.

"But he has to get sober and strong again."

"And we have to figure out why this isn't working. It seemed like it would be so easy to nail down his power. We got all those others without even trying."

"Are you sure you're all right?" he asks.

"Yeah. Why?"

"Your hand is shaking."

He's right. I didn't notice, but the bottle in my hand is practically sloshing beer. I down the rest. "I'm fine. Totally happy. I'm just shitting rainbows all over the place."

"That sounds attractive. Where the fuck did you get that expression?"

I shrug. "I read it in some book. It seems applicable here. 'Bucking up in the face of tragedy and whatnot.' You know, shitting rainbows."

"I kinda dig that. Here's to shitting rainbows." He clinks his beer against mine. "But you're still all wonky. Give me your arm."

"I said, I'm fine." I can hear how irritable I sound.

"No, you're not." Costa takes my arm and begins kneading his fingers into me.

"Ow!"

"Shut up. It'll help."

I let him dig into my muscles and nerves, and it actually does work to soothe my agitation. "Why is this happening to me?"

"Being around a death tripper who is dying or who has been dying a lot is a trigger."

"A trigger for what?"

"Don't you feel it?" he asks with a smirk.

"Feel what?"

"The urge to trip, to die. That's what your body is after."

I yank my hand away. "Don't say that."

"You're a death tripper, Stella. You need to trip occasionally. At least once a month, if not more. I don't know how this power-augmenter thing is going to play into it. Tripping enough but not too much keeps you sharp and stable."

"That's bullshit. Sam hadn't tripped in months and months when I first got here."

"Yeah? And what was he like?"

Costa has a point.

"He was…angry, cold."

"Probably drinking a lot?"

I nod. "But he had a lot to be angry about."

"That's true. He had a lot of good reasons to act however he was acting. But the need to trip was one of them, whether you like it or not."

"But then, we got together."

"Right. And he got better."

"Yes," I say. "So, he doesn't need to trip."

"Well, it might be less true now that you're in the picture. But you're his power augmenter, so you're giving him something, some kind of influence or energy. You're feeding the death tripper in him, so it might satisfy his craving enough that he can go without tripping—until he gets a taste of it."

"Oh, like when you shot him," I say snarkily.

"Well, yes."

"Sorry, that was mean. Sort of."

"I can take it," he says. "Now, give me your arm back."

"Fine." I rest my arm across his legs while he tries to rub away the craving. "So, I'm going to need to start tripping regularly?"

Costa doesn't look at me. "At some point. Maybe."

I finish my beer and take his. All this talk of tripping is only upping my desire. "Maybe that point should be now."

"No way," he says quickly.

"Why not? You could trip me again, Costa."

"You're just still hungry for death from being around Sam."

"So what? I can't do it myself. I'm too scared." I stare at him until he's forced to look into my eyes. "But you could do it for me."

"You're being crazy. And I'm already on thin ice with Sam, so there's no way in hell I'm tripping you."

"Maybe it'll make me stronger. Then, I can focus on Sam, on getting him a vision."

"Nice try. I'm *not* tripping you. When Sam's back in his right mind, you can talk to him about this. But I'm pretty sure he won't trip you either. Sam believes in only doing it yourself. Well, obviously, except when he's like this. He's just desperate though. He resents me enough for tripping you in the first place."

I can tell there's no getting Costa to budge on tripping me, and it's probably for the best. I just have to ride out this craving. "Sam says we're tied together—you and me. Do you think that's true?"

He freezes.

"Costa?"

"Yeah. I mean, I don't know. Probably a little."

"When I was under the surface, you reacted to my touch—"

"That wasn't because I tripped you." He takes his beer back. "Or maybe it was. I guess that makes sense."

"Is there something else that you're not telling me?"

"No." He looks at the sky and smiles. "Check out all the stars tonight."

"Costa, I'm serious. I feel like there's another piece to this whole death tripping. What else is there?"

"I'm telling you what I can. Fuck, I don't know everything," he says with a scoff. "I might have tripped more than Sam, but we're all just winging it."

"There has to be someone who knows what we are, what the rules are. The guy who tripped you? Haven't you tried to find him again?"

"No. He was just some dude. I don't know who he was, so there's no way to find him."

"But maybe he could help us with Toby?"

Costa throws the bottle off the roof, and it shatters on a rock below. "I'm doing the best I can in this, okay?"

"I'm sorry. You're right. I know you are. We all are."

"No, *I'm* sorry. Don't you know that it rips my heart out to see Sam like this? Especially because I'm sober. It hurts me as much as it does you, but I'm stuck. Do you see that, Stella? Christ, I'm damned if I do, damned if I don't."

"I get it. I get it. We're going to figure this out. But we have to get him clean first. Sam can't continue like this."

"Fine. I agree. We'll get him clean, and then we'll…come up with a new plan."

"If Toby can be surfaced, we will find a way. I swear to you. Look, you had Toby after you were a death tripper. Maybe our DNA changes after we've been tripped, so you could have passed on a genetic component. He could be strong already."

"You know, you're right. I didn't think about that." He lets out an exhausted laugh. "Right now, it feels like everything is a possibility, and nothing is a possibility."

I put an arm over his shoulders. There is a bond between us. I don't know what it is or where it came from, but I feel that strongly today. Maybe it's our mutual love for Sam. Maybe it's from watching him care for Sam, the mix of capability and concern and vulnerability Costa brings. Maybe it's because he made me a death tripper. Maybe, despite so much, we just have a true friendship.

But my connection to Costa is real. I just can't get clear on why.

"Show me pictures of Toby again," I ask.

Costa takes his cell out, and we spend the end of the day looking at the little boy who makes all of this worth it.

TWENTY-EIGHT
ties

FELICIA IS TAKING A BREAK on the inn's outdoor seating area—the place where we first met—when I find her the next morning. The breakfast crowd has cleared, and she's having coffee and looking out at the water. The sea is rough today, and the waves make white caps as they roll across the surface. She glances up when I come onto the deck but turns back to her view.

Shit. She knows something is wrong.

"Hi." I pull out a chair and sit at the table.

"You're here to tell me that Sam isn't coming in to work today."

"Yes."

"He's already four hours late, so I figured. And he's been a sloppy mess when he has been here." Felicia takes a sip from her mug and carefully places it back on the saucer. "Are you going to tell me what's going on?"

I don't want to lie to her, but I have to. "He's not feeling well."

For the first time, Felicia raises her voice at me. "Don't bullshit me. Are you going to tell me he's drinking?"

I run my hands through my hair. God, I hate what I'm about to do, but I do it anyway. "Yes."

Sam drank to cover up his death tripping before, and then he drank after Toby died. But now? He hasn't been drinking enough to make me worry. It is, however, the easiest excuse to use now.

Felicia focuses on the waves. "How bad is it?"

"He went on a bender."

"Is it over?"

"Yes. Costa and I are cleaning him up. I swear to you that he's going to be okay."

She nods. "I don't want him back here until then. He knows where I stand. His father and I went through hell with him last time, and we understood then. We were supportive and did everything we could. There was Toby and all…it was a nightmare. So, what's going on now? Does this have to do with Costa?"

I don't know how to answer this. "Maybe a little. It's hard to say."

"Does this have to do with you? Because I really like you, and I'd hate for that to change."

I like that she's so protective of Sam. My mother never was with me. "Sam and I are good. It's not because of me."

"Okay. How much time does he need?"

"At least a few weeks. He just needs to dry out and get his head back on straight."

Felicia folds her napkin and sets it on the table. Then, she moves her chair back and faces me directly. "Sam hasn't smelled of alcohol at all. Something else is going on here. However, I'm going to trust you and assume you have a very good reason for feeding me this story. Get a handle on whatever this is, and you tell me the second you're in too deep. Fair enough?"

Apparently, I'm not the best liar. "Fair enough. Thank you."

"Don't fuck this up." She stares at me, but then her face slowly softens to a hint of a smile. "Do you need anything, Stella?"

"I do have a favor." I wait for her to nod. "I'd like to take Sam up to your family's cabin. Get out of town for a bit with him and Costa. Would that be all right?"

"Sam and Costa agreed to this? They haven't been there since…"

"I know. Since the accident. But they want to go." This isn't exactly true because I haven't told them yet.

"You'd be taking my two best employees, not to mention my two favorite boys." The wind blows her hair across her face, but she doesn't move. "I'll get you the keys and the address. I'm guessing that Sam is in no condition to direct you. Or to drive."

I look down. "Something like that."

"And we both know that Costa drives like a maniac and can't be trusted to follow directions. So, here's the deal. You'll take our SUV, and only you are allowed behind the wheel. Sam's truck has no backseat, and frankly, I don't trust the cars you and Costa have."

"Thank you. For everything."

Felicia stands up and starts to walk past me. Then, she stops and lifts my chin. "I know how much you two love each other and how strong you are together. Take care of my son."

For the first time in days, warmth and hope run through me. "I promise, I will."

She leans in and hugs me so hard that it almost hurts. Her concern is as great as mine.

Sam, her son and the love of my entire world, is now my responsibility.

When I get back to the house, I find Costa heating up some broth on the stove.

"Where have you been?" His clothes are wrinkled from sleeping on the couch.

I don't remember the last time any of us slept well. "Is Sam up?"

"Just woke up a few minutes ago. He's hungry, but I'm starting him on something really light because I don't think either of us feels like cleaning up his puke again."

"I hear you on that." I toss my keys onto the table. "Meet me in the bedroom. I have an idea."

Costa raises his eyebrows. "Sounds sexy. I'm there."

I laugh, and it feels wonderful to have even a moment of distraction. "History will not be repeating itself."

"You never know," he calls after me.

Sam is half-sitting against a pillow, and he shuts his eyes when I walk in. "I'm so sorry, Stella. Oh God, I'm so sorry."

"For what?"

"I can't even look at you. You must hate me."

I take a pillow and sit beside him. "Sam, stop."

"What I said to you yesterday…I wish I didn't remember, but I do…every awful word."

"That was you detoxing and trying to get what you thought you needed. I know you didn't mean it."

"There's no excuse. I'm so sorry."

"Will you look at me now? Please?" I ask.

Slowly, he does.

"Do you see that I'm fine? Really. I'm here. I'm okay."

Weakly, he lifts a hand to mine. "I love you. Always."

"And I love you, too. Always." I assess his appearance and notice that he's gotten at least a little color back, but he still looks pretty wrecked. "And I have a plan."

"Room service!" Costa says cheerily. "I have the high-class bouillon you ordered, sir."

"I think I asked for a turkey sandwich."

"Persons who are prone to vomiting all over the place do not get sandwiches of any variety. They get the aforementioned high-class bouillon prepared by a world-renowned chef. Me."

Sam laughs silently. "Fine." He reaches for the bowl but drops a hand. "Sorry. I'm just so tired. Give me a minute."

Costa pulls over a chair to Sam's bedside. "I gotcha." He lifts a spoon to Sam's lips. "I know you've always dreamed of me spoon-feeding you. Today is your lucky day."

Sam takes another sip. "Thank you, Costa. Really."

"You got it." Costa runs his hand through Sam's hair and gives him more broth. "So, I heard something about a plan?"

I take a breath. "Yes. I've been trying to figure out why it's been so tough to get this vision power. We're all focused on seeing Toby, right? So much of death tripping seems to be hooked into emotion and…ties, connections. I think that we might have a better chance if we tried at the last place Toby was." I pause while this sinks in. "At the Bishops' cabin up north."

Costa keeps lifting the spoon to Sam, and I wait out the quiet while the idea settles.

"I don't know," Costa starts.

"I can't imagine either of you wants to go back there, but...do you see that this might work?"

Sam finally speaks, "It's up to you, Costa. What do you think?"

He clears his throat and swallows hard. "I...I think it's a good idea." He is on the verge of crying, but he stops himself. "I have some of Toby's things at my place. I'm going to bring those up. It could help."

"That's good," I say. "It's a great idea. Pictures, clothes, toys...anything of Toby's. The more familiar things at the cabin, the better. Doesn't that just feel right? We'll go up there, let Sam heal completely, and try again. If we're all in the right frame of mind, we'll have a better shot."

Costa nods, his eyes shining with tears. "Thank you. It's really smart. Death tripping really is about mood."

"It's going to work. It will." I know I'm right about this. I have to be. "Sam, just rest some more, and I'll pack us up. Costa, get your stuff, and we'll meet back here in a few hours."

Sam groans. "Work. I have to work. My parents—"

"I talked to your mom. She gave me the key to the cabin and her car."

"I don't want to know what you said to her."

I smile. "No, you don't."

Sam swings a leg off the bed. "I can help pack."

"No, you can't," I say firmly. "You stay in bed until we roll you into the backseat of the car, okay?"

Sam sighs but agrees. "I'm so useless."

"You're anything but." Costa pats his hand. "I'll be back."

I help Sam finish the rest of the broth and then insist that he sleep a little more. He's too tired to protest, so I tiptoe around his room and gather clothes for him before heading to my place to do the same. I look up the cabin location online, and it should take us just under three hours to get there. Whether it's a rational thought or not, I feel the need to leave as soon as possible. As much as I love Watermark, we're all suffocating here right now.

Costa scowls when I inform him that I'm driving, but I'm not the thrill seeker out of the bunch. The last thing I'm up for is Costa drag-racing north. He pouts while we help Sam into the backseat. While I'm a big believer in always wearing seat belts, I relent this one time and agree that Sam is better off lying down across the seat and being comfortable.

"If we have an accident and he dies"—Costa winks—"we can just start this detoxing fun all over!"

"Shut up," Sam grumbles as he falls against the leather seat.

Felicia and Micah handed over a luxury SUV, and I won't deny that it's a treat for me to get to drive a fully loaded car. The GPS befuddles me though. Costa finally gets irritated with my inability to properly enter the address in Willow, Maine, and he slaps my hand away. As I'm pulling out of the driveway, he starts blasting music.

"We're not listening to Bret Michaels!" I insist. "It's not happening."

"Technically, this is Poison. But fine."

"Corby," Sam says hoarsely. "Corby."

Now, it's my turn to slap Costa's hand. "Put on Matt Corby, or I'll find a way to kill you for real."

"Okay, okay. Sam's the boss."

Sam pulls a blanket over himself. "I hate Springsteen."

Costa laughs. "Close your eyes and rest, buddy."

But under his breath, Costa starts humming "Born to Run," and I giggle despite myself.

The drive is smooth with little traffic midweek, and we get to the town of Willow in good time. Sam has slept nearly the entire drive, and he only awoke moments ago. He says that he has enough energy to come into the local market with us. We really have gone from one small town to another, but the upscale grocery store has a very nice selection, and we load up two shopping carts with fresh produce, meat, and pantry items. Also, we pick up enough liquor to get the three of us through the next few weeks. I have a feeling we're going to need it.

"Hey, remember that guy who sold seafood from that stand on the side of the road? We should stop there, too," Costa says enthusiastically. "Are you getting hungry, Sammy?"

I'm happy that Sam nods.

"A little." He coughs hard. "Good crab."

"Totally. I could be up for a crab and shrimp boil." Costa gathers a few more ingredients that we'll need.

"Firewood," Sam says. "Cold at night."

He's still so pale, and I can see that this walk through the store is exhausting. I want to get him to the cabin as soon as possible, so I hurry us along until Costa stops. He's staring at a shelf. Sam and I move to stand on either side of him.

Costa shoves his hands in his pockets. "Guys, it's okay. I just…I don't know if I should bother buying diapers and wipes and Cheerios and stuff. A sippy cup. I shouldn't…I mean, that's dumb. I don't even know how old he might be, if he's aged. You know, if he's even still down there."

Sam takes a package from the shelf in front of us and puts it in his cart. "He used to like these."

Costa brightens. "Applesauce. I forgot."

"And yogurt." Sam is starting to labor hard.

"Blueberry." Costa puts an arm around Sam and helps him stand.

"And peach."

I promised Sam's mother that I would take care of him, so I'm officially calling time on this shopping trip. "I'll get the yogurt and some of these other things. You help Sam to the car. Right now, please. Maybe we'll run out later to get the seafood?"

"You got it. I'll go after we get settled," Costa says.

The drive from the market to the cabin is about twenty minutes, and Sam is passed out cold for the short ride. Costa signals me to make a right at a small red sign, and we drive through evergreen trees that form a tent of foliage over us. The dirt road ends, and I park the car.

This cannot be right.

"Costa?"

"Yeah?"

"Where's the cabin?"

"What do you mean? It's right here." He squints at me. "What the hell is wrong with you?"

"What the hell is wrong with all of you for calling this a *cabin*?"

I blink at the log—I don't know...log *mansion* in front of us. Apparently, they all think that just because it's made from wood that it's considered a cabin. It's not. Cabins are small rustic vacation homes. Unless the inside differs radically from the outside, I don't expect to walk in and find a vintage stove and dishes from the sixties.

Sam rouses from the back. "It's not that big."

"How many square feet?"

"I dunno."

"How many bedrooms?"

"A few."

"You're delirious," Costa says. "There are six along with a library and a hot tub and—"

"She gets the idea." Sam pulls himself up. "I need some water." Before we can help him out though, he opens the door and retches out the side. "Now, I really need some water."

Costa gives Sam a hand with getting to the house while I punch in the alarm code that Felicia gave me. I unlock the big front door, and I take a step inside. My mother has money for sure, but her house became a cold, sterile pretentious prison after my father left. This house? This is a *home.*

I wander in awe through the main living area, an open-concept wood wonderland connecting the kitchen, living room, and dining area that invites warmth and comfort. Above me are high ceilings with rafters crossing the width of the house and lights hanging from long spindles. Cushy couches and floor pillows are positioned by the grand fireplace, and a picture window and sliding door overlook the lake.

Of all places to detox one death tripper and strategize to save the son of another, this one ain't too shabby.

Costa practically carries Sam into the house and across the room toward the staircase. He slows, however, by the big window, and both he and Sam eye the lake with trepidation. As glorious and posh as our surroundings are, this is not a vacation. It's where Toby died, and I'm quite sure that despite Costa's singing the praises of this house moments ago, he and Sam are consumed with painful memories.

I help Costa get Sam to the foot of the stairs. "I know the past is everywhere," I say. "But the future is everywhere, too."

TWENTY-NINE
feel everything

IT TAKES SIX DAYS for Sam to fully heal and death-trip again.

Costa hands him a bag of pills and says, "Don't ask. It'll be fast."

Sam and I sit together and talk about Toby. We use the words *see* and *vision* about a hundred times. Then, Sam takes the pills, and I hold him on the couch until he stops breathing, until his body turns into glittering dust and sinks into the cushions and through the floorboards. Although I know he'll come back, and I know this death isn't permanent, I cannot help the ache and loss that I feel.

Costa joins me on the couch. "He's focused and prepared. He'll surface quickly. This isn't a trip that he'll drown in or prolong. His surge will be short, too, I'm guessing."

"We didn't bring the sandbag," I point out.

"So, either I'm getting the shit beat out of me or—"

I smile. "Why don't you make dinner?"

I want Sam's surge this time because I also have steam to burn off. The pressure and importance of trying to get this vision power has taken its own kind of toll on me even though it's hardly comparable to what the boys are going through.

Costa rolls his eyes. "I'll be in the kitchen."

"I'll be in the bedroom."

I go upstairs to our room where I strip off my pants and crawl into the king-sized bed. I'm surprised at how tired I am, so I use Sam's trip as an excuse to nap. I'm probably only out for a little more than an hour when I'm awoken by Sam pushing up my shirt.

He's breathy and hot, and I run my fingers through his hair as he travels his mouth over my stomach and to my breasts. I keep my eyes closed and focus on the sensation of his touch, how connected we are when we make love. Sex during his surges amplifies everything I feel for him, and today is the first day we've had sex since this tripping with a purpose started.

I arch my back and groan when he pulls down my underwear and moves on top of me. Right now, I don't want or need a lot of foreplay. I just need Sam inside me. My hands go to his ass when he enters me, and I lift up and pull him hard against me, making both of us let out sounds that I'm sure cut through the music Costa is playing downstairs. I couldn't care less what he hears right now. That's how much I'm glued into the chemistry between Sam and me.

His rhythm starts hard and fast, and he pulls out nearly all the way before thrusting back in, over and over until we're both ready to change the pace. I bend my knees and tuck them under his chest so that he gets even deeper. I love when we do this because Sam keeps himself pressed against me, grinding slowly and lifting his cock up inside me. I finally open my eyes to take in how he looks when he does this.

Only, when I do, he's not there, except that I feel him. I close my eyes again and then look. I know I'm awake.

Something is massively wrong with me. Again.

"Sam?"

"Baby…" he breathes heatedly.

I reach out into the empty space above me until my hand stops on where I know his chest is. I move my palm up against his skin and feel my way to his shoulder. Then, I touch his face, feel his lips sucking on my fingers. I can feel everything.

I just can't see him.

Sam is invisible.

"Look down," I tell him.

He stays inside me, but his pace slows as understanding creeps through him. "Holy…shit."

"I know," I say, tightening my muscles around his cock. "Don't stop. Please don't stop."

He doesn't. Later, I roll him onto his back and feel my way to straddling him. I don't know where his hands are going to move, when he's going to take my nipple between his fingers, when he might sit up and rock his hips into me before grabbing my hair by the roots and pulling my head back so that he can kiss my neck and suck on my skin.

It's only after we're done—when we're both sweaty and panting, recovering, and while I'm draped over an invisible Sam—that reality strikes.

"It didn't work," Sam says softly.

"It worked for me," I start. Then, I realize what he means. "Oh. Damn it! The vision power. Why didn't it work?"

Under me, the skin on his arm begins to show through. I sit up to watch as his form slowly becomes visible. It's as though long thin strokes individually take their turn over his body, and I'm once again fascinated by the fantastical nature of his powers. Some nonexistent artist is painting him right in front of me.

When he's fully back, Sam looks over his own body. "So…that was fucked up, huh?"

"Yeah, a little bit."

"But we got closer," he says. "Invisible? Vision? Not that far apart really. They're in the same family."

I sigh. "I guess so." But this is a defeat, and my frustration is hard to contain. "We're missing something. I have no idea what, but we're fucking missing something."

"I'm sorry. I know this is really surge-y of me, but I have to eat."

He pats my back, and I climb off of him and the bed before grabbing my robe.

"Death tripping makes for terrible bedside manners," he says apologetically.

"It's okay. I get it."

"You all right?" Sam pulls on jeans and a T-shirt.

"No, not really."

"I know you're frustrated. But I think this invisibility thing is a good sign. It's progress."

"Progress isn't good enough. You're doing your part. You're death-tripping. I'm the one doing something wrong. Apparently, I'm the worst power augmenter ever."

"Stella, stop. This is not your fault. You are doing more than anyone could, and you're doing it well." He does a little dance in place and shakes his body until he disappears. "Check me out! I can go all invisible on your ass!"

I laugh in spite of my crummy mood.

Sam repaints himself and takes me against him. "I smell good things wafting up here. I gather you put Costa to work?"

"Some kind of creamy seafood casserole with parmesan topping."

"Oh, man. He's good."

"And homemade biscuits and blueberry cobbler."

Sam races down the stairs, and I follow at a more normal pace. While Sam might be fired up about a big meal, I know that Costa is going to be crushed that the vision power is still proving to be unattainable.

I grab a bottle of wine and a glass and leave the guys in the kitchen. The sunset is gorgeous tonight, and I feel as though sitting out on the tiled patio area in a lounge chair might be just the thing to lift my mood.

The sunset is just starting, and the sky is layered in tiers of color and clouds.

Vision. Clarity. Sight.

What am I missing? What the hell am I missing?

Invisible, I think. My memories scream at me, memories from being in the stairwell at the hospital so many years ago. *I'm good at being invisible.*

When the sun has sunk halfway to the lake and my glass is half gone, Costa joins me outside. "What's up, pussycat?"

"What's up, CJ?"

"Nice outfit."

I'm still in my robe. I pull the fabric more over my leg, and I shrug. "Too lazy to get dressed. Sunset was calling."

He leans back in the lounger next to me and squints into the view. "Sam told me. Just so you know."

I put my hand on his. "I thought it would work this time. It's the right power to go after, and I'm trying so hard." I can feel myself getting upset. "I am doing everything I can think of to will him to see."

"Hey, hey. Easy there. I know that."

"I made you come up here, probably the last place where you want to be, and I can't fucking make this work!"

Costa turns to me. "It's not your fault, Stella. And being in Willow isn't as bad as I thought. I'm closer to Toby here, and that's a good thing."

We sit together silently until there is just a sliver of sun left.

What am I missing?

Sam steps onto the patio and seats himself on my other side. I'm relieved to see that he doesn't look particularly hungover from his trip or surge.

"Costa?" For some reason, I'm hesitant to ask him what I'm about to.

"Yeah?"

I take another drink from my glass, stalling. "I think that you're not telling me something."

"What do you mean?"

"Please tell me." There is a truth that I need to reach. I can feel it. "I want the whole story. I know you have it. I just do. Tell me."

He doesn't say anything for a long time. Then, finally, when the tension becomes nearly unbearable, he speaks, "This is going to hurt. Don't say I didn't warn you."

Ice runs through me at his words.

"What the hell are you talking about?" Sam is less relaxed now.

I glance at Sam, confirming that he has no idea what we're about to hear.

I say what I know to be true, "Costa has our missing piece."

"If you're fucking with her—" Sam starts.

"I'm not. I swear. I didn't want to ever talk about any of this."

"Talk about what?" Sam's edginess concerns me.

"The story about who first tripped me—the guy by the cliffs." Costa rubs his lips together and then takes a breath. "I made that up."

"Why?" I ask.

"Because I don't like how I became a death tripper. The story I told is better. It's how I wish it had happened, so it's what I told you both. It should have been my choice. It should have been beautiful. Instead, it wasn't. It was a nightmare that I've been in. I don't love death tripping. I never have. But I'm trying to make the best of this. Maybe I'm trying to fall in love with it. Maybe I'm just an addict. I don't know anymore. Anyway, I didn't understand the importance of how I'd first tripped until recently, the connections that link us all together."

"Get to the point, Costa," Sam snaps impatiently from his chair.

I am less impatient and more terrified. I can feel the build that Costa is leading up to something that I will not care for one bit. Something damaging is coming.

"The day that I was hit by a car in Chicago, when I was with you, Sam—"

"Wait, you were the friend? Sam, when I met you in the hospital, you were there to see Costa?"

Sam nods. "Yes. You didn't know that?"

"No. Why didn't you tell me?"

He shrugs. "I don't know. We've hardly talked about that day. It just really hasn't come up. I don't know what that has to do—"

Costa cuts him off in an explosive confession. "That's the day I was tripped." He looks at me. "I was hit by a car when I was crossing a side street. I'd met a girl, and I'd left in the dark during an ice storm to go see her. I hadn't been paying attention, and I'd stepped out in front of a car. It'd hit me, skidded, spun out, and hit a tree. And I died."

"Okay, so…what?" I ask.

Sam's expression gets dark. "A car accident," he says flatly. Then, he looks at me. "Oh, Stella…"

My stomach drops. "My father and sister were in a car accident that day. That's why I was at the hospital."

"Yes," Costa says. He waits for me to begin to process. "It was the same accident."

"My father hit you." I feel sick.

"Yes." Costa looks sad now. "He killed me and your sister, so he tripped us."

I can't form words or think or begin to understand what he's saying.

"When I went into your apartment to get your sweatshirt, I saw a picture that was facedown on the mantel, so I righted it and saw it was of your family. I know your father and sister."

I shake my head. "No, you don't. You can't. Shut up! Costa, shut the fuck up!"

Sam moves his chair closer to me and takes my hand.

"I don't know why you're making up this shit!" I'm furious with Costa for whatever twisted game he's playing.

"I'm not making up anything. It's why I got so crazy that afternoon after I saw the photograph, and it's why I tripped you. I was lashing out for what was done to me." Costa sits up in his chair and faces me. "Your father is the one who tripped me, and he tripped your sister, too. He didn't mean to kill me in the first place, but he brought me back on purpose. And your sister? Amy is not suicidal, and she's not a drug addict. She's a death tripper."

The bottle and glass fall from the arm of my chair and shatter on the tile. Sam restrains me before I can fully reach Costa, so I only get in one hard slap across his face before Sam pulls me back.

But he can't stop me from screaming and unleashing my full fury at the lies Costa is spewing. "Fuck you! Fuck you! I hate you!" I can't stop throwing every four-letter word I know at him, and neither Sam nor Costa tries to calm me down.

They must know it'd be futile to fight my rage. So, Sam just keeps his hold on me until my emotions eventually morph into devastation and uncontrollable tears. I close my eyes and fall apart.

Costa continues, "Amy and I went under. She was right next to me in the darkness, and she held my hand. We were freaked and terrified and…just waiting to…finish dying, to get through whatever this transitional stage was. It felt eternal, but Amy never let go of my hand. Your father appeared. He put his arms around both of us and pulled us to the surface. We were right near the car when we came up.

"I guess it was only a matter of minutes because right after there were ambulances and sirens and fire trucks…all hell broke loose. The EMTs had to strap me down to the gurney. I know now that I was surging, but…who knows what they thought? That I was having a seizure or going into some kind of crazy shock?

"Your father rode with Amy, of course. Even after my surge stopped, I didn't know what had happened to me. If I'd made it all up, had some sort of weird near-death experience. Your father came to my room only once—for a grand total of thirty seconds. He apologized and cried, both of which were goddamn useless. Then, he told me that I could save someone if I needed to, do for another person what he did for me. That's the only information he gave me, and it didn't make any sense to me at the time. He left me all alone and in a private hell.

"I spent the next six months being haunted by that first trip. Tortured by it really. You mix that in with my shitty parents, my shitty life…so I tried to kill myself. For good."

I just keep crying and crying. Every word out of his mouth makes my heart splinter further.

"I took an entire bottle of my mother's prescription painkillers because I thought that dying was the only way out. But I came back. A week later, I tried slitting my wrists. Then, I drove my car into a brick wall. So, I just kept going and going until I understood that I couldn't die.

"I never knew who your father was, and I never wanted to see him again. Even seeing the picture was too much. He destroyed my life—or the little that I had. But it was mine, and he turned me into this." Costa stands up and walks slowly. He pauses near me before he leaves. "I'm so sorry, Stella, for everything. I didn't want you to know."

I want to scream more, but my throat is constricted and filled with the mayhem of my sorrow, so I couldn't speak even if I wanted to.

And I don't. There's no place to begin.

chains

SAM LETS ME CRY until my body is totally spent. I fake being asleep so that he will drift off because I know that he needs to rest and refuel. There's no chance my mind will settle, and I don't know how to talk about this, even with Sam. The shock is too strong.

At four in the morning, Amy's words from the day of the accident replay in my mind.

"And what about that other kid? I saw it. That poor kid. I wish we were all dead! What is this?"

The *poor kid* was Costa.

And *this* is death tripping.

I'm ashamed that I never thought more about her words after that day, but maybe that denial was part of how I shut down and coped. I didn't want to know what Amy had meant.

My father had started this chain of events.

Everything goes back to him. Without him, Costa wouldn't have lost his son, Sam wouldn't have been a death tripper, I wouldn't have been his power augmenter or a death tripper myself. Amy would have still loved me, and my father would never have abandoned us.

Of course, Amy and Costa would be dead. There would be no Toby and no sister or father to lose.

The impact of what he'd done by tripping Amy and Costa must have been too much for my father, and he left us all. That was a huge unforgivable mistake. Not only could he have helped Amy and Costa come to grips with what they are, but he could also have been a wealth of understanding for us all.

I hate my father, and I love him more than ever. Maybe he didn't give up on his family. Maybe he gave up on himself.

I throw on sweatpants and a tee and take my phone into one of the spare bedrooms.

The call I make rings and rings and eventually goes to voice mail. I call again and again. Finally, my sister answers.

"What?" she barks groggily.

"Amy," I say, "it's Stella."

"Jesus Christ. What do *you* want?"

"I need to talk to you."

"Screw you. You left. Nobody cares. Don't call again."

I know that she's about to hang up, so I have to keep her on the line. "I know about Dad."

There's silence. "What do you mean?"

"I know about Dad, about the car accident…how you…died, how he saved you." Speaking has never been so hard. "And the other boy. His name is Costa."

Amy doesn't say anything, but I can hear her breathing.

"I went to Watermark, Maine, to find Sam Bishop. I met him that day in the hospital. He was Costa's friend. I drove to The Coastal Inn that Sam's parents own, and I found him. Costa and Sam can do what you can do. They call themselves death trippers." I pause. "I'm one now, too."

Amy finally makes a noise. A gasp or a cry, I'm not sure. But it's enough to let me know that she's listening.

"I know you're not using and that you're not suicidal. I know that. When you surface after dying, Sam and Costa call it a surge. That's the rush we get. It's how I found you at your condo. I understand everything now, Amy." I'm getting teary, but it feels good to say some of this out loud. I can hear Amy crying, which I find momentarily reassuring. "Do you know where Dad is?"

"No, and I'm fucking happy about it. Our mother hired a PI to find him, and that turned up nothing. I hope he's dead. For real." Amy's venom crawls through the phone. "Don't call me again." She hangs up.

The quiet is deafening. I whisper to nobody, "Please come back to me, and be my sister again. I miss you. I need you. You are my only family left."

I sit alone in the dark bedroom for a while. Amy is as bitter as Costa is. As we all are. We're victims of someone else's power. Tonight, it feels as though there is nothing but heartache and hate in all of us.

There just has to be beauty somewhere.

I go downstairs. A light is on in the kitchen, and Costa is sitting on one of the barstools at the island. When he hears my footsteps, he turns and gives me a look of such apology and misery that I immediately fall apart again.

He looks down. "Stella…"

"Why didn't you tell me?" I stop a few feet from him, my emotions vulnerable and raw. "How could you not? You hate me that much?"

Costa just shakes his head. "I don't hate you. Are you crazy? I didn't tell you because…look at you. Look at what this has done. I didn't want you to know. What was the point?"

I wipe my eyes and shoot him a look of disbelief. "The point? So that I could have understood that my sister is not a drug addict who despises me, that my father had a reason for disappearing and leaving me alone with a mother who did nothing but try to destroy me. And I would have understood why you tripped me and turned me into a death tripper. It's payback for what my father did to you."

"It was a stupid reactive thing to do."

"What should my father have done? Let you and Amy die?"

Costa's eyes flash with anger. "Yes. Exactly. Then, I wouldn't be living in this hell."

Now, I go to him. "Costa…" He spins his stool to me, and I put my hands on his face. "Don't say that."

"It's true. You know it. I hate this life, this world, yet I passed it on to you and Sam." His face is hard, bitter. "If I could die for good, I'd do it this minute."

"You didn't want to be alone."

He nods.

"You're not alone anymore."

"I should be."

"But you're not."

I encircle him in my hold, trying to comfort both of us. So much of me resents the hell out of this stupid, broken, selfish boy, but an equally large part of me can now empathize with everything he is. Costa, whether I like it or not, is bonded to my father and to Amy, and he's therefore bonded to me. My father tripped him, he tripped me…Costa is in my world. He's part of my fiber, my makeup. It makes sense why he reacted so strongly to my touch when we were under.

Suddenly, one bit of this circle makes sense to me. After I found Amy in her condo and after she told me to get away from her and Mom, she spoke the same words that Sam had said to me.

I whisper to Costa now as I hug him, "*Go find your good.*"

He actually laughs lightly. "You know about that?"

"Sam said it to me when I first met him. Then, Amy did years later. You passed it to her, didn't you?"

"Yeah," he says softly. "When we surfaced, before they separated us. Sammy used to say that to me when we were kids…when things were hard for me at home. I don't know that I ever listened to him though."

"You'll find your good, Costa. You will."

"I'm a mess, Stella."

"We're all in this now. None of us chose it, and even though you tripped Sam and me, I get how lonely and angry you were. Maybe I'll never forgive you entirely, but I understand. I have to. What other choice do I have?"

His arms tighten around me, and I feel him shake silently in my embrace. "I'm so fucked up. I can't get a handle on anything."

"That's why you had to tell me the truth. Even though it hurts to know, you needed to let it go, and I needed to hear it. I spent a long time not seeing truths because my mother manipulated so many of my experiences. Knowing that my father started this for all of us? It burns like poison, but the truth lets me see. The truth makes everything clear."

I stop as I'm hit with yet another piece of the puzzle—a very significant one.

Truth. See. Clear.

Oh my God.

"Costa…" I start. It's hard to breathe. "Costa." There is sudden joy in this tumultuous night.

He sniffs. "What?"

I push him from me and look into his sorrowful blue eyes. "Death tripping is very tied to emotions. It's affected by our moods, our relationships, our minds. Everything, right? All connected, all intertwined."

"It seems to be. Where are you going with this?"

I start to smile as my brain puts it all together. "Listen to me. I didn't see the truth before. I didn't have *insight.*"

He frowns. "Okay."

"Not until I had all the facts, the real story of what happened in the past. Now, I *see.*"

Costa starts to smile, too. "You can see. Stella, you can see."

I nod and watch as what I'm saying sinks in.

"And now you can help Sam see."

"Yes," I confirm breathlessly. "I can help Sam see. Literally."

In an instant, our destruction turns to hope.

"It's so obvious now." Costa's cheeks are flushed with excitement. "It makes total sense. God, Stella. This could really work."

"It will work. I'm sure."

"We can find Toby."

"Yes," I agree. "We can find Toby."

"You are incredible." Costa's eyes are wet, but this time, it's from joy.

He puts a hand on the back of my neck and leans in, kissing my cheek. For a moment, he keeps his lips on my skin, perhaps for too long, but I don't pull away. I should, but I don't.

"We can do this," he says with conviction.

"Okay."

Costa leaps up and scurries to the coffee maker. "We need fuel. Should we wake up Sam? I'll make breakfast. Lots of eggs. Protein, right? That seems like a good idea. Get us all ready."

His manic energy is making me nervous.

"We should let him sleep, don't you think?"

"Why? Let's do this. What's the point in waiting? If we can get Toby, then—" Costa stops himself. "Oh. Stella, I'm sorry."

"What?" I take a seat at one of the stools. Apparently, I'm not hiding my worry very well.

"You're going to have to trip with us if this plays out the way we hope."

"I know," I say softly.

"You scared? Or you want it too much?"

I'm scared *because* I want it too much. "It's okay. It'll be fine."

"I know Sam hates the idea of you tripping, and if there were any other way…"

"There's not. It's a good thing that you tripped me because I'm the only one who can augment Sam's vision while we're under. It's our best chance."

"Don't worry. I'll make it fun for you." He winks. The old Costa is back.

Sam's voice echoes throughout the room. "Has Stella already told you? I don't have a vision power. I have invisibility. Don't kill me for being so awesome."

He comes into the kitchen area, and I smile. His hair is sticking every which way, and he looks totally adorable.

He quickly kisses me and looks back and forth between Costa and me. He frowns. "You okay, Stella?"

"Yeah, actually, I'm good."

"Dude, can you seriously make yourself invisible?"

Sam kisses me again, and then with his hand in mine, he grins at Costa. I didn't see him transition the last time, so I am in absolute awe as he fades away in front of us. His body becomes just slightly sheer at first and then slowly, slowly becomes entirely see-through. Costa rounds the granite island and inches to where Sam was—or is, rather. I can still feel his hand on mine, but it's hard to reconcile his touch with the absence of the visual.

"Wow, Sammy. You're going to knock this vision thing out of the park."

Sam filters himself back into being visible. It's the most fantastic paint job I could imagine, and Costa is noticeably impressed.

Sam, still not fully awake even after that, yawns. "We tried for vision. We got invisibility."

"Your girl here figured it out. She might be more superhero than you are." Costa is practically giddy.

"Huh? What's going on? Last I knew everyone was miserable and hateful."

"Grab a seat," Costa says, pouring Sam a cup of coffee. "We'll fill you in."

Costa and I detail what we know—or really what we're guessing.

I also tell them about my call to Amy. "It didn't go well. The only thing I learned is that my father seems to be living off the grid."

"I don't want his help anyway," Costa says quickly. "We don't need him."

"I hope not."

"I'm not screwing around here. I don't ever want to see that man again. I know he's *your* father, but he's *my* enemy."

I glare at him. "He's not exactly my best friend either, CJ."

Sam takes a sip of his coffee. "Ease up, you two. Do you still have enough pills, Costa?"

"You want to trip today? You're ready?"

"I am. This is a good strategy, and Stella can send me into a good trip. Besides," he says, smiling, "can't you feel it? It's a good day for death."

THIRTY-ONE
no demons

"I SEE EVERYTHING NOW. I see everything so clearly. The tangled knots of my past have been undone, and while it is difficult, seeing without lies settles the heart. My history makes sense for the first time. With the truth laid out, I cannot hide. I can only run to it, embrace it even. Because now no demons are chasing me. There's nothing else to run from." This is all I say to Sam when he dies.

The pills are the most peaceful way for him to die and the easiest for me to watch, so I'm glad he chose that again. My hope is that when I'm calm and not anxious about his dying, that I can focus and send him into a productive trip.

Costa waits for me on the patio, and together, we sit without talking for the few hours it takes Sam to surface. The crash from inside makes both of us jump, and when we get to the kitchen, Sam is holding his head and fighting his surge.

"Hit my skull on the fridge," Sam says with irritation.

We all agreed that we've got to find a way to control the surging. If we find Toby, we can't all surface in states that are so *not* conducive to being around a child. I'll probably have the least control, but the guys might be able to restrain themselves if necessary. Maybe.

Sam, however, has surfaced hard right now, and he's hungry in more ways than one. Costa offers him a deli platter, but trying to thwart Sam's surge proves useless, and Costa nearly gets yet another black eye when Sam swings at him. Costa tosses up his hands and goes down to the water, leaving Sam and me alone for a while.

I really can't complain because, even though I'm not surging, holding him while he's died so many times has built up a charge in me that needs a release, and I'm more than happy to work out his surge in the bedroom—or in this case, on the kitchen island.

My legs are wrapped around Sam's waist, and he's fully dressed with only his pants undone and lowered enough. The counter is hard underneath my back, but I like this because the solidity lets me feel everything about Sam moving inside me. I let myself get lost in him and his rhythm, and I focus solely on my physical pleasure, blocking out everything else. There's too much to face right now, and my past and future are colliding in a way that's verging on unmanageable. I don't want to be here, so I let myself disappear until there is only the fluid motion of sex and my love for Sam. I need a break from being too present, so I allow myself to vanish into him. I will come back to reality though. It's not like before.

It's only when he stops moving and says something that I jar from my own world.

"What? Don't stop..." I murmur. When I open my eyes, I see that he's resting his hands on the counter and staring out the picture window.

"A rainy day at the lake is better than a sunny day anywhere else," he says, smiling.

"Huh?"

"Swim during daylight hours only. No lifeguard on duty after six p.m." He squints a bit. "*The Joy of Cooking*...*The Firm*...*The Catcher in the Rye*. Oh. *A Different Blue* and *Ten Tiny Breaths*. You read those last two, didn't you? This summer?"

I'm pretty sure that Sam is having some kind of a horrible seizure that's causing him to rattle off nonsense. I tap his arm. "Look at me. Are you okay? Bishop?"

"Sorry." He grins through his surge haze. "The sex is outstanding. But I couldn't help noticing that I can read the signs at the public beach across the lake and that I can see inside someone's house. They have a lot of books."

I'm flooded with disbelief. "You got it? You got vision?"

Sam looks down at me and begins moving his hips again. "I got it." He leans over and nuzzles into my neck. "I got it." His breath is hot on my neck, his lips and tongue wet as he starts kissing and sucking on my skin.

I lift up into him, my arousal now soaring even more. The strength of us together scares me and exhilarates me, and my body reacts to our intensity by needing more and more from him. My fingers dig into his shoulders as I work myself against him until I can barely breathe, and then my body tightens and climaxes. The groan that I release is nearly a howl, and I'm still shuddering when Sam thrusts into me harder and harder, soon working toward his own. Surge sex is raw and so animalistic in the base needs and sounds it creates in us. Death tripping might be addictive, but surge sex might be even more so.

After, when Sam has finished polishing off most of the deli platter, we go down to the lakeshore. Costa is a few feet from the water. It must have been torture for him to wait out Sam's surge to find out if this worked.

Before I can tell him the news, Sam stops us twenty feet away. "Hold up your phone."

"What?" Costa looks nervous.

"Open a web page, and hold up your phone to me."

Costa bites his lip and controls a smile. The look he gives Sam melts my heart. He does what he's asked to and lifts the phone. I can't begin to see what is on the screen.

Sam, very casually and without straining at all, reads to us, "Bret Michaels was born on March fifteenth in nineteen sixty-three—Costa, seriously?" He laughs but keeps reading, "As the lead singer of the band Poison, Bret enjoyed international success in the eighties, and to date, the band has sold over forty-five million records worldwide. Bret relaunched his career with his reality dating show, *Rock of Love*." Sam tosses up his hands. "Okay, I can't take anymore!"

Costa makes a beeline for Sam and jumps into his arms, latching on to him like a koala baby, and Sam stumbles back.

"You can see, Sammy! You can see!"

Sam rolls his eyes, but he hugs his friend close.

The boys are both laughing and crying.

While I'm as happy as they are, I'm also cautious about preemptively celebrating too much. There are too many unknowns. "Sam, let's find out if you can see in the dark."

He sets Costa down and points to the sky. "You might not have noticed in all the excitement, but it's still light out."

"Funny, funny." I pause because they're not going to like this idea. "I think you should go into the lake, Sam. Try to see in that darkness. It's the closest thing to being under." Toby died here, so I hate the suggestion, but it seems necessary.

Costa is somber now, but Sam agrees instantly, "Of course. That's good." He takes off his shirt and heads to the water as he undoes his pants. "You coming?" he asks me. "I need you."

I'm not much of a lake person myself, but I know I have to go in. The closer that I am to Sam, the stronger his vision will be.

"Let's hope no one else has a bitchin' vision power," I say as I strip down to my bra and underwear. I glare at Costa to stop him from saying anything lewd. "It's the same thing as a bathing suit. Shut up."

Costa holds up his hands in surrender. "I didn't say a word." He crosses his arms. "Hey, I'm going to wait up at the house, if that's okay."

"Of course," Sam says.

Watching us in the water here would be too hard. Without the hot summer sun, the temperature is a bit chilly, but we dunk in and swim out until we're treading water.

"Ready?" I ask.

"Ready. Hold my hand, and we'll go under."

We swim for a bit, and I try opening my eyes to see what I can make out, but I can barely see Sam, and he is right next to me. The water is for sure murky, so it's a good test. We break through the surface, and I look to Sam.

"God, it's so easy, Stella. I can see clear across to the other side, down to every pebble on the bottom."

I smack my hand against the water and splash him. "Show-off," I tease.

He splashes me back, but then he gets serious. "It's because of you, you know. You're the only reason I can do this."

"It's because of *us*." I tread water for a second. "If we find Toby, you're going to lose your powers when you surface him."

His expression sobers. "I'm not worried about that. Neither should you."

"I know it's a trade-off worth making, but I love your powers," I say.

This is true. There is something so special about them because they are determined by the union of the two of us. It's a physical manifestation of our bond.

"And without them, you won't need me. I won't serve a purpose."

"Stella, don't you dare think that. Never. Your purpose is not to be my power augmenter."

"Why do you think I'm your power augmenter? Did I become that *because* we fell in love? Or…" I don't want to say this, but the thought feels like more than I can contain. "Did we fall in love because I was…I don't know…*fated* to be your power augmenter because of my dad?"

"The chicken and egg question." Sam shakes his head. "Stella…"

"Come on, it's a possibility. Maybe we met in the hospital years ago because we were supposed to. Because I was already your power augmenter or I became that because my father tripped your best friend. The fates knew Costa would later trip you…I don't know. Maybe the way we feel about each other hasn't been our choice. What if the way we feel is just a fabrication?"

"Is falling in love ever a choice?" He swims closer and touches a wet hand to my face. "I don't think so."

"It's a possibility though, isn't it?" I go on my side and start to lead us into shore. "It happened so fast between us, an instant connection even when I was only sixteen."

"With death tripping though, doesn't it seem to you that things happen because of how we feel and not the other way around? We affect experiences. Like, we have bad trips when our emotions are out of whack."

This makes me feel a little better. "That's true."

"I know, without a doubt, that you being my power augmenter is a natural consequence of our love. Even if I have no powers to augment, you're still going to be the absolute love of my life." He flashes a smile. "And my death."

It seems unimaginable, but even in the upheaval and chaos that has come with the introduction of death tripping into my life, I am more present and grounded than I've ever been. My heart is lighter, my head less hazy. Our love is proof that, against all odds, together, we can see in the dark.

When I can set my feet on the sand below, I stand with the water lapping gently against my chest. "We came first."

"Yes, we came first. I can't be tricked into loving someone. Everything that I feel for you is real. It comes from me."

Sam Bishop, the boy who brought me Wonder Woman socks and who subsequently rocked my world into a hundred shades of clarity, kisses me and floods me with belief.

THIRTY-TWO
bleed

WE WAIT UNTIL NIGHTFALL TO TRIP, reasoning that maybe Toby would be asleep at night and in one location. It's possible that he's never been far from where the initial accident took place, but maybe Sam and Costa simply couldn't see him.

I'm edgy and walking the length of the open living area—going back and forth from the fireplace, passing the soft couches, passing the farm table where we've eaten dinner together every night, stopping in front of the pictures on the wall that are lit by small showcase lamps. Gorgeous pictures of the Bishop family, all in black and white, cover this wall, and I study the prints—Sam and Kelly as kids growing up in Maine, Micah and Felicia on their wedding day, the family in front of the inn during a party.

I see only one picture that makes me pause. It's of Sam, when he was fully grown, and I know for sure that this must have been taken after Toby died and before I met him. I can see the surly, angry person he was when I first came to Maine. It's hard to believe now how cold and shut down he was.

I'm tempted to call Felicia, but I'm afraid that she'll hear the emotion and nerves in my voice, and I don't want to alarm her. We've been in touch via text, but I haven't spoken to her. Once Sam, Costa, and I get through this last trip, I'll want to hear her voice. I'm nervous and fragile now though, and her love would be too much.

We need to be careful with death tripping. That's very obvious to me. Toby is a drastic example of what can go wrong, but there are plenty of other repercussions I don't want to even imagine.

But I'm so ready to trip. The desire in me that has been teased by all the tripping Sam's been doing has built to such a degree that I can hardly think about anything else.

"How are we going to do it?" I ask. "The pills, right?" I turn and start walking the room again, but then I stop when I see what Costa is doing. "Oh, CJ...do you think that's a good idea?"

He's kneeling by the coffee table and pulling out things from a bag. I watch as he folds a fuzzy green blanket and sets it down. Then, he takes a worn teddy bear and holds it up. "Toby loves this guy. He'll want to have him when he gets back."

I don't know what to say as he continues adding to the collection on the table—board books, a set of plastic blocks, some clothes. He's included the beginnings of everything a toddler would need.

Then, he snaps his fingers and rushes to the kitchen. "Hungry. Toby's going to be hungry." He takes Cheerios from a cabinet. "I shouldn't leave the yogurt out though, right? I don't know how long we'll be gone."

Sam is eating dinner at the table and looks up from his book. Then, he puts a finger to his lips to tell me not to bother trying to dissuade Costa.

"What did Toby call that bear?" I ask.

Costa smiles warmly. "*Ba*. He called the bear *Ba* and a bottle *baba* and a nap *bee*. I have no idea where that word came from, but most of his words started with B." He looks at the table. "I bought diapers and clothes in case he's grown. I don't know what he's going to be like, how old. But…what else am I forgetting?"

Sam backs up his chair and goes to Costa. "We'll figure it all out. And we can get anything else you need later, okay? One thing at a time." He looks at me. "Did you eat?"

"Not really hungry."

"You should try to get something in your stomach."

"I'll eat after. I want to do this. Now."

"Okay. Costa, you all set there?"

He rubs his hands together and stands. "Yeah. Did you, uh…talk to Stella?"

I look between them. "Talk to me about what?"

The apologetic expression on Sam's face scares me, and my edginess increases by a landslide. "What is it?"

"It's about how we should trip. Or really, how you should trip."

"The pills. You've been using them. It's fast, easy. That's what we're doing, right?" I confirm. Sam gestures for me to sit down, but I shake my head and rub my hands over my arms. "Just say it. How?"

Sam has trouble answering, so it's Costa who walks to me. "We need you at your strongest, your most reactive."

I understand now why they both appear hesitant. "Blood," I say. "You need me to bleed."

"I'm so sorry, but yes," Costa confirms. "Blood is your trigger. Without it, the death tripper in you is less responsive. With it, you'll trip harder, and you'll pass that to Sam. Based on the little we know, this is the smartest approach. We think…"

"It's okay. It's fine." I think they're right, but my voice is shaking horrifically, and there's no way I can conceal my fear. Again though, underneath this is a fervent ache to get what my body is screaming for. I'm desperate to see blood. "How? Just say it. I can't do it myself. You know that. I don't have the willpower."

"Knife or gun is the easiest. We need it to take a little time though, so neither can be instantaneous. You pick," Costa says.

"Sam? Which one?" My heartbeat must be visible through my shirt. "You're going to do it, right? You choose. I can't. I don't know."

"Stella…"

"You are going to do it, aren't you?" I demand.

Costa touches my arm. "I am."

"What? No, no. Sam should. I want Sam to do it." There's growing panic now that I'm in the moment.

"You'll trip harder if I do it because I tripped you first. That's the theory we're going on."

Shit, he's probably right. I swallow hard. "Then, use a knife. That's how you did it last time."

Costa nods. "Don't forget. It's going to feel good. I know you're freaked, but remember that. Neck again?"

Sam jumps in. "I don't think that's necessary, do you? It's a little more grotesque than we need."

"Fair enough." Costa shrugs. "I like a good neck slice but whatever. Up to you guys."

"How about you ease up on the crassness?" Sam is controlling his irritation.

"Let's do it now," I say calmly. "Sitting around and thinking about it won't help me. Let's do it now."

"You want me to do you, too, Sammy?"

It's with good hesitation, but Sam shakes his head. "I got this."

Although he just said no to Costa, I can tell he was tempted to let Costa knife him. Sam throws another log on the fire and turns off the lights.

Sam guides me to the couch and stretches out so that he's leaning against the arm with one foot on the floor. He pats the seat in front of him. "Sit."

But I can't move from my spot.

"Sit. Lean back against me. I'll hold you."

Now a spark is in his eyes, a charge from what we're about to do, and it passes to me. The thought of the blood—and that fuzzy, euphoric state I'm going to have—lures me to lie down between his legs and rest my back on his chest. He runs a hand through my hair and kisses my cheek. He's already sounding drugged because he knows even better than I do what's coming.

This is death-tripping foreplay.

Costa takes a knife from the mantel and pulls it from the sheath. When he kneels on the floor between my legs, I put my hand on top of Sam's, and he moves our touch over my waist.

"You first, Sam?" Costa asks.

Wordlessly, Sam takes the knife. "Don't look, Stell. I don't want you to see."

Instinctively, I turn to watch, but Costa puts a hand on the side of my head. "He said, don't look. Just focus on me, and let Sam do what he needs to do. Breathe, breathe…in and out."

Under me, I feel Sam's body arch as he pushes the knife into his side.

"Sam…" Even in my lust for this moment, I can't help my worry.

"Sam is fine." Costa's deep blue eyes haven't left me. "He's more than fine. Keep looking at me. There you go. Good."

Sam's body shifts again as he moves the knife, and his arm tightens around me when he grunts. "Inhale," he tells me.

So, I do. The smell of blood is intoxicating. Fumes invade my throat and lungs, and for a moment, I can barely keep my eyes open as the rush hits me.

"She's good, Sammy. Don't worry." Costa's arm moves in. "I'm going to take the knife, okay?"

"Yes." Sam's breath practically burns my skin.

Costa's hand is still on my face when he leans in to Sam, and he turns me to the side so that I can watch now. As his mouth touches Sam's, he starts to glide the knife out. Costa runs his tongue over Sam's lips, and I inhale again, torn between watching their kiss and watching the knife being pulled from Sam's body.

"Your turn, Stella." Costa's voice is so soothing, yet I realize that I'm closer to panting than slow breathing.

Costa kneels again. His hand is on the side of my jaw, and he traces his thumb over my lips. "Just keep looking at me."

His eyes are dark, glimmering, and it's easy for me to stay fixated on them. I feel Sam's hands move to the hem of my shirt, and he raises it, exposing my stomach. In my fog, I see Costa undo the top button of my pants and lower the zipper just a few inches so that he can tuck the corner under. The knife is still in his hand, and colors from the fireplace flash in the metal. I push Sam's hands higher under my shirt until he has my breasts in his hands.

"Costa, please," I hear myself say. "Please do it."

"Whatever you want, pretty girl." His gaze travels over me, cradled in Sam's arms. "The three of us again…"

Two fingers stroke my lips and then slip into my mouth just as his body thrusts a few inches toward me. The knife goes into my abdomen, and I moan sharply and suck as his fingers move in and out.

"Good girl," Costa breathes. He takes his wet fingers from me and covers Sam's hand with his, their hold tightening around my breast.

"Again," I murmur. The knife is still inside me, but it's not enough.

"You're just like me, aren't you? Always wanting more." He checks with Sam though. "You want to go first? Easier to catch her when she trips?" He waits until Sam can speak.

"Yeah. Not yet though." Sam breathes hard for a moment.

"It's good today, isn't it, Sammy?"

"Yes."

"Sometimes," Costa says, looking at me, "the longer it takes, the deeper you can go under. And you look like you're just fine taking your time."

I can hardly see, but I drop my hand to the side and soak myself with Sam's blood. "More. Do it again."

Costa gives me a wry smile. Then, just a hint, he jiggles the knife a fraction inside me. "Like that?"

Every nerve reacts with gratification to the movement, and I would do anything to stay like this forever. The sensation is beyond provocative, beyond just sexual. It's everything.

"You really do have a thing for this, don't you?" he coos. "Being with you makes this so much better for Sam. I've never seen him enjoy it this much. And I don't know that I've ever enjoyed it this much either."

Costa presses his lips together, and with two hands, he rips the knife from my stomach, immediately plunging it into his own stomach. His focus stays on me, and I'm further intoxicated by the mix of heat and death on his face. He doesn't make a sound, even when he moves the blade back and forth the way he did for me. He blows me a kiss and takes it out, blood beginning to stain his shirt, beautifully soaking into the fabric.

"Oh God…" He braces himself on the couch as the rush overtakes him.

As though he can read my thoughts, he raises his shirt a bit. Then, he takes my hand and presses it to him so that I feel his blood. It's like velvet—so thick, so soft. Slowly, I rub my hand over his abdomen, coloring his skin. He gives me time to explore the shape of him, the brilliance of the red, the feel of the thick liquid.

When my charge level has left me breathless and nearly blind, he speaks softly, "Sam's ready. Are you?"

"Yes, Costa," I hear myself talking, but I'm not sure how I'm making it happen. "I want to go under now."

Costa moves my arm out of the way and angles his body over Sam and me in an embrace. "Go get my kid, Sammy."

"With everything I have," Sam gets out.

Costa drives the knife into Sam one final time, and when the love of my whole world stops breathing, the taste of his death pours into me.

Costa whispers, "He'll be right there when you go. Don't be afraid of the dark. You're not alone."

"I know…" I want that knife back. Now.

Costa touches his lips to mine. "Make Sam see." He gently kisses me, and just as his tongue eases into my mouth, the knife enters my side. He shakes it inside me, sending vibrations through my entire body, as he presses his tongue deeper into my mouth.

And then, the darkness comes.

It's such a fast transition. The pleasurable experience is taken from me as I'm tossed into the heavy gel of the underworld. Immediately, Sam has me against him though, so there's no time for any panic to set in. Slowly, I lift my head. He looks at me, and I'm able to move enough to indicate that I'm all right. I want him to do what he needs to do. I let myself float in his arms while he scans. I watch him and wait.

It's exhausting for me to narrow my thoughts, but I fill my mind with the idea of vision and truth—and of Toby. I think about the pictures I've seen of him, the way Costa has his own childlike side that tugs at my soul and makes me know what a wonderful father he must have been. And could be again. I think about how Costa and I both have parents who disastrously failed us and how he would never do that to Toby. He's done so much already for the sake of his son. Despite his flaws, Costa is deserving, and he should be with his son.

It's then that Costa shoots into my sight. Unlike the last time I saw him under after he first tripped me, his eyes are clear. He touches a hand to Sam. Even in the haze of the dark world, I can see their shared determination.

Sam repositions me so that we are holding on to each other's wrists, and he can maneuver more easily. The under substance we are in is pressing against my body, making me claustrophobic, even as Sam is able to fluidly guide us. While I know that I'm here to augment Sam's vision power, I nonetheless feel utterly useless, like a weight that is slowing him down.

Time is again elusive, but I try not to worry about how long we've been under. This is not about my discomfort at all, so I'm more than willing to swallow this disorientation and unpleasantness. Costa takes my other hand to ease some of Sam's hindrance. Flashes of glittery light splash before my eyes for a moment.

He's my tripper, I think. *No wonder I react to him when I'm under.*

There is a brief moment in which he appears to get a wash of death-tripping pleasure from our touch as well, and his body nearly spasms, but he's able to shake it off.

Sam notices both of our responses, but he doesn't stop moving.

There's the occasional flash of lighter area as we traverse territory. While it's hard to understand distance, based on the stream of pressure that travels over my skin, it feels to be significant. Sam occasionally slows us to a stop and then darts us in another direction.

He's hunting, I think.

I grow increasingly concerned when he winces and turns away, so I again direct my energy to him. I close my eyes because the dark and the totally unsettling sensory experience here might be interfering.

There comes a point when I start to ache. At first, it's only minimal hurt, a feeling of soreness. But then later, after we've explored for what I assess to be hours and hours, a cold deep pain reaches into my bones. I feel as though I'm being drained, that my insides are turning into liquid ice and being sucked from my body. The silence under here is not my friend, but I'm happy that Costa and Sam cannot hear what I would vocalize.

With hope, I use what's left of my strength to angle my head through the current so that I can see Sam, but there's no sign that he is any closer. My eyes close again, and I no longer have the ability to straighten my thoughts or to control where they go. I need to sleep. I need the pain to stop. I need to vanish. The physical and emotional emptiness inside me becomes more than I can fight off, and I black out.

I regain consciousness to the sound of stone smashing apart as the three of us crash to the surface. Broken concrete and patio tile fall around me, and I cough repeatedly and try to take in air. There is more noise when the shattered material reforms and rebuilds the solid surface below us. I roll onto my stomach and continue coughing deeply, saliva accumulating in my mouth, until I am drooling onto fresh tile. I desperately need water, but then I remember what's happening. I push up onto my knees and look around. It's still night, but the outside lights are on, so I can see Costa wobbling to a stand and Sam on all fours with his head on the ground. I keep looking.

Oh God, there's no one else.

"Sam?" I'm raspy and raw, probably barely audible. "Sam?"

He lifts his head. I don't have to ask because I know the answer.

He didn't find Toby.

I crawl to Costa. My body is yearning for food and human contact, but I push hard against my surge impulses. They'll have to wait. When I reach him, I wrap my body over his and feel his sobbing penetrate through me.

"I'm so sorry."

Nothing but devastation is coming from him. He keeps his arms over his face, and his fingers wad tightly in his hair as he comes undone. Sam lies down on his side in front of Costa and puts an arm around him so that our friend is sandwiched between us in whatever comfort we can offer.

"I looked everywhere. I promise you. I looked until I couldn't anymore. Costa, there was no sign of him."

Costa lets out such an anguished wail that my heart threatens to never recover. Any sense of surge dissipates immediately, and I can tell from the way Sam is holding himself that his has, too.

A surge, it seems, cannot survive such grief.

I ease away from the boys and let them hold each other. This is, in many ways, pain that they share alone. I get myself inside and to the kitchen sink where I vomit and then run my face under water. I drink from the tap, but even under the noise of the faucet, I can hear Costa's cries. I really believed that we would find Toby. I did. I turn off the water and see that Costa is now standing. He shoves Sam hard enough to send him flying back a few feet, so I rush back outside.

Costa is unglued and hysterical. "He's dead! Toby is dead!" This isn't a surge. It's just raw agony. He lunges again, pounding his fists into Sam's chest. "It's happening all over. Oh God, I don't want to do this. Sammy, make it stop! I'll do anything. Just make it stop!"

Sam tries to grab him, but he has his own tears to compete with now. "I know. I'm so sorry. I'm so sorry. You're going to get through this, Costa. I'm here. Stella is here."

Suddenly, Costa stops and goes silent just for a moment. "I'm not living like this, not anymore. I don't want to be here. I don't want to be here. I won't do it."

"You don't have a choice, brother." Sam is as destroyed as Costa, but somehow, he is able to hold it together for his friend. "You *will* find a way. You will."

"I need to be alone," Costa says flatly. Then, he looks at me. "Thank you both. For everything. I just need to be alone."

"Of course." Sam hesitates, but then he walks to me.

We go through the glass door to the living room and leave Costa.

I put myself in Sam's arms. "This is my fault, isn't it? Something happened to me down there, and I couldn't hang on. Did you surface because of me? Maybe you could have kept going. Toby might be there. If you had more time—"

"No." Sam is firm. "No. I took us everywhere I could see, and he wasn't there. No sign of him at all, Stella. It's like a fucking maze there. No way to tell where you are really. No landmarks. Just space."

"But you surfaced us back here, so that means you know how to find some things."

"This is home. It's like a beacon. Same with the house in Watermark." I know by his flat tone that he's numb, in the same shock that I am that we failed. "It can be harder to find other locations sometimes, but you almost always know how to go home." Sam puts his face against my shoulder and wets my shirt with his tears.

"Sam…"

Costa is pacing outside. Something more is going on, something more than him just needing to be alone.

"Sam," I say more loudly.

"Yeah?"

Costa sees me looking at him, and he meets my eyes. There is apology and desperation in them.

"No," I whisper. "Costa, no!"

In slow motion, he moves like a panther, stealthy and silent, for the few yards it takes to reach the table by the grill.

"No!" I scream as I start running.

Sam follows me outside, but Costa has doused himself in lighter fluid before either of us can reach him, and there's a stick lighter in his hand. I make a move toward him, but Sam grabs me by my shirt and pulls me back. He knows we can't stop Costa from doing what he wants. He's too fast. Just a flick of that lighter is all it will take.

"No. Costa, no!" I do what I can to control my tone so that I don't sound as terrified as I feel.

"I'll just keep tripping," he says simply. "It's the only way to stay out of this world. I'll death-trip forever and never come out of it. I can't live like this. It's *not* living, so I'll just keep dying."

"I'm begging you not to do this," Sam says tearfully. "Please don't. It's not the answer. Stay with us."

"It's the only answer." There's a fraction of a pause. "Shitting rainbows, right, Stella?" Costa clicks the lighter and touches it to his shirt. Immediately, he ignites in a roar of fire.

Sam grabs me and hides me against his body. His hands move to my ears so that I won't hear the crackling of the flames or the yowl of defeat that Costa releases.

But I can still smell the burning flesh and taste the heartache.

THIRTY-THREE
olive juice

SAM AND I ARE STILL WAITING FOR COSTA TO SURFACE. We've been huddled under a blanket by the fireplace, drifting in and out of fitful sleeps throughout the night and into the late afternoon the following day. The sky matches our mood, and I frown at the steel clouds looming over us.

"He's been under a long time," I say.

"Yeah. He's good at controlling that. He can trip and stay down for hours if he wants. And that's what he wants right now. He's always been good with control," Sam says. "He's going to surface and trip again."

"We have to stop him."

"I don't know how. He'll be impossible to catch, and I can't think of anything to say that will get him to stop. Who would blame him for what he's doing? Cycling death trips is his only escape right now. If we're lucky, one of these times, he'll surface too drained to go again, and we can get him. But that could be weeks from now. He's being fueled by a lot right now, and that could power him through."

"What are we supposed to do if we catch him? Tie him down? Make this hurt less?"

Sam sighs. "I don't know. Maybe he won't come back. He can surface anywhere he chooses, and he might not want to see us."

He gets up and adds another log to the fire. Both of us are chilled to the core. He turns and looks at the table that is covered in things for Toby.

"I'll get those," I say quickly.

Sam doesn't need to see these toys and clothes any more than Costa does when—or if—he gets back.

"We haven't eaten since yesterday, and we have to take care of ourselves so that we can help Costa when he's ready. Let's get showered, and then I'll start something for dinner, okay?"

"Sure. You're right."

Our moods remain glum, but showering off the trip at least cleans us up. We both were saturated in the smell of death and tragedy.

I play music over the built-in speakers while I put together homemade macaroni and cheese and bacon-wrapped meatloaf. Comfort food seems in order, and it's abnormally cold this evening, so I hope a hot meal will help restore even a fraction of stability. Plus, I need something normal—and human—to do. Our conversation is either stilted or nonexistent while I cook because there is too much to say and also nothing to say. We let the music fill the space for us.

When everything is in the oven, I start to wipe down the counters and set the table. There are only two settings tonight, and we both feel the weight of the absence. The triangle that is Costa, Sam, and me is complex. There's no denying that. But Costa is important to both of us. Even when he's difficult or manipulative or exploitative, that dark prince has our hearts. I debate telling Sam about Costa's kiss, but I decide that death tripping is pretty much Vegas, and what happens during a trip or surge stays there.

The three of us came here with a goal, and we failed. Perhaps we never should have tried because the letdown has been too great. I'm not sure that Costa will ever recover from what feels like his child's second death. The pain and destruction is fresh again, and while Sam is being as stoic as possible, I know that he's being swallowed by waves of guilt all over. He's suffered enough for the negligence that caused Toby's death.

Because I understand the almost overpowering attraction that death tripping has, it's all too easy to imagine getting so swept up in it that the real world would cease to exist. It explains how Sam could have been so out of it that he'd forgotten about Toby. Sam, more responsible and solid than Costa and I put together, even fell victim to the ferocious pull of death tripping.

I make a big salad and check the oven. "Do you, um…do you know what power you have now?" I ask. It's a stupid question, given what we've just gone through, but it's a start at conversation.

Sam takes glasses down from a high cabinet and starts to shake up martinis. A little of our favorite hard liquor couldn't hurt right now. "I don't think I have one. You know how we didn't surge earlier? I think that stopped me from getting a power. Neither has ever happened before, but it's the only explanation I can come up with. I didn't realize my powers were connected to the surges that way. So, we learned something. Great." The ice crashes around in the tumbler as he chills the vodka.

I hand him a jar of olives from the fridge. "You going to be okay, Bishop?"

"Eventually." He fills the glasses and adds olive juice.

I lift my glass to my mouth and then spill half of it when there's a resounding knock at the door. I look to Sam. "Expecting anyone?"

"Nope. Who the hell could that be?" He's cautious as he walks to the front door, and he even looks around the house and through the windows to the back patio. "Wait here."

I watch from my spot in the kitchen as he peers through the peephole. He pulls back and then looks again. "You're not going to believe this."

"Costa? Why is he knocking?"

Sam shakes his head and opens the door. "No. Not Costa. But I have a guess who this is."

He steps aside, and I'm astounded.

My sister walks through the threshold, looking more ragged and worn than ever. Amy is rail thin—gaunt really—and probably hasn't showered in days. Her blonde curls have turned into a mass of frizz that she's gathered in an unruly knot at the nape of her neck, and her sweatshirt and jeans hang on her body. Her eyes are unfocused, but she peers in my direction. "I don't feel so good."

Sam catches her just as her legs give out.

"Amy!" I rush over and help Sam get her to the couch by the fire.

He pulls a blanket over her to quell her shaking and then pokes the fire to get it going again.

"What are you doing here?" I ask.

"I'm sorry I hung up on you."

"It's okay. It's okay." I hug her and nearly cry at how thin she is. "How did you get here?"

"Flew to Boston. Rented a car and drove to Watermark." She looks to Sam. "You must be Sam. Met your mom. She's real nice."

Sam is as confused as I am, but he gives her a smile. "She is nice. She told you where to find Stella?" he prompts.

Amy nods. "Yeah. Sorry I hung up on you. Did I already say that?"

I pat her arm. "That's all right."

"Death trippers, you said. That's what we are?" She's incredibly out of it.

"Yes."

"Did Dad do this to you also?" she asks.

I wipe a smudge of God-knows-what from her face. "No. It's a long story, but I'll explain later. You need to eat and sleep. Sam, do you mind pulling the food out of the oven? It should be done now."

"Of course. I'll make up a plate." He squeezes my shoulder as he walks past.

"Are you able to eat, or are you sick to your stomach?" I ask.

Amy looks grotesque, and I want nothing more than to nurture her and put her back together. I want to restore this fragile woman to the ferociously loving and protective older sister that she used to be.

"I'm okay now. Threw up on the plane a bunch, so that was cool." She smiles just enough that I feel slightly better. "Do you…get like this, too? Sick?"

"I've only tripped twice, but yeah. I'm guessing that you've been going a lot."

"Yeah. But it's been five days since…wait, maybe four…since I *death-tripped*." She laughs lightly. "Funny to have words for it now."

"I'm so glad you're here. We're going to take care of you." I pull her against me.

I'm beyond relieved that she's here but equally worried. For now, I'm going to concentrate on getting her healthy and on the fact that my sister—or whatever is left of her—has come back to me.

"Where's…where's Costa?" It seems to be taking all her energy to talk.

"He's not here. Not sure when he'll be back. Like I said, there's a lot to tell you."

We get her to eat two plates of food, and then Sam carries her upstairs so that I can help her in the shower. She's still too weak to do much for herself, and I'm amazed that she got herself here in one piece. I can only imagine what Felicia thought when my mess of a sister showed up at the inn. I'm *really* going to have to call Felicia now.

Sam asks for Amy's car keys because it turns out that she parked on top of what used to be a large shrub.

I tuck her into bed in one of the plush guest rooms, and seeing her cleaned up and in flannel pajamas under a puffy comforter makes me feel as though I've accomplished something tangible. Amy falls asleep immediately, but I can't bring myself to leave her. I get under the covers and wrap my arms around her.

Later, in her sleep, she hugs me back.

The light of day, however, brings a standoffish Amy. She clomps down the stairs and brushes past me when I go to her. "Do you have any cereal?" Her appearance is slightly less frightful, but her foul mood clouds the room.

"Actually, Sam made pancakes."

She sighs. "Fine."

"With fresh Maine blueberries. You'll like them." I try to sound cheery, but I give Sam a confused expression.

She takes a plate of food that Sam assembled for her and sits at the table.

I bravely join her with my coffee.

"Let's get this out of the way," she says between mouthfuls. At least she's eating.

"Get what out of the way?"

"Tell me what you know. About all this." She waves a fork around. "This death tripping."

I explain what I can with Sam jumping in to help me when I falter. While Amy refuses to look at me, she does seem to be listening. I tell her about Costa tripping Sam and then me and what he relayed to us about the day of the accident.

"I heard Dad in your room, apologizing. He said he didn't know what to do."

Amy slaps her fork against her plate, and I jump. "He should have let me die! That's what he should have done."

I'm too shaken to respond, but Sam pulls out a chair and sits next to her. "Costa said the same thing. I know how that feels. And you're sick right now, so that makes everything worse. You've been tripping your ass off, huh? You've been surging hard, too?"

"Surging?"

"What happens after you surface."

He explains the layers of it, and Amy eventually turns her head slightly in his direction.

"Yes," she finally says. "I surge hard."

"You're addicted," he offers.

"I can stop the surge if I want. I just choose not to," she says rather proudly.

"What do you mean, you can stop it?" he asks. So far, the only thing that's prevented us from surging was the aftermath of not finding Toby.

Amy wipes her mouth with the back of her hand. "Watermelon."

"I'm sorry. What?" Sam looks beyond confused.

"Watermelon. Stops all the craziness. I came back one time and went to a bar. I don't know about you guys, but I need to get laid when I come back. When I *surface.* It's so crazy to finally have a word for it. Anyway, I went to a bar and ordered a watermelon cosmopolitan." She moves a finger across her throat. "Cuts it off in a second. Totally sucked. But I keep it on hand if I have a shitty trip."

Sam laughs. "Seriously? Watermelon?"

"Yep. The imitation stuff works a little, too, if you're desperate or if you just want to tone it down. You know, watermelon-flavored water or even gum at least takes the edge off."

I have to smile. I remember the watermelon-flavored water that I found in her bedroom at the condo when I thought she overdosed. Everything about that day now makes sense, even down to the trash in her apartment.

"Now, tell me more about these powers you get. I don't have that—at least not that I know of. And Stella is your what? Generator?"

I roll my eyes. "*Power augmenter*, not generator."

"Whatever. Are all women power augmenters? We don't get powers? That blows. So, am I a power augmenter?"

Sam shrugs. "No idea."

Amy studies him. "Maybe I could try augmenting your powers, Sam? What do you say we give it a try?"

I don't like the way she's eyeing him. "It doesn't work that way." I drink the last of my coffee and loudly set my cup down. "Also, screw you."

Sam shoots me a look that tells me to leave it alone. Amy is not a threat.

"We don't exactly have a huge population of death trippers to interview. You and Stella are the only female death trippers we know. Costa and I are the only males, except for your missing father. You can't find him anywhere?"

"No. He's totally off the grid, which is good. I don't ever want to see him again." She's finished her pancakes, and she goes to the kitchen to help herself to more. "I want to know where Costa is." She's more solemn now.

"He's tripping. And we don't know when he'll be back." Sam goes to her and takes the pancake that she's eating from her hand, puts it on the plate, and directs her back to the table.

I smile. He's much better at dealing with her detoxing behavior than I am.

"Costa is binge-tripping because..." Sam hesitates. "It's a longer story that he can tell you if he wants. We're not sure we'll be able to get him to stop."

"He was there with me that first time. I need to see him. I've been waiting years."

"So, you'll wait here with us," I say. And since we're playing Twenty Questions, I ask her, "Why did you leave Chicago? For Costa?"

Amy blanches slightly and takes her time answering. "The only person keeping me in Chicago disappeared, so I left."

"Who do you mean? Mom?"

"Ugh, no."

"You two were glued at the hip," I say with irritation. "Don't act like you weren't."

Suddenly, Amy takes her plate and flings it across the room, shattering it against the wall. She kicks back her chair and stands up, slamming her hands on the table and leaning over to me. Sam and I are both speechless, but I can tell that he's ready to restrain her if necessary.

My sister looks me dead in the eyes. "We both know that I'm fucking crazy, but I never loved our mother. Don't you dare imply that I did. Just because I took whatever she gave me doesn't mean that I gave a shit about her. She was a monster. Dad threw us to the wolves when he tripped me and ran out of town. I didn't even tell her I was leaving when I blew out of town. So, don't look at me with that fucking accusatory face, Stella. You got off easy. I would have left ages ago, but I had to stay!"

"Had to stay for *what*? It certainly wasn't for me. I lost you, too, after that trip." I hold her stare. "Who was keeping you in Chicago?"

She backs off and goes to the window. "It doesn't matter. He's gone."

Great. A guy. I can only imagine what kind of dysfunctional moron she got herself involved with.

"Go clean up the mess you made." Sam breaks this up calmly. "You're an addict who's drying out, and you're being obnoxious. You're scared, and you've been alone in this for way too long. Now, you're not. At some point, you'll get that, but until then, watch yourself. This is my house, and I'll kick you out if I have to."

Amy's face crumples, and she breaks down. "I'm sorry. I'm really…sorry. I don't know who I am or what's been happening to me."

I let Sam go to her because she seems to respond better to him. I don't like it, but it's true.

He puts an arm around her and lets her cry. "You need to get clean. It'll be easier then."

"He's been gone too long." She is in hysterics now. "I lost him, and I haven't been able to get him back. I tried so hard. I don't know why he left."

I don't know if she's talking about Dad or Costa or this boyfriend of hers, but she's very agitated. Despite years of being mistreated by my sister, I understand it all in a new context. In some ways, Amy's responsible for her behavior, but in so many ways, she's not. I can't imagine how frightening and isolating her experience has been. I've got Sam, and I've still felt terrified. It's no wonder she thinks she's crazy.

"Amy." I try to break through her crying. "Amy, it's going to be okay. We can figure all of this out. It's just going to take a little time."

From Sam's arms, she nods. I take a few steps in her direction, and she goes from him to me. I can feel that, to at least some degree, she's letting me in. Our reunion, however, is cut short when the wall next to us blasts open, and we are thrown to the floor.

Costa's back.

Plaster dust coats his body, and he charges past us. I'm not even sure that he can see through his storm. Amy is shaking in my arms, and I realize that she's never seen anyone surface before. Costa heads to the stairs, and I yell Sam's name.

I know what's in Costa's room.

I push Amy behind me. "Stop him!"

Sam is already halfway across the room, and when he gets close, Costa spins and clocks Sam across the side of the head, delivering a blow that gives Sam pause.

"Costa, no!" I scramble to my feet and go after him.

Sam manages to shake off the hit to the head, and together, he and I are able to get a hold of Costa, and we struggle to pull him back downstairs. His surge has made him stronger than I was prepared for.

With garbled speech, he says, "My gun. Where's my gun?"

"No guns. No. You're not doing this." Sam gets an arm around Costa's neck and pulls him back.

"Give me my gun now!"

Costa is in a rage like I've never seen, and I barely recognize him. The anguished screams and moans from earlier return, and I cannot bear to hear him in this kind of pain.

"I'm gonna blow my *fucking* brains out!"

He lifts his legs in an attempt to tighten Sam's hold around his neck and cut off his own air, and Sam is forced to lower him to the floor although he keeps his grip tight. Sam stays like this until some of the fight and tears recede.

From her spot on the floor, Amy's voice shakes. "Costa?"

He opens his eyes.

"It's me. Amy." Slowly, she gets up and crosses the room until she is in front of him.

Because Costa has relaxed his body enough, Sam tentatively takes his arm away. Costa rises to a stand, his face fraught with emotion.

Amy and Costa step into each other and embrace, each silent and each reeling in the unspoken exchange flowing between them over the shared history of horror only they can understand.

THIRTY-FOUR
watermelon

AMY'S PRESENCE IS THE ONLY THING that stops Costa from tripping again. The bond between them is like nothing I've seen before, an instantaneous reconnection that has left little room for Sam or me. They are in the hammock that swings offside the patio right now, lying together side by side, their legs entwined and their eyes locked.

From the pieces of conversation that I overhear, a mutual hatred for my father is certainly part of their tie. I also hear bits of their whispered words about the accident and first trip. It's something that neither will talk about much to anyone else. I suppose there's a degree of privacy around that trauma that is theirs alone.

I want more than anything to have a complete family, one with parents and a sister whom I love and who love me. Instead, I have what I have. Resenting them all is a drain though. I do love Amy, but we are not without our troubles even though we're together again. I can't forget how awful she's been to me since our father left. Understanding the reasons doesn't erase the past. My parents though? My relationship with both of them is too fractured, and I don't want to see either of them again. Ever. Even if my father had answers about death tripping, I don't want those answers from him. We can survive on our own.

You don't leave your children—no matter what.

"Stella, can you grab my phone for me?" Costa calls from the hammock. "I want to show Amy a picture of Toby. I can't believe I haven't done that already."

"Sure." I get up from the lounge chair and go inside to retrieve his phone.

Being with Amy has brought him some degree of peace. Costa has told Amy everything about Toby, but he's done most of it out of earshot. I assume it's out of respect for Sam. I can't pinpoint how exactly, but for the past two days, Costa has been more stable than I would have imagined, considering his earlier blowup. I wouldn't say that he's *happy* exactly, but he's…thoughtful, serene. I'm jealous, I suppose. I don't love that I feel this way, but it's tough to watch Amy be so drawn to Costa—and, if I'm honest, him to her. It's petty, considering the much larger issues, so I've been trying to brush it off.

I take it as a good sign though that he's talking about Toby. He's said nothing to Sam or me about his son or our unsuccessful trip since he's come back, but something about connecting with Amy is making him comfortable. It's also the first time since we were young that I've seen the caretaking, nurturing side of her come out. The way she asks him for details about Toby as a baby, how she takes Costa's hand when he struggles to share—she's mothering him as she used to mother me.

When I hand him his phone, Costa is recounting stories about Toby's first words and first steps. "He called me *Dah-yee*, which was pretty awesome."

I see Sam smile from his chair next to me, but he doesn't look up from his book.

"Hey, Sammy!" Costa says as he rolls out of the hammock. "Remember what Toby called you?"

Sam's smile grows bigger. "Of course I do. *Ish*."

I laugh. "For Bishop? I thought I was the only person who called you that."

"He used to screech every time he saw Sam. *Ish*! *Ish*!" Costa holds out his hand to Amy and helps her from the hammock. "See how cute he was?"

Amy's hair is finally less unkempt, and she has nice color in her face again. I haven't seen her looking this good in years.

"So, let me see the pictures!" she demands teasingly, grabbing his phone.

It only takes a second for her to react. Her face freezes. Amy begins scrolling through photos until tears are rolling down her cheeks. None of us seem to know what to make of this. She is visibly shaking.

"Amy, what is it?" I walk to her.

She lowers the phone and looks at Costa. "This is Toby? This is your son?"

He nods, confused.

A mix of joy and disbelief blows over her face. "I *know* him."

Costa freezes. "You what?"

"I…*I know him*." Her voice breaks. "I've been watching him for months and months, over a year."

"Watching him? How?" I ask. "Oh my God, Amy. You mean, you've been watching him when you're under?"

She nods as the enormity of this sinks in. "He was why I couldn't leave Chicago."

"And he was why you were tripping so much, wasn't he?" I offer.

Amy grabs a stunned Costa by the arm. "Costa, Toby is not dead. He's not! I haven't seen him in a month though, and I thought he was gone. I tried to surface him, but I couldn't. We just hit a barrier, and I couldn't get him up with me. I'd stay under for as long as I could so that he wouldn't be alone." Amy's words tumble out of her so quickly that I can hardly understand her. "I used to be able to find him so easily. He was always there, and I'd…I'd hold him and twirl him around. We'd play Patty Cake and Peek-a-Boo. I always wanted to hear his laugh because I could see him giggle so hard. He has huge dark eyes, blue, just like you do. I…I should have known it the minute I saw you. And his hair is jet-black, like yours. He's wearing a brown outfit, a one-piece thing."

Costa is visibly trembling. "On the feet are—"

"Are bear claws." Amy is nodding and wiping her face. "It's a bear outfit with a little tail on the back."

"I have the matching hat with ears." He looks to Sam and me. "Is this…possible? Is it?" He's too scared to trust that this could be true.

After failing to find Toby the other day, I can only imagine how fragile Costa is right now. The possibility that Toby really is accessible feels like more than he can stand to hope for.

Sam puts his hands through his hair. He's as daunted and surprised by this idea as anyone. "I don't know…I mean…yes, yes, it's possible. In our world, anything is. Amy's been with him."

"Of course I've been with him!" She flashes anger. She's still edgy with Sam and me. "You believe me, don't you? I wouldn't make this up. Costa, I wouldn't do that to you."

Sam speaks evenly, "I didn't suggest that you made anything up. You need to relax and give us a moment here."

Costa is pacing back and forth, agitated and daring to believe this. "But where did he go? Why did he leave her? Why…why was he with her in the first place?" He turns to Amy. "*Why* was he with you?"

"I don't know. I have no idea. He's the only other person I've seen while tripping."

Something is tugging at my brain, and I run through what I know. All of death tripping seems to have meaning. It's based on emotions. That would be true for Toby also.

"Sam…"

Everyone is talking now, animated, and trying to piece together this story.

"Sam!"

"What? What is it?"

"You said it the other day…" The idea is pulling together for me.

He shakes his head. "Said what?"

"Home," I say, smiling. "Home is a beacon. You can always find your way home when you're under even if you're otherwise lost."

His face lights up. "Yes. Home." He looks at Costa. "Toby drifted from here to Chicago because that's where you were tripped. It's a birthplace, a home of sorts, for you. And Amy is part of you because of your first trip, so she is a home also. After you died, Costa, you left the state. Toby wouldn't have been able to seek you out because…" Sam struggles to figure this out. "Because his father wasn't home. Eventually, he tried another home associated with his dad. That was where Amy was. It's not just a location, but Amy must…smell of Costa in some way. They've got the same…trip residue."

"So, where is he now?" Amy asks. "Why did he leave me?"

"Because Costa's been tripping in Maine again and trying to find him. Toby must sense that. He was pulled between Chicago and Maine, between you and Costa. He's trying to find you, Costa. He's trying to find his dad."

I'm nearly bursting now. "Do you see? With you and Amy here, you'll be the brightest beacon for him. We can find him."

Costa's eyes go to Sam, his best friend and someone he depends on and trusts more than anyone in the world. "Sammy?"

"We can find him," Sam says with conviction. "We can. I can get vision again. I'm sure."

Amy nods. "Good. You'll need it. Toby can be a little skittish, and he's fast."

My spirits are lifting quickly. "So, if the four of us trip together, we'll have the best chance. I trip so that Sam has stronger vision, and you and Costa will be there to draw Toby out, right?"

"Exactly." Amy is breathless. "Costa, you can surface him, right?"

We all grow silent, but Costa finally answers her, "Sam has to surface him."

"Oh. Okay." At least she has enough tact not to say anything else.

Costa obviously hasn't detailed Toby's death as much as I thought, and I feel for Sam. He looks horribly uncomfortable in what is otherwise a moment charged with positivity. He starts to say something, but he stops himself.

Amy continues, "Anyway, like I said, Toby can be skittish, sensitive. He was always more likely to come to me easily if I'd tripped in a…I don't know…in the right mood. Calmly. Like, right now? Right now, we're all too fired up. It'd freak him out. We have to be slow and steady about this trip."

Sam agrees, "She's got a good point. That plays into the emotion of death tripping. We have to bring the right energy. And there's another thing—the beacon. The idea of location is important." His hesitation is obvious. "We need to go into the lake, to the exact spot."

Immediately, Costa nods. "Smart. Kids are literal. Their thinking is primitive, especially for a kid as little as Toby. That's the last place he was in Maine. He'll be willing to come here. There's trust."

I can see how he is fighting to remain logical, but his hope and anticipation are bubbling barely below the surface.

"Is he…Amy, is he older now? Did he grow?"

"It doesn't seem like it to me. He looks like he did in that last picture I saw. I don't think he's aged at all."

"Did he look okay to you? Did he cry a lot? Was he scared?"

"Oh, Costa, no. He's great. Smiled a lot. Slept in my arms. I'd let him nap. And sometimes, he would grab my hair and laugh. I wish I could have heard his laugh because it looked like it'd be so sweet. He's just wonderful."

Sam is fascinated. "So, somehow, he adapted to living under, huh? It's pretty amazing how resilient kids are."

"I need…to sit down," Costa says. He suddenly looks faint, and Sam walks him to a chair. "The thought of him down there with no one…God, until you. Thank God for you, Amy. You took care of my son. I'll never be able to thank you…this is a lot. This is all possible? This could be real? I can't hope again, not after last time when I was so sure."

Amy kneels in front of him. "Toby is under. I've spent many months with him, and he's real."

Costa holds back tears. "I'm scared."

"Stay calm," she says. "Toby needs that."

"Okay." He pushes a smile through his worry. "We're gonna need a lot of watermelon."

Sam ruffles Costa's hair. "I'm gonna buy every watermelon I can find."

THIRTY-FIVE
just keep swimming

SAM WAS INSISTENT that we wait until the next day to trip in search of Toby. All of us were too nervous and heightened in every way, and there was no way that would be conducive to a strategic search. He also felt that a night trip was smartest. Toby would be asleep and easier to find.

Sam tripped yesterday, and he got the vision power back like it was nothing. All that work to get it the first time…

He's been overly attentive and protective with me today, and I've had to repeatedly reassure him that I'll be okay tripping. I won't pass out again.

It actually feels quite likely that I will, but I don't want him to know that.

The four of us stand side by side, holding hands on the pebbly lakeshore. It's a clear night, and the moon is throwing white light that ripples across in the water.

"Are we ready?" Sam asks.

"Yes," Amy and I say immediately.

"Costa?" Sam shakes his friend's hand. "You good?"

"Yeah. But there's one thing."

"What's that?"

"Stella is going to need help tripping," he says.

"Shit," Sam mutters.

"What do you mean? Can't you just, you know…" I mime a gun to my head and then a knife across my throat. I know that we're swimming out to where Toby fell through the ice, but I didn't think about the actual dying part, which seems rather inconsequential in the scheme of what we're doing. "One of those. Why can't we do that?"

"We should trip the way Toby died." Sam takes a deep breath. "Drowning."

I don't like the sound of this, but I try to stay relaxed. "Okay."

Costa lets go of Amy's and Sam's hands and stands in front of me. "The rest of us have tripped enough that we'll be able to drown ourselves. Your instinct will be to fight it, to live."

"So, you'll do it, CJ. You'll drown me then." We can repeat what we had before. This should be simple.

He stares at me for a minute. "I can't do it."

"Why?"

He raises an eyebrow, and a bit of a smile peeks through his lips.

"Oh." I can't look at Sam right now. What happens when Costa trips me doesn't exactly set the right mood to go into this trip. Now that we have a better handle on what we're doing, tripping while overloaded with sexual energy doesn't seem appropriate. "Sure. Amy then?"

"You'll fight hard. Amy isn't strong enough," Costa explains.

Shit. It's no wonder Sam has been sticking particularly close to me today.

I squeeze his hand. "It's okay, Sam."

He doesn't say anything, but I know how much he doesn't want to do this.

"You're not really killing me," I say. "It's all right."

"It's not going to be like the other times," Sam says quietly. "You'll feel it at first. Drowning…it takes longer for the sensation of death to kick in."

I squeeze his hand. "I understand. This is still my choice."

"Sam…" Costa's eyes are full of apology. "You know I can't do it, or I would."

"Why? Why can't Costa do it?" Amy is at a loss.

"I'll explain later," he says, taking his place next to her again. "Just trust me."

I pull Sam to face me, and reluctantly, he looks at me.

"You can do this. I'm *telling* you to. I know that it goes against everything you are, but this is the only way. Unless you know someone else who wants to step in and kill me, you're up, Bishop."

"I'm going to have to hurt you. How can I do that?"

"Because you're going to. That's the deal." I lift up on my toes so that I'm closer to his height, and I rub my nose against his. "And then you'll make up for it later," I whisper.

He gives in and lets a smile come through. "You're something else, Stella."

I turn back to the water and confidently take his hand. "Let's go."

Together, we walk into the water, only letting go of each other's hands when our feet leave the sand.

Costa swims to a spot a good forty-five feet from the shore and stops. "About here."

The way he's looking at Sam pains me. This is where it happened—where his son died. Of course he'd remember the place where his world crashed. How could he not?

Sam swims in behind me, and I flinch sharply.

"Hey, hey, easy," he says. I have no idea how he can remain so solid in this place of hell. "I'll tell you when."

"Sorry." I hate that I just reacted that way to Sam's touch. "I'm just a little jumpy."

"You can't be," Amy says with too much of a critical tone.

"It doesn't help that you've been such a bitch to me," I say angrily.

We all tread water, the only sound the small splashes we make.

"You're right," she says. "I apologize. I have a few bad habits to break."

"Like your hideous snoring?" I'm apparently still able to grin in the face of tragedy.

"That's not a habit."

I splash her full-on, and she laughs.

She wipes lake water from her eyelids. "Okay, okay. Like…treating you as if you're the worst sister in the world when you're really the best?"

I just look at her. I don't want to answer this.

"Just say yes. I know it's true. And you are the best," she says.

"You *used* to be the best," I say. "I want you to be that again."

"I'm going to try. I swear, I will." For once, her sincerity is undeniable.

"Then, say it," I demand.

"Say what?"

"You know. Say it."

She sighs. "Oh, fine." Amy paddles for a few moments, and finally, she relents. "I love you so *mush*."

"Good." I wink. "I love you so *mush*, too."

"You ready to die with me, sister?"

I smile at her. "I'm ready to die with all of you. Sam?"

His nerves are hidden well, but I know this is difficult for him. "I'm going to move an arm in front of you, okay?"

"Okay." I watch his hand caress the water as he swoops it across the surface.

"Costa and Amy? Go under together. We'll be there in a few minutes."

Costa takes Amy's hand. "Stella? Thank you. And, Sam…" He falters.

"I know, I know." Sam wavers but holds it together. "I'll see you soon."

Amy and Costa sink under the water, and my heartbeat picks up.

It's time.

"The fastest way is for me to block your mouth and nose and hold you under. I might need to use two hands though, but I promise that you'll go first." He's trying very hard to sound logical, but I hear the hurt in what he's saying.

"Okay. I'm all right."

"Apologies in advance for what I'm going to do."

"I forgive you in advance."

"Here we go."

Sam uses one hand to pinch my nose and cover my mouth, and he puts the other on my shoulder and pushes down until I'm underwater. I keep my eyes closed. For a time, I just hold my breath and try to relax into it. But soon, I feel the desperate need to breathe. He was right. I'm not actively dying. I'm struggling against it.

Drowning is, ironically, about living.

I try not to push against him, but I can't help it. I want oxygen more than anything, and I grab at the hand he has over my mouth. Immediately, he clamps down on my other shoulder and wraps his legs around me to weigh me down. I hate him right now because I'm suffocating under water, and my lungs are burning. I keep grabbing at his legs, trying to get him off me, and I'm in a full panic.

But then, my brain centers me. This is for Toby. My approach going under matters, and battling against death is the wrong way in. I can stop fighting this, and I can just sink into it. The only way to find this little boy is to just let my death happen.

My palm goes to Sam's hand on my shoulder, and I give it a quick rub to let him know that my fight is over. It doesn't take long. There is dizziness…then bordering on unconsciousness…

Then, finally, there is my death.

I barrel into the dark under, and Amy catches me by the shirt before I drift past her and Costa. It's only seconds later that Sam crashes in. Amy pushes me hard so that I get through the heavy gel and reach him.

He takes my hand. Even under here, I can see how traumatized he is by what he had to do. I touch his face and look into his eyes, trying to convey that I'm not suffering, that I got through it. He kisses my hand, and under here, the sensation is so magnified that I am filled with more of his love than I thought possible. My smile must convince him because he smiles back.

Now, he begins his scan. Amy and Costa are holding hands still, trying to magnify their lure as a homing beacon. I let Sam pull me through the viscous fluid as he searches. This trip, I don't question time or even acknowledge it. All I need to do is ride and do what I can to power up Sam's ability to see through the dark. Allowing myself to surrender here makes the experience better for me, and I'm noticeably less unsettled. So, I let time go on, occasionally closing my eyes when the blurry rush of light and dark tones makes me too dizzy. The familiar cold ache begins to develop in my bones, and I will not forgive myself if I pass out again and destroy Sam's ability to see.

I catch sight of Costa and Amy, who are trying to stay as close to Sam as possible, but he's faster today than he has been. When he brakes short though, they slam into us.

I look up. Sam is on high alert. His focus darts from one location to another until he appears to hone in on one spot. Without shifting his eyes, he reaches and moves my hand from his so that I'm touching Costa's body. He presses down, I think reminding me to stay here.

Oh, wait. I understand. He wants me to…to *power* Costa's and Amy's presence somehow. I don't know if I can. Costa did react strongly to me the first time that I tripped though, so maybe I can use my connection with him to do so.

I hold tight to Costa and concentrate on him—as a father, as someone who adores Toby, and as a parent who has suffered so much because of his loss. He is home. He is the only home Toby should go to…

Sam swims us through more territory for what feels to be hours. I'm hurting, and just before I feel my body screaming to shut down because the freeze in my bones is too much, he motions for us to stay still. He cocks his head and gives a wry smile. He covers his eyes for a moment and then opens his hands and covers them again.

What is he—

Oh my God.

He's playing Peek-a-Boo.

Costa starts to swim forward, but Amy hauls him back hard and holds up her hand, telling him to stay, to be patient. Costa nods, but it must be excruciating for him to hold still.

Sam points ahead. I can't see anything, but I don't need to. Costa's face tells me that he has Toby in sight. Amy does not let go of him, but her own expression is also one of pure joy. Soon, even I can make out the figure of a small child swimming in our direction, his grace in this underworld immeasurably touching.

Amy was right. He is incredibly fast. His black hair swirls in the waves of the under substance, and his eyes stand out against his fair skin. *Of course* this is Costa's child. Toby looks just like his father.

It feels like it takes forever for Toby to reach us, but we all remain still. When he's only a few feet away, Costa holds out his arms, and the young boy swims smoothly into his father's hold. I don't need to hear Costa to know the sounds of this reunion.

Amy gives them a moment, but then she taps his shoulder and gestures up. We need to surface. He nods. Amy takes my hand. Her smile is so genuine, and I'm struck by how strong our love is despite such a ragged history. We start to move with Amy pulling me through the dense gel.

When there is more light and we've hit the ceiling, Costa gestures for Sam to go with Toby first. Tentatively, Sam takes Toby. I'm not sure what his hesitation is, but he must not want to remove Toby from his father's arms so soon. But still Sam doesn't budge, so Costa gives him a reassuring smile and a light push until he gets Sam moving upward. His arm goes through, but then he bounces back.

He shuts his eyes for a moment and tries again. It's clear that he cannot get past the ceiling.

Oh God. We can't surface Toby?

There is something we don't know that's preventing this child from leaving.

Slowly, Sam lowers back down to Costa's level. His face is beyond pained as he hands Toby to his father and points up. With this simple action and in a moment that should be overwhelmingly happy, Costa is again destroyed with understanding.

Sam cannot surface Toby because he did not trip him.

Costa did.

Now, Costa is frozen in place, and his grip on his son is slipping. Sam swoops over and pushes Toby back against Costa and secures his arms around his son. Then, he grabs Costa's face and forces him to pay attention. The two silently exchange an unspoken language of their own, and it's enough to get Costa moving. His feet begin to kick hard, and he swims to the light, soon vanishing into the surface above us.

Amy pats my shoulder and goes next, moving me into Sam, before she soars up.

Then, Sam and I are alone. I love him so much right now that it hurts. In this dark place, my heart feels lighter than ever. I'm glad that I only needed Costa to surface that first time because I want this moment alone with Sam. I embrace Sam, and together, we leave the bleakness of being under and burst through to the real world.

We've all crashed onto the small sandy beach by the lake where the four of us stood not so long ago, preparing to die. Only, this time, there are five of us. Amy is lurching to the cooler that we set out earlier. I'm still in Sam's arms, trying to catch my breath, when she shoves a piece of watermelon in my mouth. Costa is on his back, eating a slice, with his son lying across his chest.

"*Dah-yee*! *Dah-yee*!" Toby giggles.

Costa is hardly able to talk, but he says, "Yes, buddy. *Dah-yee* is here." He presses watermelon against Toby's lips. "Eat."

Amy sits next to them. She touches a hand to Toby's face and then leans down and softly kisses Costa. When she lifts, I see the smile they share, the connection. Just as Sam and I waited so long for each other, so have Costa and Amy.

Toby smacks his mouth as he eats. "*Ish*! *Ish*!" he calls.

"Yeah. Sam is here, too. Bishop's here." Costa laughs when Toby touches his little hand to his father's face. "You got my nose, huh?"

"Toby…" Sam says, gasping. "He's here? Is this real? Is it him, Stella?"

"It's him. Bishop, it's him." I struggle for breath. "It's Toby."

I hear Sam sucking on the rind. When I roll over, it's easy to read the emotion on his face. Yes, he is so full of denial that it slays me.

"Watermelon. Shit, this really works," he mutters.

I roll over to face him. "Sam…" I whisper.

"Shh. Don't. It doesn't matter."

"It does matter." I push the hair from his eyes. "You took the fall for Costa. He was the one who was tripping too much, wasn't he?"

Sam doesn't need to answer me.

"You were sober." I think for a minute, trying to clear my head of the trip. I take another bite of watermelon. "Thrill seeking. Costa was thrill-seeking on the ice. Jumping, testing how solid it was. Oh God, with his son." For a moment, I shut my eyes at the horror of the image. "So, it was easy to retell the story and get him to believe your version."

He tries to smile. "There was no reason for him to know the truth. He had enough to suffer through."

"It was a big sacrifice. It was everything." I brush my lips over his. "You're wonderful, you know that? So brave and so strong. It's why you're my good."

"And it's why you're my good. Always, Stella."

THIRTY-SIX
bubbles

FIVE WEEKS AGO, we tripped Toby.

Five weeks ago, we learned the truth about his death.

Five weeks ago, our chaos settled.

It's quite warm for late October, and Sam has the windows down in the truck, letting our hair blow freely. The air rushing through the cab feels invigorating, and I'm even more energized to get back to the Bishops' place in Willow. There's been little traffic on this Tuesday, so we've had a smooth trip.

Sam's hand is in mine, and I trace my fingers over his skin. Callous on his palms show the physical labor he exerts every day, but the top of his hand is smooth and soft. There are two sides to his hand, two sides to him—tough and hard, eternally sweet and gentle.

Many nights, I am awoken by the memory of when he tried to surface Toby and couldn't. His loyalty to Costa astounds and moves me. The way he immediately chose to protect Costa from knowing that he was responsible for his son's death was a choice that not everyone would make. Sam knew exactly what he was doing with that decision. Costa had been tripping so often that he was in a state much like he'd had too much alcohol to drink and couldn't remember what actually happened. Sam took advantage of Costa's trip haze and easily fed him a story that released Costa of fault. The details that I've pulled from Sam haunt me—Costa whooping and jumping on the ice, the sound of more cracks ripping through the only partially frozen lake, the sight of the dark water showing where Toby slipped in, the utter agony in Costa's cries.

I understand Sam's motivation. When you love someone enough, you do anything to guard that person from harm even if that means taking a hard hit yourself.

I also understand Costa's current frustration. How could he possibly thank Sam for what he did? It's impossible. He knows the destruction the false story caused Sam, but Costa also knows that it saved him from completely falling apart after Toby had vanished under the ice. Sam was right that no one should have to survive causing a child's death.

In time, I hope that all our nightmares will subside.

We pull into the driveway of the Bishops' house, and my heart soars. We left Amy, Costa, and Toby here six days after we all surfaced. None of us have tripped since. But we will. We'll have to.

Costa was correct that we need to trip on occasion to discharge the buildup we all feel, and I can tell we're getting close. My body chemistry has changed, and my physical demand to death trip is getting intense. It'll probably be another week until it'll become necessary.

Sam and I have agreed that when we do trip, we will try to make it…beautiful. Nothing about death tripping should be beautiful, but we're determined to find a way to sculpt it into something that we can make peace with. As much as I've responded to and crave blood, I'm trying to curb that urge. It feeds a darker side, the addict in me. We haven't decided how we'll trip yet, but there won't be knives or guns. I will do what I need to maintain who I am, but I will not go out of my way to heighten it. Sam and I both desperately want normal lives for ourselves.

Costa and Amy? They're okay with the gore. It suits them. It's one of the reasons that Sam and I are here for four days—to take care of Toby while they death-trip. They're driving into Boston for a long weekend and holing up in a hotel. I haven't asked how they're going to trip, and I don't want to know.

Sam parks behind Costa's car, a used Volvo with one of the highest crash-test ratings out there. He's got Toby to protect now, and his son's safety is his priority. The little boy might be a death tripper, but Costa is not taking any risks. None of us can tell if Toby will ever have to trip again, but the idea is atrocious. We're waiting to see how he continues to do, but even maintenance death tripping for a child is beyond what we can stomach, and it's our hope that he won't need to.

We grab our bags and head into the house. Through the big windows, I see Costa and Amy on the patio. The same spot where Costa once lit himself on fire is now the place where he sits with his son in his lap and the girl he loves only a few feet away.

"Look at them," Sam says happily. "They're a family."

They are. And while they might look like an instant family, they are anything but. Each of them fought long and hard to get to where they are today. They've earned this happiness.

I can't control my smile when we walk outside, and Toby squeals, "*Ish*! *Ya*!"

I love how he calls me *Ya*, which seems to come from the "la" at the end of my name.

"Toby!" I scoop him into a snuggle when he toddles over, and then I pass him to Sam after I get in some good kisses.

Costa bear hugs me and spins me around. "God, I missed you guys."

"You going stir-crazy here?"

"Well, yes." He sets me down and takes my hands in his, kissing each of them. "But I really did miss you anyway."

Given that Costa can't run the risk of being seen with Toby, even this far north from Watermark, he hasn't been out much because he hasn't wanted to leave Toby.

"You look very happy," I say. "Cabin fever or not. Or rather, mansion fever or not."

"It's a good place to hide out."

"Amen to that." Amy moves to us and touches my arm. "Hey, sis."

"Hey, sis," I say back.

"It's good to see you again."

"Yeah?"

"I'm getting better. I'm trying."

"I know, and you're doing great."

Awkwardly, we briefly put our arms around each other. We talk every few days. So far, our conversations have been on the more casual end. How our days are going, what toys Toby loves—it's nothing too heavy, but we'll get there.

"You look really healthy, Amy." Her hair is shiny and full, her skin tone is pink and fresh, and she's even put on some much-needed weight.

I'll take those as good signs.

"I've been feeding her like crazy. Death-tripper recipes and all," Costa says proudly.

She smiles at him and lifts her mouth for a kiss.

While my relationship with her might not yet be solid, she and Costa are mad for each other. He manages to bring out her softer side, and Toby brings out her mothering side. They are all healing each other.

"What? No love for *Ish*, brother?" Sam demands loudly.

"*Ish bruddah*!" Toby squeals from his spot on Sam's hip.

Costa and Amy pull apart from their kiss and laugh, and Costa lunges at Sam and Toby, throwing his arms around them both.

"Dude! You know I totally love ya!" He gives Sam a noisy wet kiss that makes a high-pitched squeal.

Sam manages to push him away with a groan, but Costa gets him into a hug.

Their hold goes on for so long that Sam finally starts tapping Costa's shoulder. "Okay, let's calm down. I'm not that exciting of a person."

Costa talks softly, but I can still hear him, "But you're the best person."

"It's over. Stop," Sam protests in a whisper.

"Love you, Sammy."

"Love you, too, Costa."

Costa pulls back finally, and Toby reaches for his father. The joy—the *purity* of the joy—in Costa's face as he lifts his son into the air makes everything that we've gone through more than worth it.

"Felicia and Micah still okay with us staying here?" Costa asks.

Sam nods. "Of course. They've been insistent actually that you stay here for as long as you need to."

"That's a little odd," Amy says.

"I know," I agree. "I thought the same thing. Is there any chance that your mom knows something?"

I'm reminded of the conversation I had with her when I asked about coming up here in the first place. I still work at the inn two days a week, and both of Sam's parents have been incredibly relaxed. I know that our relief and serenity radiates from us, and that has seemingly been enough to fend off concern or questions—at least for now.

"There's no way she knows about death tripping," Sam says confidently, "but she knows us enough to figure something is going on. She's trusting us to handle it."

"And we are handling it," Costa says.

We walk down to the lake, now a place of celebration and not fear, and sit in beach chairs. Although an assortment of pails, shovels, and other toys litters the sand, Toby immediately goes for a giant red ball.

"Ball?" Amy asks. "You want to play ball? Okay. Kick it to me!"

She runs down the shoreline, and Toby wobbles through the sand after her. Amy, I can tell, never tires of playing. She talks about him almost as much as Costa, and it's nice to see how connected she can be. For the next hour, the five of us kick and throw the ball and build sand castles. This is likely the last day it'll be warm enough to come down here for long, so we milk the afternoon.

Later, Costa sits between Sam and me. "This might be paradise, but I wish Toby and Amy and I could come home, back to Watermark. But I can't exactly show up with my formerly dead son who hasn't grown at all."

"I know you miss home," Sam says. "I have had one idea…"

"What's that?"

I glance at Sam. I have mixed feelings on this possible plan, but I smile and silently tell him to share his idea. It might be the only solution.

"If you wait a little bit longer, say another eight months until Toby is technically almost two, you might be able to tell people that he's a second child of yours." Sam raises a hand. "I know. It sounds crazy, but if he's older and doesn't look exactly as he did, you can say he's a son you didn't know about until his mother brought him to you because she didn't want him anymore. Yes, yes, it's insane. But it might work. You'd obviously have to change his name. Maybe call him by his middle name."

"A brother could easily look a lot like Toby," I add.

Costa watches his son laugh as he bends over to lift the ball. "Evan isn't a bad name," he says slowly.

"You'd need paperwork, social security number, and such. You will anyway though since Toby Jorden is officially deceased."

Costa smirks. "I got a guy who can get me what I need."

"Of course you do," Sam says with a laugh.

"That actually might work." A smile begins to take over Costa's face. "I want to be able to go home. For me, for Toby. I want to show Amy the places that are important to me and be near you two again."

I lean back and stretch my legs, pushing my feet into the sand. "Sam and I talked. If you don't think that will work, we'll go where you need us. The five of us need to stick together. We have to keep each other in check."

Costa's face tells me how touched he is. "You'd leave Watermark?"

"Of course. If that's what has to happen, of course we would," Sam says.

"What about college? Neither of you wants to go back?"

Both of us shake our heads.

"Nope," I say. "At least not yet. Maybe one day, and maybe we'll be forty when we do it but not now."

"Now," Sam says, "is all about adjusting and finding stability. Let's just live. Well, you know, with the occasional death, but let's just live."

"Okay. I don't want you two not doing what you want because of this."

"We are doing what we want, Costa. Really," I say. "We're staying with family."

Costa thinks for a minute. "Let's wait and see what Toby looks like in six months. I bet we can pull this off. We should all be able to stay in Watermark. It's where we belong."

"Okay. Then, we'll wait." Sam looks seriously at Costa. "We're staying on schedule, right? Tripping once every five weeks or so?"

Costa nods immediately. "Yes. If we can taper down, we will. Oh! I did want to show you something cool that we figured out yesterday. Watch this." Costa hops from his chair and waves to Amy. "Ready?"

"Again?" she asks with a laugh. "Okay." Amy tucks her hair behind her ears and narrows her eyes toward Costa.

He calls Toby's name, and when his son turns, Costa puts out his hands and makes a circle with his fingers. Bubbles, just like the ones blown through a plastic wand, begin to rush out, floating gently through the air right to Toby. The little boy laughs and claps his hands, and then he begins chasing them as they blow in the breeze.

Sam looks astonished. "You got your powers back?"

Costa lifts his bubble-making fingers higher and grins. "I got me a power augmenter, Sammy, just like you."

"Amy?" I ask delightedly. "Amy is your power augmenter?"

"So, it seems."

Sam looks at me. "What did I tell you, Stella? Love comes first, and power augmenter comes second."

"You might just be right about that, Bishop." I can't take my eyes off him.

I'll never get tired of the way he looks at me, the love he gives, the many ways in which he builds me up and lets me thrive. And I'll also never tire of loving him back. To get to wholly give myself to another person—it's monumentally fulfilling.

"When we ate that watermelon when our surge started, it shut down you getting a power, Sam, right?"

Sam nods.

"I didn't have one to lose, and then I think Amy activated mine." He swoops his hands through the air and produces a series of giant bubbles. "Check me out being all powered up!"

For a moment, I'm concerned. Costa has always liked tripping too much, and having powers again could be dangerous.

But before I can say anything, he says, "I don't want you to worry. If all I can ever do is blow bubbles and make my son laugh, I'm cool with that. Maintenance tripping only. I promise. For you guys, for myself, for Toby. I'm okay."

"I'm glad to hear that." Sam stands and brushes sand from his shorts. "I'm going to shuck the oysters we got and start dinner. Half shells to start and then grilled swordfish with basil mayonnaise, green beans, and fresh bread."

"Oysters!" Costa rubs his hands together and raises his eyebrows. "Oh. Aphrodisiac night!"

"None for you!" Sam yells with a laugh. "Stella, you want to come?"

"You bet." I get up to leave, but Costa takes my hand.

He waits until Sam is a few yards away and pulls me down to whisper, "I might be a good boy now, and you might be a good girl, but I will always miss that knife."

I'm reassured that Costa is still very much Costa. I turn my head and softly kiss him on the cheek. "I will, too."

"Who knows? Maybe once a year, we can have a throwback? Reminisce a little, the three of us?"

I smile. "Maybe we do. Maybe we don't." I walk to Sam and turn back to Costa. "Or maybe we do."

He laughs. "Atta girl!"

I catch up to Sam and take his hand. "I'm ready for my oysters."

"Good."

I follow him inside and hop up onto the counter to watch him shuck the oysters. Expertly, he wiggles the thick oyster knife between the two sides of the shell and jimmies it open. As he did the first night that he cooked for me in my apartment, he moves to stand between my legs.

He smiles at me as he lifts the oyster shell to my lips. "Drink."

So, I drink the briny liquid and groan at the rich flavor.

Now, his smile gets more flirtatious. "Swallow…" He tilts the shell more, and the oyster slips into my mouth. "Don't chew."

These are just as good as he promised. "I can't believe that I'm finally getting my raw oysters. A lot of our plans last summer got interrupted."

"Yep. Seal Cove. We still haven't been there."

"Then, that's what we'll do when we get back into town."

"Deal," he says. "And painting your apartment. I never finished that."

"I don't want you to paint it. I want my patches of color and your words."

"Then, I'll just keep adding to them. I'll cover all the walls." Sam opens another shell and lets me drink from it. Then, he downs the oyster and kisses me.

"When we trip next week?" I start.

"Yeah?"

"Maybe we'll go to Seal Cove in the early evening. We can hope to get lucky and see actual seals. Then, we'll watch the sky begin to turn to night. When it's dark enough, we can swim out to sea, and we can death-trip at sunset. I can do it myself, I think."

"We'll make it beautiful," he says.

"We'll make it beautiful. And we'll get you the light power back."

"I like it."

"And I like you," I say teasingly.

"You *like* me?" He pretends to be offended.

"I *love* you, Sam Bishop. When we're alive, when we're dying, when we're under, when we're surging. Always. I love you always."

"And I love you always."

Sam leans in and embraces me around the waist. My hands go around his neck, and I rest my head on his shoulder. I am happy and loved at long last. I have built a life for myself, I've found people who are family, and I no longer doubt who I am.

My bracelet begins to warm my skin, and I rub the letters. Something is different, very different. I go over them three times to be sure and then lift my wrist to look.

Adored is still there, the familiar word etched into the silver plate.

There is also another word etched below it—*Always.*

Instantly, I jerk back. "Sam." I show him my bracelet. "Sam, look."

He studies the lettering, looking as stunned as I am. We're silent for a long time.

Then, his face relaxes, and he lifts my chin. "Do you see?"

"No. What is this? How is this possible?"

"You wanted beautiful? Here's beautiful." He kisses my bracelet and then kisses me. "This is from your father. He did this. He does adore you. And he knows that I adore you. *Always.*"

Sam is right. Inexplicably, as it is with all of death tripping, this is from my father. I feel that truth beyond any doubt. Somehow, someway, he is watching over me and continuing to be my father, even from afar. There will always be a great distance between us, but now, there is also great forgiveness.

"We found our good," Sam says definitively.

"Yes. We found our good." I smile through my tears.

After years of fog, my head, my heart, and my world are finally clear.

ACKNOWLEDGMENTS

WRITING A BOOK is an enormous undertaking, and doing so would be impossible without the dedicated help of so many.

Author friends are lifelines during the writing process. Jamie McGuire, Abbi Glines, Tina Reber, Tracey Garvis Graves, and Michele Scott all listened to my pitch during lunch one year at BEA. It is their enthusiasm that helped keep my book idea alive for so many years.

Tracey let me vent and ramble and rage numerous times as I fought with this story, and I am most grateful for her unfailing enthusiasm.

Rebekah Crane is the brainstorm queen, and her many what-if questions guided me to the plot that I wanted. Few have the wild imagination and bottomless creativity she does.

Years ago, Heather Webber read a convoluted outline and gave brilliant insight and advice that impacted even this final version.

Andrew Kaufman…oh, Andrew Kaufman swooped in at my darkest moments and surfaced me over and over. His patience, intelligence, and unfailing encouragement saved my sanity over months of struggle. It takes a strong person to put up with my crazy, and he never once buckled—or at least, not that he let on.

Huge thanks out to Autumn Hull for…well, for everything—moral support, skilled PR work, editing genius, humor, understanding, common sense, and so much more. She's the total package.

Maryse Courtier Black was kind enough to talk to me over the phone and let me bounce ideas off her well-read mind, and Alexa Lewis and Tom Cullinan are both faithful friends who were constantly available to me when I needed smart consultants. Maria Milano and Liis McKinstry have emotional pom-poms that they waved enthusiastically at every opportunity.

There are so many wonderful readers and bloggers to whom I am eternally in debt for their continued loyalty and cheering. I'm terrified to list any because I'll invariably leave out someone I adore, but I have been overwhelmed over the years by a most amazing community.

As always, my husband, Bill, and son, Nick, remain troopers. Living with an author often means living with a lunatic, and they both deserve awards for their ability to cope.

Thank you to Jovana Shirley from Unforeseen Editing for being absolutely dynamite and a true joy to work with.

And finally, to Tracy Hutchinson, whose honesty and openness were crucial in helping me find the heart of this book.

ABOUT THE AUTHOR

JESSICA PARK is the author of *Left Drowning*, the Flat-Out Love series, and *Relatively Famous*. She grew up in the Boston area and attended Macalester College in St. Paul, Minnesota. After spending four years in the frigid north, including suffering through one memorable Halloween blizzard, Jessica hightailed it back to the East Coast. She now lives in relatively balmy New Hampshire with her husband and son. When not writing, Jessica indulges her healthy obsessions with Facebook and complicated coffee beverages.

OTHER WORKS

Left Drowning

What does it take to rise from life's depths, swim against the current, and breathe?

Weighted down by the loss of her parents, Blythe McGuire struggles to keep her head above water as she trudges through her last year at Matthews College. Then, a chance meeting sends Blythe crashing into something she doesn't expect—an undeniable attraction to a dark-haired senior named Chris Shepherd, whose past may be even more complicated than her own. As their relationship deepens, Chris pulls Blythe out of the stupor she's been in since the night a fire took half her family. She begins to heal, and even, haltingly, to love this guy who helps her find new paths to pleasure and self-discovery. But as Blythe moves into calmer waters, she realizes Chris is the one still strangled by his family's traumatic history. As dark currents threaten to pull him under, Blythe may be the only person who can keep him from drowning.

Flat-Out Love

He was tall, at least six feet, with dirty blond hair that hung over his eyes. His T-shirt read *Nietzsche Is My Homeboy.*

So, that was Matt—who Julie Seagle likes. A lot. But there is also Finn—who she flat-out loves.

Complicated?

Awkward?

Completely.

But really, how was this freshly minted Boston transplant and newbie college freshman supposed to know that she would end up living with the family of an old friend of her mother's? This was all supposed to be temporary. Julie wasn't supposed to be important to the Watkins family or fall in love with one of the brothers, especially the one she's never quite met. But what does that really matter? Finn *gets* her, like no one ever has before. They have a *connection.*

But here's the thing about love. In all its twisty, bumpy permutations, it always throws you a few curves. And no one ever escapes unscathed.

Flat-Out Matt

A *Flat-Out Love* companion novella for true fans! You saw geeky, damaged, loveable Matt Watkins through Julie's eyes in *Flat-Out Love*. Now, go deeper into Matt's world in this *Flat-Out Matt* novella. Live his side of the story, break when his heart breaks, and fall for the unlikely hero all over again.

Take an emotional skydive for two prequel chapters and seven *Flat-Out Love* chapters retold from his perspective, and then land with a brand-new steamy finale chapter from Julie.

Flat-Out Celeste

For high school senior Celeste Watkins, every day is a brutal test of bravery. And Celeste is scared. Alienated because she's too smart, her speech too effected, her social skills too far outside the norm, she seems to have no choice but to retreat into isolation.

But college could set her free, right? If she can make it through this grueling senior year, then maybe. If she can just find that one person to throw her a lifeline, then maybe, just maybe.

Justin Milano, a college sophomore with his own set of quirks, could be that person to pull her from a world of solitude. To rescue her—that is, if she'll let him.

Together, they may work. Together, they may save each other. And together they may also save another couple—two people Celeste knows are absolutely, positively flat-out in love.

Whether you were charmed by Celeste in *Flat-Out Love* or are meeting her for the first time, this book is a joyous celebration of differences, about battling private wars that rage in our heads and in our hearts, and very much so, this is a story about first love.

CPSIA information can be obtained at www.ICGtesting.com
Printed in the USA
LVOW06s2210160715

446585LV00016B/416/P

9 781508 453420